2017

W9-BOA-862

IVY

a novel

M. G. Slind

Ivy

©2017 by M. G. Slind

All Rights Reserved
No part of this book may be reproduced
without the written permission of
M. G. Slind

Cover photo: Kieren Welch © 123RF.com
Cover Design: M. G. Slind

Photo on p. 443 by Hannah Rosholt,
Courtesy of Luther College

This is a work of fiction. Characters, places, and events are the product of the author's imagination or are used fictitiously. Any resemblance to real people, living or dead, companies, institutions, organizations, or incidents is entirely coincidental.

ISBN-13: 978-0-9990971-0-6
ISBN-10: 0-9990971-0-5

For more information about M. G. Slind, please
check his website: www.norse.org

For Mickey, with love

Contents:

The Day in Question

Friday, February 21

WINTER STILL HELD NIEUW NEDERLAND COLLEGE firmly in its grip, even though it was the third week in February. The last few days had seen the temperatures slip briefly above freezing. But every night, the snow that melted during the day refroze into a solid layer of boilerplate ice. Optimists were hoping the milder weather meant spring was near. But anyone who'd lived through a Minnesota winter knew better. Consistently warm weather was still weeks away—months, more likely. For the past twenty-four hours, the National Weather Service had been issuing warnings that a severe winter storm would hit late that afternoon. They predicted at least a foot of new snow overnight. To make matters worse, there would be high winds and sub-zero temperatures, with wind chills at least fifty below zero.

Snow started falling just before 4:00 Friday afternoon, but only after an hour of freezing rain formed a layer of ice. The first flakes were huge, wet, and heavy, driven in sheets by the initial blasts of icy wind. But as the bottom fell out of the thermometer, the snow became lighter, and the crystalline flakes sparkled in the lights around campus. By 5:30, there were already several inches of new snow. City crews were working on the main streets, with the emphasis not so much on plowing as on spreading a mixture of sand and salt on the ice. The smaller byways would have to wait until the storm abated. On campus, everything was quiet.

Henrik ("Hank") van Daam looked out of the President's Office on the top floor of the Carroll Center. After surveying the terrace, he glanced farther off to his right, checking the parking lot outside the Central Union Building —the "CUB." There were only two cars left there. He saw the headlights flicker on one of them, and he could just make out a faint puff of exhaust; the engine had just started. In a few minutes, his would be the only car left. He should have been expecting it, but the knock on his door startled him.

"You still here?" he asked.

Annika van Rijn, his Executive Assistant, stuck her head around the corner. "Not for long," she said as she was putting on her coat.

"I suppose Sarah's already gone—you'd think the Dean would be the last person to leave wouldn't you?"

"She left about half an hour ago."

"Doesn't she have work to do? I'm beginning to think it was a mistake to hire her. She worries too much about keeping the faculty happy. That's not going to win her any points with my successor." He nodded toward the parking lot. "Is that your car in the lot? I couldn't be sure in the snow. I noticed the lights flashing a minute ago."

"I just started it," she explained, rattling her car keys and the remote starter. "I'm letting it warm up a bit before I head for home. Pieter called; his shooting competition was cancelled because of the storm, so he didn't have to get on the road this afternoon. Given the weather forecast, and the police bulletins telling everyone to stay off the streets, he's more than a little pissed that I'm not home already. The last forecast he heard was that we'll be getting 'Thunder Snow,' with plenty of thunder and lightning, in addition to 'very heavy accumulations' of snow—maybe a foot or more overnight. I want to get home before it gets any worse. It's already snowing hard enough that you can't see the warning lights flashing on top of the windmill."

"It's a snow storm, for Christ's sake—how many of those do we get every winter? You've got 4-wheel drive, so don't worry about it. I'm not."

"Easy for you to say. You live close enough that you could walk home if you had to. You obviously don't have much respect for Mother Nature. But I do! I know that in the long run, my resources don't compare to hers. Besides, it's not <u>MY</u> driving I'm worried about—it's all those idiots who never seem to learn how to drive on snow. How many winters do you have to spend in Minnesota before you figure out what snow does to your traction? At least we've gotten the campus emptied out. And letting everyone go early this afternoon helped cut down on the number of cars out on the streets."

Hank glanced out the window again. "Now that I look more closely, I see you've got your skis on top of your car. If you get stuck, you can always ski home," he chuckled.

Annika didn't laugh. "You're not very funny. I went out to the course during lunch today, remember? I wanted to get in a round before the storm hit. My racing skis wouldn't do me much good cutting a track in fresh snow, especially as heavy and wet as the first snow was. I don't look forward to driving through it. I would've preferred to go home when everyone else left."

Hank grunted. "If it were up to me, they'd have all stayed until 5. With the Trustees meeting tomorrow, all I need is to have one of them stop by campus early and find no one home—including the damned Dean. They keep badgering me about 'increased productivity.' Sending people home early doesn't fit anyone's definition of that. But I had staff representatives in here early this afternoon. They were whining about how many of their kids were going to be sent home from school early, milking the 'stay off the streets' announcements for all they were worth. All they wanted was to get off work early. If it put me in a bad light with the Trustees, they'd be even happier. If it weren't for the basketball games tomorrow night, most of the students would have left, too. But now we have to deal with dorms full of students who'll have cabin fever within an hour or two. They've probably cleared the shelves of any beer that could be found within walking distance of campus. The party's started somewhere, I'm sure."

"Look at it this way: the Trustees won't be here until tomorrow—if then. Nobody's going to be dropping in this late in the day; even without the storm, everyone would have gone home by now. I wouldn't be surprised if they postponed the meeting until next month. Sending everyone home seems like a 'win-win' situation for you."

"How do you figure?"

"To the staff, you look like you've made a generous decision in favor of their welfare. And Chief van den Hoek has to be happy that you responded proactively to his bulletins, and helped get people home and off the streets before the storm hits."

"That asshole wouldn't give me credit for anything! He's had something stuck in his craw with me ever since we first met."

"Maybe this'll help change that."

"I wouldn't count on it. Besides, I'm leaving here by July, so I'm not really concerned about what Carl thinks of me. Once we get through 'Hans Brinker Days' next week, I hope I won't have to run into him again. That's something else I won't miss when I leave here. It's bad enough having to dress up in wooden shoes and a 'Dutch Boy' hat, but then to have to freeze my ass off watching a third-rate speed skating race makes it even worse. Why can't New Leiden celebrate its 'cultural heritage' when it's warm? If they had it in the summer, I could just drive my car in a parade, instead of all of the hokey nonsense we have to put up with at this time of the year."

"It would be pretty hard to have an ice skating race in the summer. I can't see anyone coming up with enough money to build an indoor speed skating rink around here. What do you think, that we could have a tulip festival in this part of Minnesota? Ice skating, ice fishing—how much more Minnesotan can you get? And don't forget the youth hockey tournament. It's a local celebration. The more you get into the spirit, the more good feeling you build for the College."

"I just hope students can keep a low profile this spring. I don't want to have to listen to Carl complain about another student party spilling out into a nice, quiet residential neighborhood. That definitely doesn't build good feelings for the College. The 'town and gown' relationship is bad enough already. Hopefully that won't happen this weekend with this storm blowing in, even if the basketball games are tomorrow night. By the way, did you hear from anybody at Chartwell about the games?"

"No, . . . I don't expect to. Since they're our home games, they're probably waiting to see if we want to cancel them," she replied.

"They're the ones who'll have to drive in this crap. If they don't want to do that, they should cancel. If we pull the plug, Thompson will probably say I'm afraid of getting beat again." He laughed, "He'd be right on that count. The women might come close—maybe even win for a change. But I don't think the men have a prayer."

"But if you suggested it, and worded it right, you could steal the initiative from President Thompson, and show him how much you're concerned about the safety of the Chartwell students."

"Yeah, right . . . ," Hank grumbled. "Let me think about it. If it looks like we're going to get as much snow as they're predicting, I'll call Thompson later this evening and suggest it. Besides, if we do cancel it, I won't have to worry about any students showing up with those damned 'Chuck Fartwell' t-shirts again. Last year, the Trustees who saw those at the game were pretty upset."

"You can't control what students say or wear—freedom of speech, or expression, for that matter."

"They're students at a private institution, of which I'm the CEO. If the Trustees are upset at something students do, it's my ass they're going to chew on. Students need to remember that 'you can't have freedom without also

5

taking responsibility for your actions.' How many times do I have to remind them of that?"

"Apparently more than you have."

"The Trustees want me to make sure student behavior is 'appropriate,' no matter how hopeless that task might be. Don't forget: some of them still have trouble accepting the fact that students have dances on campus, even though those have been allowed since the 60s. I've managed to pack the Board with people who share my vision, but there are still a few of the 'Old Guard' that I have to worry about. Even so, I've got a good relationship with most of the Board. That's especially important to maintain now, when I'm retiring at the end of the semester. I don't want some pimply-faced sophomore with an offensive t-shirt screwing that up for me."

"Hank, you're a college president, not a 'CEO.' If any of the faculty heard you say that, you'd have more problems with them than you do already."

"That's the problem around here. This college is a multi-million dollar enterprise, and I'm in charge of it. If it's not managed efficiently, it'll go broke. Would the faculty rather have everything run like we're still in the nineteenth century, until the bank closes the doors and they're out of a job? Or do they want a viable college? They've got to make some changes. The old paradigms aren't going to work anymore."

"You know that. I know that. But you're not going to convince most of the faculty—especially if you talk about 'paradigms,' 'increased productivity,' and 'cost effectiveness.' They don't appreciate business jargon. But this isn't the time to rehash your feelings about the faculty. The roads aren't getting any better, and I've got to get home. I'll see you before the Board of Trustees meeting tomorrow. You should get out of here, too."

"I'll head home as soon as I finish my presentation for the Trustees."

"You're still working on that? You should be finished by now! I wrote most of what you have to say yesterday.

All you needed to do was add some concluding comments, and it would be ready to go. What the Hell have you been doing all day?"

Hank looked out the window. "I got off to a pretty good start, but I had a few interruptions. A couple times, I thought I heard someone outside on the terrace. But when I went to the window to check, I couldn't see anything. That's what I was doing when you came in."

"It was probably just wind blowing the snow around. With the changing weather conditions, we'll probably have big chunks of snow sliding off the roof. We're expecting that problem at home, too. Pieter wanted to go up and clear some of it off, but I warned him: if he tried that and anything happened to him, he'd have to get himself to the hospital—and I wouldn't be a willing or tender nurse when he got back home. Don't worry about the sounds of winter outside. You need to wrap up your presentation and go home."

"I'm just about done with it. I should be able to get it finished in another half hour or so. Then I'll close up here."

"Did Hannah get back yet?"

"No, she called from the Cities about fifteen minutes ago. Their flight was delayed, and just after they landed, they heard that the storm had already closed several stretches of highway between here and the Cities. So she and Gene got a couple of rooms in a hotel near the airport, and they'll come up first thing in the morning. As Board Chair, he wanted to get here tonight, but there's no way that can happen. I'll go over my presentation with him in the morning, and tweak it if he has any suggestions. He's got a good sense of the Trustees' feelings on most things."

"Okay, I'm out of here. The meeting's at 1:00. If the roads are cleared early enough, I'll try to get here by 9:30 or 10, at the latest. If you need anything in the morning, I can take care of it before the meeting starts."

"See you then—but make sure you close the outer door on your way out! I don't want any janitors coming in and interrupting my train of thought."

"I'm sure the custodial staff have all gone home, too. The idea was to get the campus cleared out before the storm really socked us in, remember?"

Hank grumbled, "They'd better have someone around in the morning to make sure everything's cleaned up well for the Trustees. And somebody'd better have the snow cleared off the terrace outside my office before anyone drops by on the way to the meeting. You reminded them about that, didn't you?"

"Yes, yes! They know all about it! The cleaning staff learned long ago not to even think about coming in when your outer door is closed. They won't start anything as long as you're here. And don't worry—the facilities crew will have the terrace cleared first thing in the morning. Now, for the last time, I'm out of here. It's almost quarter to 6, and I told Pieter I'd be on my way more than 20 minutes ago."

Hank watched her close the door behind her, and then listened as she closed the double door between the outer office and her own. He went back to the window. A few minutes later, he saw her make her way through the new snow to her car. Since the engine had warmed up, she was able to clear her windshield with a few swipes of her wipers. She backed out carefully, testing the icy surface, and slowly drove out into the street. In the blowing snow, her tail lights were barely visible in the parking lot. They disappeared as soon as she turned past the Field House and started up Campus Avenue.

Hank went back to his desk, and gathered up the few notes that he'd left himself earlier in the day. He crumpled most of them and tossed them in the wastebasket, but left two on his desk. The first read simply: "Sabbatical." When he finished his presentation for the Trustees, he could toss that one, too. He slipped the other one into his desk calendar, to remind himself to take care of it on Monday.

Then he sat down in front of his computer and went back to work on his presentation.

He'd only been at it for about ten minutes when he heard the phone ring in Annika's office. He pushed the flashing light on his phone to connect to that line. "President van Daam speaking. May I help you?"

"Hank, this is Pieter. Is Annika still there? She was supposed to be home at least half an hour ago."

"She's fine, Pete. She --"

"It's Pieter, dammit," he yelled into the phone. "How many times do I have to tell you, I don't like being called 'Pete,' or 'Petey,' or any other diminutives you like to call everyone?"

Hank smiled to himself. It was one of his ways of keeping people off balance, making sure that conversations flowed in directions that he preferred. "Sorry, Pieter. You know I'm not one who's big on formalities. She was finishing up a few things for the Board of Trustees meeting, and finally left about ten minutes ago. She should be there soon. Campus Avenue was plowed early, and it's still pretty clear. And there's almost no traffic. It's still not quite 6. Even in this snow, she should be there by quarter past."

"She damned well better be. The College was supposedly closed down at 3. She should've been home before the snow started—before the freezing rain, for that matter. If she runs into any problems, I'm holding you responsible. You can cover any towing costs or car repairs if she slides into a ditch coming up the hill to our house."

"Relax, Pieter. It's just a snow storm. We've all driven in dozens of them. Why don't you open a bottle of wine, pour a glass for each of you, and by the time you get started fixing dinner, she'll be home."

"I'll do that," Pieter mumbled as he hung up the phone.

"Of course HE's fixing dinner," Hank laughed to himself. "What a wuss!"

About forty-five minutes later, Hank looked up from his computer. Twice in the last half hour he'd thought he'd heard someone outside, but each time he went to the window to check, there was nothing there. He'd even opened the door to look outside. The terrace ran the length of the building, but as far as he could see, there was nothing but snow. No tracks—just unevenly piled snow. In a couple of places, the snow piles were a little higher than on the rest of the terrace. And above them, there were no icicles hanging from the eves. So Annika must have been right—that was probably snow that had slid off the roof.

When he glanced outside now, he could see that the snow had stopped, and he heard voices somewhere in the distance. He walked back to the window, and saw about a dozen students in the middle of the football field, in what looked like the beginning of a good-natured snowball fight. He smiled as he watched one couple pair off and lock into a deep embrace. "Nothing like a good tonsil massage to warm you up, is there, buddy?" he laughed.

But as he watched, the students started trampling paths in the snow. *"What the hell are they up to now?"* At first he thought they might be making some kind of geometric pattern—maybe a maze. But after they finished in one spot, a student with a spray can started applying orange paint to what Hank now recognized as letters tramped in the snow. At first, he thought they might be spelling out NNC. But as the letters took form, he knew that was wrong: "C – H – U – C . . ." It didn't take much imagination to recognize that they were using school colors to spell out what would soon be "Chuck Fartwell," where it could be seen by anyone going into the gymnasium. *"Not while I'm around, you won't, God damn it!"*

He threw open the door to the terrace and charged outside, slamming the door behind him. A moment of panic hit him: *"Damn—I hope to Hell I have my keys with me,"* he thought. *"But I've got my cell phone. If I've locked myself out, I can get Campus Security to let me back in."*

Just as he was about to yell at the students, he heard something behind him. "Who's there?" he barked. He heard the sound again, and as he started to turn around, he felt a sharp blow to the back of his head. He put his hand at the source of the pain, and he could feel blood running down his neck. When he looked at his hand, it was covered with blood. This was obviously more than "just a flesh wound."

"I said, who's there? What do you want?" he shouted again. Hank heard another noise behind him, this time even closer. He turned quickly to see who was on the terrace with him. As he spun around, his leather-soled loafer slipped on a patch of ice. With the combination of motions, turning and slipping, his body contorted, and he fell. The last thing he was conscious of was something hitting him at the base of his skull. Everything went black as he crumpled to the deck. And then the snow began to fall again, gently covering him as he lay bleeding on the terrace.

As if to punctuate what was happening outside the President's office, the sky erupted in a flash of lightning, the light diffused by the clouds and falling snow. The whole horizon turned white. That was immediately followed by the deafening crash of thunder. Down on the football field, the students scattered with the flash. They'd succeeded in trampling and painting "CHUC," but suddenly realized that they'd only been enjoying a brief respite from the snowfall. The next wave of the storm would soon completely cover their efforts. They may have been having a good time, but none of them was crazy enough to stay out in the middle of a thunderstorm, particularly one that was obviously about to turn into the heaviest blizzard of the winter. A couple of the seniors in the group offered to share what was left of a case of cheap beer back in their room, and most of the group headed in that direction. A few wandered back to their own rooms. The couple headed off on their own—a group event wasn't on their agenda that evening.

The clock on top of the Carroll Center ticked ahead to 6:45, and the bell chimed accordingly. When they heard the bell, a couple of the students glanced at their watches. The evening was still young. They might not be able to get downtown tonight, but there was still plenty of time to get a party going back in their dorm.

The snow that had earlier been slipping off the roof of the Carroll Center in small sections now released completely. It covered the entire terrace, including Hank van Daam, under a pile of snow about two feet deep. Soon, the mound covering Hank looked no different from the rest of the terrace. There were a few more flashes of lighting, followed by loud crashes of thunder. Then the snow began to fall again in earnest, with the increasingly violent wind blowing it into every nook and cranny. Any tracks outside Hank's door were soon buried under a steadily growing layer of new snow.

*   *   *   *   *

ANNIKA DIDN'T MAKE IT HOME until almost 7:30. When she pulled into her garage, she was cursing the bad road conditions she'd just survived. She was surprised to see that Pieter's car still had snow on it.

"Thank God you're home! Where have you been?" he asked as she came in the door. "I tried calling you at least a dozen times, but you never answered. Did you turn your phone off?"

"No, it was on," she grumbled. "But there was a car blocking the road, and what little traffic there was, was backed up for over half an hour. And—of course—I was in that low area where there's no cell coverage."

"Was there an accident? How'd you get by it? I heard there was a 'no tow' order tonight."

"No . . . fortunately there wasn't an accident, and nobody was hurt. Someone just lost control when they were headed down that long hill. They didn't go all the way off the road, so there were no injuries. But another car tried to slip around the first one, and it got stuck on the other shoulder. So traffic was stopped both ways. We'd probably all still be there if a carload of students hadn't shown up. They'd made a last minute run to stock up on beer for the weekend. When they got to the traffic jam, they all piled out of their car, and helped get the cars out of the snow and going again."

Before he could respond, she asked, "What's the deal with your car? I thought you were home before the storm hit—but there's fresh snow on it, and it hasn't melted yet. Did you go out?"

"When you weren't home, and I couldn't raise you by phone, I thought I should go see if I could find you. If you'd slid off the road, or had been in an accident, I didn't want you freezing to death in your car. But before I'd even driven a mile, it was clear that I'd made a stupid decision. I decided I'd probably be more valuable to you at home. I didn't want to take the risk of both of us getting stuck. So I turned around and came back home. I've got dinner ready for you, and there's a bottle of wine chilled just the way you like it."

She'd been hoping that Pieter would have dinner started. That was one of the things she'd been looking forward to ever since she left Hank's office. When she opened the door to the kitchen, the aroma made her cry. When he pulled a bottle of her favorite sauvignon blanc out of the refrigerator, she all but forgot about Hank and the Trustees.

*   *   *   *   *

IN THE TWIN CITIES, Hannah van Daam and Gene Graandsma met in the lobby at 7:45, and headed to the restaurant attached to their hotel. Hannah pulled out her cell phone, and nodded to Gene, "Let me give Hank a call, and find out what the conditions are like up there." Hank's office phone rang until his voice mail kicked in, so she left a message: "Hi, Hank, it's Hannah. Gene and I are just going next door for a bite to eat. I'll call you when I get back to my room." After they were seated in the restaurant, she tried his cell phone, and left the same message. "Maybe he went to the Men's Room, and left his phone on his desk. I'll try again after dinner. Since we can't get anywhere tonight, we might as well enjoy dinner. It's a good thing Hank's not in this situation. He'd be bitching about the quality of restaurants you get when the College won't pay for more expensive hotels. The College has a special 'Park and Fly' rate here. Since it won't reimburse faculty for any more than this rate, he feels he's stuck staying here, too. When it's decent weather, you can at least go someplace else for dinner, but with the storm tonight, this is our only real option."

"He could stay somewhere else and pay the difference out of his own pocket. With the salary we pay him, he could easily afford that."

"You've got to be kidding! Hank doesn't pay for anything himself if he can help it. 'That's what the President's Entertainment Expenses are for,' he says. Can you think of anyone who's ever seen him pick up a check?—unless he's hosting a potential donor. And then, of course, the tab's actually picked up by the Institutional Advancement Office."

By 9:00, Hannah and Gene had finished dinner and were headed back to their rooms. Hannah dug her cell phone out of her purse. "Let me try calling him again, just in case he has something he wants to talk to you about regarding tomorrow's meeting." Again, she got no answer on either phone. This time she tried their home number as well, with no success.

"That's strange—still no answer. I'll call Annika and see if she has any idea where he is."

Pieter answered the phone: "Annika's having a hot soak in the tub right now. Is there anything I might be able to help you with?"

"I'm trying to reach Hank, but he doesn't answer, either at his office, at home, or on his cell. Do you have any idea when he left his office this evening?"

"I don't know when he left, but I know he was still there just before 6. Annika left about 15 minutes before I called. The weather had slowed her down, and I was worried when she wasn't home yet. I tried calling her at the office, and Hank answered. From what Annika said, I got the impression that he was still working on his presentation to the Trustees. But we haven't had any contact with him since then. Why don't you call Campus Security and see if they can track him down. At least they can tell you if his car's still in the lot. Even if it is, he might have decided to walk home with the roads the way they are."

"That's not very likely—just the walk from the Carroll Center to his car would be treacherous enough in his dress shoes. He wouldn't try that without taking his boots to campus, and I doubt he did that—not wearing his suit. Besides, he'd much rather go home in the warmth of his SUV. He loves to use the four-wheel drive—'Vroom, Vroom, Vroom,' you know. I'll give Campus Security a call. I'm sorry to have bothered you."

When she called the Campus Security office, Tom Olsson, the Director, answered. That surprised her. "We sent almost everyone home early" he explained, "and those of us who live within walking distance are holding down the fort. Right now, I'm the one answering the phones. Fortunately, it's been a quiet evening. Everyone's hunkered down until this storm blows through. What can I do for you, Mrs. van Daam?"

"I've been trying to reach the President for a couple hours now, and can't raise him. He doesn't answer the office phone, our home phone, or his cell."

Tom turned to look out his window. "I can see his parking spot from here, and his car's still there. That means he's probably still in his office—it wouldn't be likely for him to try walking home in this storm, even if your house is just on the other side of campus. But if he's got his door closed, you know he doesn't like to be disturbed."

"Don't worry about that. I'll be happy to take responsibility for you interrupting him. He's got me worried now. I can assure you that if he doesn't have a good excuse for not answering any of my calls, what he's going to face from me is far worse than his reaction to being interrupted."

That brought a smile to Tom's face. "Okay, I'll check his office, and call you right back."

After passing telephone duty along to one of the staff members who were still in the office, Olsson bundled up and headed across the parking lot to the back entrance of the Carroll Center. He shook off the snow that had accumulated even in that short walk, and took the stairs to the third floor.

He found the front door to the President's office locked, and the room dark. Elke Spoelstra, the President's Secretary, had heeded the warnings and closed down her office early. Annika van Rijn's office was dark as well, but there was light shining under the door to the President's office. He took a deep breath, built up his courage, and knocked on the door. "President van Daam? It's Tom Olsson. Campus Security. Are you in there?"

When he got no reply, he knocked again, and when he still heard nothing on the third try, he carefully opened the door, and called out again: "President van Daam? It's Tom Olsson. Campus Security. Are you okay?"

When he opened the door, he could immediately see that the office was empty. He was relieved that he wouldn't have to deal with an angry president, barking at him because he'd been interrupted in the middle of some 'important task.' But that was tempered by his concern that something might have happened to him. His worries deepened when he checked the closet, and found Hank's suit jacket and winter coat. Then he noticed Hank's keys lying on the middle of his desk. *"That doesn't tell me much,*" he thought. *"We already know he didn't drive home. But then again, it probably means he didn't walk home, since his house key is here, too. And he sure as hell wouldn't walk home without his coat. So where is that son of a bitch? I don't want to have to spend all night tracking him down."*

Tom opened the door to the terrace and looked out. All he saw was snow—trackless snow, with a long pile several feet high where it had slid off the roof. He turned and went back into the office. Just after he closed the door, the message tone on Hank's cell phone went off, indicating that he'd missed several calls from Hannah. But from inside Hank's pocket, muffled beneath the snow, and outside the closed door to the office, it went unheard as Tom headed for the hallway.

Tom searched every office in the building before he called Hannah. "I don't know what to tell you, Mrs. van Daam. I checked his office, and he's not there. But his jacket and topcoat are still in his closet, and his keys are sitting on top of his desk. His computer's on—it looks like he's in the middle of writing something. But I checked every office and every rest room in the building. I even checked the Ladies' Rooms—just in case he had some kind of emergency and ran into the closest one. There's no sign of him. And if he went out on the terrace, his tracks have long since been covered up by all the snow we've gotten tonight. As I told you, I'm working with a short staff tonight, but I'll send the guys who are here around to all the other buildings. Maybe some students invited him to their dorm for hot chocolate or something." *"More likely a beer,"* he thought. "I can also swing by your house and see if he's there—maybe the phone's not working or something. We have a key for the President's residence for emergencies. If you give me permission to go in, I'll be happy to check there. Would you like me ask the city police to keep their eyes out for him, too?"

"Thanks. I'd forgotten about that key. Hank never liked the idea of that, but as a couple of the Trustees frequently

17

remind him, the house belongs to the College, not to us, and you need access in case of an emergency—and this might qualify as one. Yes, by all means, please check the house. But if you talk to the police department, please try to do it carefully—Hank and Chief van den Hoek aren't the best of friends. And please call me back when you've finished checking the house and the rest of the campus. Don't worry what time it is. I'm not going to be able to get to sleep until we track him down. He'd better have a damned good explanation for this, or he's going to catch Hell from me!"

Tom was able to track down one of his student workers to come in and answer the phones while he and his skeleton staff went to all of the buildings on campus. To lighten their load, he contacted the head residents and asked them to check every room in their dorms. While they interrupted a few scattered parties in the process, there was no sign of President van Daam. And none of the students had seen him. Campus Security didn't have any better luck in the other buildings. City police patrols had no reports of him, either. Tom felt Chief van den Hoek's voice had a little too much sting in it when he asked if Tom had checked the local bars and motels, but he kept his thoughts to himself. Whatever the problem was between Hank and Carl, it was none of his business, and he wasn't about to let it keep him from doing his job.

*   *   *   *   *

BY THE TIME TOM CALLED HANNAH AGAIN, it was just after midnight. As she predicted, she hadn't slept yet, and whatever anger she felt about Hank's mysterious disappearance was overwhelmed by worry that something serious might have happened to him. It had stopped snowing in the Cities, and she planned to leave for home as soon as she heard the roads had been cleared. She hoped she could be in his office by 9 the next morning.

Just as Tom ended the call, Max Cuypers knocked on his door. As Head of the College's Buildings and Grounds Services, it was his responsibility to make sure the campus was kept in the kind of condition that Hank deemed suitable. That included plenty of flowers—and no dandelions—in the summer, and clear sidewalks in the winter. Unfortunately for Max, Hank not only had high standards, but also definite ideas about how certain things should be done.

"What's going on? I've run into Security staff in three buildings tonight, obviously doing more than their usual building walk-throughs. But when I asked them what they were doing, they told me to ask you. It looks like we were lucky with this storm. The snow is already starting to let up, and if I'm going to make any headway, I've got to get started. With the Trustees coming tomorrow, I've got to get the snow cleared in the key areas of campus, but until the President leaves, I can't get much done."

"What do you mean, you can't get it done 'til he leaves?"

"We've got to plow the parking lot, but he doesn't like plows near his car—afraid we'll scratch it. I told him we'd use a blower near his car, but he's afraid it will pick up sand and blow it onto his car. And he doesn't like us usin' a blower on that damned terrace of his unless it's absolutely necessary, since it might drift all the way down to his car, and even then, never when he's in his office. The noise of a blower 'disturbs him.' Damned 'Princess and the Pea,' as far as I'm concerned. So I've been sittin' in my office waitin' for him to drive home so that we can clear the lot and the terrace—I'm still waitin'."

"That's the problem."

"What is?"

"Well, he's not in his office. We don't have any idea where he is. His wife's been calling him since before 8:00, with no answer—he's not in his office or at home, and he's not answering his cell phone. Nobody's seen him since Annika left about quarter to six."

"I wonder where that crazy bugger's run off to. If you find him, let me know. In the meantime, I'm gonna start clearing the parking lot. And when I can spare someone, I'll have someone take a blower up on the terrace. If we don't have that cleared before the Trustees show up, he'll want my head on a god-damned platter."

"Sounds like a plan to me. Plow the lot, but use the blower 'delicately' around his car. And tell whoever blows the terrace to make sure they always keep the blower pointed away from where his car is parked. His keys are on his desk, so we could move his car, but he'd probably raise even more Hell if we tried that."

While Max would have preferred to have the terrace cleared in daylight, that would have given them too late a start. If Hank came strolling in at 8:30 and found any snow still on the terrace, they'd never hear the end of it. So at 6:00 a.m., he sent his best student worker up to the terrace. He gave him strict instructions to carefully avoid blowing any snow in the direction of the President's car. Fortunately, the wind was blowing from the Southwest, away from the lot, so that wouldn't be a problem.

It was almost 6:30 by the time Denny Bakken had worked his way close to the President's office. He'd once been chewed out for running a leaf blower while van Daam was in his office, so he kept one eye on the office window, while he carefully kept the snow blower on a precise path: the President also expressed his displeasure when lawnmower or snow blower tracks weren't straight. And of course, Denny also had to watch to make sure no snow was drifting in the general direction of his car.

Even with a bottom layer of heavy snow, on top of a thin layer of ice, the blower was working well. And the wind kept blowing in the right direction. But suddenly, Denny saw something that made him stop in his tracks. Instead of the clean, white snow that he'd been spraying off the rest of the terrace, there were now small blotches of dark, mushy snow coming out of the blower. In the dim light of the terrace, there was no color, but he could tell it

20

wasn't "pure as the driven snow." He killed the engine, and bent down to take a closer look. He was standing by a drain. It was frozen over, but it was still the lowest point in this part of the terrace. And something other than melted snow had been collecting there. Even in the dark, it looked like blood. Just as he bent down to look at it more closely, he heard the muffled sound of a cell phone under the snow, signaling messages and missed calls. Denny didn't know whose phone it was, or where the blood came from, but he knew that he shouldn't be the one to dig any further. He ran back to the office to find Max.

Max wasn't in his office, but he'd left a sign outside his door indicating where he could be found: in the coffee shop with Tom Olsson, trying to figure out what to do next if Hank didn't turn up soon. Denny ran to the coffee shop. Since it had only been open a few minutes, it was easy for him to find Max and Tom. From the look on his face when he came through the door, they knew something was wrong.

"Max! Max! Up on the terrace. Up on the terrace. Come on – now!!"

He'd already started back out the door when Max stopped him. "Hey, Denny, slow down! What's goin' on? Have you finished clearin' the terrace already?"

Denny took a second to catch his breath, and then tried to explain what he'd just seen. "Did you ever see 'Fargo'? The guy stuffing the body in the wood chipper? It reminded me of that, but I didn't see a body—just some dark slush. Still, it looked red, even in the dark. And there's something beeping under the snow. Come on—I didn't touch anything. I wanted you to see it. But be careful when we get to the terrace—there was a thin layer of ice under the snow. I was going to spread some ice-melt when I got done with the blower."

Max and Tom gave each other a skeptical look, and followed him out the door. "If it were anybody else," Max said, "I'd think they'd been smokin' funny cigarettes or somethin'. But Denny's my most reliable worker. If he says somethin's screwy, then somethin's screwy."

While the sky was starting to lighten a bit, the sun wouldn't be up for almost another hour. He figured he'd need all the light they could get, so on the way to the terrace, Tom made a detour past his office, where he picked up a couple of heavy duty flashlights. They showed that Denny had been right. The slush was indeed dark red. There was blood coming from somewhere on the terrace. And then they heard the phone beep.

Max started to move into the pile of snow when Tom stopped him. "It's my guess that we've probably just found Hank. But if we did, I doubt we'll be able to do anything to help him, from the looks of this. We need to see if there's any possibility that he's still alive, but we've got to do it carefully. I don't want to mess up something that may be important. I'm just a Campus Security Director. And half of this community has never felt comfortable with a Swede in charge of Security here, so they'll all be second-guessing anything I do. As soon as we find out what's under that snow, we need to get some real police here right away."

The two of them carefully brushed snow away in the area the beep was coming from. When they found Hank's body, Tom felt Hank's throat, hoping to find some hint of a pulse.

He frowned and shook his head. Then he took a deep breath, and turned to Max: "Can you call Chief van den Hoek? Explain what we've found, and tell him to get his ass over here right away! I know he can't stand Hank, but I also know he's not going to want to do anything that would make him look like he screwed something up. I'll make sure no one else comes out on the Terrace."

*   *   *   *   *

CARL VAN DEN HOEK MADE IT ACROSS TOWN in less than ten minutes, with lights flashing and siren blaring the whole way. Thanks to the lights and siren, he was able to maneuver quickly through the traffic backed up at the stoplight on campus. Even though it was Saturday morning, and there wasn't much traffic because of the storm, that was still a bottleneck. After he pulled into the parking lot by the CUB, he crossed over to the Carroll Center as quickly as he could on the icy sidewalk. He took the stairs two at a time. Carl slowed his pace when he got to the terrace, but he was still trying to catch his breath when he got to where Tom and Max were huddled by the snow blower.

"Okay, what the Hell's going on? What's this about blood, snow blowers, and cell phones? Max, the officer you talked to said you were a little confusing on the phone. And what's this got to do with Hank? Did he somehow grind his foot in a snow blower? I can't imagine him doing any manual labor on this campus."

Tom answered before Max could say anything: "The snow blower's not the cause of the problem—it provided the answer to something we were trying to figure out all night. Max, move so the Chief can get close enough to take a look for himself."

Carl peered over the snow blower, and saw the swath of reddish snow that had spooked Denny. Then he looked at the thin layer of red ice over the drain—what had earlier been slush was already hardening in the frigid air. As if on cue, the cell phone beeped again. That's when he saw Hank's body.

"When you called last night," Carl said, "I thought you were worrying about van Daam for no reason—that somebody had invited him for a drink or bite to eat, and when the storm hit, he just decided to stay over at their place. I figured he'd turn up this morning, bright eyed and bushy tailed. I wasn't counting on something like this. You've checked to make sure there are no signs of life?"

Tom shook his head. "I couldn't find any pulse, and the body's cold. Hank's definitely dead."

"Then I don't want anyone to touch anything else," he continued. "And I want to make sure we get photos of everything. One of my officers should be here any minute. She usually has her camera in her car—I'll call her to make sure. In the meantime, don't let anyone touch ANYTHING up here!"

Carl went back to his car and called Laura van Klees on the radio. She assured him she had her camera with her, and she was only a couple blocks from campus. He then put in a call for a couple more officers to get to the campus as quickly as they could. As he started to head back to the terrace, Officer van Klees's car was already pulling into the parking lot. He waved her over, and she joined him as he raced back up the stairs.

Carl immediately put her to work taking pictures, starting with the snow blower and its gruesome trail of red snow. She quickly worked her way to the pile of snow and Hank's body.

"Laura, I want pictures of all of this," Carl barked. "Get as many close-ups as you can, but without messing up any of that untracked snow! It looks like there's a big gash on the back of his head—probably the source of the blood. And look at the contusion on the base of his neck, just above the hair line—it looks like he took a pretty good blow there. Make sure you have plenty of pictures of all of that. And get pictures of everything else you can think of—around the door to his office, the railing, . . . everything!"

To no one in particular, Carl said, "We've gotta make sure this doesn't get screwed up. There are enough 'town and gown' problems around here already, and everybody knows Hank and I didn't get along. If anything slips through the cracks, I'll never hear the end of it! Whatever happened here, I'm not willing to leave it to our little one-horse police department. We're used to dealing with students peeing in someone's yard on the way home from the bar, or fights between neighbors when one of them forgets to return a rototiller or snow blower. My force and

I may have listened to a few presentations about violent crimes at training seminars, but we've been lucky to only have to deal with small town problems. For something like this, we need some real expertise."

He took out his cell phone, and called the desk sergeant at the police station. After he explained what they'd found, he said, "Larry, call the Bureau of Criminal Apprehension in St. Paul. Tell them we need someone out here from BCA Homicide to look at this. Hell, tell 'em to send Lucas Davenport, if he's available. Just tell 'em we need some help asap!"

"Who's Lucas Davenport, Carl?"

He shook his head. "Forget that part, Larry. It was a poor attempt at humor, at an inappropriate time. But you need to broaden your choice in reading materials."

A few minutes later, Carl's cell phone rang. It was Larry. "Good news, Chief! The woman I talked to in St. Paul told me to call Bemidji, since that's the closest field office. Turns out a BCA agent from there was down in St. Cloud yesterday—his mom fell on a patch of ice on Thursday, and was in the hospital overnight. After he got her home yesterday afternoon, he was heading back to Bemidji when he got caught in the storm. When he'd passed the third or fourth car in the ditch, he figured he should hole up somewhere for the night. The first motel he came to was the New Leiden Inn. When I told them what you needed, they called him right away. They caught him just as he was finishing breakfast, and was about to get back on the road. She told him to go to the campus instead. He should be there in ten or fifteen minutes. They'll also send down a crime scene team right away. But the woman I talked to first, in St. Paul, also said to tell you they don't have anybody named Davenport working in their office, and that she's tired of people asking for him."

"Christ, you didn't actually ask them to send Lucas Davenport, did you?"

"That's what you told me to do, so I did. Did I do something wrong again, Chief?"

25

"No, Larry, don't worry about it. I'll talk to you later. And I'll give you a couple of Davenport mysteries to read in your spare time. Christ! I can't believe a police officer in Minnesota doesn't know who in the hell Lucas Davenport is!"

After Carl hung up, he went back to where Max was still working to clear snow. Laura van Klees was documenting every step with her camera. Tom soon joined them, with his cell phone still in his hand. "That was Hannah van Daam," Tom said. "She said she got a late start out of the Cities—a semi had jackknifed, and blocked both lanes just after they got on I-94. And they were stuck between exits, so they couldn't pull off to get around the accident. She thinks she should be here by about 10:30 or 11:00."

"Did you tell her that we found Hank?"

"No. When she asked what we were doing, I just said we were following up a couple more leads, and hoped to know something by the time she got here."

A few minutes later, they saw a short, ruddy-faced man walking toward them on the terrace. He was bundled up in a parka and bomber hat, with the flaps pulled down over his ears. "Good morning," he grumbled. "I'm Frank O'Leary, from the Bureau of Criminal Apprehension. I got a call from my office in Bemidji that you've got some kind of problem here you wanted checked out. What's going on?"

Carl introduced himself, as well as Tom and Max. Then he led Frank to where Hank's body was still lying in a shallow layer of snow. "They tried to uncover it as carefully as possible, but they wanted to make sure he was really dead. Officer van Klees here has been taking pictures of the whole area. But we made sure nobody touched the body, other than to brush enough snow off of it to see what was there, and feel for a pulse. I wanted someone with expertise in something like this to have a look. The only bodies I've ever been around have been at funerals."

O'Leary knelt down next to the body, carefully examining the laceration on Hank's scalp, and the contusion at the base of his skull. "My office said they have a crime scene team on their way already. They'll go over this terrace with a fine-tooth comb. Do you have any staff who can help us control this area?"

"Sure, I can assign a couple of officers to help with whatever you need. Just don't expect someone with experience dealing with something like this."

"Don't worry about that," Frank replied. "They won't have to do anything technical. As long as they don't mind doing some grunt work, they'll be fine, experienced or not."

He turned to face Carl directly, and asked, "Who're we looking at here? I assume you know him. From what little I can see of his clothes, it looks like he's probably not some underpaid philosophy prof. I'm guessing Dean or higher, right?"

Carl couldn't help but laugh. "You're right there. Definitely not a poorly paid prof. That's Henrik van Daam—until this morning, President of Nieuw Nederland College. Or as he would've introduced himself to you, 'Just call me Hank.' He always liked to tell everyone that he was 'just one of the guys.' But he never mixed with the 'little people' unless he absolutely had to. As a result, instead of Hank van Daam, he's better known to some of us as 'that damned Hank.'"

Frank thought about Carl's response, especially the tone of his voice. "Can you think of anyone who might have wanted to see him dead?"

Carl laughed again. "Where do you want to start?"

Then, as if in protest, Hank's phone beeped again.

2
Birds of a Feather

The Previous Summer: Monday, August 12

SIX MONTHS BEFORE HANK'S UNTIMELY DEMISE, no one in New Leiden was thinking about snow storms. The summer weather had been its usual mixture of heat and humidity. The heat index would build to a point where no one went anywhere that wasn't air-conditioned. Then a thunderstorm would clear everything out, and everyone would enjoy a brief respite of relatively dry, warm weather.

Dean Sarah Christiansen stormed into her office. She threw her briefcase down with such force that it bounced twice before hitting her desk. That knocked over the picture that had been set near the edge of the desk. She was barely able to catch it before it fell off. She took a few deep breaths to compose herself, and set the picture back in place. Then she walked back to where her secretary, Mary de Smet, was sorting the morning mail.

"How'd your meeting with President van Daam go?" Mary asked.

"It didn't! He had a fundraising meeting this morning, and he didn't bother to have Elke let us know. She said he told her that he'd get the word to me, but it apparently 'slipped his mind.' She was going to call you about it anyway, just to make sure we knew, but he got her busy doing something else, so she didn't get a chance. She was as surprised as I was when I showed up and his office was empty."

"Do you want me to try to reschedule it?"

"That's what I was just going to ask you to do. Elke said that he needs to meet with me before next week's

Faculty Assembly meeting—that it's 'really important.' This doesn't seem like any way to run a railroad."

"Oh, I'm sure it's just a normal 'beginning of the school year glitch.' Things'll start going better once you get into a rhythm. Just you wait and see!" Sometimes Mary's cheerfulness could be almost too much for Sarah to take.

"I sure as Hell hope so!" Sarah said to herself. Then she took another breath, smiled at Mary, and said, "I'm sure you're right. Thanks."

She walked to her desk and looked at the picture she'd almost knocked to the floor. It showed her twin daughters at their college graduation in May. Anyone could tell at a glance that she was their mother. They had her bright blue eyes, and naturally blonde hair, though without the streaks of gray that were now evident in hers. Like her, they were both tall and trim. Their athleticism was evident even through their graduation gowns. They'd been the stars of their college volleyball team, which had gotten to the semi-finals of the Division III championship the previous year. Now they were starting post-graduate studies: one was beginning medical school in Illinois, and the other was entering a graduate program in anthropology in Virginia.

She picked up the photo, and said, "We all thought it would be exciting to start the 'new chapters of our lives' at the same time. I hope yours are off to a better start than mine is! I've only been here since July, and I'm already wondering if becoming Dean here was a mistake." She shook her head, put the photo back on her desk. Then she sat down at her computer to get back to the project she'd been working on the previous afternoon.

*   *   *   *   *

CHRIS VAN ZANT WAS SETTLING into his office in Macalester Hall. He'd just taken the last few books out of his packing boxes, and was putting them on a shelf when he heard a knock on his door. He looked up to see Marty Dykstra leaning against the jamb, blocking most of the doorway with his huge frame. "Welcome to the Nieuw Nederland Department of History, Christiaan," he said, stepping into the office with his right hand extended.

"Just 'Chris' is fine, Doctor Dykstra," Chris replied, feeling the strength of Marty's grip. He noticed that his hand seemed almost twice the size of his own. "The only people who call me 'Christiaan' any more are elderly aunts and classmates from high school. I always preferred Chris, and ever since I started college, that's how I've introduced myself."

"I can relate to that. I prefer Marty. But all of my aunts are long gone, and I only see people from high school if I go to reunions every five or ten years, so I don't run into that problem much anymore. About the only person who calls me 'Martin' is Hank van Daam—because he knows I prefer 'Marty.' It's just one of his little quirks. If you want him to call you 'Chris,' introduce yourself to him as Christiaan. That might work, but it's no guarantee. "

"It's probably too late for that. When I was on campus for my interview in February, I introduced myself to him as 'Chris.'"

"I doubt he'll remember. The next time you meet him, just introduce yourself to him as Christiaan, and you'll probably be Chris from then on. But if not, don't worry about it. You probably won't run into him that often."

"Thanks, I'll try to remember that."

"And you can drop the 'Doctor' stuff, too. It's Marty. We're colleagues. If faculty in a department our size can't call each other by their first names, this won't be a very pleasant place to work." He looked around Chris's office and asked, "Are you getting settled in okay?"

"Sure, no problems so far. Tech Services got my computer set up this morning, and I've just finished unpacking my books. I'll need to organize them sometime, but at least they're out of the boxes."

"Then it looks like I caught you at a good stopping point. Before you start a new project, do you have time for me to buy you a cup of coffee? Since I'm your department chair, at least for the coming year, the Dean wants me to be your 'mentor.' She hopes that I can help you avoid some of the more obvious problems that might crop up between now and your tenure review. I've got a meeting with her next week, and I'd like to report that I've already gotten started. A coffee break's as good a place to begin as any."

"That sounds great to me! Is there someplace here in the building to get coffee? I didn't notice anything when I was looking around earlier."

"Nope! There's nothing here in Macalester, or any of the other classroom or office buildings on campus, for that matter. There are machines in the dorms, with really bad instant coffee, I'm told. And once the semester starts, there'll be a coffee pot going in the department office. But unless you don't mind stale, weak coffee, I'd avoid that, too. For a cup of decent coffee, you have to go over to the CUB."

"The CUB?"

"Sorry—Central Union Building. You won't find it listed as 'the CUB' on any campus maps. But at the same time, you won't find anyone referring to it by any other name if they've been here more than a few days. So, you've gotten your first lesson in campus geography. Let's go get some coffee. It'll give you a chance to meet a few faculty from some other departments. A couple of emeriti faculty might be there, too. I'm sure you've already met most of your cohort of new assistant professors, but you should meet some of the more senior faculty, too. We don't claim to know everything—at least most of us don't. But we've been around the block a few times. Maybe we can help your generation avoid trying to reinvent the wheel every time someone comes up with an idea that they think is 'new.' You'd be amazed how many times I've heard some new faculty member propose something in the

Faculty Assembly that they think is 'new,' when it's already been proposed, if not necessarily tried, many times before."

As they were walking out of the building, Marty stopped for a moment and asked, "How familiar are you with the campus?"

"Aside from Macalester, the only building I've been in so far is the administration building—the Carroll Center, right? I had to fill out the forms for payroll and insurance. Then yesterday afternoon, we had our first 'orientation for new faculty' session in one of the classrooms there."

Marty laughed: "'The Carroll Center for Teaching and Administration'—without doubt, the most aptly named building on campus."

"In what way?"

"It's not named after Lewis Carroll, but it could just as well be. Most of the ideas that come out of the administrative section of that building remind me of *Alice in Wonderland* or *Through the Looking Glass*. Listening to the Dean or President lay out some of their 'brilliant ideas,' I sometimes expect to see the Mad Hatter chasing a white rabbit into the building. They may sound great when the Dean or the President is describing them, but when you think about them for a little while, you realize that they're closer to fantasy. They're more like smoke and mirrors. When Hank's talking about faculty positions, you can almost hear him yelling, 'Off with their heads!'

"And including 'Teaching' in the name of the building is increasingly becoming an exaggeration. While our teaching staff hasn't increased to go along with our increased enrollments over the last decade or two, the number of administrators in that building seems to have expanded exponentially. A few of the administrative offices, like the Vice President for Student Affairs, have spilled over into the CUB, using offices that were previously dedicated to student organizations. In addition, several of the classrooms in Carroll were carved up to make more offices. So there's less and less teaching done in that building, and the administration's gradually taking over the CUB, too. I wouldn't make any bets about the amount of genuine, productive work that actually gets done among the administrators in either place," he laughed

Marty pointed back in the general direction of Macalester Hall. "Have you had a chance to meet anyone else in the building?"

"Just the other members of the History Department, when I was on campus for my interview in February. But no one since I started moving in this morning. Who else is in the building besides History?"

"International Relations and Political Science, though the former would just as soon that we were somewhere else. They don't have any problems with Political Science—there's quite a bit of overlap between their courses. But some of them have the idea that 'Ancient History' means anything before World War II, and that none of it's worth studying. For that matter, to them, the Cold War is 'Medieval History.' It doesn't help that van Daam has an even more limited view of our relevance."

"Really? When I met him in February, he didn't give any indication of that."

"He wouldn't. But trust me: if your field were something other than modern European history, we probably wouldn't have been able to keep your tenure line."

"You're kidding me! What would've happened to it?"

"He'd have probably sent it over there," he said, pointing at Drake Hall. "The Department of Economics and Business Administration. Either there, or to that bright, shiny building with all the chrome and glass: the Mudd Center for Science and Technology. Biology and chemistry majors make up the vast majority of our pre-med or pre-dent students. Doctors and dentists are much more likely to become big donors than high school history teachers will ever be—once they've paid off all of their student loans, of course. And he's still hoping one of our computer science majors will become the next dot-com 'gazillionaire' and show some big-time gratitude to their alma mater. But it takes a lot more money to offer lab science classes than business courses. So fundamentally, he thinks our financial future lies with building up the Business faculty—even though we don't have an accredited business department, and we can't offer an M.B.A."

Like many small liberal arts college, NNC only has one degree: a Bachelor of Arts, regardless of major. There is no Bachelor of Science, Music, or anything else. It also only offers undergraduate courses. There are no graduate programs—much to President van Daam's dismay. On a couple of occasions, Hank had suggested that the college should start 'outreach' programs to offer courses in the Twin Cities. His ultimate goal was to offer graduate programs there as well. But the Faculty Assembly had been strongly opposed to that idea--even at the undergraduate level. And there was no interest in expanding to offer graduate degrees. So the idea went nowhere. That faculty opposition solidified his negative views about the Faculty Assembly and the idea of "shared governance."

When they got to the CUB, Marty steered Chris toward the back of the coffee shop, where large thermoses held several varieties of coffee. "There's 'regular' coffee, decaf, dark roast, and a 'flavor of the day.' Looks like it's hazelnut today. Or if you'd prefer tea, they have several kinds of that, too, including herbals. There's also iced tea or sodas if you'd prefer something cold. Take your choice. If you'd like a snack, I highly recommend the cinnamon rolls. My treat today."

"Thanks! I wasn't expecting more than one variety of coffee—maybe with decaf as an alternative. I'm surprised to see so many choices."

"That's been a nice change over the past few years. And once classes start, the smaller coffee shop on the second floor—the 'Bean Bag'—will also have made-to-order espresso drinks. This one has a machine that dumps out what is euphemistically referred to as 'cappuccino,' but it's essentially an expensive cup of instant coffee with powdered milk and flavoring in it."

"An espresso machine? That sounds great! It reminds me of the Pacific Northwest 'coffee culture.' I was afraid I'd be leaving that behind when I moved to the Midwest."

"It's one of the few positive results of the switch to this food service. About three years ago, van Daam decided we needed to 'privatize' a number of things that the College had run for itself for decades. The food service was his first—and most successful—effort. One of the big national food service providers took it over, and by and large, it's worked pretty well. Students still complain about some things in the cafeteria, but you'll never avoid that. And they're hosting receptions and big events for people from town, which adds to their bottom line. Not surprisingly, van Daam soon found himself serving on their board of directors. I don't think he really does anything, other than to go to meetings a couple times of year, and deposit an occasional check for his services. Nice work if you can get it! He didn't have as much luck with the bookstore. He wanted to bring in a franchise from one of the national bookstore chains, but they did a market analysis, and thought it wouldn't be worth their time."

Marty swiped his faculty card through the scanner to pay for their coffee and rolls, and pointed toward a couple of tables that had been pushed together in the opposite corner of the coffee shop. There was already a small group there, engaged in what was obviously a light-hearted conversation. Occasional bursts of laughter could be heard across the room. While they represented a range of ages, Chris could easily see that he would be the youngest person at the table. There were still a few empty chairs around the tables, so he figured that more people were expected.

When they got to the table, Marty bellowed, "Good morning, everyone!" The group immediately quieted down as everyone looked up to see who had arrived with Marty.

"I'd like you to meet the newest member of the History Department, Chris van Zant. I think a couple of you might have seen him when he was on campus last winter, but hopefully this won't be quite as much of a nerve-wracking experience for him as that was."

He then turned to Chris: "This isn't a 'set' group. The faces that show up here change from day to day. Some of us come here a couple times a week, and one or two are here every day—the ones with the lighter loads," he laughed. "Let me introduce you to today's line-up. Going around the table, we have Terry O'Brien, from Math. To his left is Johanna Jacobsen, Education—she specializes in social studies at the secondary level, so she works with quite a few of our majors. You'll probably have a lot of contact with her. You'll notice that she has a slight hint of a southern drawl. Johanna did her graduate work in Tennessee, and occasionally slips in an occasional 'y'all' when she's not careful—not all the time; just enough to add a little spice to the dominant Midwestern brogue you'll find around here. If she really gets wound up, though, she sounds like a finalist in a 'Miss Magnolia' pageant. Her husband, Al, works in the library. He handles the Social Sciences collection, so you'll probably want to meet him soon, too. Next to her is Ed Coonradt, who teaches Finance in the Business Department, and then Marianna de Han, from Chemistry. Despite her name, she's not Dutch—her husband is. She's 100% Minnesotan, and has the strongest 'Scandahoovian' brogue you'll hear among the faculty. When she really gets rolling, she can get three syllables—and almost two octaves—out of the word 'No.'"

"You bet!" Marianna laughed. "And I can even throw in an occasional 'Youbetcha' when I really want to show off my Norsky roots."

Marty finished his introductions: "The guy at the end is Dirk de Vries, from Political Science. His office is right above yours in Macalester."

As Marty introduced each person at the table, Chris moved around and shook hands with each of them. Terry was the first of the group to speak up after Marty finished the introductions. "Before you ask: No, Marianna and I aren't the only members of the faculty who aren't Dutch. But I was one of the first. And as near as I can tell, I was the first Irish Catholic. I think a few of the old guard are still suspicious of my intentions—probably afraid that I'll turn over some classified information that will lead to a takeover by the Knights of Columbus, or something like that."

Ed responded next: "As Marty said, I teach Finance." He chuckled, "I tell my students at the beginning of every semester, we're the ones who don't have the personalities to become accountants."

After a few of the others chimed in, Dirk asked, "To turn to a more serious topic, are you A.B.D., or have you finished your dissertation?"

"I finished it in May, and defended on June 5. So I'm a full-fledged Ph.D."

"Bet he's still signing everything with 'Ph.D.' after his name, right?" Marianna laughed.

Chris blushed. "I suppose that's common, isn't it?"

"Sure, we've all been through that," she said. "There's nothing wrong with being proud of your accomplishments. But after a while, you won't be quite as concerned about everyone knowing you have a doctorate. You'll still be proud of it, but once the novelty wears off a bit, you won't worry about it or wear it like a badge. So, are you straight out of grad school, or have you had a chance to get some full-time teaching experience?"

"I had a temporary—but full time—position the last two years. There were quite a few course preps, but I was still able to finish my research and get the writing done to finish my dissertation. It's a relief to have that behind me."

"Congratulations!" Dirk seemed to visibly relax. "That's one potential problem out of the way. Just out of curiosity, what kind of proof did you have to give the Dean's Office that you've finished your Ph.D.?"

"The registrar sent an updated transcript of my grad work, which had the completion of my degree officially noted on it. But the Dean's Office also had me bring in my actual diploma so they could make a copy for my file. That caught me a little by surprise."

Ed laughed, "Once burned, twice scared!"

"What do you mean?" Chris asked.

Marty answered before anyone else had a chance. "It's a long story, but the gist of it is that the former Dean screwed up big time. One of his 'golden children' didn't finish her dissertation."

"That has to happen occasionally, doesn't it. How is that a 'big time' screw-up?"

"Well, first of all, it wasn't that she just missed a deadline. She never got her Ph.D. But it goes deeper than that. She wasn't her department's first choice, but the Dean and the President were both enamored of her, and overrode the department's ranking. She was tall, blonde, and very athletic-looking. Just the way both of them like to see faculty: young and nubile. She was hired as an A.B.D. in the Economics Department, and was given three years to get her dissertation finished. A little over two years after she started here, she told the Dean that she was done. That's the problem. She really wasn't. Unfortunately, her mentor was also in on the scam—he wrote a letter saying that she had successfully defended her dissertation. That was good enough for the Dean, so she wasn't asked to provide any more proof that she had her degree. Three years later, she slipped through tenure review based on the same 'documentation.' She'd gotten an article published, which was one of the key things the committee was looking for, I guess. They didn't see any reason to question the degree. The Dean's Office had already okayed that."

"So, how'd she get caught?"

"She was applying for a grant to fund a sabbatical, and her department head was putting together a letter of support. He noticed that the date she'd listed for her degree wasn't what he'd remembered from her tenure application. So he called her grad school to get clarification of the date. They informed him that her degree was still 'pending.'"

"Why would he remember the date she got her degree, several years after the fact?"

"The date she was supposedly awarded the degree was the same date as his wedding anniversary. If she'd made up just about any other date, she'd probably still be here. Might have even 'climbed the greasy pole' and become a Dean somewhere else by now."

Dirk spoke up again: "That's obviously something they watch pretty closely now. It was pretty embarrassing for the Dean, as well as the members of the Tenure and Hiring Practices Committee. I'm just starting a term on that committee now, so I'll still be on it when you have your Third Year Review. It's nice to know they're making sure we don't have that problem again."

Marty's voice showed a bit of irritation: "But the Dean and van Daam didn't experience as much embarrassment as they should have. They just hushed it up, and swept it under the carpet. When she left here, she told everyone she was going to go into the private sector, which sounded reasonable. Economists and business faculty have more options that way than most faculty at a liberal arts college. Her department head wasn't very pleased with the way they covered it all up, though. Like most of us, he thought she should have had to pay more of a price for committing academic fraud."

"You know that was never going to happen," Marianna said. "Neither 'el Deano' nor 'el Presidente' would ever allow anything to happen that showed that they'd messed up that badly."

Chris waved his hand to catch her attention. "Excuse me. 'El Presidente' is obviously President van Daam—and 'el Deano' is the Dean?"

"Right on the first count," Marty laughed. "But not the current Dean, Sarah Christiansen. El Deano is her predecessor, Paul Rothman—he's now the President at Zwingli College, one of the many small liberal arts colleges down in Iowa. He teased us all that he would be in a milder climate than we have here, but he's close enough to the Minnesota border to freeze his ass off there, too. He's starting his second year at Zwingli. Rumors are, the honeymoon didn't last too long, and the bloom is off the rose as far as most of the faculty are concerned. First of all, it's a pretty conservative school. I'm not sure how well he's going to fit into that. Because of NNC's Dutch heritage, the folks down at Zwingli apparently figured we're much more conservative here than we are. But we don't fit the mold of most Dutch colleges. By Zwingli's standards, we're probably considered screaming radicals. But even if he could finesse that part of it, his managerial style is reportedly rubbing people the wrong way. Instead of sticking to fundraising and ceremonial events, he's tried to micromanage everything. Sticking his nose into an on-going curriculum review didn't win him any points. And that's apparently just one example."

"Micromanaging was always his style," Johanna added. Chris noticed the slight drawl that Marty had mentioned. Her pronunciation of "style" sounded more like "stahl." She continued, "If he hadn't spent so much time here trying to direct the tiniest of details in every department, he might have had time to read some of the departmental reviews he had us do, year after year. And we might have had time to actually do what we were supposed to be doing in the first place: teach and do research. El Presidente's almost as bad, but at least he generally has the sense to stay out of the faculty's way when it comes to academic issues."

Dirk turned to Chris, and said with a very serious tone, "I wouldn't let anyone hear you refer to van Daam as 'el Presidente.' There are some faculty (especially his 'Golden Children') who really like the guy. He gives them everything they want, and they don't see how he walks all over the rest of us. If they heard any of us (particularly a young, untenured assistant professor, like yourself) call him that, they'd probably try to have us run out of here on charges of *lèse-majesté*—behead us, if that were possible. And if HE heard you do it, he'd definitely make life difficult for you. You wouldn't have a chance when tenure review came along, regardless of what the faculty committee had to say. Theoretically, he can't override the committee, but he'd find some way to accomplish that."

Marianna picked up her story where she'd left off. "If she'd been anyone other than a 'golden child,' the problem would have never happened. Marty's right: 'young and nubile.' Someone older, or less attractive, probably wouldn't have been hired in the first place. They stuck a department with someone they liked, without regard for her real qualifications—or lack thereof. This is the price the College had to pay. And they stood there pretending to have clean hands in the whole affair."

"Chris, welcome to the world of higher education," Ed laughed. "I don't know how much experience you have working with administrators, but let me give you some insight: it was no coincidence that Laurence Peter formulated the 'Peter Principle' after observing college administrators at work."

Chris looked puzzled. "Peter Principle?"

"I'm sorry, I just assumed you were familiar with it. If you're going to have a career in higher education, you'll quickly become familiar with the phenomenon, so you'd better know what it is. Peter pointed out that in any management hierarchy, people rise to what he called their own 'level of incompetence.' We hire you as an assistant professor, and you're expected to teach and do research. Do that well, and they'll make you Department Chair, with a new set of responsibilities. Manage a small department well, and they'll promote you to Dean, with expectations well beyond what any Department Chair ever has to deal with. Be a successful Dean, and you'll end up as a Provost

41

at a larger school, or maybe even a President, like 'el Deano' did. But at each step along the way, you're promoted on the basis of skills you have at one level, which don't necessarily fit the next job higher up the pole. When you get to the point where you can't do the job well, you don't get promoted any higher. You reach your level of incompetence. That's the 'Peter Principle.' At that point, if you move at all, it will only be horizontally. Otherwise, you'll be stuck where you are, and everyone under you pays the price."

"That doesn't sound very encouraging!" Chris replied.

"It's not," Marty said. "But unless you want to start climbing the greasy pole, you can usually avoid most of it. In a department our size, the odds are you'll eventually have to spend a few years as Chair, which increases the contact you have with the Dean's Office. Hopefully that won't happen until you've made Full Professor. But most of the time, you'll be able to do your research and teach to your heart's content. If you keep your head down and your mouth shut, they'll generally leave you alone."

"Ha!!" Johanna laughed, almost choking on her coffee. "That's strange advice coming from the likes o' you, Marty! I can't think of anybody who's spoken up against the administration more than you have, at least for as long as I've been here."

"Guilty as charged! But there comes a point when you can only put up with so much B.S. I have no ambitions of going anywhere else. I wouldn't even be Chair now if Johansson hadn't taken an endowed chair in Michigan. But then we wouldn't have Chris with us, either. So I have to handle administrative duties for another year. At the same time, we have a bright young scholar in our department instead of that stuffed shirt Johansson. Reasonable trade-off, as far as I'm concerned."

"There's not a touch of jealousy, is there Marty?" Dirk asked.

"No, not at all. I was getting tired of hearing Johansson tell us all how great he was. You couldn't ask him a simple question without getting a 20 minute lecture, which may or may not have had anything to do with your original question. At least he convinced someone of his talents. And it sounds like he's got a cushy deal with that endowed chair. I wish him well—particularly if it means he's boring someone else to death instead of me. And he won't have to spend much time teaching now—something that's undoubtedly good for both him and his students."

"Wasn't he a good teacher?" Chris asked.

"It wasn't just that he wasn't very good. He essentially had disdain for teaching. He only wanted to do research. He just did the minimum in the classroom, in order to devote more time to his research. On one infamous occasion, he showed one of his classes a video of him lecturing, while he went back to his office to work on his latest book."

Johanna decided it was time to change the subject. "So, if ya replaced Tim Johansson, your field must be Modern European History. What's your specialization?"

"Twentieth century Europe—my dissertation was on the Dutch resistance in World War II."

"He also had a field in Asian history," Marty added. "So in addition to our Modern European courses, he'll occasionally teach some general Asian history courses, too."

"How's your Dutch?" O'Brien asked. "I know you have a Dutch name, but so do three-quarters of the faculty here—and most of them don't speak the language at all."

"I'm pretty close to fluent. Both sides of my family came from Holland in the early '50s, when my parents were in grade school. They wanted us to speak English without an accent, so we were supposed to use English most of the time. But with my grandparents having lived through the Nazi Occupation, they didn't want to see our heritage disappear. So they made sure that we learned Dutch, too. I'm glad they did, for many reasons. For starters, it was easier to understand my grandfather when he spoke Dutch than when he spoke English with his strong accent. In the community where I grew up, there were so many Dutch families that it was hard not to hear the language around you. When I was little, I thought that's what an 'old person' was—someone with gray hair, who spoke with a Dutch accent. When we'd go to church, the older generation always spoke Dutch with one another before and after the service."

In response to a few more questions, Chris quickly summarized his personal background. He'd grown up in Western Washington, about half way between Seattle and the Canadian border. There are a number of farm communities there with large Dutch populations. Most of the Dutch came a lot earlier, but his parents were part of a postwar wave. At first, almost all of them were dairy farmers, and that continued into his generation. Both of his brothers were dairy farmers, and his sister had married one as well. He explained that except for a year spent studying in the Netherlands, he'd spent most of his life in small towns. Even in grad school, he hadn't lived in a big city. Seattle's urban sprawl was finally getting there, but even so, the outlying areas still weren't like being in a metropolis.

Marty laughed: "You may have lived in small towns, but not Midwestern small towns! I think you might find things a little different here."

"How so?"

Marianna laughed: "Didn't you know that Lake Wobegone is only about 20 miles east of here?"

Dirk gave her a stern look and snapped, "You know that's not true, Marianna. You shouldn't be saying things like that about New Leiden." Then he turned to Chris, and, barely suppressing a smile, he said, "She doesn't know what she's talking about. Actually, Lake Wobegone is about 10 miles south of here."

Marty shook his head. "Don't believe either of them, Chris. If you want to know the truth, it's right here. New Leiden is 'Lake Wobegone with a college.'"

Ed chuckled, and added, "There's a waitress at 'The Korner Koffee Korral' who describes it pretty well. She calls this 'the little valley that time forgot.' By the way, Chris, if you're looking for a good breakfast, that's the place to go."

"Johansson had a similar view of New Leiden," Marty added. "I didn't agree with him often, but he was 'spot on' with this. Considering some of the local attitudes toward race, as well as gender relations, he said it was 'Minnesota's largest open-air museum of the mid-twentieth century.'"

Almost everyone at the table nodded in agreement. Then Johanna spoke up again: "To get back to your story, Chris, what gotcha off the dairy farm? Ya didn't want to join your brothers in farming?"

"I decided early on that I didn't want to have to milk cows twice a day, every day, 365 days a year. College sounded more promising. Like many of my classmates who grew up on dairy farms, from the time I was in grade school, I wanted to be a veterinarian. Most of them didn't do well enough academically, even in high school. By the end of their freshman year, the majority of them could tell that they wouldn't be going to vet school—or even college, for that matter. So they saved up their money, bought a car, found a girlfriend, and focused on a future close to home. They were all Future Farmers of America, and in their FFA projects, they raised a few dairy cattle. By the time they'd graduated from high school, they were hoping to start their own herds.

"I didn't have a problem with the academics," Chris continued, "but when I got to college, I quickly figured out how hard it would be to get into vet school. More significantly, though, during my freshman year, I was trying to get my general education courses out of the way. When I got closed out of a few that I really wanted to take, and couldn't find anything else that fit my schedule, I wound up in a history class. I'd never had much interest in history before, but I had a great professor. She really lit a spark in me, and before I knew it, I was a history major. I took my required seminar fall semester of my senior year, and the topic was European colonialism. Because of my family heritage, I focused on the Dutch empire—the significance of the Dutch East India Company's presence in Indonesia and Japan. I continued that Dutch emphasis when I went to graduate school, though I gradually developed a more modern emphasis. Then I parlayed that into a Fulbright to Utrecht University, where I was based while I was doing my dissertation research. I also took a few courses at the University."

"Where'd you study here in the US?" Dirk asked.

"I did my undergraduate work at a small liberal arts college, sort of like Nieuw Nederland: North Puget Sound College. It also has a Dutch background, and I was able to take courses in Dutch language, which polished up what was previously mostly informal, colloquial Dutch. Then I got my M.A. and Ph.D. from Northwest Washington University—NWWU. Since I was the first one in my family to go to college, my parents—especially Mom— were a lot more comfortable with me staying fairly close to home for my B.A. And NPSC's Dutch connection helped in that regard, too. I ended up at NWWU more or less by default. I got admitted to several other schools, but none of them offered me an assistantship. NWWU didn't, either, but if I went there, I could pay in-state tuition. I told myself I'd do that through my M.A., and if I didn't get a T.A., either there or somewhere else, I wouldn't go any farther. At the end of my first year of grad school, my Department Chair called me in and told me they had a T.A. for me, so I stayed there until I left for Utrecht. With the T.A., I was able to get out of grad school with no additional debt—which is good, since I still have to pay off some student loans from my BA."

"You're lucky," Dirk said. "I've known some Ph.D.'s who were paying off their graduate programs for twenty years. Did you have any fields outside of Modern Europe?"

"As one of my secondary fields, I chose East Asia, building on what I'd started with my undergraduate seminar. I'm looking forward to the chance to teach Asian history here."

Terry O'Brien spoke up again: "Where'd you spend the last two years?"

"At one of the smaller colleges in the Oregon state system. It was originally a one-year sabbatical replacement, but the woman I was replacing got a grant that extended her leave for another year, so I was able to stay on. That really helped me get my dissertation finished. I knew my chances of getting a tenure-track job wouldn't be very high in this job market if I were still an A.B.D.— there are too many people with degrees in hand, plus teaching experience. A lot of them already have publications—not only journal articles, but some even have books already. I've gotten started on an article, but I need to get back to the Netherlands to finish a little more archival research. I hope to be able to go for a few weeks next summer."

Marty excused himself to get more coffee for himself and Chris. Just as he was about to leave the table, Alf Thompson showed up. "I hope I'm not too late—I had a dentist appointment this morning, and just got back to campus. You're not all ready to leave, are you?"

"No, I'm just getting a refill. Make yourself comfortable. Dirk, can you make introductions while I'm getting coffee? Alf, I'm feeling generous today—can I get you a cup of coffee?"

"Thanks! I should probably mark this on my calendar," he laughed. "You're not usually so generous."

While Marty was getting the coffee, Dirk introduced Alf and Chris. "Chris is the new modern European historian—'the new Tim Johansson.' Alf's from Biology—the 'bird man of New Leiden.'"

Marianna laughed, "And not just because he's an ornithologist. He looks at everything as if it were avian, including faculty members and administrators."

"He gives new meaning to the description of someone being a 'strange bird,'" Ed added.

Chris raised an eyebrow, as if it were a question mark. "There's obviously a story there. What do you mean?"

Alf smiled, as everyone looked at him, waiting to hear his explanation—which they'd all heard many times before, but enjoyed every time they heard it. "Do you have a bird feeder, Chris?"

"No, but my parents do. I don't think the apartment I'm renting would allow one."

Before Alf could continue, Ed spoke up: "I assume you're probably not in a position to buy a house yet, but do it as soon as you can. It doesn't have to be big, just something you can build equity with. As my Dad used to say, 'renting is like making payments on a dead horse.'"

Marianna glared at him. "Oh, for cryin' out loud, Ed! Chris asked Alf to tell him about his 'bird perspective.' Can you let Alf do that?"

Marty was just returning with their coffee, and as he set the tray down, he said, "As you've already noticed, there's a lot of 'give and take' in this group. If you don't stay on your toes, someone will put you in your place. Alf, pardon the interruptions. Can you please enlighten young Chris here on the 'Alf Thompson theory of bird personalities'?"

"Okay, picking up where I left off," he continued as he glared at Ed. "If you've ever watched a bird feeder, you see different personality traits. You find pretty much the same thing with any group of people, including college faculty. So when I look around me at a Faculty Assembly meeting, I can't help but look at people's personalities as if they were birds out on my feeder."

"Give him some examples," Johanna said.

"Sure. When you're at the Faculty Assembly meeting next week, watch the other faculty members. Most of us will be like the sparrows, chickadees, and finches you see grouped around a bird feeder. They'll hang around, moving as the mood strikes them. Sometimes they'll get on the feeder, while at other times they'll just perch on a nearby branch, taking in all the action.

"But then," he continued, "there are a few oddballs, like nuthatches, which land on the side of the tree upside down."

"That would be our friend Jean, right Alf?" Marty asked.

Before Chris could ask for clarification, Alf answered his question for him: "Jean Lemieux is the senior member of the French Department. I don't know how many French profs you've been around, Chris, but he fits the mold pretty well. 'About half a bubble off level,' but with no shortage of self-esteem."

"Arrogance, you mean," Dirk snarled.

"Yes, that too," Alf replied. "But definitely an unusual character.

"Then we have the song birds—our friends in the Music Department over in Oberlin Hall. Some of them stay out of sight, content to make their music. Most of them are simply content to please themselves with their music, without worrying about what anyone else might think of it. But there are a few who are a lot flashier—the Cardinals. Not only do they make sure you can hear their music (beautiful as it may be), but they also make sure they're seen as well. No hiding in the background for them. We also have a few hummingbirds on campus. Have you met Maria Hendrix yet—the Head of Information Services?"

"In other words, Head Librarian," Marty laughed.

"But Information Services also includes the campus computing resources, Information Technology, and Tech Services, so it deserves a more representative title," Johanna added, defending her husband's department.

"No, I haven't," Chris said.

"Well, she's about 5'2"—"

"In high heels," Johanna interjected.

49

"—and she moves about 100 miles an hours. It seems like she never stays in one place for more than a few seconds," Alf said.

"She's not quite that bad," Johanna said. "But she DOES fidget and move around a lot—and quickly. So I see your point. Please continue, Alf. I'm sorry for being so defensive."

"No offense taken," Alf continued. "Then you have a few faculty members scattered around the campus who are like robins in the spring. You're happy to see them at first, and you enjoy hearing them the first time they speak up, but after a while, you get tired of them. At home, the robins are always trying to build nests above my gutter pipes, making a mess of everything around them. Likewise, these faculty are always trying to get something for themselves, but messing things up for everyone else.

"There are few well-trained technicians, like in Chemistry or Biology. They're like the orioles, who build their nests like baskets hanging up in the long, skinny branches. They're highly skilled, and generally keep out of sight, though you can usually hear them, and they show up at your feeder—but only if you put out what they want."

"What's your assessment of van Daam this week?" Dirk asked, adding with a laugh, "That seems to change every month or so."

"In his opinion," Alf said, "he's an eagle, of course. He's up there, soaring high above the little people below him, with his sharp eye keeping track of everything that might affect the great institution that's been entrusted to his gifted leadership. But you know, from a distance, when you see a large bird circling, riding the updrafts, it's hard to tell if it's an eagle or a turkey buzzard, which is what I used to think he was. But lately I've come to the conclusion that he's a parrot. Teach him to say a few things, and he'll repeat them over, and over, and over again. He doesn't really know what they mean, but he likes the sound of his own voice when he says 'em."

Dirk turned to Chris: "Wait 'til you hear his 'The State of Nieuw Nederland' talk next week. He'll be at his 'inspirational' best. And you'll hear more clichés strung together than you can imagine. At the beginning of the last major fundraising campaign, he had a committee come up with a new slogan for the college, and he never tires of repeating it. It wasn't too bad the first time he did it, but after a while, it got very tiring. I wish I had a hundred dollars for every time I've heard him say, 'Enlightened and Inspired.'"

"How would you describe Marty, Alf," Marianna asked.

"Near the feeder outside my kitchen window, there's occasionally a big 'ladderback' woodpecker. He doesn't intimidate the other birds, but when he flies onto the feeder, the others give him space. He's not one that any of the others want to tangle with. I think that fits Marty pretty well."

"What about the English Department?" Ed said.

"I guess you could say that they're an exception. All the other birds are more or less peacefully minding their own business around the feeder. And then the English Department shows up: the blue jays. Squawking, fluttering around, and driving everyone else away while they dominate the feeder. They may even throw half the seed out of the feeder, but as long as it's done by one of them, they don't care. Then they fly away, and it takes a while before everything settles back to normal. Now, don't get me wrong. Not everyone in the English Department is like that, but they do suffer from a 'group mentality.'"

"More precisely," Marty said, "they hunt in a pack."

"Marty's right," Alf nodded. "You'll hear people talk about how much the English faculty love to have 'lively intellectual exchanges.' They do—among themselves. And they can go on forever. Most department meetings on campus last an hour. But theirs go on for at least an hour and a half. And for some of them, that's not long enough. But let me warn you: if you're in a situation where they're all bantering back and forth about some issue, that kind of thing could go on indefinitely—as long as it's just them. If someone else jumps into the discussion, particularly saying something some of the senior faculty disagree with, then look out. They'll all 'circle the wagons,' and you'll have them coming at you from all sides."

"To mix metaphors," Terry said, "last winter, I was watching a nature program with my kids. It was about wildlife up in the Arctic stretches of Canada. There was a herd of muskox, with calves jumping around, and young bulls butting heads. Then one of the older bulls caught scent of wolves nearby, and they circled up into a defensive ring, with the cows and calves in the center. They were able to hold off the wolves for a while, but then they decided to make a run for it. As the wolves were closing in on the herd, one of the old bulls bumped into one of the younger ones, knocking him off balance, and he went down. The narrator said it wasn't possible to tell whether the bump was accidental or intentional. But the result was that the wolf pack stopped to feast on the young bull, and the rest of the herd got away. Many of the English faculty are the same way. Among themselves, it's 'lively banter.' But let someone else get into it with them, and they circle up, and if necessary, even 'sacrifice' one of their own to maintain the 'right ideas.' Kind of an informal 'thought police.' But your example of blue jays fits, too, Alf."

"Ouch!" Chris said in amazement. "The English Department obviously isn't very popular at this table! I notice there are no English faculty here this morning. Is that part of the reason?"

"Only partly," Marty replied. "Actually, some of the department are among my best friends on campus. Occasionally a few of them will join us, but usually most of the English faculty aren't that interested. We occasionally talk about such mundane things as sports. That doesn't fit with their ideal of 'living the life of the mind.'"

Dirk added, "And I think it's safe to say some of them have a rather 'imperial bearing.' Take Francine Reim, for example. She once told the Faculty Assembly that if you gave her the textbook with a week's lead time, she could teach any class on campus."

Chris asked, "Does that include differential equations or quantum physics?"

"Apparently," Dirk laughed. "You just read the chapter ahead of time, and then you can sit around and discuss it in class. Then maybe write a paper about it. I think she could probably teach a phone book, if students today even knew what those are."

Marty shook his head. "Their last external review said that there were tensions with other departments on campus. Francine replied, 'We can't help it if everyone else on campus is jealous of us.'"

Ed started to get out of his chair. "I can't say that we've solved any of the world's problems this morning, but I need to get back to my office." Turning to Chris he added, "I've been gone all summer, and I need to get to work on my course syllabi."

"Ed teaches finance," Johanna said. "That means that he spends his summer consulting. He manages a couple of good sized portfolios, which adds significantly to what he gets paid here."

"And I've been able to use examples from my work as case studies in publications. If I were neglecting my academic work here at NNC, then you could complain. But I hold up my end of the research production in my department."

"Whoa, Ed! Jack down!" Johanna exclaimed. "I wasn't criticizing you, just explaining to Chris what you do all summer. I can't help but be a little jealous that your field lends itself to consulting."

"Okay, I'm sorry I overreacted. I get a little sensitive at this time of the year when some of our colleagues snipe at me for what I do in the summer. A few years ago, van Daam tried to tell me that I had to stay around campus in the summer so I could be here if the Registrar needed summer advisors. I told him I wasn't required to do it—it wasn't in my contract. He tried to argue that my contract had a vague clause about 'other duties as assigned.' I told him that if he wanted to pursue the matter, I could give him my lawyer's phone number. He's spent the last couple of years trying to figure out how to get back at me for that, but since my classes are always full—with great student evaluations, I might add—and I publish regularly and keep serving on faculty committees, there's not much he can do. Fortunately we have a salary scale that moves everyone along without anybody (like el Presidente) being able to play favorites."

"I noticed a section in the College Manual about a salary scale. That's not common is it?" Chris asked.

"Hardly—we're one of relatively few schools with a set faculty salary scale," Ed said. "It was created back in late 60's or early 70's, long before any of us got here. When I started at NNC, one of the older Economics faculty told me that he was on leave the year it was voted in. He said he'd have probably voted against it, but once it was in place, he came to realize its advantages. If we didn't have it, you'd see departments like Art, Foreign Languages, or History getting much smaller raises every year than Computer Science, Biology, or Business. Considering the fact that the two previous Deans had Ph.D.s in English, our friends in English would have probably fared pretty well. But at most schools, that wouldn't have been the case for English, either. I have colleagues at other colleges who are amazed when I say we have a fixed salary scale, where everyone, across the board, moves up at the same rate. Some say that they wouldn't work at a school with that kind of a system, because they wouldn't get paid as much. They're obviously colleagues in business, and would fare well without our scale. I figure that being able to concentrate on my consultancy in the summer, which gives me additional income all year, more than makes up for not getting higher raises. Having a more collegial faculty to work with is worth it. I can't imagine going into committee meetings with colleagues who would be getting annual raises much lower than mine. And the gap would get bigger every year. But van Daam would prefer to reward his favorites. He'd love to have more ways to play one group off against another."

"Or punish anyone who disagrees with him," Marty said.

Marianna laughed: "You'd probably be at the top of his list in that category."

That brought a smile to Marty's face. "I suspect you're right about that. But it gives me some pleasure to know that my mere presence here irritates him. At this point in my life, there's nothing he can do to me. And I plan to wait him out, and not retire until he does."

Dirk nodded in agreement: "In terms of your department, that's probably wise."

"Why's that," Chris asked.

Marty replied, "Hank believes that there's no reason for us to offer courses in early modern European history, and particularly not courses focusing on Dutch history. He and el Deano had great plans to replace me with someone specializing in Italian history—they'd both heard of the Renaissance (which I teach a course on, by the way), and thought that would be better represented by someone specializing in Italian history. There's such a strong contingent of Italians here, you know, in comparison to our meager Dutch connection—I'm sorry, I shouldn't be so sarcastic. But he essentially told me that if I retired, my position would go to another department. That was the bonus of hiring you, Chris. You're qualified to carry on the Dutch history courses, though he'd like to see those phased out, too. Johansson thought the same thing, so I delighted in the fact that we replaced him with someone who could teach Dutch history. Considering the school's heritage, I think it would be a shame not to continue to offer at least one course related to Dutch history every year. So with your expertise, now I don't care what specialty they replace me with, as long as the early modern courses get covered. If I retired before he did, they'd be gone. But I've heard rumors that he's going to retire at the end of the next academic year. So, hopefully, we'll only have to put up with him for two more years. As soon as he's out the door, I'll announce my plans to retire. I think I can make a good case that if they were to get rid of my early modern European courses, we would be the only one of our peer schools not to offer those. The administration loves to compare us to our peer schools, at least when it involves something they want that our peers have, and we don't. But I won't even consider retiring until he's out the door."

"On that cheery note," Marianna said, "I need to go, too. It was a pleasure meeting you, Chris. I hope to see you around here often. You can probably guess: we're a veritable font of wisdom! As a new faculty member, I realize you can't take the time to join us every day, but hopefully you'll see you here every week or so. We'll also see each other at the monthly Faculty Assembly meetings, but that doesn't count!"

"Don't forget the Faculty Club on Fridays!" Ed added.

"What's the Faculty Club?" Chris asked.

"I'm sorry, Chris," Marty said. "I haven't had a chance to tell you about that yet. Back in the 60's, a couple who lived on the edge of campus donated their house to the College. It was used for a few years as the Student Health Center, and then as offices. In the early 80's, the College sold it to the Faculty for a nominal fee. The 'NNC Faculty Association' is an incorporated legal entity—and we maintain the building, among other things. There are several guest rooms available for off-campus speakers or other visitors, and the main floor is perfect for small receptions. The basement—what used to be the family room—is the Faculty Club."

Ed laughed. "That's the most frequently used area. A lot of people show up there for an informal gathering on Friday afternoons. It's a nice way to interact with colleagues from other departments whom we don't normally see on campus. We don't have a liquor license, so we can't charge for drinks. Somebody found an old spittoon in a flea market. They polished it up, and that's where you throw your 'free will donations' for drinks. We take turns using that money to stock the 'fridge with beer and wine, as well as tending bar. And there are even a few small lockers where people with 'really refined tastes' can keep their single malt scotch or small batch bourbons. If someone wants something in particular to drink that's not in the normal selection, they're free to bring whatever they want."

"You'll be getting an invitation to join in the next few days," Marianna said. "Dues are how we pay the property taxes and routine maintenance. Don't worry, they're not too high, particularly considering the fact that we have such a convenient faculty gathering place. You're not required to join, but there are only a few faculty who aren't members. I hope we'll see you there. And now, I really have to get going. See you all soon!"

The others joined her in bussing their empty cups, and everyone headed back to their offices. Dirk joined Chris and Marty as they walked back to Macalester Hall. "I hope we didn't scare you off with our comments about the administration," Dirk said.

"Not exactly 'scared,'" Chris answered. "But when I was in Oregon, as an adjunct I didn't have much contact with most of the faculty outside my department. Instead of a Faculty Assembly, there was a representative Senate, which I obviously wouldn't be elected to as an adjunct. Campus politics pretty much went on without my knowledge of them. It's obviously going to be a little different here."

"That's true," Dirk agreed. "But don't let yourself get sucked into them, at least until you're tenured. If there's an important issue that you strongly believe in, you should speak up. But in general, I suggest that you keep your head down and your mouth shut on most issues. If you speak up too much, or weigh in on something too controversial, you may end up pissing off someone who could vote against you for tenure, just to pay you back for something you said. Theoretically the tenure review committee leaves all personal feelings out of their decisions. But if you believe that, I've got a bridge in Brooklyn that I'll sell you, real cheap."

When they got back to Macalester Hall, Marty and Chris went down the hall to their respective offices. Dirk started up the stairs to his. Before he got to the first landing, he called down to Chris: "Don't worry—this place isn't as strange as it may have seemed this morning." He paused a moment, and then added, "It's worse!" He laughed, and continued up the stairs.

Before he went on back to his own office, Marty stopped when Chris opened his door. "An interesting lot," Chris said.

"It could be much worse," Marty said. "That bunch this morning is a pretty good group. They're hardworking, dedicated to the College, and they don't take themselves too seriously. Actually, I think you'll find most of the faculty here are like that. . . . I think that's a good note to leave on this morning. If you need anything as you're settling in, let me know. I'll be around every day from now until fall break. I'll have my office hours posted on the door, so if I can help you out in any way, feel free to stop by."

Chris watched him as he continued down the hall. As he started organizing his book shelves, he heard something outside his window. A group of blue jays were in the tree outside his window, and they started a ruckus before flying away.

*　　*　　*　　*　　*

HANK TOOK OFF HIS JACKET and hung it in his office closet. He looked out his window, down toward the football practice field, where the team was just finishing

58

its warm-ups. *"Now there's an exercise in futility!"* Hank said to himself. *"Harry Westbrook couldn't coach his way out of a wet paper bag. I should've fired him at the end of last season, and put the team out of its misery. If we have another season like that again, I promise, he's gone—and all of his assistants with him!"*

Annika brought him a cup of coffee and he settled in behind his desk to enjoy it. "How'd the trip go," she asked. "You look like the cat that swallowed the canary!"

"Great. I finally got old man van der Kellen to loosen his grip on some of the money he's sitting on. Actually quite a bit of it. That's the good news."

"Is there bad news, too?"

"I wouldn't say 'bad,' but not exactly what I'd hoped for. But the important thing is that he was willing to part with $5 million."

"Wow! Congratulations!"

"But, unfortunately, he was very specific. He's one of those guys who are so full of their Dutch heritage that they can't see anything else. He insisted that it go to fund a Center for Dutch Studies. Just what we need!" Hank sneered. "But he wasn't about to give me the money for anything else. The Center would have needed about $3 million, but I convinced him that if he really wanted it done right, it should be headed by someone with an endowed chair. And he agreed. So starting next year, we will have the 'Paul and Cornelia van der Kellen Center for Dutch Studies.'"

"Have you told the Public Relations Office?"

"Not yet. Call Terry Daalmans, would you? And ask him to come by this afternoon so I can give him the details. But I don't want it released yet. And don't tell anyone else about this! I want to make the announcement next week in my 'State of Nieuw Nederland' speech. Terry can write up a news release, and send it out immediately after my talk."

"But you'll let Institutional Advancement know—or have you already told Mike Nagel about it?

"He told me last week that he'd be out of town until tomorrow. Can you have him stop by sometime tomorrow afternoon? If I don't tell him, he'll have a cow. And he can keep his mouth shut. I want this to be a surprise for the campus. I can't wait to see the look on that asshole Dykstra's face. He's been complaining that I haven't been supportive enough of programs related to the College's heritage. This should shut him up."

"If you're looking to see a reaction from Marty, I doubt this will do it. He's pretty good at keeping a poker face."

"But I haven't told you the best part yet. This will really kill him. I insisted that the Center be named after the van den Kellers. It took some talking. As you know, the old guy's pretty shy, and his wife's even more so. But when he agreed, out of appreciation for agreeing to his request to establish the center, he insisted that the endowed chair be called the 'Henrik and Hannah van Daam Endowed Chair of Dutch Language and Culture.' I can't wait to see Dykstra squirm when he hears that."

"Well, congratulations, to both you and Hannah. That's quite an honor, indeed! But as I said, I wouldn't count on seeing any big reaction from Marty Dykstra."

3
One Less Barricade

The Following Week: Thursday, August 22

CHRIS WAS ON HIS WAY FROM THE LIBRARY back to his office. He'd just put several books on reserve for his history course, and he was ready for a coffee break. Except for running off copies of his syllabus, he had everything ready for the first day of classes on Monday. So he decided to see if anyone he knew was in the coffee shop. When he got there, he found most of the group from the previous week, plus a couple new faces. Marty wasn't with them.

He poured himself a cup of coffee, picked the last cinnamon roll out of the case, and paid the cashier. When he neared the table, he realized there was a fairly lively conversation going on, so he was hesitant to join the group. Just as he was about to look for another table, Dirk saw him, and waved him over. "Good morning Chris! I was hoping you'd be joining us again soon. But I imagine you've been pretty busy with course preps and new faculty orientation meetings. Come . . . sit down! There are a couple of people here that you may not have met. Let me introduce 'em to you."

Dirk caught the attention of the group and said, "Most of you met Chris last week. But Casey and Sharon—you both just got back on campus this week, didn't you?" They both nodded in agreement. "Okay, Chris, this is Casey van Pelt, Chair of the Physics Department. Across the table from him is Sharon Dickinson, from Psychology."

Chris shook hands with each of them. Then Dirk asked, "Have you seen Marty this morning?"

"I've been in the library most of the morning," Chris replied. "He wasn't in his office when I left Macalester."

Casey smiled, "I've got some news that I'm sure he'll want to hear. I was hoping he'd be here this morning, so I wouldn't have to repeat it too many times."

As if on cue, Marty walked into the building. "Let him get his coffee," Ed said, "and then you can tell us your hot news. Whatever it is, it must be good. You're grinning like the cat that swallowed the canary."

Marty went straight to the coffee urns and poured himself a cup. Finding the cinnamon roll case empty, he grabbed an apple fritter, paid the cashier, and joined the group. "That'll teach me to get here too late—no cinnamon rolls this morning." He noticed that Chris immediately turned bright red, and saw the uneaten cinnamon roll on his plate. Chris made a gesture, offering it to Marty, but Marty shook his head: "Don't worry, Chris. I'm happy with an occasional apple fritter, too. If you'd taken that right from under my reach, I might think differently. But I don't expect everyone to save something for me if I'm not here in time to get it for myself."

He turned to Casey. "You obviously have something juicy this morning. You look like you're about to burst," he laughed. "Go ahead. Spit it out!"

Casey looked around to see who might be within earshot, and with a conspiratorial tone said, "I got an e-mail from a colleague down in Iowa this morning. He had some very interesting news. I'm sure you'll be interested, Marty! It concerns our beloved former Dean, and how well he's fitting in at Zwingli."

"What's el Deano been up to this time? Micromanaging himself into some kind of trouble, I hope."

"Not so much micromanaging as bullying, as usual. But Rothman apparently tried it on the wrong person this time."

"Now, this I've got to hear! Out with it, Casey! What'd he do?"

"Apparently he didn't like the way one of the grounds crew was grooming the lawn. The lines from the mower weren't straight enough, or some picky thing like that. But instead of just asking him to be more careful with his work, he got into the guy's face. Started yelling at him, including using quite a bit of profanity. But he picked the wrong target."

"How so?" Sharon asked.

"The grounds crew guy was a relatively new hire. He's an Iraq and Afghanistan war vet, who just got out of the Army after a couple of tours of duty in combat zones."

"What did he do, punch him out?" Marty asked.

"No, fortunately—that would've cost the guy his job, and probably would have landed him in jail. He did something even better. He spent most of the last year in counseling for Post-Traumatic Stress Disorder. The counselor he worked with focused a lot on how to deal with situations in which he might lose his temper and react violently. So he took a deep breath, and focused on what his counselor had told him. Then he looked Rothman square in the eye and said something like, 'When I was in uniform, I had to stand there and take it when some shave-tail second lieutenant wanted to throw his rank around. I got yelled at enough when I was in basic training. And then I had to live with it for the next three years. But this isn't the Army, and I don't have to take this kind of abuse.' Then he climbed off the mower and marched straight over to the Human Resources Office, where he filed a formal complaint. At a conservative school like Zwingli, use of foul language is a no-no. And this will come as no surprise to any of you: Rothman hadn't earned himself any favors with the HR staff, because of the way he meddled in—and messed up—a few job searches last year. So Rothman was required to issue a formal apology to the guy, and then participate in a series of anger management seminars. And he's on probation—if there are any similar incidents in the next two years, they'll recommend to the Board of Regents that he face at least a six-month suspension—without pay. If there's retaliation of any kind toward the worker, they'll recommend suspension immediately."

"Well, that certainly brightens up my day," Marty laughed. "I guess there are indeed some limits to the 'van Daam/Rothman School of Management.'"

"I guess I'm lucky I wasn't here when he was Dean," Chris said.

"If he were still Dean, it's highly unlikely that you'd have been hired," Marty replied.

Chris looked at him quizzically, and was about to ask for an explanation, when Dirk spoke up: "He wouldn't have hired you with a degree from what he would disparagingly refer to as a 'directional school,' or a 'school with a geographical point in its name.' He thought we should fill our faculty with Ivy League Ph.D.'s, perhaps with a few from Stanford, Berkeley, or Chicago, to give a little 'institutional diversity.'"

Marty grumbled: "He couldn't understand why we didn't want to hire someone who just wanted to focus on the third week of September, 1871, and who would complain if we wanted them to teach something outside their narrow area of specialization. We had a few applicants for your position who would fit that description. It's like they were physicians, who thought the job was for a specialist at Mayo, when we're more like a family practice—we need people who can teach outside a narrow area of specialization."

Dirk continued: "He would reluctantly hire someone from a Big-10 school, which is what he usually ended up doing. He did manage to hire a few Ivy Leaguers, but every one of them left before they even came up for tenure review. They'd get an article published, or maybe even a book, and that, plus a few years of teaching experience here, helped them land jobs at bigger schools. In a couple of cases, he was willing to go outside the Big-10 and hire someone from one of the larger state universities on the east or west coasts. But History would've had a tough time hiring anyone from Northwest Washington University, unless you were particularly 'young and nubile.' And no offense, Chris—you may be young, but he wouldn't consider you nubile."

"So what's his background?" Chris asked.

"As you might suspect, not one that would fit the criteria he set for a hire," Dirk replied. "Like many of us here, he got his B.A. from a small liberal arts college, a lot like NNC. Then he got his M.A. and Ph.D. from a large state university out East. He's a specialist in Victorian literature. That was part of the problem: he was our second consecutive Dean with a Ph.D. in English. That only added to the arrogance of some of our friends in that department. They almost always got whatever they wanted, and if there was ever some controversy that needed resolution, he'd invariably side with the English Department."

Johanna added, "He was also a classic micromanager. He loved to keep us all busy, doing departmental studies or evaluation reports, but most people felt that he never read any of them. Every department has to do a self-study every seven or eight years, in preparation for an external review. That's been the case here for decades. But I'm sure he never read most of the ones done while he was Dean— either the self-studies or the reports of the external reviewers."

"Or if he did read them," Marty said, "he only paid attention to the parts that fit his pre-conceived ideas. Our last reviewer said basically the same things that we've been arguing for a decade or more. But Rothman simply ignored it. When I tried to point that out to him, he simply said, 'Well, I'm not convinced of that yet.' End of discussion."

Casey agreed: "He was always 'too busy' to meet with a department or to actually get something done. But then he'd turn around and get involved in minor details of departmental administration which he should have left us to work out. And he somehow had enough time on his hands to wander the corridors of the CUB with a marking pen, correcting spelling or grammar on posters that student organizations had put up on the bulletin boards. Then he'd call the president of the offending group and tell them to correct the rest of their posters around campus."

"You're kidding me!" Marty snorted. "That's a new one! Where'd you hear that?"

"The director of the Career Placement Bureau and my wife are both in a women's group at our church. One evening over coffee, she had the group in stitches as she described how she'd seen him going up and down the hall with his red felt pen. She apparently does a pretty good imitation of him. Fortunately for her, neither Rothman nor van Daam ever heard about it, or they'd have made her life Hell for making fun of one of them."

Marty turned to Chris and smiled. "Trust me. You didn't miss anything by never meeting Paul Rothman."

"The Dean I met when I was here for my interview was an interim, right?" Chris asked.

"Correct. The search for the new Dean was just about over when you were on campus," Marty said. "If first impressions are any indication, I think the search committee did a good job on this one. I was holding my breath for a while, because one of the candidates looked like she'd be a real disaster. And of course she seemed to be Hank's favorite. Fortunately, she got a job at a bigger school."

"What didn't ya like about her?" Johanna asked.

"She was the type who had definite answers about things she didn't really know anything about. Higher Ed is full of the type. They roll into a school determined to 'make their mark.' They upset everything, usually firing anyone who's competent, because they feel threatened. They run around 'peeing on every bush,' then, on the basis of their 'decisive leadership,' they get a job somewhere else. There, they start the whole process of destruction all over again. They keep climbing the greasy pole, leaving a trail of broken careers in their wake wherever they go."

Dirk gave Marty a questioning look. "What makes you think Sarah Christiansen is any different, Marty? We've all heard of plenty of deans who fit that mold. And we've all seen colleagues whose careers were ruined by some ambitious dean or VP. That would fit nicely with Hank's management style, too."

"Obviously we don't know anything for certain yet. Probably won't for a while. If Hank were going to be here longer, I don't think he'd have hired her. But my guess is that he's going to retire in a year or two—maybe three years at the most. He just finished a major fund-raising campaign, so this would be a good time for him to leave. And if he were to leave in the midst of too much chaos, that would cast a dark shadow on his 'legacy.' Building his legacy seems to be his top priority lately. I take it as a good sign that she's asking questions, and not telling people what to do when she just got here this summer. And she's a physicist, not an English Ph.D. So I suspect she'll want solid evidence to back up any arguments or requests that we make. That would be nice, for a change!"

Casey interrupted him. "I took that as a good sign, too. I've got an appointment with her tomorrow. She said she wanted to go over our last external review."

Marty nodded in agreement. "She told me the same thing. My appointment's this afternoon. That's why I was a little late this morning. I had to re-read our review. If she's read the History Department's review, I think that's more than could ever be said about Rothman. And she sent me an e-mail asking me to serve as Chris's mentor, to help make sure he earns tenure without any problems. That's a good sign, too."

Ed said, "After my run yesterday, I was just finishing my shower when Matt van Baak came into the locker room." He turned to Chris and explained, "He's Director of the Global Studies Office. He said he had his appointment with Dean Christiansen last week. Apparently the external review of his office had been very critical of the way they run faculty-led programs overseas. She asked him if he'd made the changes the reviewers suggested. When he said he hadn't, she asked him very directly, 'Why not?' To which he replied very simply, 'I was going to implement them immediately, but Dean Rothman specifically told me not to.' Matt said she looked him straight in the eye and said, 'It looks to me like FORMER Dean Rothman's approach opens the College up to a number of liability issues. Those would be financially devastating if anything happened to a student or faculty leader on one of our programs. He's no longer Dean here. I am. And I'm directing you to implement the recommended changes . . . immediately.' Then, just to drive the issue home, she added, 'Just so you know: if you'd told me that you didn't agree with the reviewers' suggestions, and that's why you hadn't done anything about them, I'd have asked for your resignation this morning. But I've been around the block enough times to know that if you'd made those changes against Rothman's instructions, that would have put you out of a job. As I said, I'm the Dean now. Do what the reviewers recommended, and we'll get along just fine.' He was still looking a bit pale when I talked to him."

"What a novel idea!" Dirk laughed. "Do what's right, and not what's least expensive. It sounds like you wouldn't want to cross her, but it also sounds like we might be dealing with a rational Dean, who functions on the basis of facts, and not ego, for a change. 'Rational Dean'—based on our two most recent experiences, I was beginning to think that might be an oxymoron."

Marty laughed, too: "Let's hope that we've finally found an exception. That would be nice, for a change. That's a good note to leave on this morning. Are you heading back to Macalester, Chris? If so, I'll go with you."

"Sure, but first, can someone explain to me what's involved in this 'Investiture Convocation' this evening?"

Johanna spoke up first. "It's one of the few ceremonial things around here that I actually look forward to. It's a public recognition for everyone who just got tenure and promotion to associate professor, as well as those who were promoted to full professor. In addition, there'll be a brief introduction of all o' you new faculty members. Besides the faculty, some of the staff, or at least the ones in 'lead' positions in their areas of responsibility, will be there. And most faculty spouses or partners attend as well. Are ya married, Chris? Or do ya have a partner or 'significant other'?" Chris noticed that her drawl was in evidence this morning, as she pronounced "other" like "utha."

"No, I'm totally unattached. I was dating a woman in my graduate program for a while, but nothing came of it, and we went our separate ways. She left grad school when she finished her M.A. The last I heard, she was working for the California State Archives."

Before Johanna could continue, Dirk commented, "In case you're wondering about her reference to 'partners,' that's a relatively new development at NNC. As with most institutions, there have always been gay faculty members here. But until about five years ago, they couldn't be open about it. In fact, Rothman rejected one department's top choice in a search because she made no secret of the fact that she's a lesbian. Just after that—probably in reaction to it, actually—a full professor decided he didn't want to 'hide in the closet' any longer, and 'came out.' The administration's initial response was to fire him. They thought they could use an 'elastic' clause about 'moral turpitude' to break his contract, but his attorney convinced them otherwise. The next thing we knew, gay and lesbian partners were showing up at events like this, and despite el Presidente's fears to the contrary, the sun keeps coming up in the East every morning, and donors keep writing checks to the College. A few faculty still aren't comfortable with it, and I'm sure some of the more conservative alums have written letters of protest. But I can't see any way of turning back the clock now. Even el Presidente has brought himself to talk about the importance of tolerating what he awkwardly refers to as 'diverse life styles.'"

Marty couldn't hold his tongue: "Speaking of van Daam, one of the nice things about the evening is to watch him start to get red in the face as the Dean recognizes everyone who got tenure. If it were up to him, and many of his appointees to the Board of Trustees, the College would abolish tenure, so he could hire and fire as he sees fit."

Johanna let the interruptions pass without comment, and continued: "Dale Haak, The Director of Student Recruitment and Retention, follows the Dean's recognition of faculty with a brief overview of what our incoming freshman class is like—you know, the number of Merit Scholars, Honor Society Members, class presidents, yearbook and student newspaper editors, Eagle Scouts, and anything else you can think of. Remember, as Marty says, we're in 'Lake Wobegon with a college.' So tonight y'all will be hearin' glowin' testimony to prove that all of our students are truly 'above average.'"

Ed added, "Then all of that's followed by the President's 'State of Nieuw Nederland College' speech. That's usually pretty much just 'boiler plate,' extolling the virtues of this 'Harvard of the Northern Prairie,' and telling us how we need to keep our collective belts tightened. As you listen to his presentation, you can always tell what he wrote, and what his Executive Assistant, Annika van Rijn, wrote for him. She writes well. Her words usually jump off the page. He's never been accused of that. His paragraphs plod along, with mixed metaphors, run-on sentences, and no clear sense of direction. Fortunately, she writes most of what he says. But unfortunately, he makes her stick in his favorite clichés all over the place."

"For the last few years," Marty said, "I've been waiting for him to announce his retirement. Then I can start planning my own. Maybe this year I'll finally get lucky."

"We're supposed to wear 'cap and gown,' right?" Chris asked.

"If you have your own academic regalia, yes, by all means wear it." Marty replied. "If you don't, just wear a coat and tie."

"I have it. When I finished my dissertation, Mom told me that she and Dad wanted to buy my academic regalia for me. But then they found out how much it cost—I thought Dad was going to have a stroke! I told them they could just buy my hood, and I'd get the rest. And I got lucky: when I got the job here, my major professor asked me if I'd be needing a cap and gown. He had a colleague who was retiring, and wanted to sell his. So it didn't set me back nearly as much as a new one would have. I had to get a new cap, but the gown was in great shape, and it was my size. And my parents were pleased to buy the hood. So everybody was happy with that deal."

Before they all got up to leave, Marianna threw out one more question: "Are we going to have a pool this year to guess how many times Hank says 'Enlightened and Inspired' tonight?"

"No," Johanna laughed. "It gets too complicated. Y'all have to set too many variables. How much does it count if he says 'Enlightened' but not 'Inspired' in the same sentence? Or if he says 'Inspired and Enlightened,' instead of the other way around? Or if he gets creative, and slips in 'Enlightening' or 'Inspiring.' I think the correct answer, in any case, would be 'too many,' and y'all never let me pick that."

"I get your point," Marianna said. "But to make his talk more interesting, we should have something to keep track of."

"We know he'll mention the 'intellectual commons' and 'shared inquiry,' or how we're 'all here learning together.' None of Hank's talks has ever left those out! Those are too easy. We could always try to guess how far into his speech he'll get before he mentions how much he loves browsing through bookstores," Marty laughed. "But the winner should also have to guess which of the latest 'pop-managerial' handbooks he'll quote from this year."

Sharon turned to Chris and explained, "To put my psychology training to good use, and try a little 'quickie-psychoanalysis' here: Hank apparently suffers from a case of 'book envy.' He doesn't seem to read anything particularly intellectual. But he's always speaking in glowing terms about anything that's part of a campus-wide reading—that's part of the 'intellectual commons' and 'shared inquiry' that he loves to talk about. For example, when we have convocation speaker come to campus, everyone is invited to read their latest book, or most famous one, in some cases. But he seems to feel uncomfortable discussing anything intellectual. He always says that when he travels, he likes to browse through bookstores. But the only titles he ever mentions are pseudo-business manuals—popular distillations of current business or personnel management theories. And no one's ever seen him darken the door of the 'Northern Prairie Book Haven' downtown."

"I saw that shop when I was opening a bank account last week. It looked like an interesting place, but I haven't had a chance to go in there yet."

Marty said, "Since you're from the Pacific Northwest, I have to caution you not to set your hopes too high—it's no Powell's. But I don't know any other place that is. Still, it's a great local bookstore. I try to give them as much business as possible, rather than ordering on-line. They have a pretty good selection, and they'll special order anything for you. When you have a little spare time, I'll take you in there and show you around. I think you'll enjoy getting to know the owner, too. You'll have a chance to meet him when we have a departmental get-together. His wife, Marcia, teaches Early American history, as well as an occasional course for Women and Gender Studies."

Dirk pushed his chair back from the table, and stood up. "Unless you have any more questions this morning, Chris, I have to get back to my office. I'll see all of you tonight. Don't forget, as usual, you're all invited to our house for a

'*Nachspiel*' after the convocation. I picked up a case of Argentinian wine when I was in the Cities last weekend, and Karen said she was going to experiment with some new hors d'oeuvres that she wants to try out before she offers them commercially. Chris, I'll e-mail you directions to our house. It's easy to find. I hope you can join us."

"If Karen's making the food," Johanna said, "y'all can be sure it'll be good. She has a local catering service, and we often get to be Guinea pigs for her new creations. Given tastes in this community, she doesn't try anything that a local would consider too 'weird'—though a lot of it might be viewed as 'exotic.' This is Minnesota, after all. You'll love it. I hope to see ya there. It'll give ya a chance to meet Al. After we had coffee last week, I told him about you, and he's looking forward to getting to getting to know you. This'll be a good opportunity for that."

"It's also a nice way to put things in focus before tomorrow's Faculty Assembly meeting," Ed added. "Hank will undoubtedly say something that will get someone's dander up—usually Marty's. Talking about it among friends over a glass of wine tonight is a better way to work out one's frustrations than it would be to fuss about it in the meeting tomorrow."

Everyone bussed their dishes, and started back to their offices. As they headed toward Macalester, Marty turned to Chris and asked, "How much research do you have left to do in the Netherlands in order to get that article finished? Last week you mentioned that you hoped to spend several weeks there next summer. Could you get it done during January term?"

"Sure, and it would probably be cheaper for me to go then. But can I be gone in January—just take off? I assumed I'd have to be on campus, even if I'm not scheduled to teach J-term this year."

"It was scheduled that way intentionally. Normally, you'll teach six classes a year. You either teach three courses in the fall and spring, with January off, or teach January, and only two classes in one of the semesters. But for new faculty, the College will give a release from one course, sometime during their first two years. That way, A.B.D.'s can have more time to finish their dissertations, or new Ph.D.'s like you can make some progress on a research project. I scheduled you for two classes this fall, and nothing in January, in the hopes that you could use that to get some work done on an article."

"Thanks. I really appreciate that."

"I wasn't sure whether to do it this year or next, so I just went ahead and gave it to you this year. After you said you only needed a few more weeks to get your research finished, it looks like that was the right decision. As I told the others, I have to meet with the new Dean this afternoon. If you think you can get your research finished by going to the Netherlands in January, I'll see if I can get her office to come up with some funding to help toward a plane ticket. I can pretty much guarantee that the College won't pay for the whole thing. But I may be able to scrounge up a couple hundred dollars. That's better than nothing."

"That would be great! I have some friends who've offered to put me up any time I go back to Utrecht, so it wouldn't cost me that much to be there. Any help you can come up with to get me there would be wonderful!"

"I can't promise anything, but I'll do what I can. Now, I have to get back to my office and read through that external review one more time before I meet with the Dean this afternoon."

*   *   *   *   *

THAT EVENING, HANK VAN DAAM SAT IMPATIENTLY as the Dean read through the list of faculty who'd been awarded tenure and promoted to Associate Professor. Listening to the list of new faculty members was less galling to him, but he could tell that the color of his face probably showed his frustration. In his mind, tenure was a carry-over from horse and buggy days. It had no place in the modern world.

Dale Haak's description of the new freshman class was more tolerable. But Hank felt like much of it was intended to cover up the fact that the College didn't have as many new students as he and the Regents had planned for when they worked up the budget. Although the numbers weren't down much—only two or three students in the incoming freshman class—if Dale didn't start raising them more consistently, he'd be looking for a job somewhere else in the not too distant future. But that would be someone else's problem. Hank just had to get through one more year, and then he wouldn't have to worry about enrollments or the College's budget any more.

When Haak finished, the Dean returned to the lectern. "As I said in my opening remarks, it is an honor for me to begin my term as the Dean of Nieuw Nederland College. And tonight it is my privilege to introduce a man who I'm sure needs no introduction here: President Henrik van Daam. Like the rest of you, I'm sure, I'm looking forward to hearing his assessment of the state of our college, and his vision for its future. President van Daam."

The faculty joined the rest of the audience in a round of applause. It was not particularly enthusiastic, but was suitably polite and long enough not to embarrass either the President or the audience. As he approached the lectern, he shook the Dean's hand enthusiastically, and laughed, "Thanks, Sarah. But please, just call me Hank." Marty and Dirk, seated at opposite ends of the same row, looked at each other and grinned. Dirk had seen Marty mouthing the words, "just call me Hank," before the President had gotten to the microphone. They both had seen it coming as soon as the Dean had introduced him.

Then Hank addressed the assembled faculty: "It is my pleasure to welcome you all to the beginning of another exciting year at Nieuw Nederland College. I hope you enjoyed a summer that was both reinvigorating and productive. The year ahead of us should prove to be one of the most memorable in the long and venerable history of this institution. Opportunities like the ones that lie ahead of us now do not reoccur often."

Marty groaned to himself. *"It's recur, Hank! 'Reoccur' isn't a word! That obviously wasn't part of what Annika wrote,"* he thought.

It took Hank another few minutes before he got to the part of the text that Annika had prepared for him. He managed to avoid any other grammatical or linguistic errors. But when he mentioned "Enlightened and Inspired" and "Inspiring and Enlightening" in consecutive sentences, Marty and Dirk looked at each other and rolled their eyes.

The majority of his speech was what most people had expected. Enrollments were steady, but not as high as the administration had hoped. The Board of Trustees had agreed that faculty would receive a 1.5% salary increase. While that wasn't much, he admitted, it was a full percent more than they had gotten the previous year. The economy seemed to be improving, and the Office of Student Recruitment and Retention was implementing new approaches to attract students. If those were successful, he hoped that salaries could be increased more significantly the following year.

It was clear that Hank was nearing the end of his speech, and the faculty started shifting in their seats. Everyone was ready for the evening's program to end. Hank usually saved some surprise for the end of his talk, and conjecture over what that might be was now the only point of interest for most of the audience. After making some general allusions to "exciting news" and "important developments," Hank finally came to the point.

"As most of you know, I've been working for many years to strengthen our Dutch language program."

That immediately struck a nerve with Marty. He turned to Ed Coonradt, who was seated to his left, and whispered bitterly, "No, he hasn't. He's done just about everything short of killing it. Where's he going with this now?"

Meanwhile, Hank was building his announcement into a crescendo. "Many of you know Paul and Cornelia van der Kellen. They are both active members of our Alumni Association, and they have been generous donors to the College for many years. They are particularly proud of their Dutch heritage, and like all of us, want to see that heritage honored and maintained at Nieuw Nederland College. It is my great honor this evening to announce that they have generously offered to fund the establishment of a new center to promote the study of Dutch language, literature, and culture. Nieuw Nederland College will soon be the home of the 'Paul and Cornelia van der Kellen Center for Dutch Studies.' And to provide the driving inspiration for that new center, they have also generously offered to create a new endowed chair of Dutch Language and Culture."

The audience started to applaud, but he immediately waved for silence. "That's not all." He had picked out where Marty was sitting, and as he continued, he kept looking in that direction in order to see Marty's reaction. "I am humbled, and I'm sure you would expect, embarrassed, to tell you that Paul and Cornelia have insisted that they will only provide the support for the center and the endowed chair if it is called the 'Henrik and Hannah van Daam Endowed Chair of Dutch Language and Culture.'"

The applause resumed, and he turned to watch the look on Marty's face. Much to his surprise, and to the surprise of nearly everyone in the audience, Marty immediately leapt to his feet, and urged everyone in the audience to join him in a standing ovation. Hank looked in disbelief. When the applause finally died down, and everyone sat down again, it took him a moment to regain his composure and resume his presentation.

"Thank you very much. Your response is overwhelming, to say the least. But there is one more important announcement I wish to make this evening. As you all know, it has been my great honor to serve as

President of Nieuw Nederland College for the past seventeen years. We have made great strides in developing one of the finest colleges in the United States. We have continued to enlighten and inspire our students to be examples of dedicated leadership in their communities."

When he said "enlighten and inspire," Marty and Dirk looked at each other and rolled their eyes again. Then Marty raised his eyebrows and mouthed the words, "Where's he going with this?" To himself, he asked, *"Can we hope that he's actually going to retire?"*

"I had several extended conversations with the Board of Trustees this summer," Hank continued. "We've been working hard to build on the strong legacy of the College. Our latest capital campaign was a major success. The Trustees and I agree that it's time to pass the leadership of the College on to a new President, who can lead it to even higher levels of excellence. After giving this long and prayerful consideration, I have decided that I will retire at the end of this academic year. I've asked the Board of Trustees to begin the search for my successor immediately. In this day and age, that is a long and time-consuming process, but they hope to be able to announce a new president early next semester. Thank you for the privilege of serving as your President. I have always tried to follow God's plan for my life. And I believe God has new opportunities for me ahead, just as He gave me the opportunity to serve Nieuw Nederland College."

Once again, he saw Marty leap to his feet, and the rest of the auditorium followed his example in a standing ovation. The College organist began playing the recessional, and Hank joined the other members of the stage party to lead the faculty out of the auditorium. As he walked past Annika, she whispered, "I told you not to expect anything from Marty. That definitely wasn't something I'd have anticipated."

"That son of a bitch never does anything I'd expect," Hank grumbled.

*   *   *   *   *

CHRIS HAD NO TROUBLE finding Dirk's house. When he got to the porch, he saw a note on the door: "Come right in—don't bother knocking."

When he came through the door, Dirk saw him, and came over to take his jacket. His wife was carrying a fresh platter of hors-d'oeuvres from the kitchen, and he waived for her to come to meet Chris.

"Karen, I'd like you to meet Chris van Zant. He's the newest member of the History Department – the 'new Tim Johansson,' I guess you could say."

She offered him a sample of her newest culinary creation. "You're not allergic to shrimp, I hope."

Chris shook his head. When he took a bite, he moaned with delight. "Oh, my God! I don't think I've ever tasted anything like it. It's amazing! Is all your food this delicious?"

"She'll probably say no, but don't believe her," Dirk laughed. "I'm obviously a biased judge, but I think she's the best cook in town—and one of the best you'll find anywhere."

Karen beamed with pride, and laughed, "Flattery will get you anything, my dear!" She looked at Chris again, and smiled. "If first impressions are any indication, Chris is clearly more sociable than Johansson ever was—I can tell that already. It's also nice not to have to worry about what his wife could—or would—eat. Are you married, Chris?"

"No, he's single—and don't start!" Dirk said. Turning to Chris, he cautioned, "Be forewarned: Karen considers herself something of a matchmaker. She doesn't go overboard with it, but if she meets someone who seems like a good match for someone she knows who's single, she'll usually try to 'facilitate' things for them."

"That's just my way of drumming up business—I'm always looking for a wedding to cater," she laughed.

79

Chris helped himself to a few more hors-d'oeuvres and excused himself. He wandered into what looked like a study. Terry O'Brien was standing near a table that held several empty glasses and two opened bottles of wine: one red, the other white. "Can I offer you a glass of wine, Chris? Dirk always has some pretty nice offerings. He's kind of a master of finding good prices on wine, which is important when you're living on a faculty salary. He usually strikes a good balance with wines that have high ratings but reasonable prices. Tonight's 'special' seems to be this red—an Argentinian Malbec. The other one's a New Zealand Sauvignon Blanc. If you'd like something else, soft drink, beer, iced tea, whatever, Karen always has a good supply laid out in the kitchen. As with most parties, everyone usually ends up there at some point in the evening, anyway."

"This is all rather surprising," Chris said, gesturing toward the bottles of wine. "At my alma mater, there was never any alcohol. An individual might have wine at home, but not at something that involved anyone else from the college. The conservatism of the Dutch Reformed Church was dominant. I was surprised when I got to the Netherlands, and saw people drinking beer and *Oude Jenever*. I assumed it would be pretty conservative here, too."

[handwritten margin note: How about Christian Reformed? — almost like pharisees .]

[handwritten note below "too.": Gin]

"There have been a few occasions when people have tried to instill that kind of conservative atmosphere here. A president back in the '70s said that it was his mission to make NNC the most conservative Dutch college in the country. Fortunately for the college—and obviously unfortunately for him—he had some medical issues, and had to retire after only a few years on the job. Everyone breathed a sigh of relief—both for his health, which improved after he left office, and for the direction the College would no longer be going. But generally speaking, NNC doesn't fit the stereotype of most Dutch-heritage schools. In some ways, the founders were reacting against that conservative model. They leaned more toward the heritage that brought us Heineken and *Oude Jenever*. It's not a party school, by any means. But it's not completely dry, either. You might get wine at an occasional event on campus (particularly if it's a private party that hires the catering service), but never if there it's something that students might be attending. But this is a private party, so if Dirk wants to serve wine or beer, he's free to do so. Which brings me back to my initial question: what can I get you to drink?"

"I'll try the red. I'm not familiar with that variety. In grad school, anything with a cork was considered 'top shelf.'"

Terry poured him a glass, and glanced at his empty plate. "I see you've already had a taste of her cooking. What do you think of her special hors d'oeuvres tonight?"

"I've only tried the shrimp, but they're out of this world. Does everything she make taste this good?"

"Almost always. Her cooking is a good reason not to piss off Dirk. You don't want to get taken off his party list. Don't worry—just disagreeing with him wouldn't do that. But if you do something he considers really egregious, you won't be invited again. The first couple of years that Hank was President, Dirk invited him every year. And every year, he had some excuse why he couldn't come—mostly quite legitimate, I suspect. He finally managed to come once—and only once. He and Hannah made no effort to hide their boredom. They obviously didn't enjoy slumming with the *hoi polloi*. So they never got invited back again. Rothman and his wife came a couple of times, but after a while Dirk got fed up with his 'administrative style.' He dropped him off the list, too. I'll be curious to see if the new Dean comes tonight. I'm sure Dirk invited her."

As if on cue, the front door opened, and Sarah stuck her head into the entry way.

"Speak of the Devil," Terry laughed. "There she is now!"

81

Chris watched as she went through the same ritual that he had: Dirk hurried over and took her coat. Then he introduced her to Karen, who offered a plate heaped with samples of another delicious-looking appetizer. After a few words with Karen, he led Sarah into the study, and asked Terry, "Would you mind getting the Dean something to drink? You seem to have fallen into the role of bartender tonight."

"Would you like a glass of wine, Dean? Or a beer?" Terry asked. "That's all we have in here, but there's quite a range of other options in the kitchen."

"A glass of red, please. And all of you, please—call me Sarah. I grew up in a Navy family, and I've always thought college faculty and administrators were kind of like military officers. If it's something that involves the 'line of command,' then I'm 'Dean.' I'll be happy to listen to differing opinions, and welcome opposing views. But when you get right down to it, I'm the one who'll be making decisions, and I expect my faculty colleagues to respect my authority. But outside of that official setting, we're in the 'Officers' Club.' If I'm looking at you over a plate of hors d'oeuvres with a glass of wine in my hand, I hope we can function amicably as colleagues, and ideally as friends. We can't be very sociable if I'm simply viewed as 'Dean.'"

"Speaking of which, here's your wine, Sarah," Terry said. "Have you met Chris van Zant? He's new this year, too."

"No, I haven't had the pleasure. But I've already heard a great deal about you. I look forward to working with you, Chris."

Chris looked puzzled, and was obviously taken aback.

"I had a nice meeting with Marty Dykstra this afternoon, and he was saying great things about you."

Chris blushed, and wasn't sure what to say in reply. He didn't have a chance, as Sarah quickly continued, "It sounds like you're working on an interesting research topic. Marty says you should be able to finish up your research with a few more weeks in the Netherlands. I'm curious: is this something different from what you were working on when you were there on your Fulbright? You couldn't have gone through those documents then?"

"I wouldn't call it different—more of an outgrowth of my dissertation work. There's a set of archival holdings that were closed when I was there. The man who donated the documents to the archives specified that they could not be opened to researchers until 20 years after he died—and last spring was 20 years. My Fulbright was just a couple years too early for me to get to see that collection. With the move here, and getting ready for a new teaching appointment, I didn't have time to get back to Utrecht this year. I'm planning to return next summer and go through those files. From their description, it looks like that should only take me a few weeks. They'll let me make digital copies of the documents, but I have to do it myself. They don't do any copying."

"That's pretty much what Marty told me. He said you might be able to go in January, is that right?"

"That's what he suggested. I didn't realize that I could go then. Even though I'm not scheduled to teach in January, I figured I had to be on campus."

"I don't know how it's been in the past, but if you're working on a research project, I certainly would have no objection. I should probably wait to let Marty tell you this himself, but since we're talking about it now, I'll go ahead. After Marty left this afternoon, I checked some of the funds that my office has to support research. I assumed that they'd probably all have been allocated by now, but I was able to piece together $400 for you to use toward air fare. Will that help?"

"Of course! In January, that would be a great down-payment for a round-trip ticket to Amsterdam. As I told Marty, I have friends in Utrecht who've invited me to stay with them whenever I'm in the area, so with this, I shouldn't have any problem going. Thank you!"

"My pleasure!" she smiled. "But you realize that we'll expect a good return on this investment. This is intended to help you get that first article, and get you well on your way to tenure. I don't want to have to run a search for your replacement if you don't get that done! With a new president coming in next year, I hope to see as much continuity as possible in the coming years."

"That shouldn't be a problem. That new collection of documents should be all that I need to get this article finished. Again, thank you!"

"When I came in, Dirk told me that his wife—Karen, is it?—had even more appetizers floating around. So if you'll excuse me, I'm going to try to track down some of those."

After she'd left the study, Terry turned to Chris. "What a refreshing change that is! Unless you were a 'Golden Child,' el Deano generally wouldn't give you the time of day, much less any money. Let's hope that she stays that way. Based on what I've heard and seen today, I already get the impression that she's going to expect everyone to produce. And she's not going to give you what you want just because you blow smoke up her skirt. But the only thing most of us have ever wanted is to be treated fairly. I get the feeling that she'll give us a fair hearing. I've never expected to get everything I want from a dean. But I do expect to be treated like everyone else. If first impressions mean anything, she's definitely going to be a nice change from Rothman."

They watched Sarah as she worked her way toward the kitchen. Just as she was passing through the entryway, Marty came in through the front door. The two of them spoke briefly, and she leaned her head toward the study. Marty smiled and nodded approvingly, and the two of them continued on to the kitchen. Chris figured that she must have mentioned to Marty that she'd given Chris the good news about his travel money.

Marty came into the study a few minutes later, emptied a bottle of Heineken into a beer glass, and set the empty bottle on the table next to the wine bottles. He turned to

Chris and said, "In case you're wondering, I do like wine. But I'm generally a beer man—especially tonight. I thought Hank's announcement deserved a Dutch beer in celebration. I'll be back in a minute. I'm going to track down some of Karen's hors d'oeuvres. What kinds of delicacies does she have in store for us this evening?"

Chris spoke up first. "I don't know what else she has, but her shrimp are 'to die for.' But before you head out in search of appetizers, I want to thank you for getting me travel money! Sarah just gave me the good news."

"That's what she said. I'm glad I could be of assistance. But all I really did was to let her know what you needed. She was pretty insistent that it should be something that we'll see the results of pretty soon, so don't let me down!"

"Don't worry about that. Now that I won't be making a trip to Utrecht next summer, I can have an uninterrupted couple of months to get the paper finished. Unless I find something that runs counter to what I already have, I should be able to get the first draft written during spring semester."

"Before you send it off to a journal, be sure to have someone in the department read it first. It's always best to have at least one other pair of eyes go over an article before you send it to an editor. You'd be amazed how helpful that can be—and how much embarrassment it might save. If you'd like me to, when the time comes, I'll be happy to go over it for you."

"To give you advance warning," Terry said, "you should know that Marty's a very demanding editor. But that's the bad news. The good news is that if you can get something by him, it will probably be acceptable to most journal editors. Be sure to take him up on his offer."

"I will, thanks. Marty, I think you've got the right idea. I'm going to find some more food to sample. I hope you don't mind, Terry."

"Not at all. I'm sort of a surrogate bartender tonight, but my wife will be bringing me a plate of munchies pretty soon. You should go mingle, and meet a few people. I know Johanna was hoping you'd have a chance to talk to Al."

After he found several trays of appetizers to sample, Chris located Johanna. She led him to Al, who was chatting with some other librarians out in the screened-in porch. After she introduced them to each another, she went back to her friends inside, and left Chris with the librarians.

"Johanna said you're new to the Midwest," Al said. Chris noticed that his Southern drawl was even stronger than Johanna's. "Ya seemed to be observing this porch area with a great deal o' curiosity. I take it ya didn't have many mosquitas where you're from."

"A few, but not as many as I've seen here. I take it that's why this porch is screened on all sides."

One of the other librarians laughed, "That's right. It's intended to keep out the 'state bird.' 'Minnesota: The Land of Ten Thousand Lakes'—but also ten billion mosquitoes."

Al continued, "I think I saw ya in the library the last couple of days. Did ya find everythin' ya needed?"

"Yes, thanks. It's not as big as the library I used in grad school, but I wouldn't expect that here. It's very comparable to what I had as an undergraduate—even a little bigger, I think."

"I appreciate that attitude! Johansson was always complainin' that we didn't have everythin' he needed. We're not a research university, for cryin' out loud! I always told him that if he needed somethin', we could almost always get it through interlibrary loan. But that wasn't 'quick enough' for him. It would've helped if he didn't put everything off until the last minute."

After about twenty minutes, Al suggested they refill their glasses and replenish their hors d'oeuvres. When they got to the study, Dirk, Terry, and Marty were there. Sarah followed them in, just to say goodbye to Dirk, and to thank him for his hospitality. "I'm sorry I have to leave so soon, but I'll be chairing the Faculty Assembly meeting tomorrow, and I want to get ready for it."

Dirk interrupted her: "Isn't Hank going to be there? According to the College Manual, he's supposed to chair Faculty Assembly meetings. I know he doesn't like doing it, but unfortunately, that's the way it is."

"Last week he told me I needed to meet with him before the Faculty Assembly meeting, which we did yesterday. That's when he told me I needed to chair the meeting in his absence. There's apparently another potentially large donor who's about to take off on an extended trip, and if Hank wanted to meet with him, it was now, or not until spring. So he felt he had to be gone."

"And he didn't mention that as a result, you might find yourself stepping into a hornets' nest? There are some faculty who have been very vocal about how important it is that he follow the College Manual. So be forewarned!"

"Thanks! I appreciate the heads-up. That's another good reason for me to go over the agenda again tonight, and then get a good night's sleep so I don't make any slip-ups on my first day in front of all the faculty. From the looks of the agenda, it doesn't look like it should take too long. Everything seems pretty straightforward, and nothing seems very controversial, at least from a newcomer's perspective."

Marty laughed, and almost snorted beer out his nose. When he'd regained his composure, he apologized and said, "From your perspective, I'm sure it looks that way. But after more than thirty years of hard experience, let me assure you, we'll be lucky to get out in time for lunch. I hope we won't have to reconvene in the afternoon."

Sarah gave him a look of disbelief, and was about to ask for a fuller explanation, but she thought better of it. She decided it would be best to experience it for herself, without letting anyone else's opinions color her views.

Dirk seized on the brief lull in the conversation to change the subject. "We're all glad you could join us, Sarah. I've been hosting these for over twenty years, and I plan to keep it up until I retire. So remember that next year, too. Hopefully your husband will be able to be with us then. Let me walk you to the door—I need to turn on the porch light so nobody trips on the stairs on the way out."

"I really appreciate you inviting me tonight, Dirk. I'm sorry Owen couldn't join us, but he's working in the Cities today and tomorrow, and won't be back here until Saturday afternoon. He's made arrangements to 'telecommute,' but some things need to be done in person. I had a chance to thank Karen, too, but can you tell her again for me how much I enjoyed this evening? She's a marvelous cook. I'm told she does professional catering, is that right?"

"Correct!" he laughed. "And if you look on your way out, there's a stack of flyers strategically placed on the table by the door. Feel free to take one. If you have an event you need catered off-campus, she'll be happy to give you a bid. As you probably know already, everything on-campus has to be handled through Dining Services, but they limit themselves to the campus. That keeps a pretty good relationship between the College and local food establishments."

After Sarah had left, Dirk raced back into the study. "Okay, Marty, now that the Dean's gone, I have to ask: what in Hell was that all about tonight?" Several others in the room nodded in agreement with Dirk.

"What do you mean?"

"A standing ovation for Hank van Daam? I never expected to see that from you!"

"Look, what was I supposed to do? I've been bitching at him for the past five years because he's been undercutting and underfunding the Dutch language program and our Dutch history courses. This means they're secure. Now there's one less barricade for me to fight on."

"But for Christ's sake, Marty, an endowed chair named after them? That's pretty hypocritical, don't you think?"

"Of course I do. Naming an endowed chair in Dutch Studies after the two of them is about like establishing a 'Heinrich and Margarete Himmler Chair of Holocaust Studies.' It's hypocritical as Hell! Remember: this is the guy who was opposed to a community effort to establish a Dutch Heritage Center on campus. His argument? 'Because we don't want to look like we're catering to any particular ethnic constituency.' The word 'hypocritical' doesn't really do him justice. If anyone had asked my opinion, I'd have told them that. But they didn't. And first and foremost, I was applauding Paul and Cornelia van der Kellen. I'm sure he wanted their money without strings attached. If they'd agreed to that, it would've gone to Business, or one of the sciences. Certainly not to one of our departments, and definitely not Modern and Classical Languages. But with a gift that big, he's now committed to maintaining something he's spent much of the last decade trying to dismantle."

He took a sip of his beer, and continued, "Now I won't have to worry anymore about him cutting Dutch language, or having my courses in Dutch history go by the boards. If applauding the van der Kellens, and letting Hank think I was applauding him, is the only way to accomplish that, I can live with it. Besides, did you see the look on his face when I stood up? As they say in the credit card ads, 'Priceless!' I'm sure he was expecting me to sit on my hands. But as I say, I wasn't applauding for him. I was applauding the fact that the school's heritage isn't going to be chopped by some administrative hack."

"But you were also the first person on his feet when he announced that he was going to retire after this year. I could understand you grudgingly getting up after some of his brown-nosing 'golden children' started it. But you beat them all to the punch."

"I'll explain that in a minute. But first—I know you always have a bottle of good sour mash bourbon stashed someplace around here. Would you pour me a glass, please? With a couple of pieces of ice in it, if you don't mind."

"Yes, sir!" Dirk grumbled, as he gave a weak salute. He gave Marty a funny look, but found a glass and some ice, and poured him a hearty serving of bourbon. "I'm sure this is going to be a good explanation. So I gave you a generous 'snort.' Since you live within walking distance, I won't worry about you driving home. And if this is good enough, you might even merit a second one. Now, tell us: why'd you give him a standing ovation when he announced his retirement?"

Marty took the glass, swirled the ice cube a few times, and held it up to the light to admire the amber color. "Think about it, Dirk. What have I been saying for years? 'I'm not going to retire 'til el Presidente does,' right? Well, he essentially announced MY retirement for ME tonight! I can't do it at the end of this year—even if we started right now, we probably couldn't get a decent search organized in time. I can't be sure he'd approve a replacement for my position; I don't know how many times he's said it should be cut. There's obviously no guarantee that his successor won't want to do the same thing. But if we get a decent president, I think we can make a convincing case so the department can keep my position."

He raised the glass to his nose, and sniffed the bourbon. "And there's the added bonus: now I know that my last year here will be spent without Hank van Daam around! In my opinion, that's worth a standing ovation. So, please join me in a toast: to a bright future for NNC, without the dark shadow of el Presidente hanging over it. He said he believes he's following God's plan for his future. To which I say, 'The Lord giveth, and the Lord taketh away. Blessed be the name of the Lord!' Proost!"

4
The Calm Before the Storm

The Next Day: Friday, August 23

BY NNC STANDARDS, THE FACULTY ASSEMBLY MEETING
went fairly well. When she called it to order, Sarah could
feel the tension in the room. But thanks to her conversation
with Dirk the night before, she was ready for it. She
apologized on Hank's behalf for his absence, and stressed
how much she was looking forward to working with the
faculty in the coming year. She made appropriate
references to the College Manual, and the importance of
following that. She could feel the tension gradually
subsiding. Looking back on it later, Marty considered her
initial interaction with the faculty "charmingly disarming."

The only moment of real friction came when Mary de
Groet, Vice President for Finance, gave her presentation
about the financial outlook for the coming year.
Enrollment numbers were down slightly but not enough to
create much worry. Unfortunately, the current budget had
been based on rather optimistic projections, so there would
have to be some "belt-tightening" somewhere.
Nonetheless, faculty would be receiving a 1.5% salary
increase over the coming year. At that point, several hands
went up among the faculty. Mary pointed to one,
seemingly at random.

"So, last year faculty got a 0.5% raise, and this year it's
1.5%. Can I ask what raises were for administrators?"

Mary stiffened a bit, but reacted as if she was expecting
the question: "The overall average for administrative raises
over the past two years has been just slightly more than
one percent." Although several other faculty tried to elicit
more information, that was as much as she was prepared to

say. "Unfortunately, President van Daam isn't here today. He might have been able to give you more details."

"But YOU'RE the Vice President for Finance, aren't you?" someone at the back of the room asked. "Aren't you familiar enough with salary information to give us a little more insight as to how that breaks down?"

"Salaries are part of personnel information, so I can't give you more specific details without violating someone's privacy. I'm sorry, but that's as much information as I'm permitted to give you at this point."

When Mary returned to her seat, Sarah could feel the tension that she'd sensed when she opened the meeting. She realized that while she may have defused it, that was only temporarily. Now it was back. She had a sense of what Dirk and Marty warned her about. It would have been nice if Hank had given her some advance warning. *"I wonder what that's all about,"* she thought.

After the financial report, the rest of the agenda was fairly straightforward. Dale Haak gave another rendition of the presentation he'd given the night before, highlighting a few more details concerning the incoming freshman class's accomplishments and awards in high school. A few faculty members asked questions about the percentage of students who might not be quite as "outstanding," reflecting concerns that admission standards might have been compromised in order to achieve adequate enrollments, but Haak was able to address those fairly effectively. One or two faculty questions made him feel like he'd been called before the Inquisition, but overall, he survived his ordeal without serious damage.

At one point, however, Dale couldn't help thinking to himself, *"If they only knew about the students that Hank pressured me to admit—underachieving children of wealthy alumni."* Fortunately, their SAT and ACT scores were much higher than their grades would have suggested. He could rationalize their admission on those grounds. Maybe "the nurturing environment of NNC will ignite that spark of inspiration and enlightenment," as Hank had put it. He'd stood his ground against letting one of them start in the pre-med curriculum, even if his father—a doctor, of course—threatened to withdraw his son's application and send him somewhere else. Dale knew that was an empty threat. There weren't many other schools that would admit him at all, at least not without parents who were wealthy alumni. If he proved himself capable of doing high quality work in other introductory college classes, he could easily start the pre-med program. But that didn't seem very likely. He'd probably be one of those who would finish the first year with a g.p.a. below 1.0, and start the next year at a community college close to home, where it wouldn't cost his parents 40 grand for an extended, beer-soaked vacation. He might finally figure things out and make it back to college. If he did, Dale would be among the first to congratulate him and welcome him back into the fold. But he wouldn't hold his breath until that happened.

The Faculty Assembly then had to deal with some relatively routine academic matters. There were a few new courses being proposed, as well as some modifications to existing courses. Sarah figured those would be easily dispensed with. But she was wrong again. A woman from Chemistry raised a few concerns about an English course. She didn't question the overall content of the course, though she did suggest a book to be read instead of one of those on the proposed syllabus. Her main concern was with the number of core requirements that could be fulfilled by one course if the proposal were approved as it was now worded. Instead of simply addressing the chemist's concerns directly, the Chair of the English Department offered a long defense of the importance of "imaginative literature" in the curriculum, even going so far as to suggest that this specific course ought to be made a requirement for all students. At that point, several faculty members from other departments, who had barely been paying attention while they browsed through their e-mail, closed their laptops and entered the discussion. After nearly an hour, during which it became clear that the course's fate was uncertain in its current form, someone moved that the proposal be tabled. The Curriculum Committee was directed to review the proposal in terms of the requirements it could fulfill. That prompted another motion that the Committee once again review the whole question of courses fulfilling more than one requirement simultaneously, an issue that had been festering for several years. After the discussion of the English course, the rest of the Curriculum Committee's presentation went fairly quickly. The meeting finally adjourned at 12:45. Since it was scheduled to end at 12:00, and actually ended within an hour of that deadline, most faculty considered it a success. Most importantly, they wouldn't have to reconvene after lunch.

The faculty then filed over to the cafeteria, where a buffet lunch was set up. The cafeteria staff hadn't really expected the meeting to actually be over by noon, so the 45 minute delay didn't upset any of them. When the meeting seemed to be drawing to a close, the Chair of the Faculty Assembly sent a text message to the head of catering, alerting her that they would soon be on their way. So when the first faculty members came through the door, lunch was waiting for them.

Chris filled his plate, and followed Marty to a table by one of the large windows looking out toward the athletic fields. They could see that the football team was just finishing a morning practice, and was heading to the locker room. Chris and Marty were soon joined by Dirk and a few of the other "regulars" from the coffee shop.

"So, Chris, what'd you think of your first Faculty Assembly meeting?" Dirk asked.

"Are they always so contentious?" Chris replied.

"Contentious? That was one of the least contentious meetings I've been to in years. You should've been here when we were going through the curriculum review a few years ago."

"But over an hour to approve—no, make that 'not approve'—one course? That can't be normal, can it?"

Marty laughed. "There's an old saying that 'The politics of the university are so intense because the stakes are so low.' I think you saw a good example of that this morning."

Just then, Sarah came up to the table, carrying her lunch tray. "Do you folks mind if I join you?"

Marianna pointed to a vacant chair next to her, and said, "Of course not! Please have a seat."

Sarah settled into the chair, unwrapped her silverware, and spread the napkin on her lap. She looked around the table, shook her head, and said, "That was one of the strangest experiences I've ever had in my professional career. Are Faculty Assembly meetings all like that?"

Marianna shook her head. "No, not at all," covering at least an octave in her Minnesota brogue, before she laughed, "They're not always that uncontroversial. For your first one, I think this wasn't too bad."

Sarah looked at Marty and Dirk. "First of all, I want to thank you for tipping me off about the faculty attitude toward Hank chairing the meeting. I'm glad I was aware of that. Otherwise I probably would have walked into a buzz saw. I don't know why Hank didn't let me know that when he asked me to chair it in his absence."

Everyone else at the table looked at each other, but no one said a word. Their silence was not lost on Sarah.

"I'll have to ask him about that when he gets back to town. But I'm curious: is it normal for someone from the Chemistry Department to suggest what should be included in an English course? As a physicist, I'd never consider telling someone in another department what they should or shouldn't include in a course, unless they asked me what I thought should be included in a history of science course." She paused a moment, and then smiled. "In that case, of course, I'd suggest that it should probably focus on physics." She waited a second, and much to her relief, a ripple of laughter moved through the group. "That was a joke, of course. A little physics humor—probably about as much of that as you'll find anywhere. We're not known for our joke telling."

"Don't worry about bad jokes," Dirk laughed. "Marty's got everyone beat on that."

Marty held his hands up. "Guilty as charged! When I was in grad school, there was a departmental coffee room, where some of the faculty members used to congregate every morning before class. They also welcomed grad students there, too, and some of us would venture in there every once in a while. I had a reputation that I could 'clear the coffee room with three jokes.' I have to confess, they haven't gotten any better."

"That's because you're still telling the same jokes," Dirk taunted.

"Jokes aside," Sarah said, "in that discussion this morning, there was obviously something going on that was more than a simple course proposal, right?"

"Very insightful," Marty replied. "None of that is limited to any specific department, but some are worse than others. The questions from Chemistry about the English course were a brief, symbolic pay-back. Most of the English faculty feel like they're defending the last bastions of civilization against the onslaught of the barbarians. They want to make sure that NNC doesn't abandon its mission, and that it 'keeps the beacon of the liberal arts burning ever bright.' I'm sorry to sound sarcastic, but for over thirty years, I've been listening to some of them preach to us as if we're the great unwashed, and they're the only ones who care about this college, or about learning in general."

"Wanting to maintain the College's integrity and standards certainly can't be something you'd complain about, can it?" Sarah asked.

"No, of course not. But for most of them, there's only one form that can take, and it's the model that they use. Watch the next time a course proposal comes up in the Faculty Assembly. If it's a history course, for example, someone from English will ask some questions that point to the amount of time spent in lectures, as opposed to 'discussion.' They won't come right out and ask that directly, but they'll get to it in a roundabout way. And then someone else in the department will comment about how more effective learning takes place in group discussion, rather than lectures. Their model is essentially: 'read something, talk about it, and then write about it. Then read something else, talk about it, and write about it.' To spice things up, after you've done that a few times, instead of just writing about one work, you compare two or three: 'How is Odysseus' circuitous journey home similar to the path of Calvin's intellectual development?' (Ignoring, of course, the fact that Odysseus is a fictional character, while Calvin is an historical figure. No problem comparing apples and oranges.)"

"That obviously varies from subject to subject," Sarah said. "I can't imagine asking students to sit around in a physics class to discuss how they feel about quanta."

"Thank you!" Dirk exclaimed. "When they were renovating the Mudd Center a few years ago, some of the science courses—lectures in chemistry, physics, and biology—were in classrooms in several different buildings around campus. Whenever I'd walk by one of them in Macalester, I'd see my colleagues from those departments lecturing, and no one seemed to have any problems with that. But when I lecture in a Political Science course, I get criticized for not having more discussions in class. And not just by English faculty—just about everyone from the Humanities Division seems to follow their lead."

"Which brings us back to your question, Sarah," Marty said. "The questions from Chemistry involved much more than just that specific course. A few years ago, there was a chemistry course being proposed in Faculty Assembly. One English professor questioned the wording in the course description, and didn't seem quite convinced that while the terminology wasn't normal English usage in a literary work, it is in Chemistry. Then there were some other questions about how the course was going to be taught. The Chemistry faculty thought the whole discussion smacked of 'academic imperialism,' as they described it. I tend to agree."

"That's something else it would've been good to know about before the meeting," Sarah sighed. No one at the table responded. They thought it best to leave it as a rhetorical comment.

Johanna took the opportunity to change the subject. "Chris, do ya have your courses ready to go? Or will ya have to spend the weekend gettin' 'em finished?" The influence of her time in Tennessee was more noticeable than usual today.

"No, they're set. I'm only teaching one history class this semester: 'Nineteenth Century Europe.' I made copies of the syllabus the other day. When I was a TA in grad school, I had to print off copies of everything else, too— study guides, outlines, and the like. The last two years, I used a web-based course management program, so students got all of that on-line. I was relieved to see that NNC has something similar. I finished uploading all of that yesterday, so I won't have to spend the weekend on any of it. I still have some things to organize in my apartment, but otherwise, I can relax."

"Take advantage of the weekend," Marty said. "This is 'the calm before the storm.' From Monday until the end of the semester, you'll find yourself scrambling to get something done. During the course of the semester, I suggest you follow the advice my major professor gave me. He told me to 'always keep a Sabbath for yourself, every week.' But he didn't mean that I had to spend it in religious activity—he wasn't particularly religious himself. He just believed that if you work every day, which it's easy to do when papers and exams start coming in, you'll quickly find yourself 'running on overload.' Your work suffers, and then your health suffers. And you won't enjoy what you're doing."

Dirk added, "And it's not all just preparing lectures and grading papers and exams. As you probably noticed, new students started arriving yesterday. Today, tomorrow, and Sunday, the Office of Student Affairs will be holding its New Student Orientation—essentially 'how to survive college.' There are sessions on alcohol abuse, time management, and social relationships. While some of the more conservative Trustees are scandalized by this, they also address things like birth control and sexually transmitted diseases. Although they do touch on academics a little, not much of what they provide gives any attention to the 'scholarly' side of the college experience. That's up to us. Hopefully we'll succeed—and if we do, the students will, too. But it's as much of an effort on our part as it is on theirs. If you work yourself into the ground, you won't succeed, and neither will they."

Chris heard the staccato sound of hard heels clicking on the cafeteria flooring. He looked up to see a tall, blonde woman approaching their table. She looked very athletic, and well-conditioned. Her hair was short enough to be easily managed after a mid-day workout and shower. Her blouse and slacks were not tight, but they clearly confirmed the appearance of fitness. Her posture was rigid. She looked like someone who was busy, with a task to complete. She didn't waste any time getting to her point.

"Excuse me, please, all of you. I just need a quick word with Dirk. I hope you don't mind."

Everyone at the table nodded cooperatively, and motioned for her to continue. They politely started quiet conversations among themselves, so that they didn't look like they were eavesdropping on her and Dirk.

"Dirk, I'm terribly sorry we couldn't make it to your place last night. You know how much Pieter and I both look forward to it every year. But his mother is staying with us . . ."

"You know you could've brought her along," Dirk interrupted. "I'm sorry you didn't. We missed the two of you."

"No, that's not why we didn't come. After the Investiture Convocation, we were going to take her over to a friend's house. She'd been invited to play bridge last night, and was really looking forward to it. We told her she'd be welcome at your party, but she said that as much as she'd probably enjoy it, she'd prefer bridge with her friends. That would be much more relaxing for her than making conversations with academics, even as gracious as you and Karen are. But that didn't work out, either. As we were walking to our car, she tripped on the curb and sprained her ankle—quite severely. We were afraid she might have broken it. We spent most of the evening with her in the ER. Fortunately, it turned out to be 'only' a bad sprain, with nothing broken. But by the time they'd gotten the x-rays evaluated and the sprained ankle wrapped up, she just wanted to go home and get to bed. As nerve-wracking as the evening was, a glass or two of wine and some of Karen's hors d'oeuvres would've been a great way to end the evening, but she didn't want to go out then, and we didn't feel comfortable leaving her alone. She wasn't managing with the crutches very well."

"I'm sorry to hear about her accident, but it's a relief to know it wasn't more serious."

"Thanks. I knew you'd understand. I've sent Karen a note explaining why we weren't there, but please convey my apologies to her as well, would you."

"Sure. And don't worry, you're still on the list for next year," Dirk laughed.

To no one in particular, Annika asked, "How did the meeting go this morning? Hank called a little while ago, and he was curious to know if anything came up he should be aware of. Pieter couldn't be there—he was at the doctor's office with his Mom getting a follow-up evaluation—so I haven't heard anything about it yet."

Sarah started to say something, but Marty spoke up before she had a chance. "Things got off to kind of a rough start, when everyone found out that Hank wouldn't be there. I was afraid Sarah would have trouble getting through that, but she was able to handle the situation pretty effectively, wouldn't you agree?" He motioned toward the rest of the group. They weren't sure what he was up to, but they nodded in agreement. Sarah covered up her confusion with an agreeable smile, but she made a mental note to herself to bring this up the next time she had a chance to talk to Marty.

Annika started to excuse herself and turned to leave. But before she could, Terry O'Brien spoke up. "While you're here, Annika, have you met Chris van Zant? He's the new historian."

"No, I haven't had the pleasure."

Terry turned to Chris: "This is Annika van Rijn, the Executive Assistant to the President. She's the reason most things get done on time on this campus."

Annika blushed slightly, and as she shook Chris's hand, she said, "I'm sure you've already figured out that Terry's blessed with the 'gift of Blarney.' Don't believe everything he says. It's a pleasure to meet you, Chris. I'm sure we'll see each other around campus a lot in the future." Looking at everyone at the table, she added, "Don't forget next Friday afternoon. The Langbroeks are hosting another 'back to school' reception for faculty at their house."

Annika turned to Chris to explain, "Betty Langbroek was a long-time member of the Board of Trustees—she just recently finished serving as Chair before she stepped down from the board. For the last ten years or so, she and her husband, Arnold, have hosted a reception for faculty at the end of the first week of classes. It's a nice way to kick off the semester. I hope to see all of you there."

"Looking forward to it, Annika," Terry said. "I'll be sure to have the right nametag this year," he laughed.

Chris noticed that her posture seemed to stiffen, if that were possible. But she kept a smile on her face, and excused herself. Sarah took the opportunity to leave then, too. "I've got to get back to work, so I'll leave the problems of the world for the rest of you to work out. Thanks for sharing lunch with me."

As soon as they were gone, Chris asked, "What was that last bit about a nametag. Was it my imagination, or did that hit a nerve?"

"No, you're not imagining anything," Marty laughed. "Terry could've spared her that last shot."

"I'm sorry," Terry replied, a bit defensively. "But it was just too good a 'straight line' to pass up."

"You've noticed the big windmill on campus, I'm sure," Marty said. "Its image is now plastered on just about everything associated with the College." He pointed to Chris's nametag as an example. "It's one of Hank's 'great accomplishments.' One of the things you have to understand around here is that Hank's a bit paranoid, especially when it comes to the Lutheran colleges in the Upper Midwest—which are legion. Several of them put up windmills to generate power on campus—all part of the national race by college presidents to try to prove whose campus is 'most sustainable.'"

Dirk added, "For over a century, the College's symbol was a windmill, but one of the old-fashioned, Dutch kind. You've seen the one in New Leiden, just as you come into town. That was pretty much a shared symbol of New Leiden and NNC. But when the Lutheran colleges started putting up windmills, Hank had to have one, too. And once it was there, all of the graphic materials on campus that showed the old, Dutch windmill had to be replaced with newer versions, all featuring the new windmill, and a new, jazzier font. Two years ago, Terry showed up at the reception wearing his old name tag—with the old logo on it. The following Monday, Annika sent out an e-mail to faculty reminding us all of the importance of maintaining a 'coherent graphic image,' and telling everyone to be sure to only use up-to-date materials, with images of the new windmill. She specifically mentioned name tags as an example. While I suspect Hank was partly responsible, she's 'Type-A' enough to worry about something like that on her own. I've heard that a few people teased her about it—surprisingly, I guess, no one from this group that I know of. So she's been a little sensitive about it ever since. I guess Terry was just making up for not being among those who teased her when it happened."

Terry held up his hands: "I'm sorry. I just couldn't control myself. At least I didn't refer to the new windmill as 'Hank van Daam's Final Erection,' as some people call it."

"Watch yo' mouth, Terry," Johanna said, with a drawl that was even more noticeable than usual. "Remembah, there ah ladies present!"

"Again, my apologies," Terry said. "I think I've stuck my foot in my mouth enough today. I'm going to head back to my office. I'm not in as good a position with my courses as Chris is. So if I don't want to spend the weekend working, I'd better get going now."

Chris turned to the rest of the group and said, "President van Daam clearly isn't the most popular person on campus. If he's so bad, how did he get to be President?"

Marianna laughed, "Oh, he is naïve, isn't he?"

Dirk was the first to respond. "Remember our discussion the other day about the 'Peter Principle?' Well, Hank's a good example of the Peter Principle, combined with a healthy dose of being at the right place at the right time."

"How so?"

"For most of his life," Dirk replied, "Hank wanted to be a college president. The story is that when he was in grade school, back in the mid-50s, there was a tv program called 'The Halls of Ivy.' It was a remake of an old radio show, as I understand it. His parents had listened to the radio show, and when the tv show started, the whole family used to watch it. He became enthralled with the idea of an ivy-covered college campus. Notice how much ivy there is around NNC? Much of that was planted after he became president."

Marty snorted, "You should get Max Cuypers started on that sometime! According to him, the ivy that Hank ordered him to plant is wreaking havoc with buildings all across the campus. He told me that the mortar on most of the brick buildings will have to be repaired before too long. And some of the newer concrete facades, like on the Carroll Center, are a mess, too. As far as Max is concerned, the ivy is a plague on the campus. He tried to explain that to Hank, but Hank insisted that the campus would look better with more ivy. So we got more ivy."

Dirk continued: "When he was still in grade school, he decided he wanted to be a college professor, and eventually that evolved into ambitions of becoming a president. After he graduated from college (a small liberal arts college in Michigan), he went on to get a Ph.D. in Child Psychology."

Marianna picked up the narrative: "According to a friend of mine who teaches where he got his first teaching job, he was lucky just to get tenure in the first place. He'd barely met the department's minimum standards for publication. He had an article published in a second-rate journal—that was edited by a friend of his, no less. The department was evenly split. But when the faculty met to decide on his tenure, one of the senior members who didn't like him was in the hospital with gall stones. Hank's tenure was approved by one vote. Two years later, the department chair died of a heart attack. The dean had to appoint a replacement, and everyone else in the department had apparently pissed him off so many times that he appointed Hank, partly out of spite toward the rest of the department. Most people, including the dean, figured he'd fall flat on his face, but he apparently did a decent job steering the department between the rival factions—maybe a result of his child psychology training.

"After a year and a half as chair, he was contacted by another school, telling him that he'd been nominated to be Chair of their Psych department. They wanted to know if he was interested, which he was. It was a bigger program, with more prestige—and more money. So he went for an interview, and got the job. He never knew who nominated him, but most people on campus felt that someone from his department had done it—partly in the faint hope that they could get rid of him, or failing that, that he'd be embarrassed when he tried to get the job and didn't make it. He got the last laugh. He apparently made a great impression in the interview, and they loved him. He served there several years, and then started his way up the greasy pole.

"He left there to become a dean at a small college, then provost at another, and on the basis of his supposedly sterling credentials in those positions, we got him. His colleagues at each place apparently gave him glowing recommendations in hopes of getting rid of him. If it weren't for his Dutch name, we might have selected somebody else. There was another candidate, apparently very well qualified, whom most of the faculty liked. Unfortunately, he didn't have any Dutch ancestry. Up to that point, Hank never cared anything about his, either. But he did his homework, and figured out that was something folks here would like. By the time he got on campus for an interview, Hank was 'Mr. Netherlands.'"

Marty spoke up next. "The first couple of years here, he was fine. He didn't try to mess anything up, and generally just stuck to fund-raising, which is what college presidents spend most of their time doing these days, anyway. But then he started reading his own press clippings. He loaded up the Board of Trustees with a bunch of business types who 'shared his vision.' He wanted their money, and figured the best way to get it was to have them on the Board. The problem with that is, most business people don't have any understanding of how a college operates. They don't necessarily care about 'ambiguous' issues like academic freedom, and they hate tenure. 'If you have an economic downturn, just deal with it by laying off faculty.' They have no problems giving him more money for his 'visionary leadership,' but faculty salaries are another issue altogether. And listening to all of that didn't improve

Hank over the years. You haven't had much experience with college administrators, have you, Chris?"

"No, this is really my first contact with administration. As an adjunct, I was pretty much out of the loop."

"Well, let me give you some advice in case you ever decide to climb the greasy pole yourself: in my opinion, deans and presidents shouldn't stay at one school more than ten years. Closer to five is even better. Six or seven, . . . maybe. But definitely not more than ten. Like Hank, they start reading their own press clippings, and actually think they're good, forgetting that it's the college's own PR machinery that's putting out that spin. They forget that they're stewards of the institution. They want to build a 'legacy.' But they don't realize that their legacy will ultimately be based on how well they actually serve the school as stewards of its resources."

"And more significantly," Dirk added, "They hear 'Yes, Sir!' too many times. They come to equate their own opinions with 'THE ONE, TRUE WAY,' and woe be upon anyone who disagrees with them. That's another reason Hank doesn't like tenure. And he also doesn't like our salary scale. He says he just wants to be able to reward 'exceptional performance.' But I have no doubt that his definition of 'exceptional performance' would be limited to his favorites. His criteria would include a significant amount of ass-kissing."

Marty continued: "His 'Golden Children' would get everything, and the rest of us would be left to suck eggs. But with tenure, and the salary scale, I can stand by my beliefs without fear of reprisal—at least to my own position now. But if I were to retire before Hank did, he'd get back at me—and my colleagues in history, by extension—by transferring my position to another department. He's let me know that on a couple of occasions. So I continue to toil in the vineyard."

"Speaking of salary scales," Marianna said, "what was that crap that Mary de Groet threw out this morning about administrative salaries only increasing by about one percent? The *Chronicle's* listing of presidential salaries had Hank getting over six percent."

"Now, now, Marianna," Dirk laughed. "If you're dealing with administrators, you need to be more precise. First of all, I'm sure Hank would point out that the latest *Chronicle* listing is for salaries earned two years ago. Current figures, of course, are 'unavailable.' But more significantly, administrators don't have a set salary scale. And the young recruiters in Admissions, for example, probably got no raises, even though they're responsible for keeping this place afloat. With people like them in the mix, her estimate of one percent may have been fairly accurate."

Marianna shook her head. Then she added, "That makes sense. And I suspect that Sarah's salary is much less than el Deano's was. Not only is she new—she's also a female, and Hank probably feels he should be paying a woman less than a man."

"On that cheery note," Johanna said, "I've gotta get back to mah office, too. Y'all have a good weekend. See y'all next week!"

The rest of the group followed her example, cleared their dishes, and returned to their offices. As they walked back to Macalester, Marty told Chris, "Don't be discouraged by the discussion of administrators. You would probably find that at almost every school, at least to a certain degree. Faculty distrust administrators, and administrators think that faculty don't understand how to make the school function efficiently. They're both right, to a certain degree. My best advice to you is, just do the job you were hired to do. The nice thing about NNC is that salary scale. You don't have to worry about favoritism in that regard. There will be other 'plums' handed to people who seem less deserving than you are, but there's nothing you can do about that. The important thing is, get that article finished, and do a good job teaching. We'll also get you on a couple of committees in the next few years, so you can fulfill the 'service' part of your responsibilities.

Once you get tenure, that'll be one less thing for you to worry about. For now, though, just concentrate on classes. Oh, before I forget: I'll be sending out an e-mail to everyone in the department on Monday, but just so you know, we'll be having a departmental picnic next Saturday afternoon. I hope you don't already have something scheduled then. I should've told you about it earlier."

"No, I don't have anything planned. First there's the reception on Friday that Annika was talking about, and then the picnic on Saturday. Are there always so many social activities going on for faculty?"

"Hardly!" Marty laughed. "This will just about be it until the Christmas season. Then we'll have a departmental dinner, and there's a college Christmas party, hosted by the van Daams. It used to be a full dinner, for all faculty and staff. But as the school's grown, it became more of a reception, with 'heavy hors d'oeuvres.' Then that got replaced by 'dessert.' Not necessarily anything to write home about, but it's still better than nothing. It's nice to maintain some kind of 'community' feeling on campus. There's a lot less of that than there used to be. That's one reason we're having the departmental picnic next week. It had almost died out, too, but I'm resolved to resuscitate it before I retire. My e-mail will spell out the details. In the meantime, have a great weekend!"

*　　　*　　　*　　　*　　　*

AFTER THEY GOT BACK TO MACALESTER HALL, Chris spent an hour or so putting the finishing touches on his opening lecture. Then he left to get a few items for his apartment. Marty spent the afternoon in his office. He was just turning off his computer when he thought he heard a soft knock on his door. He looked up to see Sarah Christiansen, looking somewhat apprehensive as she was about to knock again.

"I'm sorry, I thought I heard a knock, but it was so soft that I wasn't sure. Come in!"

"No, you look like you're about to leave. I can talk to you another time."

"It's not a problem. I'm not going anywhere special. I was just going to stop by 'Snuffy's Italian Garden' and get something to eat. If your husband's still in the Cities, would you like to join me?"

"That would be great! Owen won't get home until tomorrow afternoon. Thanks for the invitation."

They decided it would be simplest for her to follow him in her car, since neither of them would be going in the direction of campus after dinner. That way they wouldn't have to return to pick up Sarah's car. There were still several spaces in Snuffy's parking lot when they got there. "Next week at this time, this lot will be full, and we'd have to wait an hour or more for a table," Marty told her as she was getting out of her car. "But most of the students won't be back in town until tomorrow or Sunday. This is one more 'calm before the storm.' In a town the size of New Leiden, the influx of nearly 2000 students has quite an impact. It's kind of like a python swallowing a pig, to use a crude description. Next week, there will be students all over town, opening bank accounts, and buying odds and ends for their dorm rooms (or apartments, if they're among the few who live off campus). Next Friday night, you won't be able to get a seat in most of the restaurants without an hour wait. But then everyone falls into a routine, and things calm down a bit. In the spring, when the campus empties out, New Leiden goes back to being a sleepy little town. The students are our livelihood, so we can't really complain. But it's nice to have it like this for one more day."

When they got inside, Marty introduced Sarah to the owner, "Snuffy," who led them to a relatively quiet corner of the restaurant where they could carry on a conversation. "Would you like some wine?" Marty asked "The choices here don't compare to Dirk's, but they're not bad. Sort of like the table wines you'd find in a small trattoria in Italy."

"I'll have to take your word for that. I've never been to Italy," Sarah replied. "Owen and I have been to England a couple of times. I spent a year there when I was on a sabbatical leave, working in a physics lab in Durham. We've been back a couple of times since. We had some great Italian food there and in London, but I've never been to the continent. That's something we hope to accomplish in the next few years."

Snuffy sent a waitress to take their order, and after she'd left, Marty said, "When you showed up outside my office, you looked like you wanted to ask me about something. What's up?"

"I've been here for little more than a month, but I've already gotten the impression that you're someone whom people on campus respect."

"Not everyone does, I can assure you," he laughed. "But I'm flattered that you think some people do."

"You don't need to be so modest. But I thought you'd be a good person to talk to, after what I've experienced in the last day or two. What in the Hell have I gotten myself into here?"

"In what way? I thought you did a great job this morning, and you certainly charmed everyone at Dirk's last night."

"But if you and Dirk hadn't tipped me off about the faculty attitude about Hank chairing Faculty Assembly meetings, I'd have been hung out to dry. Hank didn't give me any heads-up about that. And when I mentioned that at lunch, the silence spoke volumes."

"You mentioned that your father was in the Navy, right?"

"Yes. He retired as a Commander. Why?"

"I've never been in the military. But I've seen a lot of old movies with military settings. I don't know if they really say this in the Navy or not, but in the movies, someone in my position right now would say, 'Permission to speak freely, sir?'"

Sarah laughed. "Of course. That's why I stopped by your office."

"But the other part of the equation is that this conversation stays at this table. Agreed?"

"Don't worry about that. After this morning, I figure that Hank's left me on my own, so I'm not going to do anything to compromise my position. Anything you say won't leave this table."

"Fine. For starters, let's just say that Hank's administrative style is very different from my own."

"For example?"

"He likes to be in charge, and that's sometimes accomplished most easily by other people being caught off guard—like you'd have been if you'd walked into that meeting 'blind.' If I were you, I wouldn't mention anything to him about what Dirk and I said last night. If he thinks you're developing a good relationship with faculty, he won't be pleased. When he asks you about the meeting, just say something about how difficult the meeting started out, but that things calmed down eventually."

"That's what you told Annika."

"Which will get back to him—probably has already. She's not a 'snitch,' but when he asks for something, she provides the information. She's an innocent 'messenger' in this situation. Since Pieter wasn't at the meeting, she won't hear anything about it from him. And she's not going to ask anyone else for corroboration, since you were at the table with us, and you didn't contradict me. If any other faculty mention the meeting to him, it will simply be to bitch at him for not being there. So let him think you got into a bind today. Then he'll think he's got a slight advantage over you, and leave it at that. If you were to ask him why he let you walk into a potential buzz saw, he'd be embarrassed, and then look for some other way to get the advantage. And your relationship with him would 'go South' from there. I'm curious: has he referred to you by any names besides Sarah?"

"Not exactly. But he mentioned something about a grade school friend whose name was Sarah. He said she preferred to be called 'Sally.'"

"And how did you respond to that?"

"I said, 'No one has ever called me that. It's not a name I would answer to.'"

"Good response. If he ever does call you Sally, call him 'Henrik' in return. Then, if he says, as he undoubtedly would, 'Just call me Hank,' say something like 'And just call me Sarah.' He likes to call people by names other than what they prefer to go by. He often says 'Hi, Martin' when he sees me on campus, for example. When he does, I say 'Hi, Henrik.' And then we go back to Marty and Hank for a while. It's one of his little quirks. I'm also curious: did he tell you before last night that he was planning to retire at the end of the year?"

"No, that caught me by surprise. When I interviewed for my position, he told me he was thinking about retiring 'in a year or two.' He said it was important to get a dean in place and well established, so there would be some continuity when a new president came on board. But I wasn't expecting that announcement last night—maybe next year or the year after."

"He probably had this in mind all along. Having a new dean in place has the potential of giving a good continuity for the new president's administration. But if you're only here a year before his successor starts his term of office, there might still be a few fits and starts before everything begins to run smoothly again. And his presidency will look good in comparison."

"That's what I was thinking," Sarah groaned.

"Don't worry about it. Much of what goes on around here happens almost by itself. The Faculty Assembly isn't likely to bring up anything unusual for you to deal with. We went through a gruesome experience with curriculum reform about five years ago, and nobody's looking to do anything like that again for a while. And nothing comes out of his office without it going through Annika first.

She's someone with whom you should develop a good working relationship, by the way. While she can sometimes come across as a bit stiff and humorless, I think you'd find a good ally there. Don't present it to her that way. She's a loyal assistant to Hank. But she's an even more loyal servant of the College. While Hank may pull some things that she doesn't agree with, he has to do that on his own. Very few things happen on campus that don't go through her. Sometimes he catches her by surprise, and puts something in gear that she doesn't know about it. Unfortunately, when that happens, there's not much she can do to stop him. But that doesn't happen often.

"A word of caution, though," Marty continued. "Don't let Hank realize that you're developing a good working relationship with Annika. He prefers the 'divide and conquer' method. The nice thing is, now you know that you'll only be working with him for one year. Concentrate on doing things the way you think they should be done, and establish your own 'system.' If he questions anything you're doing, just use the excuse that you're trying to build the transition to the new administration. Suggest that the better that transition goes, the better he'll look. Hank will eat that up. Otherwise, keep your head down and don't cross him. You'll be fine. And he'll be gone before you know it."

"I had a very different picture of him when I was hired. He seemed much more easy-going then."

"Hank can be a little 'passive-aggressive' at times. But the bottom line, in my opinion, is that he's a bully. A couple of years ago, everyone on campus had to attend one of the anti-discrimination workshops that we have every few years. Only this time, the focus wasn't on race or gender discrimination. The 'facilitator' dealt with 'bullying in the workplace.' She talked about how bullies play favorites, downplay or insult the contributions of those who aren't favorites, belittle people, and the like. Then she gave suggestions about how people could report bullying to their superiors in the administration, and what those people should do in response. On my way back to my office, I kept thinking, 'She just described the 'van Daam/Rothman School of Management.' So the next morning, I sent her an e-mail. I thanked her for her 'valuable presentation,' and then asked, 'But what do you do when the bullies are the ones in charge of the whole operation: the Dean and the President?'"

"How did she respond?"

"She didn't. I figured she'd gotten her check, and didn't need to worry about us anymore."

"That's too bad. So Rothman functioned the same way that Hank does? No wonder I've picked up on some bad feelings towards the Dean's Office."

"They each had their own personalized approach, but yes, essentially they functioned in much the same way. If you can show the faculty that you're not cut from the same cloth as Rothman, that will go miles to make your relationship with them smoother. But you'll be walking a fine line. Hank has strong views about the relationship between faculty and administration. If he thinks you're siding with the faculty too much, it will be tough sledding for you. But if you follow his example, it will immediately sour your relationship with them, and after he's gone, you'll never be able to dig yourself out of that hole. That's the bad news. The good news is, now we know you'll only have to walk that tightrope for one academic year."

The waitress brought them a carafe of wine—the house chianti. Then the conversation shifted to more pleasant topics. When they finished their pizza, Marty started to reach for his wallet. Sarah stopped him before he could pay. "No, this is my treat. You gave me a wealth of information this evening, and an important perspective on my forthcoming experience at NNC." Then she laughed, and added, "Besides, I don't want you coming to me sometime in the future, asking for a new copy machine or something, and saying, 'Remember, you still owe me for that pizza.'"

"You're an astute administrator!" Marty chuckled. "I was going to make it my treat—without any future strings attached, by the way—but since you insist. . . . I'll agree to that, only on the condition that it's my treat next time. But one word of advice, all kidding aside: don't <u>EVER</u> mention to Hank that you and I are on speaking terms, much less that we shared a pizza at Snuffy's! As far as he's concerned, you're administration, and I'm faculty, 'and n'er the twain shall meet.' In his mind, there could never be a smooth working relationship between the two."

"This is our little secret," Sarah said. "Thanks for the advice."

When they walked back to the parking lot, Sarah stopped before she got into her car. "Thanks again," she said. "You gave me some valuable insights. I feel kind of like Humphrey Bogart at the end of 'Casablanca': 'I think this is the beginning of a beautiful friendship.'"

"I hope so," Marty replied. "Have a great weekend. The 'circus' starts on Monday, so try to be well-rested before it does."

5
It's Not the Heat . . .

Monday, August 26

MONDAY MORNING STARTED OUT HOT. Not just hot—hot and humid. "Muggy" barely described it. Chris had never experienced humidity like this. When he opened his garage door, the floor looked like a light rain had fallen—but it was just from the humidity. As usual, he'd gotten up at 6:00—a carryover from his days on the dairy farm, when he would already be milking cows by that time. He was hoping to enjoy a cool, crisp morning. Unfortunately, as he'd already learned in the short time he'd been in Minnesota, that wasn't likely. Instead of a clear, bright blue sky, there was a haze. It wasn't quite fog, but if the dew point got a little higher, it would be.

Chris took a quick shower, using cooler water than usual. Even then, he'd no sooner dried off than he was already wet again. Just the effort of drying himself seemed to work up a sweat. After he got dressed, he decided to take an extra shirt to school with him. By the time he got to his afternoon class, the one he'd just put on would probably be soaked.

Macalester Hall was air-conditioned. But the previous week, he'd discovered that was a relative term. Marty told him to consider himself lucky: when he was a student at NNC, most of the buildings on campus weren't air-conditioned, and the first chiller in Macalester wasn't very efficient. This one did a pretty good job, but there was still a general feeling of dampness that permeated everything. On Friday, Marty had printed a copy of his daily schedule and taped it to the inside of the window of his office door. By Monday morning, the ink had spread in blotches that made it almost unreadable.

Although he wasn't ready for the humidity, Chris had prepared himself well for his first class of the semester. The students all seemed enthusiastic, though he sensed that some weren't quite as excited after he handed out the syllabus. He didn't consider two exams and a 10-page research paper excessive for a 300-level course. Most of the students didn't, either, but a few were apparently hoping for considerably less. In one of his "New Faculty Orientation" sessions, a panel of experienced teachers had talked about that very issue. One of them cautioned, "For many students, anything more than a 'classics comic book' will be too much. But as much as they might grumble and groan when you hand out your syllabus, if you don't have a decent workload, you'll get no respect, which is even worse than the grumbling."

Having taught at a larger, public university, Chris wasn't sure how NNC would compare to his last two years in Oregon. Marty's advice had been simple: "Don't expect a classroom full of Rhodes Scholars, but set the bar high enough to challenge them. Not only will most of them rise to that challenge, but some will also surprise you with how much they can do. Hank talks about this place like it's the 'Harvard of the Northern Prairie.' It's hardly that, but don't underestimate the students. Igniting a 'spark' in them is one of the real joys of teaching. And I'll pass along some advice I picked up from a young woman who was a sabbatical replacement here a few years ago. At the end of the year, someone asked her, 'What's the most important thing you've learned this year?' Her answer was very simple: 'That the students aren't us.' All of us here have spent countless hours pursuing our disciplines. The students are just starting out. Even if they're really excited to learn about the subjects that we love so much, they're still just beginners. Don't ever forget that."

When he got to his office, Chris checked his e-mail, and found the invitation that Marty had promised:

After the hiatus of the last few years, I'm happy to be reinstituting the History Department's "Back to School" picnic!

Location: My back yard (and family room if it rains or gets too muggy)

When: Saturday, August 31, 4:30 to ??

What to bring: appetizers, side dishes, or desserts. There will be a sign-up sheet outside my office (with spaces for each category)

The Department will provide burgers and brats, chips, and soft drinks. Let me know if you want a "veggie burger" or meatless hot dog.

I'll provide a case of Heineken and some samples of my latest home brewing efforts. If you want wine or different beer, please bring some along.

Marty

After his first class, Chris was on his way back to his office when he ran into Marty, who was coming back from a department chairs' meeting. As they walked back to Macalester together, Marty spotted Tom Olsson, and waved him over to them. "Chris, here's someone you need to meet. Tom Olsson's our Director of Campus Security. Hopefully, the worst problem you'll need his help for will be if you've locked your keys in your office. Even then, you'll probably be dealing with one of his staff. But there isn't much that happens on this campus that he doesn't know about."

"Marty, if you're flattering me, you must want something! What's it this time?" Tom laughed.

"Not at all, Tom, I just want you to meet Chris van Zant, the newest member of the History Department. He's Tim Johansson's replacement. If the impressions of the first couple of weeks are any indication, I think you'll find him a much more agreeable colleague than Tim was."

"That's not saying much!" Tom laughed. "I pity my counterpart where he is now."

"What are you up to this morning?"

"Do you really have to ask, Marty? It's Monday morning—almost 10:30. And as you can see, I'm headed for Middlebury Hall. What else would I be doing at this hour?"

"Oh, Christ, are they still making you go to every meeting?"

"You bet! Nothing's changed yet! I've heard that Juan Carlos may be retiring at the end of this year, so maybe I'll get a reprieve next year. But until then, I'll be there every Monday morning—unless Hank has something more pressing, in which case I'll send one of my staff. But if I don't get there pretty soon, who knows what will happen! Glad to meet you Chris. I look forward to getting to know you."

Tom hurried off. Seeing the confused look on Chris's face, Marty explained: "Middlebury houses the Department of Modern and Classical Languages. That's broken down into separate language sections: French, German, Spanish, Dutch, and Classics (Latin & Greek). They each essentially function as mini-departments (and most of us even refer to them as departments). If they weren't separate, nothing could ever get done over there; German would be arguing with French, and they'd both be in competition with Spanish. All of them would gang up on Latin, which in turn looks down its nose at everything except Classical Greek. It would make debates at the UN look efficient.

"But Spanish is a world of its own," Marty continued. "In addition to a couple of adjuncts who help with the introductory Spanish language classes, there are four tenured faculty. Two of them are from South America— Peru and Argentina. The other two are from Spain. The same battles that raged for centuries in the Spanish Empire continue today in our Spanish section. The Spaniards don't think the other two speak with 'proper' accents. The

Peruvian and Argentinian think the Spaniards are overbearing and imperious. It doesn't help any that Juan Carlos—one of the Spaniards—has the same name as the former King of Spain. That just adds to his 'regal aura.' The tensions simmered under the surface for a long time, but three or four years ago, the South Americans had finally had enough. Anna Maria—the Peruvian—got up in the middle of a meeting, and started to walk out. Juan Carlos stepped in front of her to block her exit. In the process, he bumped her, and she started to lose her balance. Edmundo—the Argentinian—thought Juan Carlos had shoved her, so he took a swing at him. Fortunately, he missed. The ruckus caught the attention of the Chair of the whole department, Hannelore van Leuven. She came running into the room just in time to keep the situation from deteriorating into a free for all."

"Hannelore teaches German," he explained. "She likes everything to be '*in Ordnung*,' and departmental fisticuffs don't fit into her world view. So she insisted that the Spanish section's meetings had to be attended by someone from Campus Security. While Tom could delegate that to someone else, he's well aware that some of the younger members of his staff don't have enough '*gravitas*' to intimidate Juan Carlos. Also, his wife is from Honduras, and he's pretty much fluent in Spanish. In other words, the faculty can't say anything 'behind his back.' So every Monday, he hauls himself over to their meeting and serves as referee. Hopefully the rumors of Juan Carlos's impending retirement are true. The general consensus is that he's well beyond his 'sell by' date."

"Wow! I'd never expect that from professionals."

"Just because they have advanced degrees, don't expect academics always to act professionally. You'll be amazed at the amount of pettiness there is in higher education— and not just at NNC.'"

Having exhausted the subject of the Spanish section, Marty changed the subject: "Did you see my e-mail about the picnic on Saturday?"

"Sure—I'm looking forward to the chance to spend some time with the rest of the department and get to know them a little better. It'll be nice to be with them outside of the campus. Is there anything in particular you'd like me to bring?"

"Anything you'd like—if you don't have something special in mind, just check the sign-up sheet to see what isn't being covered by someone else. If were up to me, I wouldn't even bother with a sign-up sheet, because things always seem to sort out by themselves. But some members of the department worry that we'll have problems without a list—you know: too many desserts and no salads, or vice versa. As I mentioned, the department will provide burgers and brats, as well as chips. If we didn't do that, a couple people might only bring a bag or two of chips. And some salsa, if we were lucky. That's not fair to those who devote some time and effort to fixing a favorite recipe."

"Your e-mail indicated that it's a tradition that's being 'reinstituted.' I take it that you haven't been doing it for a while."

"It essentially died out when Johansson was Chair. It's traditionally been hosted by the Department Chair, but his wife had a fairly high opinion of her social status. So she wasn't very happy having all of us *hoi poloi* in her house—especially not anyone's children. When she decided to become a vegetarian, she didn't like the smell of burgers and brats cooking on a grill in her back yard. It became even worse when she tried being a vegan. And Johansson wouldn't spend any departmental money on food for department functions, even though every department has a small budget line for such things. He was such an inept administrator that he thought he could win points with the higher-ups if he didn't use all the money in our budget. Every year, he was amazed when the end of the budget cycle came around, and the administration just sucked up any leftover funds. As my Dad used to say, they didn't give him a 'thank you, kiss my ass, or nothin'.' What's worse, he couldn't figure out that when they found leftover money at the end of one year, they'd look at his budget request for the coming year and say, 'You obviously don't need as much as we allocated last time-- we're cutting your budget accordingly.' One of the fundamental rules of academic budgeting, Chris: 'Use it or lose it.'"

"I'll try to remember that. But from what I've seen of administration at this point, I hope I never have to deal with it personally."

"In a department our size, I wouldn't count on that. It's rare that someone doesn't serve at least one three-year term as Chair. The real problems come when someone gets their turn in the rotation and thinks it's a result of some spectacular accomplishment on their part, without realizing that almost everyone else has been in the same boat. The really ambitious ones use the opportunity as the first step up the greasy pole. While he wasn't a particularly good teacher, Johansson was a productive scholar. He cranked out more monographs and scholarly articles than anyone else on campus. Combining his publication record with four years as department head, he was able to parlay that into the endowed chair where he is now. I always had the feeling he was just 'marking time' here until something better came along. I'm sure he'll do well there, and I have no doubt that his wife feels he now has a position more representative of their true status—or at least hers. I wish them good luck, though I can't say that I'll miss either one of them.

*   *   *   *   *

ACROSS CAMPUS, HANK GOT UP FROM HIS COMPUTER and poked his head into Annika's office. "What time's the meeting with Nagel and that Summerfield guy?"

"1:30"

"Why didn't Nagel have him come for lunch. I'm generally more successful at fundraising when I can 'break bread' with a potential donor."

"And get them over-fed and a little groggy, so that you can talk them into anything," Annika laughed. "That's probably why Mr. Summerfield specifically said that he would be coming AFTER lunch. Mike said he was most insistent about that. After he meets with the two of you, Mr. Summerfield will be going over to Edison to meet with President Thompson. Apparently they invited him to dinner at Chartwell, but he told them the same thing."

"Can you tell me anything more than is in Nagel's 'executive summary?' I know he's the head of some 'dot.com' outfit in Silicon Valley, but not much more than that. Why's he interested in giving us his money? He's not an alum of either NNC or Chartwell."

"You need to read the summary more closely," Annika said, punctuating her comment with a heavy sigh. "It's not HIS money he's giving away. It's his parents'. They own a big farm near Allendale, about halfway between here and Edison. They used to go to concerts and sports events at both colleges, and decided to give their land to them in appreciation for all the enjoyment they had at both schools. They left it up to their son to decide how to divide it. Since retirement, they've been living in the Cities near their daughter, leasing the land to a neighbor. He wanted to buy it from them, but they're insistent that they want to show their appreciation to Chartwell and NNC. If either school wants to sell its share to the neighbor—or anyone else, for that matter—we can go ahead. It will be ours to dispose of as we see fit."

"How's Dick feel about his parents giving the money to two schools that he never attended?"

"My God! Didn't you even read the first paragraph of Nagel's summary? Right there, in ALL CAPS, it says 'MR. SUMMERFIELD PREFERS TO BE CALLED "RICH"—OR IF YOU PREFER TO BE MORE FORMAL, "RICHARD." BUT HE DISLIKES BEING CALLED "RICK," AND HATES THE NAME "DICK." UNDER NO CIRCUMSTANCES SHOULD YOU CALL

HIM ANYWHERE OTHER THAN "RICH" OR "RICHARD."'" So don't try to be cute with his name!"

"Don't worry about it. I'll be fine. But you still haven't told me how he's reacting to his parents giving us the land, when he was never a student here."

"He founded a very successful 'dot.com,' and he's looking for places to give his own money. He graduated from Stanford, but he doesn't expect his parents to send their money there. His donations to his alma mater are apparently substantial, but his parents don't have any personal attachment there. If this is what they want to do with the land, it's fine with him. Before you meet with him this afternoon, I'd suggest you re-read Nagel's 'executive summary.'" She thought to herself, *"Or more likely, finally get around to reading it for the first time."*

"Okay, I'll see if I can find some time. Meanwhile, can you run over to the 'Bean Bag' and get me a latte? The usual—'skinny' with a double shot—and one packet of artificial sweetener?"

"And who's going to answer the phone? Elke's home sick this morning, remember? And we won't have student workers lined up for another day or two."

"I'm capable of answering the God-damned phone!" Hank barked. "Anything that rings into the main office line lights up a button on my phone, too. And there's nothing on my schedule before lunch today, so there's not likely to be anyone coming into the office while you're gone."

"Okay, I'll be back as soon as I can."

As she headed out the door, she mumbled under her breath, *"Just don't screw anything up. And a simple 'please' would be appreciated once in a while."*

As soon as Annika was gone, Hank picked up his cell phone, and pushed an auto-dial number. When Mike Nagel answered, Hank asked, "What do I need to know for this meeting this afternoon? I read your 'executive summary,' but Annika seems to know a lot more about this guy— Rich, right?—than I saw in what you gave me. . . . No, I don't have time to read the damned thing again. Just tell me the important points that I need to know."

While Annika was hurrying down the back stairs, a tall man in his mid-40s was stepping out of the elevator at the far end of the hall. He was wearing dirty jeans, muddy boots, and a blue work shirt that was soaked with sweat. His battered seed cap was also waterlogged. He had obviously been working hard in the morning heat and humidity. And he looked like he'd been frustrated by whatever he'd been doing.

He stopped to read the registry opposite the elevator. He found the office number he was looking for, and started down the hall. When he reached the President's Office, he stepped inside. The outer office was empty, but there was a sign on the desk that read, "For Assistance, Please See the President's Executive Assistant." An arrow pointed toward Annika's Office. That, too, was empty, but he could hear someone talking on the phone in the next room. He tapped lightly on the open door. When the talking continued, he knocked, trying not to make too much of a disturbance, but loud enough to catch the speaker's attention. When that still didn't work, he knocked harder, and coughed politely.

Hank was looking at his computer, with his cell phone pressed between his shoulder and his ear. It was hard to tell whether he was concentrating more on the phone or the computer. The cough caught his attention, however, and he looked up impatiently. "Yes?" he grunted.

"Institutional Advancement?"

"What?"

"Institutional Advancement," the man repeated, this time more as a statement than as a question.

"No," Hank grunted.

"I'm looking for Institutional Advancement."

"This is the President's Office," Hank growled

"I know. But I'm asking about Institutional Advancement."

"They're in Carlton."

"Carlton?"

"Institutional Advancement is in Carlton Hall."

"Why didn't you tell me that to begin with?"

"You didn't ask."

"Where is it?"

"Carlton?

"Yes, specifically Institutional Advancement."

"Next building over, second floor," Hank said, pointing vaguely in the general direction of Carlton Hall.

"Thanks . . . I guess," he said, as he turned to leave.

"Sure," Hank growled, and turned his attention back to his computer and the cell phone.

Mike Nagel, who had been cut off in mid-sentence, asked, "What's going on?"

"Oh, nothing. Just some dufus in a seed cap babbling away about nothing. He was looking for your office, so I sent him over to Carlton."

The "dufus in a seed cap" hadn't made it through Annika's office yet, so he heard Hank's comment clearly. It didn't improve his disposition. Just as he stepped into the hall, Annika came up the stairwell, carrying Hank's latte. When she saw him coming out of the office, she asked, "Have you been helped, sir?"

"You might say that, in a roundabout way. I just simplified my afternoon."

"What do you mean?" Annika asked, trying to hide her growing concern.

"I had an appointment with President van Daam scheduled for 1:30 this afternoon." Annika immediately noticed his use of the past tense. "But I spent the morning helping my parents' neighbor try to get a herd of cows back in a pasture after they broke down a fence. I was on my way to my hotel to clean up and change clothes, and was hoping to push the meeting back to 2:00. I guess I left my cell phone in the neighbor's pickup, so I couldn't call. Since I had to drive by campus on the way to the hotel, I just popped in here to talk to someone about rescheduling the meeting."

"You must be Mr. Summerfield. I'm Annika van Rejn, President van Daam's Executive Assistant. I'll be happy to reschedule the meeting for you."

"That won't be necessary. I just had what was essentially a monosyllabic conversation with the person I assume is President van Daam. The arrogant son-of-a-bitch could hardly be bothered to look up from his damned computer screen. My parents have always had good feelings about Nieuw Nederland College, but they obviously haven't met the current president. I can assure you, this isn't what they want to support with their land. You can cancel the meeting. I'll spend my time with President Thompson at Chartwell. I'm sure he'll be able to carry on a polite conversation with a potential donor— regardless of how he's dressed."

"I'm sorry you feel that way, but of course I'll respect your wishes."

"I don't envy you having to work as his assistant. I can imagine you have to try and undo his screw-ups all the time."

Annika didn't reply, but she told herself, *"You don't know the half of it!"*

"He'll undoubtedly want to call me to make up for this morning. Tell him not to bother. I won't be returning any of his calls—or Mike Nagel's, either. My staff will be informed of that as soon as I get my hands on my cell phone again."

As Summerfield walked quickly back to the elevator, Annika took a deep breath and went into Hank's office. He was still talking to Mike Nagel, but most of his attention was directed toward his computer screen.

"Hang up the phone . . . now!" Annika said, her voice almost cracking.

"But it's Mike Nagel. He's briefing me about this afternoon's meeting." As he spoke, he clicked the mouse to minimize the application on his computer.

"Hang up the damned phone! Now! There is no meeting this afternoon!" She was almost screaming.

"What do you mean? We have the dot-com guy, Dick— I mean Rich—Summerfield, at 1:30." The look on Annika's face told him that he should follow her directions. He told Nagel that he'd call him back later, and ended the call.

"What are you talking about?" he asked.

"What in the Hell did you do while I was getting you your damned latte?"

"Nothing. I called Nagel on my cell phone, and he was briefing me. Nobody called. I didn't mess up any calls"

"What about people who came into the office?"

"What people? There was just one guy, some hayseed fresh off the farm. He asked about Institutional Advancement, so I sent him over there. I have no idea why he came looking for them here."

"Because he had an appointment with you at 1:30. That was Rich Summerfield."

"That can't be Summerfield. He's a dot.com exec, not a farmer—especially not one in muddy boots and a sweaty work shirt. And from the smell, I'm sure most of what was on his boots wasn't mud."

"He'd been at his parents' farm, helping a neighbor get some cattle back into their pasture. He was on his way back to his hotel to clean up, and stopped by here to push the appointment back a bit. Notice that I'm using past tense! Whatever you said to him pissed him off so much that he's going to give all of his parents' money to Chartwell, instead of splitting it with us."

"Can he do that? He's supposed to divide it between the two schools."

"Divide it as he deems appropriate! I suspect he'll give us a token amount so that it's technically 'divided,' but we're not going to get anything substantial."

She walked to the window, and said, "Come here, and look at the visitors' section of the parking lot. What do you see there?"

Hank got up and joined her at the window. "A Mercedes convertible. Whose is that?"

"Watch."

Just then, Rich Summerfield walked quickly out of the building and climbed into the Mercedes.

"See—that's not just some 'hayseed farmer.' That's Rich Summerfield. And I think you're missing how appropriate his first name is—if he's in a position to simply pass along his parents' land without a second thought, he's definitely rich."

"What are we talking about here? A couple hundred thousand, after dividing it up with Chartwell."

"You didn't read ANY of Mike's executive summary, did you? And you clearly don't have any idea of the value of land around here. His parents' land would probably sell for <u>at least</u> $10 million. We'd have probably gotten half of that. Now we'll get nothing."

As Hank watched Summerfield drive out of the parking lot, the color drained from his face. "Shit," he grumbled.

"That's an understatement. I hope you enjoy your latte. It was a pretty expensive one this morning."

*　　　*　　　*　　　*　　　*

WHEN SHE GOT HOME THAT AFTERNOON, Annika was still furious. When Pieter came in the door a few minutes after she'd arrived, he could feel the tension in the air. He was sure that he wasn't the cause of it, but until he knew for certain, he wasn't going to take any chances.

"What's going on?" he asked carefully.

"He's finally done it!" she said. The muscles in her jaw were so tight that he was afraid she might break a bone.

"Who's finally done what?"

"Hank! Who else? He's finally pushed me past the breaking point."

"What's that idiot done THIS time?"

"Oh, nothing but lose the college about $5 million, just because he's too busy being 'presidential' to actually do the things he's supposed to do as President. He's too goddamned lazy to read an executive summary! Then he sends me on a flunky errand that he could've just as easily done himself. But no—he can't get his own damned coffee! Instead, he wastes his time, as well as Mike Nagel's, because he's 'too busy' to read a summary that had all the important information in it. He's had that summary for over a week, but he just didn't get around to reading it."

"The man's an idiot. That was established long ago. It's time you get a job in another office. You need to get out of there."

"You know I can't do that."

"Why not? Because of the salary? I know you have one of the highest paid administrative staff positions on campus. But what good's a nice salary if you have to work under these conditions? Swallow your pride, and take a job in another office. I'm sure you'd find challenges elsewhere on campus. And what you have now certainly can't be considered 'job satisfaction.'"

"Give me a break, Pieter. You know me better than that. I'm not staying in this position because of my ego. If I try to get a job in another office on campus, he'll block it."

"How could he do that? He doesn't run every office on campus."

"He might as well, the way things work around here. I never mentioned this, because I didn't want to get our hopes up prematurely. Over the last year or so, I've sounded out a couple of positions on campus. I talked to the directors in each office, and everything seemed to be a 'go.' I even submitted a few applications. But every time, I got vague responses about being 'over qualified,' or how I probably 'wouldn't really be happy' there. I pushed the issue in one case, where the head of the office is someone I've known for years. He said he couldn't really talk about the position, but he strongly hinted that he'd gotten pressure from Hank not to hire me."

"What kind of pressure?"

"The obvious kind—funding for what he needs or wants, if he cooperated with Hank; 'unanticipated budget shortfalls' if he didn't."

"Did you confront Hank about it?"

"Sure, and as you might expect, he denied having done anything. And then he laid on the guilt, asking what could possibly be so bad in his office that I would want to leave. He said he was 'hurt' that I would think he would do anything that wasn't in my best interest. He claimed I was always free to go wherever I wanted to go, but then asked why I'd want to leave one of the best-paying administrative jobs on campus. He's a master of passive-aggressiveness."

"Then you should find something off campus."

"I've already looked into that, but I haven't been able to find anything, other than working the counter at a fast-food restaurant. After today, though, even that sounds good."

"Look at it this way: if you weren't working for Hank, you'd have time to finish your dissertation."

"What good would that do me? We wouldn't have my income anymore, and there's no likelihood of me teaching full time here."

"We can get by without you working full time, at least for the time it would take you to finish your degree. Then I'm sure you could piece together some courses here and at Chartwell. If nothing else, you could get a couple sections of *die Quellen*, and if you picked up a course or two at Chartwell, you'd be close to full-time. You'd still be covered under my health insurance, so that's not an issue. Give it some thought, at least."

"That does sound appealing. I don't know how much longer I can stand working for that idiot."

"Well, at least he'll only be around for the rest of this year."

"I keep telling myself that. But then I wonder if I can make it through the year without strangling the son of a bitch!" She paused a moment, and then asked, "Are you going to the range this evening?"

"Sure, there's a tournament next week. I need to keep myself in practice. I'll be going every day until the tournament. Why?"

"I think I'd like to join you for a change. Firing off a few rounds might help me relax a little. Don't worry, I won't paste Hank's picture on the targets. I won't have to—he'll be all I see every time I pull the trigger."

*   *   *   *   *

BY THURSDAY, THE TEMPERATURE HAD COOLED a couple degrees, but the humidity was still as high as it had been on Monday. About 10:00, Marty knocked on Chris's office door and asked him if he'd like to join him for coffee—or more likely, for something cold to drink. Chris didn't teach on Thursdays, and he was already pretty well prepared for Friday. So he eagerly agreed.

Thanks to a relatively recent renovation, the CUB's air conditioning was much more efficient than Macalester's. "The CUB was always adequate," Marty explained. "But several of our 'peer institutions'—read that as 'competitors' in recruiting students—got bequests to build new student centers. So Hank beat the bushes to come up with enough money to give the CUB better 'street appeal.' In the process, they also upgraded the facilities. The 'Bean Bag,' with its shiny new espresso machine, is a good example. While I might grumble about how the money could've been better spent on salaries, I also realize that donors want their money to go to something they can stick their names on. Higher salaries make faculty happier, but they're not something a donor can relate to. My biggest complaint about the renovation is that it displaced what used to be space for student organizations. They got moved out in order to make way for administrative offices."

132

When they got to the CUB's coffee shop, most of the "regulars" were already there. Chris and Marty both poured themselves a glass of iced tea and found seats at opposite ends of the table. As they sat down, Dirk asked, "Hot enough for you?"

Everyone looked at Chris, who wasn't sure how he was supposed to answer. Johanna laughed, "Ya obviously haven't been here long enough to know the proper response. This time o' year, the standard greetin' is usually some variation of, 'Is it hot enough for ya?'"

"Since I haven't stopped sweating all week, it obviously is," Chris replied.

"Of course—we all feel that way. But the appropriate answer is, 'Oh, it's not the heat, it's the humidity!'"

Chris laughed: "One of my cousins lives in Arizona. Her standard comment is always, 'Sure, it's hot here—but it's dry heat.' I guess this is the regional equivalent."

"But in the Upper Midwest, complaining about the weather is almost a professional sport," Ed added. "Part of it comes from the fact that so many people around here are farmers, or working in some ag-related business. Weather isn't only something related to physical comfort. It's also a key element of economic survival."

"Spoken like a true Professor of Finance," Johanna laughed. "But in this case, he's right." Her drawl was in good form this morning, with the last word stretching out as almost two syllables: "ra-aht."

"What do you mean, in this case?" Ed tried to look like his feelings were hurt, but he couldn't suppress a smile.

"Even a blind pig finds a mushroom every once in a while," Marty said.

"I don't need to stay here and be insulted," Ed snapped, again barely keeping his grin under control.

"No, you can get insulted anywhere on campus!" Johanna laughed.

Ed held up his hands: "I surrender! It's time to pick on someone else."

Marty looked down the table at Chris: "This is a good day to stay in the shadows. Fortunately, this is just good-natured banter. But when we get a week or two of really hot, muggy weather, people's shorts start to bind, and they get a little sensitive. Sometimes joking like this can accidently set someone off; they'll leave in a huff, and not come back for a couple weeks. But I don't think it'll get that bad this time. According to this morning's weather report, we're supposed to get some thunderstorms late tonight. There's supposed to be a cooler front moving in, bringing dryer weather. It should be here by tomorrow morning."

"Do you have a weather radio?" Ed asked.

Chris gave him a surprised look. "No. Is that something I need?"

"It would probably just be a convenience in the Pacific Northwest," Ed replied. "But around here, with 'severe storms' coming through frequently, it's a valuable thing to have. You've probably heard the city siren being tested every evening at 6:00. If you hear that any other time of the day, head for the basement, if you have one. At least stay in the lowest spot possible, away from windows. A weather radio, which will give you official weather alerts, may save you more than a lot of anxiety. If we get hit with a severe thunder storm, it could literally be a life saver. Bookmark the national weather radar site on your computer, too. That way you can track storms as they're rolling by."

Most of the color had drained from Chris's face. "That's the one real concern I had about moving here. Tornados scare the hell out of me. They aren't a worry in the Pacific Northwest. But after I accepted the job here, every news report about them in the Midwest set me on edge. Is that something we need to worry about tonight?"

Marty put his hand on Chris's shoulder. "They're always something to worry about, but the prediction that I heard for tonight didn't mention 'severe storms.' When you hear that term, make sure you pay attention to what's happening with the weather. They usually don't use the word 'tornado' unless one's actually been sighted. But any weather report that includes the words 'severe' and 'thunder storm' means they're a possibility. Fortunately, it sounds like this'll just be a mild storm, brought by cooler weather colliding with the steam bath that we've had this week. It's supposed to be clear and cooler by tomorrow morning."

"That'll be nice for Betty Langbroek," Johanna replied. "We'll be able to enjoy ourselves on her deck, without having to crowd inside. And if it cools off, everyone'll be in brighter spirits. It should be a pleasant evening. I hope you can make it, Chris."

"I'm looking forward to it. I'm trying to take advantage of every opportunity I have to meet the rest of the faculty. Those of us who are new have had plenty of chances to meet each other. But I still keep seeing plenty of faces that I don't recognize."

"How many kids do you think will be there this year?" Ed asked. "Like last year, they specifically mentioned that it wasn't an appropriate venue for children."

"I'm sure there will be a few, regardless of what the invitation said," Marty groaned. He turned to Chris, and said, "Unfortunately, some of your generation of faculty haven't figured out that they don't need to bring their children to everything."

Johanna agreed. "Why do some parents think they need to 'share' everythin' with their children? How can they ever imagine that a five-year-old would have a good time watchin' a bunch of faculty members standin' around a deck, carryin' on what to them must seem like terribly borin' conversations?"

"Besides that," Ed added, "Betty's house isn't really 'accommodating' for children. Hers have all grown up and moved away. And while she undoubtedly has a supply of toys stashed away somewhere for her grandchildren, she's certainly not going to drag those out at a reception for faculty members. More importantly, she has all those nice porcelain items that she and Arnold have picked up in their travels over the years. She shouldn't have to spend the evening worrying about those, and making sure somebody's kid doesn't knock one over."

"Keeping them safe from the faculty is worry enough," Marty laughed. "Chris, if you want to stay in the good graces of this group, you have to promise that if you marry and have children, you won't bring them to faculty events, except for the few that are specifically designed for all ages."

The conversation had obviously reached a transition point, so some of the group excused themselves and went back to their offices. Marty, Chris, and a few others continued to nurse their drinks, if only to enjoy the CUB's air conditioning a little longer. Eventually, Chris excused himself, too, and headed back to his office. "See you all tomorrow evening at the Langbroeks."

*　　　*　　　*　　　*　　　*

SARAH CHECKED HER APPOINTMENT CALENDAR AGAIN, and confirmed that she didn't have anything scheduled until 2:00. Throughout her career, her normal routine had been to swim at noon. But since she came to NNC, she'd only been to the pool once. Now that the semester was underway, she was determined to change that. She told her secretary to avoid scheduling any meetings between noon and 1:00, unless they were absolutely necessary. This week, she'd had two meetings with Hank which fit that category—at least from his perspective. She thought they were routine, and could have been scheduled any time. For that matter, they could have easily been combined into one meeting. *"He's trying to 'halter train me,' to 'house break me,'"* she told herself. She thought about Marty's advice, and sighed. *"Every day is one less day until he retires. I just hope I can survive that long."*

She hurried over to the athletic complex about 11:30, changed, and got into the pool. She was the only person there, except for the lifeguard. As she started her third lap, she was starting to loosen up. She could feel the tension leaving her shoulders. By forcing herself to think about the next stroke, the next kick, and the next turn at the end of the pool, she was finally able to start clearing her mind and relax. The exercise would be good for her body, too. She'd been too sedentary lately. She knew from sad experience that if she didn't get out from behind her desk regularly, she'd quickly pay the price in terms of muscle tone and weight. Hank had mentioned several times that he thought it was important for people to work out regularly. He didn't respect people who let their bodies "get flabby," as he'd described it. That's when she'd mentioned that she liked to swim every day at noon. The next morning, she learned that he'd scheduled two lunch meetings. That wasn't a coincidence—she was sure of that.

She made a turn, and pushed off from the end of the pool. She glided as far as she could, and then resumed her stroke. She sensed, more than heard, someone dive into the next lane; the splash was barely noticeable. *"Somebody knows what they're doing,"* she thought. That was confirmed by the swimmer's first few strokes: rhythmically steady, and powerful. Sarah briefly thought she would try to keep pace, but after swimming only a couple of strokes, she knew there was no point. Whoever was in the next lane was "out of her league." When the other swimmer came by in the other direction—before she'd gone three-quarters of a lap herself—she could see that it was a woman. A few laps later, she saw her more clearly when she made a turn. The short, blond hair looked familiar. There were still quite a few people on campus whom she didn't recognize. But she had no doubt that this was Annika van Rijn. That was confirmed soon after she had finished her swim and went into the locker room.

Sarah had just gotten out of the shower and was drying her hair when Annika came in from the pool. She was still breathing heavily after her swim, but she displayed the kind of exhaustion that comes from a workout when you're in good condition. Her muscle tone confirmed that. Sarah could tell that Annika swam regularly. And from what she'd witnessed in the pool, she was obviously good at it.

"It looks like you had a good workout," Sarah said.

Annika had been concentrating on something, and was taken by surprise when Sarah spoke to her. She almost jumped. *"She's wound a little tight,"* Sarah thought.

"I'm sorry," Annika said, blushing. "I wasn't paying attention, and didn't notice that anyone was in here yet. Most of the regulars from town don't come until about 1:00, when there's a community swim period here. I try to get my laps in and slip out of the locker room before most of them arrive. I didn't know you were a swimmer, Dean Christiansen."

"Please—it's Sarah. I suspect you and I will be working together a lot—especially in the coming year, with the presidential search. That will be much more pleasant if we can dispense with formalities."

"Thanks. I'd like that. Dean Rothman always seemed a bit uncomfortable when most people called him by his first name. But Hank likes to 'keep things informal,' as he says, so Paul had to go along with it. It's nice to have you suggest it. I'm sure it won't feel awkward like it did with him."

"It sounds like I do a lot of things different than Paul Rothman. I keep hearing stories about him, but you never know how accurate campus gossip might be. I'm curious to meet him."

"I'm sure you'll get the chance. He and Hank still keep in pretty close contact, since Hank mentored him in his quest for a college presidency. I suspect he'll be back on campus for some kind of function. Hank has Bill Logan—the athletic director—scurrying to get a football game scheduled with Zwingli College in the next year or so. If that happens, Paul will definitely be here, expecting everyone to welcome him back like a conquering hero. Now that Hank's announced his retirement, Paul will probably try to get his name into contention as his replacement. But if he were ever hired here, most of the faculty would probably quit *en masse*."

"I gather he wasn't very popular around here."

"That's an understatement! I don't think I've ever met anyone who was as universally disliked."

"But he and Hank got along?"

There was a long pause before Annika replied. Sarah thought the silence probably spoke volumes.

"As I mentioned, Hank was his 'mentor.' And as 'Hank's Dean,' Paul was a loyal and dutiful servant. If Hank wanted something done, Paul didn't hesitate to do it. If Hank told Paul to jump, the only question he'd ask would be, 'How high?'"

Sarah thought a change of subjects was in order. "To get back to your earlier comment, I like to swim, though my high school swimming coach might question whether or not I really qualify as a 'swimmer.' I was good enough to be on my school team, but that's not saying much, considering the size of my high school. I had no illusions about continuing competitive swimming at the college level. But when I was in college, I started swimming regularly on my own, and I've kept at it ever since. It helps me avoid putting on too much weight. What about you? From what I saw, you look like you've been swimming for a long time. And you were probably much better at it than anyone in my high school."

Annika blushed, and with a touch of embarrassment admitted, "Yes, I swam in college. I wasn't good enough to swim for a Division I school, but I made it to Division III nationals my junior and senior year. The last year, I won a third-place medal in individual freestyle. I also swam the anchor on our relay squad, which took second place. After that, I stopped swimming completely for a couple of years when I was in grad school. But it seemed like something was missing, so I started swimming again. I discovered that although I'd been 'burned out,' it wasn't from the swimming itself. Without the pressure of team training and competitions, I enjoyed it again. So I've been swimming regularly ever since. I try to get down here every day, unless there's something going on in the office that I can't miss."

"I'm hoping to do the same," Sarah replied. "I'd like to be here every day, and I've asked my secretary to keep this slot open whenever possible. But this week I already had two meetings with Hank, that he said could only be at noon."

"Did you mention to him that you wanted to reserve noon hours for yourself?" Annika asked.

"I guess I may have said something in passing. Why?"

"That explains a lot. He usually likes to keep his lunch hours open, too. Sometimes he's able to arrange lunches with potential donors, so he likes to have the flexibility to add those whenever they come up. He also goes to Rotary every week when he's in town. So I was surprised when he asked me to put a couple of meetings on his schedule this week. You didn't complain about having to meet with him then, did you?"

"No, and I didn't mention swimming at all, except for that one brief comment I made last week."

"Good. Don't bring it up again, and he'll forget about it. One of his unfortunate quirks is that he likes to be 'in control.' The more information he has, the easier it is for him to 'gain an advantage,' as he'd describe it. But he also gets nervous if he thinks someone's keeping something from him. The best way to function with him is on a 'need to know' basis. Don't let him get the impression that you're keeping anything from him. But at the same time, don't give him any information that might be 'revealing' about who you really are, especially not anything that he can use to get an advantage."

"Thanks. I'm coming to the conclusion that I can use all the advice I can get to deal with him effectively."

"The saving grace is that it's only for another year."

"That's what Marty told me, too."

"Marty? Marty Dykstra? You've been talking to Marty? That's definitely one bit of information I wouldn't let Hank know about."

"That's what Marty said, too. We had an interesting conversation over pizza last Friday evening."

"At Snuffy's, I bet! Quiet booth in the back corner, right?" Annika laughed.

"How'd you know?"

"He goes there regularly. And the booth in the back is his favorite. It's quiet, and it's out of the way. Most people in the restaurant don't even know you're there. You can hardly hear the rest of the clientele, and more importantly, they can't hear you. He used to go there almost every Friday night with his wife, Annette."

"They don't anymore?"

"Annette died a little over two years ago. She had heart bypass surgery about ten years earlier, and went in for what the doctor expected to be a 'minor tune-up.' Marty went home about 10:00 that evening, with the doctor's prognosis that she'd be going home in about 48 hours. Then the doctor called him about 3:00 the morning and told him that something had unexpectedly gone wrong, and that he should get back to the hospital right away. She died about half an hour after he got there."

"I was wondering if he were married. He didn't mention anything about family. But he doesn't seem like the type who'd be a life-long bachelor."

"You're right. He was very happily married. It's just in the last six months or so that he's started to get his spirit back. I think he probably would've retired right after his wife died if it hadn't been for Hank?"

"Why Hank?"

"Hank doesn't see any need to keep offering language classes on campus—especially upper division literature courses. He'd just as soon eliminate language instruction on campus all together. If it were up to him, he'd get every student one of those language programs they advertise on television, and reallocate the faculty positions to other departments. Marty's wife taught Dutch. And Marty is one of the many people who believe that NNC should preserve its Dutch heritage.

"Hank also told him that if he retired, the History Department would lose his position. For Hank, the College doesn't need another historian as much as it needs someone in business, computer science, or environmental studies. In some ways, I think Marty's feelings about Hank have been the spark that's kept him going since Annette died."

"Marty told me that you would be a good person for me to develop a working relationship with."

"Marty said that about me? I'm flattered. He has pretty high standards. But I didn't think he cared for anything in Hank's office, including me."

"Marty's obviously someone who can distinguish between Hank and his staff. And it's clear that he thinks highly of you—especially your loyalty to the college."

"That's not a surprise. What a lot of people forget about Marty is that he's not only a long-serving faculty member at NNC. He's also an alum. And he's dedicated to the college's long-term survival. He also has a low tolerance for stupidity. Unfortunately, I'm increasingly coming to share his opinions about some of the people I work with here. But please, don't say that to anyone else. If it ever got back to Hank, he'd make my life miserable. He comes close to doing that enough already."

"Marty cautioned me that if I were to start developing a good working relationship with you, I shouldn't let Hank know about it. I think the women's locker room is a good place to carry on our conversations."

"Thanks. I'll look forward to seeing you here again. And I'll see what I can do to make sure Hank doesn't schedule any 'important meetings' for you at this time of the day. I think we can agree: 'What happens in the locker room, stays in the locker room!'"

6
"Give and No"

Friday, August 30

THE WEATHER FORECAST had been very accurate. A thunderstorm rolled through town around 10:30 Thursday night. It only lasted a few hours, but it dropped about two inches of rain. Then cooler, dryer air moved in. By morning, the humidity had plummeted. Because it hadn't rained in several weeks, the ground was dry enough to absorb the rain almost immediately. When Chris got to campus, there were only a few small puddles and some broken branches scattered on the sidewalks to indicate that there had been a storm the night before.

On his way into Macalester, he ran into Marty, who immediately asked, "How'd you like your first Midwestern thunderstorm?"

"I have to admit, it was a little scary. Fortunately, I took Tom's advice; I stopped on the way home and picked up a weather alert radio. I don't think I've ever listened to a weather report as attentively as I did last night. I couldn't believe how precisely the storm was tracked."

"It's even more detailed when there's a 'severe weather' alert."

"I kept listening for that last night. But to my great relief, I never heard the word 'severe' mentioned. I couldn't believe how long that thunder rolled last night. I never experienced anything like that in the Northwest."

"Sometimes those storms will rumble all night. It's almost like one continuous roar of thunder. With a combination of a weather radio and the radar site, you can keep track of what's going on. They all have the potential of being serious, but if you keep yourself informed, you can reduce the tension a bit."

Marty was heading to class, so he excused himself. As he continued out of Macalester he said, "At least the storm broke the hot weather. It should be delightful at Langbroeks' this evening. I'll see you there!"

"I know it starts at 4, but I won't be able to get there until about 5. Will that be a problem?"

Marty laughed: "Not at all! About the only people who get there at 4 are some of the older emeriti and their spouses. They show up early for anything that includes food. Most people won't get there until 4:30, and some won't be there until 5:30 or 6. Don't worry about that at all! Just remember to wear your name tag—otherwise some of the emeriti will ask you for your name several times before it finally computes for them. See you there!"

*   *   *   *   *

SHORTLY AFTER 10:00, Hank hung up the phone. Shaking his head, he got up from his desk and walked into Annika's office. "That idiot Rothman may get himself fired if he's not careful. I can't believe how stupid he can be sometimes."

"What's President Rothman done that could possibly get him fired?" Annika asked.

"For starters, he's trying to shape the school into what he wants. That's all fine and good, but you can't do it in your first year or two at a school. I warned him: make sure you've filled your Board of Trustees with loyal supporters, who share your vision and are willing to back you up when the inevitable reaction appears. I told him that could take a few years—especially at a place like Zwingli. Hell, I tried to talk him out of going there in the first place. I warned him how conservative it is! But he wanted to be a college president so badly he could taste it."

"Disagreements about 'vision' shouldn't be enough to threaten his position there, should they? What kinds of

144

changes can he be proposing that upset people that much?" To herself, she thought, *"Just his personality alone could be enough to turn some people off. Unless he's developed a new one of those, I can't imagine he's winning too many friends there."*

"In his defense, I have to say that he hasn't really tried to implement any big changes yet. But just the suggestion of some things—like wine at faculty or alumni functions, reducing the number of chapel services each week, and the like—got everyone's guard up. But what's really gotten him in trouble is tied more to his 'administrative style.'"

"Really? In what way?" Again, she thought, *"And you're surprised by that? Of course, since he functions just like you do, it's easy to see why he would rub people the wrong way."*

"You know how finicky he can be."

Annika's first thought was, *"You mean, just like his mentor, Hank van Daam?"* But she controlled herself, and instead said, "I know some people here felt that he rubbed them the wrong way. But not to the extent that it would've jeopardized his position."

"Apparently he got a little carried away when he was trying to improve the sloppy work of one of the grounds crew. But instead of just sucking it up, and following directions from the president of the college, this guy went whining to the Human Resources Office! Apparently, the poor little thing's feelings were hurt. To make matters worse, rather than just telling him to be a man, and do what Rothman had told him to do, HR suggested that he file a formal complaint. Now Rothman has to go to some woo-woo 'anger management' course, and they've put him on probation. It'll take him years to recover from that damage. Now any chance he has of shaping that school the way he wants it to be won't happen for five or ten years, if he's lucky. He'll have trouble getting new trustees who'll support his agenda, because he's going to be viewed as 'poison' for quite a while."

"I heard he really wanted to be a college president," Annika said, "but Zwingli didn't seem like a place where he'd fit in. It's so conservative. I'm surprised he even considered going there, much less that he accepted the position."

"He was starting to get nervous that he'd be stuck here. His 'shelf life' was running out—another year or two, and he'd be older than most colleges would consider for a new president. And he knew it wouldn't be long before I retired. A new president will probably want his own dean to do his bidding."

"Or her."

"Sure, sure. 'Or her.'" Hank laughed. "The chances of our Board of Trustees selecting a woman president are pretty slim. But that won't be a factor now, anyway."

"What do you mean, it 'won't be a factor now?'"

"With a woman as dean, they'll never pick a woman president. 'Women's Lib' is all fine and good in the abstract, but a woman as president is the last thing this place needs. By picking Sarah, I pretty much eliminated that possibility," he said, with a smug grin on his face. Annika felt like she was ready to gag.

She could tell her face was beginning to redden, and she knew that if she didn't find an excuse to leave the office, she would probably say something she'd regret. She looked at her watch, and said, "I think the line should be gone at the Bean Bag by now. Are you ready for your morning latte? I'm going to run and get one for myself. Would you like one, too? Skinny, with a double shot, as usual, right?"

The quick change of subject caught Hank a little off guard, but the thought of a steaming latte got his mind off the subject of Rothman and female presidents. He didn't notice how flushed Annika looked as she bolted for the door. She stepped into the ladies' room down the hall, and took a deep breath. "I swear, one of these days I'm going to kill that son of a bitch!" she said under her breath—but, unfortunately, not quietly enough that no one else could hear her. She heard a toilet flush, a stall opened, and Sarah Christiansen walked over to the sink.

"What's Hank done this time?" she asked.

Annika's face got even redder, this time from embarrassment. She wondered if she should tell Sarah what Hank had just told her, and quickly decided that this wasn't the time. She might eventually, but with luck, that could wait until after Hank had retired. "Oh, he just reminded me what a sexist pig he can be sometimes. The things that come out of his mouth never cease to amaze me. Sometimes I wonder how he ever made it to become a college president. I'm surprised somebody didn't punch his lights out a long time ago."

"From what I've seen in the short time I've been here, I think you'd probably have to get in line to do it. We have to keep reminding ourselves: we just have to make it through this year."

"I know. I keep telling myself that. But on days like this, it doesn't sound so easy. I'm afraid that as a 'lame duck' president, he's not going to feel any of the constraints that used to moderate his behavior."

"Just try to keep your head down and stay out of his way. I think we'll both be doing a lot of that in the coming months. I've already decided that on January 1, the daily calendar on my computer is going to have a 'countdown' on it. When I turn on my computer every morning, I'll know exactly how many more days I have to put up with him."

"That sounds like a good idea," Annika said. "Thanks for letting me 'vent.' If we both make it through the day, we can toast each other at Langbroeks' reception this evening. You'll be there, I hope!"

"I'm looking forward to it. Hank was grumbling to me about how he was going to have to put in an appearance, which made it sound like he won't be there too long. If I time it right, we'll only cross paths briefly. He'll know I 'put in an appearance,' too, and I can enjoy the gathering even more."

Annika started toward the door. "I told Hank I was going to get his morning latte, so I'd better get moving or he'll wonder what happened to me."

"Don't put anything in it," Sarah laughed. "If Hank suddenly drops over dead after drinking his morning latte, they'll come looking for you first."

"I realize that. But I'd only be the first in a long list of possible suspects."

*   *   *   *   *

THE AFTERNOON WAS COOL, with a faint hint of fall in the air. Since it wasn't far from his apartment to the Langbroeks' house, Chris decided to enjoy the weather and walk. He arrived just as Marty was getting out of his car. "Great timing," Marty laughed. "I can introduce you to a few people you may not have met before. As I was driving up, I saw Bill Kaufman go in the front door. He couldn't make it to Dirk's party, and he doesn't join us for coffee very often. But I know he'd love to meet you."

"I was afraid of being late, but it looks like everything worked out fine. I've been trying to schedule a dentist appointment, and as a new patient, I couldn't get anything scheduled locally for several months. I don't have any problems that I know of, but I was long overdue for a checkup and cleaning. Then they called me yesterday, and said they had a cancellation for this afternoon—could I come in then? I didn't think I should turn that down, but I wasn't sure how long I'd be. It went more quickly than I'd anticipated—I got out early enough that I could even walk over here."

"You're here in plenty of time. It looks like most people are just starting to arrive.

As they walked up the front steps, Betty Langbroek opened the door and welcomed them in. After Marty introduced her to Chris, he took Betty's hand. "We were afraid that when you retired from the Board of Trustees, we'd miss the opportunity to share your generous hospitality. It's extremely gracious of you to have us all here again."

Betty blushed, and turned to Chris. "As you can tell, Marty sometimes likes to lay it on a little thick."

"No, I'm serious, Betty. I've always been amazed at the way you're able to put up with so many of us taking over your home like this. There aren't many people who would be so generous." He also thought to himself, *"We'd definitely never all get invited to the President's home, even though it was designed for entertaining large groups. Hank could never stand being around us this long."*

"You know it's our pleasure, Marty. Despite all the time we spend on campus, the Trustees don't get much time to interact with faculty. This is a notable exception."

"I'm glad you enjoy it. I can't tell you how much we appreciate being here every year," Marty said.

"Arnold's out on the back deck overseeing the beverages. Help yourself to the food. There are tables in the kitchen as well as the dining room. Karen de Vries is in charge of the food this evening, so I'm sure you won't be disappointed in what you find there. Then make your way out to the deck. Arnold will make sure you get something to drink. Enjoy yourselves." She took Chris's hand and said, "Thank you for coming, Chris. It's a pleasure to meet you. I hope you enjoy yourself here, as well as in your new career at NNC. I hope it's a long and productive one."

As they made their way to the kitchen, Marty told Chris, "That's one of the things Hank doesn't like about this evening. It's not an accident that Trustees don't interact with faculty very much. When they have meetings on campus, Hank controls their schedule VERY tightly. There might be a brief report from a faculty member or two. But there's never any time for idle chit-chat. On the rare occasion when they meet actual students, they've all been screened well in advance. They never meet a student who might disagree with something Hank wants. But especially with the faculty, he makes sure no one has time to get the ear of a Trustee and possibly voice some concerns or, worse yet, complaints. There are faculty representatives at the Trustees' meetings, but even they don't have much opportunity to meet with any Trustees 'one on one.'"

Although there were lines for the food, they moved quickly. Just as they got to the table, Karen brought a fresh tray of hors d'oeuvres. When she saw Chris and Marty, she stopped briefly before returning to fetch more food. "It's great to see you again, Chris. I'm sorry I can't spend time chatting this evening, but I'm 'on duty' now. When things slow down a little, though, I'd love to find out how your first week has gone. In case you didn't see them, there are a couple trays of your favorite shrimp hors d'oeuvres on the far side of the table. Enjoy yourselves— I'll talk to you later."

They quickly loaded their plates, and headed for the back deck. Arnold spotted them as they came out the door, and immediately handed Marty a bottle of Heineken. "I assume you're going with your usual—or would you prefer wine?"

Marty laughed, "Are my habits that obvious, Arnold? Sure, I'll be happy with this." He introduced Chris to Arnold, who quickly asked for Chris's drink preferences, and brought him a glass of red wine.

They found a spot where they could rest their drinks on a railing, and turned their attention to their food. Before Chris had polished off his first shrimp, they had company.

"Hi, Marty. Is this your new historian?"

"Right you are, Walt. Chris, meet Walt Braaten. He's a member of the Business Department—Marketing's his specialty. Walt, Chris is our new modern European historian."

"What are you teaching this semester, Chris."

"I've got a light load this semester, only teaching two courses: 'Nineteenth Century Europe,' and like everyone else in the History Department, a section of '*Die Quellen*.'"

"Oh, I'm sure Marty's already told you all kinds of horror stories about '*Die Quellen*,' so you probably hate it before you've even been in the course for a semester.'"

Marty set down his plate and turned to Walt. His demeanor had clearly changed. He was no longer smiling, and his jaw was taut. The veins on his neck were beginning to stand out.

"Walt, I want you to listen to me."

"What's the matter, Marty?"

"Walt, I want you to listen VERY CAREFULLY. Paul Rothman once made the mistake of saying something like you just did."

"What did I say?"

"That I bad-mouth *Die Quellen*, and turn people against it."

"Well you do. I've heard you complain about the course for years."

"That much is true, Walt. But I leave it up to anyone who teaches in that damned course to form their own opinions. I told Rothman that if I EVER heard that he had suggested to ANYONE that I tried to influence how my junior colleagues think about *Die Quellen*, he'd better seek legal counsel, because I sure as hell would. The same goes for you, Walt. I'll be the first to admit that I bitch about that course. But don't EVER suggest that I try to brainwash my colleagues against it."

"I'm sorry, Marty. But as you just admitted, you bitch about the course all the time."

"Yes, and I continue to teach in it, year after year, because the administration makes me. Unlike you, I don't have a choice. You'll notice that the people I bitch to are the ones who try to tell me what a wonderful course it is, without ever having taught in it themselves. No offense, Walt, but that includes you."

"But it's such a great course. I still don't understand why you don't appreciate it."

"How in the Hell do you know that, Walt? Just because the English Department tells you so?"

"Did I hear my department's name being taken in vain?" Bill Kaufman laughed, as he stepped between Marty and Walt. Walt took the opportunity to head inside for more food, and to get somewhere out of Marty's line of sight.

"Sorry, it was just that damned Braaten again. Telling me how much I should enjoy the course he's never taught, and never will teach."

"I suggest we change the subject," Bill said. "Is this your new department member?"

"Indeed it is. Chris van Zant, please meet Bill Kaufman. He holds the endowed Chair of Creative Writing in the English Department."

"Before you ask, Chris: yes, he said English Department! Yet, he still talks to me! Probably even more surprising, we're good friends—at least I hope we are."

"Yes, we definitely are," Marty replied. He was clearly getting back into a better mood.

"I know, I don't look like an English prof. For starters, I'm not wearing black. And before long, you'll probably hear Marty and me talk about sports. That's something most of my department would never do."

"Don't sell them short, Bill," Marty chuckled. "They've had some pretty lively activities lately."

"Sure they have! The closest thing to sports that some of my colleagues have ever engaged in, not counting required PE classes when they were undergraduates, is their annual 'Poetry Slam.'"

"They did that one better last year, remember?"

"Of course—the 'Shakespeare Smackdown.' Sure, they're a lively bunch."

"I think you'll enjoy talking to Chris. I've been looking forward to the opportunity to introduce you to him."

"Why's that?" Bill asked.

"That's up to you to find out. I can't do everything for you," Marty laughed. Then he turned to Chris, who was following the conversation with rather dazed look on his face. "It's surprising, considering the attitudes of some of his departmental colleagues, but Bill's probably the best athlete on the faculty."

"That's not saying much, considering the athletic interests of most of our colleagues."

"But you're the only one who not only played four years of college ball, but was also a pro."

"Really?" Chris asked. "What sport?"

"Baseball," Bill replied. "I was a pitcher. I played small college ball, but I was at least good enough to catch the eye of one scout. They gave me a small signing bonus, and I played one year in the minors—'single A' baseball. After a summer of bouncing around in old busses, playing in small town ballparks, and eating lots of cheap fast food, I had to make a decision: continue playing minor league ball, with the dream of sometime making it to the majors, or go on with my academic career. I came to the conclusion that I didn't have a decent slider—at least not one that was consistently good. That was also the view of my pitching coach and a couple of scouts. So I used that signing bonus to pay most of my grad school expenses. And here I am today. I don't have any regrets—I had a chance to play pro ball, and I had sense enough not to waste too much time on a dream that probably wouldn't come true."

"Well, baseball's loss was our gain," Marty laughed. "But it wasn't a total loss to baseball. Bill coaches an American Legion team here in town. They've won the district championship three out of the last four years."

Bill turned to Chris. "How about you, Chris? Do you play any sports."

Bill noticed a sly grin beginning to form on Marty's face, but he wasn't sure of its cause.

"Basketball. I used to play some basketball," he said shyly.

"I think you should define 'some,'" Marty chuckled.

"Out with it—how much did you play?" Bill was clearly interested now.

"I haven't played much since I started grad school. But I played on my high school team, and was All-State the year we won the state championship."

"And . . ." Marty said.

"And I played in college. Just Division III, though."

"Division III is a lot more than almost anyone else around here. Were you a starter?"

"For three years. My senior year, we made it to the NCAA Division III tournament, but got knocked out in the second round."

"He was also All-Conference, and Conference All-Academic for three years," Marty added. "The local paper called him 'that spunky little guard.' Apparently, he doesn't like to sing his own praises. But I knew you'd be interested, Bill."

"I sure am. There are a bunch of us who play basketball three days a week—but you've got to be an early riser. We start at 6:30, in order to get showered and make it to our classes on time. Would you like to join us? We'd love to have another player, especially someone who knows what they're doing. We also have an annual charity game with faculty from Chartwell. They have a couple 'ringers' on their team, so it will be nice to offer them some competition for a change."

"That sounds like fun. I don't have class until 9, but I'm an early riser. If you don't mind, I'd like to start next week."

"Why didn't you tell me about him sooner, Marty. It's not like you to hold out on me."

"I thought you should hear it straight from the horse's mouth."

"You know so much about his basketball career—did you bother to check his academic credentials, too?"

"It's amazing the things that you can find with just a quick internet search. After we hired him, I thought it might be easier to help him adjust to life in New Leiden if I knew a little more about him than I learned in his interview. There are only so many things you can cover in the short time a candidate's on campus. When I googled his name and his undergraduate college, I found a lot about his basketball career. I knew a little about that already: we talked briefly about his sports interests when he was on campus. But he seems to prefer to 'hide his light under a bushel.'"

Chris replied, "When I was here last spring, President van Daam asked me if I played sports. When I told him I played basketball, he said that there were faculty who played regularly, and that he sometimes joined them."

"Oh, Christ!" Bill snorted. "Hank thinks he's an athlete. He played with us a few times, but fortunately 'his schedule wouldn't permit it' any more. I always hoped that meant he realized that he wasn't the kind of player we liked having in our games. Don't get me wrong—I'm not saying he had to be a great player to be able to join us. Some of our group can't dribble and chew gum at the same time. It's just that he didn't know what he was doing, but he still always wanted the ball. To him, the verb 'to pass' only goes one direction—to him. Do you know how to work a 'give and go' play, Chris?"

"Sure, who doesn't? It's one of the first drills you run in grade school. Pass to the post, and break for the basket. Then the post passes it back to you for a layup."

"Well, apparently Hank never learned that play. We'd pass him the ball, break for the basket, and he'd stand there trying to decide where he should pass the ball. Then he'd just settle on taking a shot—and usually miss. So with Hank, it wasn't a 'give and go' play—it was 'give and no.'"

Marty added, "The term 'ball hog' comes to mind. It wouldn't have been so bad if he could shoot, but the combination of selfish play and poor execution didn't make for an enjoyable game. But he considers himself quite an athlete. So he's not willing to admit that he's not great in every sport he plays. He's apparently a pretty good golfer. At least as long as he can hold his temper. But if things don't go well for him, he starts getting mad. Then 'the wheels fall off' his game pretty quickly. At least that's what I've heard from some of my friends who've played with him at the Country Club. Several of them have managed to use that to their advantage when they're playing against him."

"What's his sports background?" Chris asked.

"Football," Bill replied. "When he waxes eloquent about his college football days, you'd think he's describing the star quarterback of a national championship team. But he was a long-snapper."

"Back-up long-snapper, at that," Marty added.

"Right, back-up long-snapper. Still, he and the starter both got a lot of playing time, because their team wasn't very good. They punted a lot. Basically, his experience on the gridiron was to look between his legs at the kicker, snap the ball, and have his face mask smashed into the turf by a defensive lineman. Unfortunately, his college experience colors his view of NNC's team. His team had a record about like what we've had the last few years. But after his last season, the head coach retired, and a few years later, they won the national championship. By the time the new coach retired, he'd won four championships. Hank's spent his adult life thinking that if they'd fired his coach, Hank could've played for the other guy, and been a member of a national championship team. Maybe that could have happened. Or maybe the new coach recruited some better players, whose talents fit his coaching scheme. You'd never convince Hank of that, though. That's why Harry Westbrook is sitting on a hot seat now. If he doesn't win a few more games this season, Hank's going to fire him. He's made it pretty clear that he doesn't think Harry has the team 'going in the right direction.'"

Marty snorted, "No, he's 'not doing the right things.' Like having a Rhodes Scholar and a couple of Fulbrights in the last 5 years. Not to mention the number of his players who have gone on to law school or med school after graduating. Or the fact that all of his players graduate, and the team g.p.a. is the highest in the conference. But none of those things are as important to Hank as the won-loss record. Hank often says, 'Sports build character.' But he's wrong. As John Wooden famously said, 'Sports do not build character. They reveal it.' And that's definitely the case with Hank."

Bill nodded. "If the 'Flying Dutch' don't start winning, we'll have a new football coach before Christmas."

Marty turned to Chris. "In case you're wondering, we used to be the 'Flying Dutchmen,' but with Title IX and the growth of women's sports, the name needed to be changed. Some people suggested that we just use the school color, and call ourselves 'the Orange,' but others argued that they didn't want the mascot to be a fruit. There were too many possible interpretations of that for some people."

"That led to all kinds of absurd suggestions," Bill laughed. "For a long time, Hank wanted to change the name of the college, translating the Dutch to English. He proposed 'New Holland,' until it was pointed out that Holland is a province, and founders of the school were referring to the whole country. But one wag suggested that Hank had an ulterior motive with that name. He hates the school colors—can't stand orange. If he changed the name to 'New Holland,' he could also change the colors to blue and yellow, and then maybe he could get some kind of subsidy from the farm machinery company by that name. Of course, then we'd also have to change our nickname from 'Flying Dutchmen' to 'The Flying Tractors,' or something along that line. Hank wasn't amused."

"'Flying Dutchwomen' doesn't have the same ring to it that 'Flying Dutchmen' did," Marty added. "And 'Flying Dutchmen and –women' would be even worse. Don't laugh, Chris, I'm not making this up. Someone actually suggested that combination. Finally a voice of reason said, 'Why don't we just call ourselves 'The Flying Dutch.' And here we are."

"I think that if Hank believed he could really get some money from the New Holland Company, our teams would be sporting blue and yellow uniforms, and that would be the name of the college. We're just lucky Hank didn't turn this place into a 'for profit' school."

"Was that a real possibility?" Chris asked.

"I don't know if the Board of Trustees would've really gone through with it," Bill replied. "But Hank had some preliminary discussions with one of the big 'for profits.' He apparently thought they'd keep him on as President, but with a substantial bump in salary. Then he found out that they'd probably have come in and cleaned house in the administration, bringing in their own 'hired guns' for all of the upper-level positions, starting with the President—or CEO, in business parlance. When he learned that, Hank dropped the idea like a hot potato."

"In case you can't tell, Chris, Bill's an invaluable source of gossip and 'insider' news. I don't know who all of his sources are, but I have to admit, he's usually very accurate."

"I'm happy that my knowledge keeps you entertained, Marty. But I do have to admit, Hank's retirement announcement caught me off guard. That was a complete surprise. I thought he'd stay for at least another year, in order to milk the school for another year's salary."

"He's obviously got something cushy lined up for next year," Marty said. "I have no doubts about that."

"Speak of the Devil . . ." Bill laughed. "Hank and Hannah just arrived. He'll make his token appearance, and then get out of here before someone decides to ask a question about something he doesn't really want to talk about. Chris, I suggest that you separate yourself from us before he comes out here. He'll think we're leading you down the path to corruption. No sense you getting off on the wrong foot with him."

Marty added, "Remember what I told you about your name. I see that your college nametag has your full name. When he sees that, he'll be sure to call you 'Chris.'"

Bill added, "But if you talk to Hannah, start out by calling her 'Mrs. van Daam.' Hank will insist that you call them by their first names, but you'll win points with her if you don't do that on your own."

"She prefers formality, I take it," Chris replied.

"That's an understatement," Bill laughed. "If you were a staff member doing any repairs at their house, she'd insist that you refer to her only as 'Madame President.'"

While Marty and Bill went to refresh their drinks, Chris got a fresh plate of hors d'oeuvres. When he returned to the deck, Hank was gesturing to illustrate something he was telling Hannah. Chris unwittingly walked into Hank's "line of fire." Hank knocked the plate out of Chris's hand, but he was able to catch it with his other hand without spilling anything.

"Good save," Hank laughed. Chris saw that Hank was reading his nametag carefully. "It's good to see you again . . . Chris. Welcome to NNC! I hope you've enjoyed your first week of classes. I always love the beginning of the school year. It always offers the promise of great things to come. Have you met my wife, Chris?"

"No, I haven't had the pleasure," Chris said. Following Bill's advice, he extended his hand, and said, "It's a pleasure to meet you, Mrs. van Daam."

"Oh, please!" Hank interjected. "We're not big on formality around here. You can call her Hannah. And of course, just call me Hank!"

Chris noticed that Hannah stiffened slightly, but she smiled and said, "Yes, please. Call me Hannah. It's a pleasure to meet you, too, Chris."

They were soon joined by another couple, who each hugged Hank and Hannah. The man was wearing an expensive, well-tailored suit. His dark tan was accentuated by sparkling white teeth. He was tall, and rather thin. He didn't look particularly muscular, but he seemed very fit, like he spent a lot of time on a tennis court or golf course—or both. She was strikingly tall, with blond hair that hung just below her shoulders. It shimmered with every move of her head. She seemed well aware of that, as she frequently turned one direction or another, giving her

159

hair a slight shake every time she did. She also had a brilliant white smile, and her suntan matched his. She was wearing a red silk dress that highlighted every curve of her body. It wasn't tight, but it clung to the key points of her figure. Chris realized that he was staring at her, and quickly looked away. When he did, he saw that Hank's eyes were glued to her. Unlike Chris, though, Hank made no effort to divert his eyes. He was clearly enjoying the view.

When it became apparent that Hank wasn't going to say anything, Hannah spoke up. She stole a quick glance at Chris's nametag, and said, "Christiaan, have you had a chance to meet the Graandsmas? Gene and Demi, this is Christiaan van Zant, one of our new faculty members. He's just joined the History Department."

Before she could continue, Hank interrupted. "It's Chris. I think he prefers Chris to Christiaan. Don't you?"

Chris nodded meekly, and Hannah continued the introductions: "Gene is chair of the Board of Trustees. And this is his lovely wife, Demi. We don't often have the pleasure of both of them joining us for campus events. They own a chain of exercise studios in Southern Minnesota, and that keeps her pretty busy."

Gene laughed, "Busy running the studios, as well as working out in them—that's Demi. She's the financial brains of the family, so she's usually tied up keeping the books. Fortunately, that gives me time to devote to some other interests, like the Board of Trustees. Now that Hank's announced his retirement, we're going to be pretty busy this year. In addition to finding his replacement, I'm sure he'll have a busy schedule meeting with alumni groups around the country. They're going to want to give him a proper send-off."

Gene gave Chris a quick handshake, and then directed his attention to Hank. Demi, however, took his hand firmly, and drew him away from the others. "I've always been interested in history," she said. "What's your specialty?" She still had not released his hand.

"Modern Europe," he replied.

"That's my favorite! I try to get to Europe at least once a year, and I'm always fascinated by all the history around me. I just wish I knew more about what I'm seeing. It would be nice to see it with someone who knew more about it. Do you travel to Europe often? If so, maybe you could be my guide to some of your favorite sites."

Since she still hadn't let go of his hand, Chris wasn't sure how to answer. He noticed that Hank still had his eyes on Demi, but he was now looking at Chris suspiciously. Chris was starting to feel uncomfortable.

Fortunately, they were interrupted by the sudden arrival of Karen de Vries. Hank assumed she was bringing fresh hors d'oeuvres, and was disappointed to see that she was carrying an empty platter.

She saw the look on Hank's face, and said, "Don't worry, Hank—I'll be right back with a fresh plate of goodies for you. I'm sorry to interrupt your conversation, but Chris, you have a phone call."

"Me? Who even knows I'm here? Are you sure it's for me?"

"Absolutely. Betty asked me to answer the phone, since she was greeting someone at the door. There's a phone down the hallway to the left as you go into the house. It will be quieter for you to take it there."

Chris freed his hand from Demi's grip, and excused himself. "I'm sorry I have to run. I have no idea who could be calling me." He looked at both Demi and Gene and said, "It was a pleasure to meet both of you."

Gene nodded, and returned to his conversation with Hank. Demi smiled broadly, and said, "It's been a pleasure, indeed. I hope we can meet again soon."

Chris found the phone, and picked it up. "Chris van Zant speaking. Can I help you?"

"Hi, Chris. This is Bill . . . Kaufman, from English. Marty suggested I come to your rescue. Stay on the line for a few minutes, then go into the bathroom. When you're done there, get yourself a fresh plate of food, and come back out to where we were on the deck. Just don't go anywhere near Hank or the Graandsmas. Hopefully they'll be leaving soon, anyway. We'll explain when you get back out here."

As Chris was adding one last hors d'oeuvre to his plate, he noticed that the van Daams and Graandsmas were at the front door, saying goodbye to Arnold and Betty. Demi's eyes scanned the room, and when she saw Chris, she smiled, and gave him a little wave.

Chris shifted his plate and waved back, and then quickly went back to the deck. Marty and Bill were where he had left them, but they had both obviously left long enough to refill their plates and freshen their drinks.

"What was that all about?" Chris asked. "Was it my imagination, or was Mrs. Graandsma hitting on me?"

"Not your imagination at all," Marty said. "That's why I sent 'Bill's Rescue Service' into action. If your conversation hadn't been interrupted by that phone call, Demi would've been sizing you up to be the next notch on her belt. And if Hank had gotten wind of it, he'd have made your life here very difficult."

"Hank? What about Mr. Graandsma?"

"Gene's apparently pretty tolerant of Demi's 'wanderings,'" Bill replied. "The money in their family comes from her side. Her Dad started a chain of high-end kitchenware stores. You see them in just about any big shopping mall in the country. He sold out to a bigger chain, and when he died, she inherited millions. They started their first exercise studio as a tax write-off, but it turned out to be a big success, and they expanded it into a small chain in Southern Minnesota. Managing that keeps her pretty busy. But that's just the tip of the iceberg in terms of their family wealth. She keeps Gene living 'in the style to which he's become accustomed,' so he doesn't complain about anything she does."

"You aren't the first new faculty member she's tried to 'cut from the herd,'" Marty added. "But she's apparently very easily bored, so her little flings never last very long.

The problem is, if Hank finds out about them, he does everything he can to get them out of here. Remember, there's a vague clause in the Faculty Manual about 'moral turpitude' being grounds for dismissal. Hank starts making hints about that, and Demi's latest conquest starts looking for a job somewhere else."

"Does he have something going on with her himself?"

"Ha!" Marty snorted. "He wishes as much! No, she goes for younger faculty. Hank's got more gray around the temples than she looks for. He's a bit 'long of tooth' for her. But that doesn't keep him from hoping. Did you notice how he was looking at her? She's lucky he didn't drool on her. He obviously noticed that she was giving you a bit of attention, so we decided to call the cavalry in to the rescue. Bill saw that Karen was near a phone, and called her. When he told her what was going on, she immediately flew into action. Be sure to thank her the next time you see her."

"I will! And thank you, too! That isn't the way I planned to start—and possibly end—my career here."

As if on cue, Karen walked up to them with a fresh platter of food. "Please help yourself to some of these. The party's starting to thin out a bit, and as soon as this platter's empty, I'm going to leave the rest of the serving to my crew. Then I'll get a glass of wine and enjoy the party myself."

"Thanks for helping to 'rescue' me," Chris said. "The conversation with Demi seemed a little strange. It felt like she was hitting on me, but I thought it was probably just my imagination."

"Unfortunately, it wasn't. But at least it happened here, where someone could help you out. I'm glad to have been of service. I'll be back in a few minutes—you're not leaving right away, are you?"

Marty, Bill, and Chris all promised to stick around for a while longer. After Karen returned, they chatted for a while, and then they were joined by Dirk. Karen told him about Chris's brief encounter with Demi.

"Probably not what you expected in your first week at NNC, was it?" Dirk said.

"No, not at all. There have been quite a few things I haven't expected, but I'd probably put this at the top of the list. Is this something I'm going to have to worry about all the time?"

Dirk replied, "No, Demi's rarely on campus. She usually doesn't accompany Gene when he comes to Trustees meetings. Besides, she doesn't keep anyone in her sights for very long. The next time you see her, she'll probably be zeroing in on someone else."

"Is that the voice of experience speaking?" Karen asked, trying unsuccessfully to keep a straight face.

"Hardly!" Dirk said defensively. "She doesn't have the same refined tastes that you do. I'd never show up on her radar."

"I think we should just consider this topic closed," Marty chuckled. "I should probably get started for home. I'm hosting the History Department picnic tomorrow, and I'd better make sure everything's ready for that. I'll see you there tomorrow, Chris!"

"Only if you promise I won't have any experiences like I had today!"

Bill laughed, "I think it's a pretty safe bet that you won't have anything like that happen at a History Department picnic. While you may end up having some esoteric conversations with a few eccentric colleagues, that can probably be said about every department on campus. I think you'll be safe."

When Marty left, Chris also excused himself, and walked home. When he was about halfway there, he heard the low hum of powerful motor coming up the street behind him. He turned to watch a bright red Mercedes convertible make a left turn at the intersection he'd just passed. The woman in the passenger seat turned to look at him; he immediately recognized Demi. She smiled and gave him a little wave. Chris waved back, but quickly turned and hurried the last few blocks to his apartment.

He didn't bother turning on the lights, but instead, just sat in his easy chair and thought about his first week on campus. He shook his head. *"That was one of the strangest evenings I've ever had. Is it too much to hope that the Department picnic will be a little less bizarre?"*

7
A Dish to Pass

Saturday, August 31

FRIDAY'S WEATHER CONTINUED through the weekend. The humidity started to climb a little. But with a slight breeze and temperatures in the mid-70s, it was still comfortable. Chris took Marty's advice, and assigned this as his "Sabbath" of the week. The picnic was in the afternoon, and he'd need some time to prepare what he was taking. So he decided to wait until Sunday afternoon to go over his lectures for the coming week. The first set of student papers was due in *die Quellen* on Monday. The rest of the week would have to be spent grading them, with no time to spend on his history lectures. Those had to be taken care of before Monday, so he couldn't take off the whole weekend. But Marty's advice made sense to him. He wouldn't do any class-related work until Sunday afternoon.

He had planned ahead. Earlier in the week, he'd put his name on a few time slots on the sign-up sheet in his apartment building's laundry room. He spent Saturday morning taking care of his dirty clothes. He was done by noon, so he fixed himself a sandwich, and settled in to watch some college football. By mid-afternoon, he was ready to start fixing what he'd be taking to the History Department picnic. He'd picked up the necessary ingredients earlier in the week, and placed an order to have fresh chicken waiting for him at the meat counter at Dick's Market that morning. Since he was still getting to know what the local stores kept in stock, he didn't want to take any chances. As it was, he had to go to two stores before he found his essential ingredients at Dick's.

He timed his cooking just right, and everything was loaded into his car by about 4:20. If he didn't have anything to carry, he'd have taken advantage of the nice weather and walked to Marty's. But with his casserole dish and a bottle of wine, walking that far would have been difficult. So like everyone else in the department, he drove. Most of them were just arriving when he pulled up in front of Marty's house.

From that point on, the rest of the afternoon and evening seemed like a whirlwind to him. He knew all of his colleagues, but not well. He'd met them all when he'd been on campus to interview for his job. He'd seen them in passing in the hall, or around campus. And he was in a department meeting with most of them the previous week. But he'd never had a chance to talk to any of them at any length, and definitely not about anything personal. With all of their spouses at the party, as well as most of their children, he had trouble remembering who was who. The addition of a couple of emeritus faculty members made him feel like he needed a scorecard to keep track of everyone.

When Chris started up the sidewalk, Marty was holding the front door open, helping someone who was trying to manage her contribution to the picnic while also herding three children. Chris estimated that they ranged in age from about 5 to 9. Marty took a basket of food from her, and pointed the children toward the back yard. When he saw Chris, he broke into a broad smile. "I'm glad you could make it, Chris. Do you need any help with anything? As soon as I get Anna straightened away here, I can give you a hand."

"No, I'm fine, if someone can just get the door for me."

The man following the woman and her children set down a bag. "Here—let me get it for you. It's more important to get food and wine inside than this bag of toys. I told Anna that Marty would have plenty of things to keep the kids busy, but she insisted that we bring some of their favorites along, 'just in case.' I'm willing to bet that Marty will keep them so entertained that these things won't even come out of the bag. You must be the new modern European historian—Chris, isn't it? I'm Tony di Marco, Anna's husband. She's already been telling me good things about you."

Chris blushed. "I'm not sure how she'd come up with anything good to say about me already. I haven't had a chance to do anything yet."

"Probably not," Tony laughed. "But you've apparently already convinced her that while you may have his job, you're definitely not 'the new Tim Johansson.' That's a relief for everyone. So you're off to a good start already."

After Chris got through the door, Tony picked up the bag of toys and led Chris to the kitchen. Marty and Anna had just unloaded her bag of food, and Marty pointed to an open counter. "You can just put your dish there, unless it's something you have to keep warm. In that case, you can put it in the oven. I've already turned it on low, but if you need it hotter, set it as you see fit. No one else has put anything in there yet. Yours is the first bottle of wine to make it to the kitchen, too. Would you like me to do the honors with that? I've got a cork screw around here somewhere," he said as he started rummaging through a drawer. "As I mentioned, I've got a case of Heineken, as well as a couple varieties of my home brew. What would you like?"

"I'll probably have wine, eventually. But your home brew sounds intriguing. I'd love to start out with a taste of that. Have you been brewing long?"

"When I was in grad school, a friend and I used to brew, following the example of one of our professors. But while it was drinkable, it was also really amateur stuff. With the increasing popularity of microbrewies in the last decade or two, the range of ingredients available to home brewers has expanded, too. That's improved the quality of my brew. I'm still definitely an amateur, but I can also proudly say that I've tried some commercial stuff that doesn't hold a candle to mine. But if you're looking for something really 'hoppy,' you won't find it here. No 'alphabet beers'—IPAs or ESBs—in my brew house! I long ago came to the conclusion that a lot of hops can cover a multitude of sins. If you're not a very good brewer, you can simply add more hops, and no one will know. Obviously, that's my prejudices showing. I spent too much time in the Netherlands and Germany. I used to say that I was skeptical of anything brewed west of the Rhine. Then my first trip to Ireland changed that. Now I say that I'm skeptical of anything brewed between the Rhine and the Irish Sea."

While Marty was pouring Chris a glass of his home brew, a few more people filed into the kitchen. They set their salads, appetizers, and desserts on different sections of the counter. Marty helped where he could, and then directed people outside: "Grab something to drink, and make yourselves comfortable out on the deck. There's a bottle of wine here that Chris brought. It looks like he stayed true to his roots—it's from Washington. What few wines I've had from there have all been great! I've also just opened a bottle of home brew. The Heineken is in the blue cooler on the deck. The red cooler's full of pop and water. I tried to get a variety of regular, diet, and caffeine-free pop. Hopefully there's something for everyone's tastes. Please help yourselves."

When Chris got to the deck, Tony was pouring a can of root beer into three plastic glasses, which he then gave to his children. "Chris, I'd like you to meet our children, Maria, Caroline, and Anthony—known to most people as 'Tony, Jr.' Kids, this is Mr. van Zant. Please say hello."

All three of the children stepped forward, shook Chris's hand, and politely said, "Pleased to meet you, Mr. van Zant."

"Now, go see what Marty's got for you to play with. And please don't break anything!"

As they ran off in the direction of a swing in the back corner of the yard, Tony added, "I'm not sure if I was referring to Marty's stuff, or their own limbs. We've managed to avoid any broken arms for over a year now. I hope we can keep that streak going!"

"They're lovely children, Tony. And I'm impressed with their manners! I wish a couple of my nieces and nephews could come and take lessons from them."

"They are well behaved, I admit. In case you're wondering, we tend to err on the side of formality when introducing them to adults. Marty's kind of like a third grandfather to them—and the one who lives the closest. After they get to know you, feel free to ask them to call you by your first name if you'd like. But for now, they probably wouldn't be comfortable with that. They're a bit lively at times, but fortunately, they never seem to get out of control. I keep holding my breath that they won't figure out that they've got us outnumbered. When that happens, we'll be in 'deep kimchi'! And before you say it, I know— they look like Central Casting could send for them to play the grandchildren in a 'Godfather' remake."

Chris laughed. "Now that you mention it, if you'll excuse a stereotype, they definitely 'look Italian.'"

"Just what you'd expect from the marriage of Anthony di Marco and Anna Maria Ciccarello, wouldn't you say? Considering that at least three-quarters of the kids in school around here are Dutch, German, or Norwegian, they definitely stand out on the playground." Tony switched to a thick New Jersey accent. "I tink summa da locals are convinced dat we gots mob connections. Don't youse worry, dough—we ain't got none," he chuckled.

"Then I assume you're not in the olive oil import business?" Chris laughed.

"Correct! Accounting. It's a lot safer. I'm a CPA downtown. The senior partner is Dutch, and his is the only name that appears on the company logo. That way I don't scare anyone away. I occasionally teach introductory accounting classes at NNC, but they hardly pay adjuncts enough to make it worth my time. I enjoy the chance to interact with the students and most of the faculty in the business department, though, so I try to teach one class a year. I usually do it in the fall, since tax season makes my springs hectic enough already."

Marty came over to them, and put his hand on Chris's arm. "I'm sorry to interrupt you and Tony, but I have a request for you. Would you mind doing me a favor, and making an old man's day? And no, Tony, I'm not the 'old man' I'm referring to."

"The thought never crossed my mind," Tony laughed. He looked inside the house, and said, "I think I can guess who it involves, and given what I've heard about Chris's background, I bet I can also guess what it is. Don't worry Chris, I think you'll enjoy this."

"Now you've got my curiosity piqued. What do you need, Marty?"

"Do you see the fellow who's just coming out onto the deck?" Marty asked. "The one with the walker? That's Klaas de Graaf. He's the oldest emeritus professor in the department—probably in the whole college by now. He turned 96 this spring. I had him for Dutch history when I was a student. He was still teaching when I started here, and when he retired, I picked up those classes. He's spent the last few years worrying that when I retire, Dutch history won't be taught here anymore. He'd be 'tickled pink' if you were to walk up to him and introduce yourself in Dutch, and chat with him in the language for a while. He doesn't get many opportunities to do that anymore. I try to stop by to see him once a week or so, but other than me, I don't think he has anyone to speak Dutch with. He's getting a little frail physically, but, mentally, he's still sharp as a tack. Just a word of warning—you may find his Dutch a little outdated. He hasn't been back to the Netherlands in about 20 years, and he always spoke a rather old-fashioned dialect anyway. Just speak up—he has hearing aids, but he still has some problems picking up conversations if you don't speak loudly enough."

"That sounds like my grandfather. And when I visited relatives in the Netherlands, most of my grandfather's generation used a lot of colloquialisms that weren't 'standard Dutch.' Hopefully I won't disappoint him. I'd love to meet him."

Chris made his way over to Klaas, put out his hand, and introduced himself in Dutch. At first the old man wasn't sure what he'd heard, but when Chris repeated himself, slowly, and a little louder, his face lit up, and he immediately broke into conversation in Dutch. Chris helped him into a chair, and the two continued to talk for the next 15 minutes. Marty interrupted them once, to bring Klaas a glass of Heineken, and to refill Chris's glass of home brew. But otherwise, he left them to themselves. Chris noticed that several more people had arrived, and that Marty had started up the grill. Soon the smell of grilled brats, hot dogs, and burgers was wafting across the deck. Marty announced that if anyone needed to do anything to prepare the food they'd brought, now was the time. So Chris excused himself from Klaas, and went into the kitchen to take his dish out of the oven.

Anna was removing cellophane wrap from a large platter of antipasto. She turned to the woman next to her and said, "Margaret, this is Chris van Zant. Chris, this is Margaret Brant. Her husband, Terry, is the Modern US historian. Margaret, Chris is our new Modern European historian. I won't color your view of him by calling him 'the new Tim Johansson.' I think you'll find him a refreshing change."

"I certainly hope so! It's a pleasure to meet you Chris. Terry was complaining to me that he hadn't really had a chance to get to know you yet, so I'm glad Marty resurrected the back-to-school picnic. I always looked forward to it. That's another thing about Johansson I won't miss."

"I keep getting the impression that he wasn't very well liked around here. I hope I make a better impression."

"I don't think that's going to be a problem," Margaret said. "I just watched you talking to old Klaas—and in Dutch, no less! I don't think I've seen him that animated and in as good spirits for ten or fifteen years. Obviously,

Johansson couldn't have done it in Dutch, but he could have taken the time to make a retired colleague feel like he still belonged. And Erika, Tim's wife, was even worse. The last couple of years we had this picnic, Klaas stopped coming. I'm glad to see he came today. Thanks for brightening his day. Now, what do you have in that delicious smelling casserole dish of yours? The smell has been driving me crazy, but I was afraid if I peeked, I might break a moisture seal or something, so I behaved myself."

"Asian chicken wings. One of my cousins married a Japanese American, and it's his 'old family recipe.' It's one of the few things I make well enough to fix for someone else."

"They smell delicious," Anna said. "I can't wait to try them. They definitely smell better than the typical 'dish to pass,' which I thought it was when I saw the casserole dish. But that was before I caught wind of them."

"Dish to pass?" Chris looked at her quizzically. "That's a term I've never heard before."

Anna laughed. "I forgot—you're new to the Upper Midwest, aren't you? That's a term you'll hear quite a bit in some parts of the region. I grew up in northern Illinois, not far from Chicago. My Mom was always bringing a 'dish to pass' to potluck dinners. The phrase isn't as widely used around here—'hot dish' is probably used more frequently. But you'll still hear it sometimes. It's self-explanatory. I would even say redundant. But it's so ingrained in my vocabulary that I can't shake it. And to be an authentic Midwesterner, you need to pronounce it like it's one word: 'a dishtopass.'"

Margaret added, "Another term you'll hear frequently in connection with potlucks is 'bars.' They're probably the most common dessert you'll find at any get-together, because they're easy to make for large groups—especially if you have a lot of kids or teenagers. I see there are a couple trays of them here today."

By now, all the food had been uncovered, and Marty brought a platter of meats in from the grill. Anna helped her children put some food on their plates, and prepared their hot dogs for them. Then Margaret fixed a plate for Klaas, and took it out to him on the deck. There were two teenagers, who everyone insisted should go next. The boy was wearing a "New Leiden Cross Country" t-shirt. When he started to load his plate, Tony joked, "Be careful Bob! I know you're burning a lot of calories on the cross country team, but please leave a little for the rest of us." Bob blushed, but didn't seem to limit his portions. "Don't listen to him, Bob," Anna said. "Tony's just jealous that he can't eat as much as he used to—at least not without adding to his spare tire. Just help yourself to what you want. Tony, however, will need to watch himself around the desserts!"

When the teenagers and younger children left the table, the adults started loading their plates, and headed to the picnic tables Marty had set up outside. Before she got to the door, however, Margaret took a bite of one of Chris's Asian chicken wings. "Chris, these are fantastic!! You said they're an Asian in-law's old family recipe? Are they difficult to fix."

"Not really. The toughest part is just finding the necessary ingredients. They go together pretty quickly after that."

Terry followed his wife's lead, and tried a bite of his own. "She's right. These are great! I think I've had wings like this somewhere before, but I can't place it. They're delicious, though. I just wish I could remember where I had 'em."

Chris blushed, and then admitted, "Probably at a sample table in a supermarket! My cousin's 'old family recipe' is a bottle of Asian barbeque sauce. I was afraid I wasn't going to find it here. When I checked the stores, it wasn't in the first one I tried. Fortunately, the other one carries that brand. I'm not sure what I'd have done if I couldn't come up with the 'old family recipe.' That's pretty much the only dish I'm confident in sharing with anyone."

"I'm not sure I'd have fessed up to that," Terry laughed. "But bottle or no bottle, they're still delicious. As far as

I'm concerned, you can bring them to History picnics any time!"

"I'm curious, Chris: which store didn't have it?" Margaret asked.

"Buywell Foods. I found it at Dick's Market."

"Ha! I knew it! But be careful you don't let Martha Braaten hear you say that. She's Walt's wife—have you met them? He's in the Business Department. In her opinion, 'If Buywell doesn't have it, you don't need it.'"

"That figures," Anna laughed. "Considering Martha's culinary skills and Walt's tastes, she probably doesn't have much trouble finding what she needs there. For her, 'spice rack' means a pair of salt and pepper shakers."

When he got back to the deck, one table had already filled up, so he took a seat at the other one. He was soon joined by several of his new colleagues. Anna, who had been right behind him in the food line, sat down next to him.

"Mind if I keep you company?" she asked. "Tony's at the smaller table with the children. He thought I deserved to have a dinner with adult conversation for a change. I love 'em for all the world, but Tony's right—it IS nice to eat with just grown-ups once in a while. How are you adjusting to NNC?"

"So far, so good, I guess. I'll probably have a better idea after Monday, when the first papers come in for *die Quellen.* That's going to be a new experience for me. I always assign papers in my classes, so I'm used to grading those, but these sound like they're something different altogether."

"You're right there," a voice to his left said. He turned to see Marcia Holt put her plate down. She held out her hand. "I'm glad to finally get a chance to talk to you, beyond our brief contact when you were on campus for your interview last spring. I've caught glimpses of you in the hall a few times, but I've always been on my way to class or to a committee meeting when that happened. And I couldn't be at last week's department meeting. I'm happy we finally have a chance to get to know each other." She pointed to the man setting his plate down on the opposite side of the table. "This is my husband, Jerry Fremont. I don't know if you've had a chance to visit the 'Northern Prairie Book Haven,' but he's the happy owner of that establishment."

Jerry reached across the table and shook Chris's hand: "Pleased to meet you." Then he laughed, "I claim to be a small business owner, but Marcia maintains it's more of a hobby than a business. Fortunately, there aren't any national chain stores in the vicinity, or I'd have to find something else to do. But with the faculty at NNC and at Chartwell, plus a literate population around both colleges, I'm able to keep my head above water."

"Who's minding the store today, Jerry?" Anna asked.

"Frank's always looking for more hours, and I can't always give him as many as I'd like. So this works out well for both of us.

Anna turned to Chris to explain, "Frank Kramer used to be Assistant Dean of Student Affairs. When our previous Dean of Students, Cynthia Reynen, came in, she immediately started 'peeing on all the bushes' to show everyone that she was in charge. Frank immediately recognized what was going on, and tried to keep his head down and stay out of her line of fire. But she decided she needed 'fresh blood' in all the top positions, and eventually pushed him out. One day the College suddenly announced that he was taking 'early retirement'—effective immediately. She had Hank's ear, so she pretty much got what she wanted. I'm sure he wanted her to have more than his ear, which is what proved to be her undoing."

Jerry saw the look of confusion on Chris's face, and added, "Cynthia's husband was an educational consultant, and spent quite a bit of time on the road. As a result, Cynthia spent quite a few evenings in her office. The Controller's office is right next to the Dean of Students' office. And then Craig Watson, the Controller, started spending a lot of time at his desk after hours. You can probably guess what happened next. The desks apparently got very close together. She got a divorce, Craig's wife left him, and Cynthia and Craig moved in together. That alone would be scandalous at NNC. It was even worse, however, because Craig is African American. A racially mixed marriage would've been a big enough controversy in this town. But for the two of them to be simply living together, without any apparent plans to get married, it was too much. Hank told her that as Dean of Students, she had to set a decent example for student behavior. He informed her that he would be terminating her contract at the end of the academic year—which was a lot more notice than she gave Frank."

"But I still think part of Hank's problem was jealousy," Anna replied. "She's an attractive woman, and I think Hank was jealous of Craig."

"So, what happened to them," Chris asked.

"She found herself another Dean of Students position," Jerry said. "They apparently figured out which side their bread was buttered on, because they got married just before they left here, and he got a well-paid 'spousal accommodation' position at her new school."

Anna groaned: "And she apparently carried on her reign of terror there as well. She came in and cleaned house, and immediately started firing long-established administrators. Some of them had regional and national reputations in their areas of expertise. But she said she didn't like the way they were doing things, and wanted to 'take things in a new direction.' A friend of mine at her new school said that Cynthia called a meeting of all the various directors who reported to her. She announced they each needed to come up with a reorganization plan for Student Affairs. Two weeks later, she called them all in and harangued them. She complained that she hadn't received any reorganization plans. One of them bravely said, 'I turned mine in two days ago,' to which she replied, 'As I said, I haven't received any plans.' He went back to his office, and immediately started sending out his resume.

Fortunately for him, he was well known nationally, and was able to land a new job before the end of the semester. Unfortunately, Frank wasn't so lucky. He was pretty much place bound; Brenda, his wife, is assistant director of the NNC library. And he's too close to retirement to have much hope of finding a new position at his age."

Jerry added, "With Brenda's position, their kids are eligible for tuition exchange, and her insurance covers them both. Although he'd be getting more if he could have waited another 5 years or so, they did let him 'retire early,' so he's able to draw from his retirement plan. In a few years, he'll also be able to collect Social Security. Working at the bookstore helps fill in the gaps, and also keeps him active. He's known many of my customers since he was a student here, and he's a personable clerk. My customers don't get the heavy-duty sighs that they might get from some younger staff. It's a huge benefit for me as well."

Marcia turned to Chris and apologized: "I'm sorry for the interruption. We got a little side-tracked. I think you were talking about the papers we have to grade in *die Quellen*. I've been teaching the course for over twenty years now, and I'm still not comfortable with them. In fall semester, it's a combination of papers where students read a text, and then come up with some argumentative thesis. It's essentially what they do in English and Modern Languages. That's why none of the faculty from those departments complain about them. What that type of paper has to do with the field I really know something about— Colonial American history—I'll never know! I don't have a problem in 'stretching' what we teach. My specialty is Colonial Virginia. But except for an occasional senior seminar, I'll never teach a course at NNC that's so narrowly focused. I teach the first half of the US history survey, a general Colonial US course, the Civil War, and sometimes courses related to one of those areas, but focusing on Women and Gender Studies. All of those could keep me more than busy. But every semester, we all teach a section of *Die Quellen*."

"It's about the same for me," Anna said. "My research focuses on Renaissance Italy. But I also teach our courses on Ancient Greece, Rome, and the Middle Ages. Our Renaissance course includes the Reformation, too, so even that class is much broader than my area of specialization. Marty's fields overlap with mine, so sometimes he teaches the Renaissance/Reformation course, which allows me to offer a broader range of courses in my areas of expertise."

Terry Brant had just sat down at the table, and he joined in the conversation. "I'm pretty lucky in that regard. My specialty is Twentieth Century US Diplomatic History, with a Latin American focus. I teach the second half of the US history survey, an upper division course on Twentieth Century US, and a few courses in Latin American History. Even the course on the Populists and Progressives isn't that far from my primary area of interest. The only problem is that I have to teach them in a two—and sometimes three—year rotation. It would be nice to offer some of those courses more often. But for all of us, *die Quellen* is given priority."

"I'm still trying to figure out why there aren't more departments represented among *die Quellen* faculty; I thought it was an 'all-campus' course," Chris said. "Except for a few faculty, the only ones I've met have been from History or English. I'm still trying to figure out what the course is all about?"

"Get in line," Anna laughed. "There's a long history that you probably don't want to hear all at once. To make it simple, back in the early '80s, the Faculty created the course to serve as the introductory writing class, as well as an introductory history course. The original idea was to introduce students to the 'Sources of Western Civilization.' Hannelore van Leuven, who was Head of the Modern and Classical Languages Department then, suggested the name *die Quellen*—German for 'The Sources.' That's the only thing she's ever contributed to the class. Until very recently, they never contributed anyone from her department, and even now, NEVER her. The idea got immediate support campus wide—especially when someone came up with the idea of making it an 'English and History' course, which meant that they wouldn't have to teach in it. By the mid-'90s, it was decided to broaden the focus to 'Sources of World Civilization.' That didn't change the make-up of the faculty. It was still just English and History. When it needed more staffing, the Classics Department occasionally contributed someone, too."

"But I met a few people from Philosophy and Modern Languages who're teaching this semester," Chris said.

"That's a recent development," Terry said. "Our student body has grown, but Hank's kept a lid on faculty size. He's consistently maintained that we can't add any faculty, no matter what kind of academic changes we make."

"That caused a pinch for *die Quellen*," Marcia added. "To make the course work—if it actually can—they have to keep the numbers down in each section. It's capped at 20. No exceptions. When the numbers started to get beyond what English and History could cover, Paul Rothman tried to get us each to add another section. We told him we were already committing a third of our faculty load to the course, and that was enough. Hank tried to put pressure on us, too, but that was farther than we were willing to be pushed. Finally, Rothman realized he was going to have to recruit *die Quellen* faculty from other departments, so he used that as a bargaining chip. When a department head wanted something from him, the price was committing a faculty member to teach in the course for three years."

"So other departments get rewarded," Terry grumbled, "for doing what we're expected to do without so much as a thank you."

Anna nodded. "One of the reasons Hank doesn't like Marty is that Marty's been an outspoken critic of the course, and our continued involvement in it at the current level. On a couple of occasions, Hank has refused to support what we want—no, make that need—because we've dared to criticize 'the College's signature course.' Marty quoted the College Manual, chapter and verse, which states that 'Faculty have the right to criticize College policies.' That's obviously not going to convince Hank to give us something that we want, but it seems to be enough to keep him from trying to take something away."

"That's why Marty hasn't retired," Marcia said. "Hank's told Marty several times that when he retires, the College will reallocate his position to another department. But Marty figures—hopefully correctly—that whoever replaces Hank won't hold the same grudge, and we'll be able to keep his slot."

"Does he want to retire?" Chris asked. "At the university where I taught the last two years, the senior member of the department has all but barricaded herself in her office, refusing to retire. From what I could gather, she has no life other than her teaching. And unfortunately, she's no longer very good at it—if she ever was. But she'll be kicking and screaming when they finally drag her out of that office."

Anna shook her head. "We've got a few like that at NNC, too. But Marty would love to retire. He's still a great teacher, but according to him, he's lost a little of his 'edge.' And he'd like to give someone else a chance at a career like he had."

"And probably more significantly," Marcia added, "he wants to spend more time with his grandchildren."

"How many does he have?"

"Five. Three in Minneapolis, and two in a western suburb of the Cities. He gets down there whenever he can, and since Annette died, his son and daughter have been great about bringing the kids up to visit him. But now the older ones are starting to get into organized sports at school, so that makes it hard for them to come up here as often. A couple of them play hockey—it is Minnesota, after all—and I know Marty enjoys watching them play.

But the oldest granddaughter has started playing basketball, so that's really close to his heart. If they lived closer, I'm sure he'd be a volunteer coach. As it is now, he gets to see a few weekend games, but he can't help out with the practices, since they're during the week."

"Do you have children, Marcia?" Chris asked.

"A son and a daughter. They're both in college. That's one of the reasons I wouldn't consider leaving here, no matter how irritating I find teaching in *die Quellen.*"

"Same here," Terry laughed. "You met my son and one of my daughters in the food line. Linda's a senior this year, so she'll be starting college next fall. She still hasn't decided where she wants to go, other than somewhere where her sister, Amy, isn't going. Amy's a junior in college, so it would only be one year at the same school, but that's one too many for Linda. Bob's just a sophomore in high school. I just hope I can afford the food bills for the next three years. But at least I don't have to worry about paying college tuition for any of them."

"Why's that?"

"Tuition exchange! Hasn't anyone told you about that?" Anna asked.

"When I interviewed for the job, the acting Dean asked if I had children. I said I wasn't married, so I had no immediate prospects in that regard. He mentioned something about tuition exchange, but said that could wait until I had a genuine stake in it. But he also implied that it might not be available much longer."

"If Hank had his way," Anna replied, "it would've been cut a long time ago. But that's one thing the Faculty will fight to the death to keep. He tried to restrict some of the benefits for staff, but the Faculty wouldn't let him touch that, either. If the College did away with that, there would be a mass exodus out of this place. Of course, Hank probably wouldn't mind that, because the replacements would have lower salaries. But even he's not crazy enough to drive out most of his faculty."

"Okay, that explains how my undergraduate profs were all able to send their kids to private colleges," Chris said. "I didn't think their salaries were that good."

"I'm sure most small college presidents feel the same way Hank does," Terry added. "They'd rather see more full-paying students. Tuition exchange doesn't help the bottom line. But it's a huge factor in recruiting faculty— especially those who have kids. When the time comes, you'll really appreciate it, Chris."

"Unless you pull a Harry Wilson," Marcia laughed.

"Who's Harry Wilson?"

"Former professor of psychology," Marcia said. "He decided he wanted to focus more on research than teaching, so he took a position at a 'Research-I' university in the Southeast. That would also give him the opportunity to work with graduate students. He said he was 'eager for new challenges.'"

Anna laughed. "He added new dimensions to the term, 'work with graduate students.' After he was there a few years, his wife came home from work early one day, and found him in bed with one of his graduate assistants. She divorced the sorry bastard as soon as she could, and he married the grad student. Last I heard, they had three kids."

Terry groaned, "So for Harry, 'working with graduate students' was an expensive proposition. When he left here, his two kids were in high school, so the tuition exchange wasn't some far-off, vague concept. But state universities don't have the same tuition benefits that we do. So that's easily a couple hundred thousand dollars in tuition money that he gave up when he left here. The three from his second marriage obviously wouldn't have been part of that, but they still represent three more sets of college tuition. I don't think that's what he had in mind when he talked about 'new challenges.'"

Chris sensed the presence of someone behind him. He noticed the others at the table looking high above his head. Then he was suddenly engulfed in a huge shadow. As he was turning around to see who it was, Anna exclaimed, "Talmadge! I'm glad you could make it! I take it the Black Studies picnic was as lively as ever," she laughed.

Chris stood up to meet the new guest. Even standing, he felt small next to him.

"Chris, this is Talmadge Sumner. He's technically a member of the Black Studies Department, and not history. But his degree is in history, and he teaches African-American and African history, so we claim him as our own, too. Talmadge, Chris is the new Modern European historian." Terry waited a second, and then added, "Perhaps more importantly for you, it sounds like he may be our secret ingredient for beating the Chartwell faculty in basketball this year. From what Marty tells me, with Chris, we'll finally have a threat from three-point range.'"

Talmadge's deep voice rumbled. "I've been looking forward to meeting you, even without knowing that you can add some flash to our basketball team. But if your hiring means I won't have to carry the rest of these slackers all by myself," he chuckled, "I'm especially delighted to meet you."

"Hey, we're not that bad," Terry protested.

"Maybe not, but you're not that good, either," Talmadge laughed again, with a rumble that came from deep within his huge frame.

Terry added, "Talmadge not only played college ball—he was on a Division I team."

"Picked up a lot of splinters sitting on the bench most of the time," Talmadge protested.

"Doesn't make any difference as far as I'm concerned. You were on a Big-10 team. Bench or no bench, you saw more high-quality time playing at that level than the rest of us combined." Terry turned to Chris. "Chartwell has several good basketball players on their faculty. We try to focus more on academic quality at NNC, with faculty as well as students." It was all he could do to say that with a straight face.

"It sounds to me like you've heard too many of Hank's pep talks," Talmadge laughed. "Next you'll be calling us the 'Harvard of the Northern Prairie.'"

"No—remember, I believe in the motto, 'NNC: Where the Ns stand for Knowledge," Terry laughed.

Talmadge nodded in agreement. "Maybe if I tell Hank that Chartwell beats us every year because they have more African Americans on their faculty, he might hire a few more here."

"I wouldn't count on that," Anna said, "unless you can convince him that something would give us an 'opportunity.'"

Chris looked a little puzzled, so she explained, "Talmadge isn't the only African American on our faculty, but he's one of precious few. A couple of times, Hank meddled in searches and insisted that departments hire minority—generally African American—candidates, even when they weren't the departments' top—or even second—choices. He said we needed to 'take advantage of the opportunity to diversify our faculty.'"

"That sounds like a reasonable goal," Chris replied. "I noticed at the Faculty Assembly that we're a pretty white group here. What's the Chartwell faculty like?"

"It's about as white as NNC," Talmadge said. "But at least they have a few minority faculty in the sciences. In Hank's defense, I do have to say that I appreciate the fact that he seems to recognize we need to have more minority faculty here. And it's an up-hill battle: there aren't too many of us 'black folk' who enjoy the winters in north-central Minnesota. But I still don't like the way he tries to solve the problem. It's probably because he's only doing it for the wrong reason: PR."

"I can't say too much," Terry said softly, "because I'm one of the few beneficiaries of his 'vision.'"

Chris was completely in the dark regarding that comment. "What do you mean?"

"Before I came here, Hank went to a couple meetings of college presidents from the Upper Midwest. They had a few sessions about 'changing demographics.' One speaker told them that in the next 50 years, there would be a huge increase in the number of Hispanics in the region. Hank figured that NNC could tap into that by offering more courses that would appeal to Hispanic American students: language, literature, history and culture—things like that. So Spanish is the one language section he's supported in Modern and Classical Languages. Thus far, the anticipated 'demographic shift' hasn't had any impact there. First, we don't have many Hispanic students. Most of the ones we get here are pretty much bi-lingual. And they're not any more interested in upper division language courses (which are mostly literature classes) than the rest of our students. It's possible the next generation will be different, but if they follow the pattern of other ethnic groups, that next generation will also be generally uninterested in learning the language. Then the generation after that will want to 'get in touch with their roots.'"

Marcia picked up the thread of the conversation: "We'd been hoping to add another US historian for quite a while, but Hank wouldn't hear of it. Then Marty suggested that we ask for someone who could teach US and Latin American history. Hank was convinced that would help to attract Hispanic students to NNC, and we got the position."

"Hank told me he was disappointed that there were no Hispanics in the applicant pool, but at least I'm not tall and blond. I studied in Mexico, and I'm fluent in Spanish. So here I am," Terry laughed. "I was able to get a faculty Fulbright to teach for a year in Chile—I lectured on US Foreign Policy. Until then, I think Hank was a little skeptical about my credentials. But since my classes are full, and he was able to get some publicity about my Fulbright, he hasn't given me any grief since then. What he hasn't seemed to figure out, though, is that my classes aren't full of Hispanic students. We still don't have large numbers of them, and I can probably count on one hand the ones who've taken my classes. That's something I'm not about to point out to him, you can be sure. Speaking of Fulbrights, Chris, I have a favor to ask of you."

"What's that?"

"As a first-year faculty member here, you don't have to serve on any committees. But since you've had a Fulbright, I was wondering if you'd be willing to help us interview the students who are applying for what NNC vaguely refers to as 'external postgraduate scholarships.' It doesn't take too much time—we usually have about eight to ten Fulbright applicants, and maybe a couple who are hoping to make it to the Rhodes or Marshall competition."

"Can I do something like that in my first year here?"

"It's up to you. I asked Marty what he thought. He's done it for many years, and he'd like to see some new blood injected into our system. He said it's up to you, but as far as he's concerned, he thinks it would be a great idea. Several of us on campus had Faculty Fulbrights. But as far as I know, you and Marty are the only ones who had them as graduate students. Since the application processes are different for faculty and students, it's a good idea to have someone who knows something about the student experience. I'm not asking for an answer right now, but please think about it."

Anna added, "That's a great idea, Terry. It'll give him a head start on 'service' for his third year review, and eventually for his tenure evaluation. This won't be enough by itself, but it'll give him a leg up on everyone else coming up for review with him." She turned to Chris and added, "This committee is another one of Marty's contributions—and one of many of the points of irritation with Hank."

"Why's that?"

"For years," Terry said, "the 'external postgraduate scholarships' were handled by an assistant dean. That's usually a three-year appointment. Marty argued that using that arrangement kept us from developing a successful track record with any of those scholarships. The first year, a new assistant dean would be trying to figure out how each application process worked. The next year, it was a little better, and by the third year, they were finally comfortable with what they were doing. But then the next year, a new assistant dean started the process all over again. There wasn't any continuity."

"Rothman didn't help matters," Anna grumbled. "His overseas experience was limited to a brief trip to England, where he visited a small archive related to one of his favorite Victorian authors. And of course he took in some plays in the West End and Stratford-upon-Avon. But he didn't really understand what Fulbrights were all about— either for the students, or for a school's academic reputation. He was also influenced by a few of our faculty who think that we shouldn't be doing anything to single out students, no matter how good they might be. Since all of our students are great, they argue, singling out any of them isn't really something we should be doing."

"That's why NNC calls them 'external postgraduate scholarships,'" Terry added. "Any school that I've ever been associated with refers to them as something like 'distinguished scholarships.' But not here. Every year, Marty kept telling Rothman that we needed to handle those scholarships more effectively. Of course, Hank then heard from Rothman that Marty was annoying him about this, so that didn't help improve Hank's view of Marty. He'd already gotten on Hank's bad side by daring to be critical of *die Quellen*, among other things."

Anna laughed, "Many other things!"

"So how did this new committee get set up?" Chris asked.

"Marty's persistence, to put it simply," Terry said. "Whenever he'd see something in one of the Twin Cities newspapers about students from other schools in the state getting a Fulbright, Rhodes, or Marshall Scholarship, he'd send Rothman and Hank a copy."

"I think the clincher was the ad with the football player," Anna added.

Terry chuckled: "I have to admit, that was a great ad! One of the Norwegian Lutheran schools took out a full-page ad in a Twin Cities magazine. It showed their most recent Rhodes Scholar in his football uniform (he was their quarterback, I think), playing his violin out in a snow-covered cornfield. In addition to his usual note, Marty asked Hank if it wouldn't help our recruitment and fundraising to be able to showcase some of our students like that. Then he made his standard pitch for creating a faculty committee to give more consistency to our recruitment and selection process. Given Hank's obsession with the football team, that ad finally convinced him."

"Of course Rothman opposed the idea," Anna said, "but Hank was convinced. So now we have the committee. In addition to Terry, there are a few other people who've had Faculty Fulbrights. (I'm planning to apply for one in a couple of years myself.) We don't have any Rhodes Scholars on our faculty, but one's a lawyer in New Leiden. Whenever we have a student make the interview stage, she helps conduct a 'mock interview.' Each year we've gotten more applicants, and more of them are successful every year. The second year we had the committee, one of our football players got a Rhodes. And as you can imagine, the Public Relations Office got a lot of mileage out of that. It apparently took them a while to convince Hank that they shouldn't run an ad showing him in his uniform, playing a violin in a cornfield. For starters, he's not a musician. And they pointed out that simply copying the other ad wouldn't make NNC look very good. Instead, they put out some 'tasteful but effective' publicity. It got a lot of reaction from interested students and alums—as well as potential donors. Hank had to admit grudgingly that Marty's idea was a good one. Rothman, of course, immediately extolled the virtues of the committee, and as usual, he tried to make it look like it was his own idea."

Marty came over to their table, accompanied by an older man. Chris guessed that he was probably another emeritus professor, which Marty quickly confirmed.

"Chris, I'd like you to meet another of our emeriti: Charles Johnson. When he retired, Johansson took his place, and now you have the position. I think you two will get along well. Unfortunately, you probably won't see him around campus too much—he and Madeline spend a lot of time traveling. Charles, Chris is the new modern European historian." Marty turned back to Chris and added, "As one of my graduate professors used to describe a colleague, Charles 'is an historian of Britain, who wishes he were a British historian.'"

Charles laughed, and with a slight, affected British accent replied, "I'm never sure if I should be insulted when Marty says that, but then I realize that he's telling the truth! I've already been hearing good things about you, Chris, and I look forward to getting to know you. But I brought Klaas this afternoon, and he's starting to get tired, so I'd better get him back home. I'm sorry you didn't get a chance to meet Madeline. Our daughter called and asked if Madeline could join her and our granddaughter for a 'girls' weekend in the Cities.' That was something she couldn't pass up. She was looking forward to meeting you, so I hope we can connect before the departmental Christmas party. We'll try to have you over for dinner sometime this semester. I hope to see you again soon."

After Charles left, Marty turned to Chris. "I'm glad to see you're getting a chance to get to know the rest of your History colleagues. While Talmadge is technically not in the History Department, he is, after all, an historian, so we consider him one of our own, too. I think you'll find them all to be a likeable bunch." He turned to the rest of the table, and asked, "Can I get anyone here something more to eat or drink?"

"No, I think we're all fine," Anna replied. "Why don't you sit down with us for a while? If you keep running around with the kids, you'll wear yourself out, and we'll all have to go home early. We've finally gotten a chance to get together for a change, so let's enjoy it!"

Marcia agreed. "Please, sit down! And tell us about your summer, Marty! Did you get to spend a lot of it at your cabin? I'm assuming you got in some quality fishing time."

"Yes on both counts. I was at the cabin most of the summer, and I had an extra bonus with fishing this year. A friend from grad school just retired from a small college in Montana. His son runs a fly fishing guide service out there. For a retirement gift, he offered to take him and a guest on a week-long fishing expedition. Since his wife doesn't like to fish, I got to be the lucky guest! We fished several of the "blue ribbon" rivers. We floated some, and waded others. With so much ground to cover, and considering the fact we're both in our late 60's, his son scheduled in a couple of 'rest days' along the way. Otherwise, I wouldn't have been able to move my casting arm! As it was, we caught more large trout than I ever have. I've always wanted to go on a guided float trip, but I always thought they were out of my price range. This was too good an opportunity to pass up—it was worth being away from the cabin for a while."

"Where's your cabin?" Chris asked.

"Should I tell him, Anna, or do you want to?" Marty said.

"It's 'up North, at the lake,' she laughed. "That's where everyone's cabin is in Minnesota. Now, when you consider how many lakes there are in Minnesota, and how much of the state is 'up North,' that doesn't narrow it down much."

"To be more specific," Marty added, "it's up near the Canadian border, in the 'Arrowhead' near Lake Superior. There's good fishing for bass, Northern Pike and walleye in the lake. And fortunately, it's not far from my cabin to some of the streams that run into Lake Superior. When I was in grad school in Michigan, I got hooked on fly fishing for trout in the Upper Peninsula—the 'U.P.' I enjoy fly fishing for bass and Northerns, too, but I really like stream fishing for trout. That's why the Montana trip was such a wonderful treat. I've never had the chance to catch so many big trout before. Do you fish, Chris?"

"When I was in Boy Scouts, an assistant scoutmaster gave us a course on fly fishing. I immediately fell in love with it. He also taught us to tie our own flies. I haven't had many opportunities to fish since I started grad school, but I do enjoy it. There's a lake not far from my parents, with some nice mayfly and caddis hatches. There's good fly fishing there. But the streams in Western Washington don't hold many resident trout. Almost all of them go to sea—either Sea-run Cutthroat or Steelhead. The same is pretty much the case in Oregon. But I was pretty busy finishing my dissertation and teaching new classes the last two years, so I really didn't have a chance to find that out first-hand. I was hoping to catch a steelhead or two when I was there, but I never had the time."

"Steelhead?" Marty asked. "Do you fish for steelhead—with a fly?"

"Sure! It's my favorite kind of fishing. One of my uncles has a farm along the Stillaguamish River, north of Seattle, and there's a nice gravel bar where I like to fish. Hooking a summer-run steelhead is the greatest thrill in fly fishing, as far as I'm concerned."

Anna burst out laughing. "Close your mouth, Marty. I'm afraid you're going to start drooling! Maybe if you ask him nicely, Chris could get you on that river." She turned to the rest of the group, and said, "I think we've found another reason why Marty's going to do everything he can to help Chris get tenure!"

"I've read about fly fishing for steelhead, but I've never had the opportunity. I almost got a chance to go to Wisconsin one year, but that fell through. The season always conflicts with my teaching schedule. But I really want to try it on some of the rivers in the Pacific Northwest. Any advice you could give me about where to go would be wonderful—and I'd especially appreciate any tricks that might help me catch a steelhead!"

"The best place I know is on my uncle's farm. And he's very generous about letting people have access through his property—as long as they ask first. He doesn't want somebody to go wandering through a field where he's just pastured his bull. So whenever you decide you'd like to go fishing there, just let me know, and I'll call him and let him know you're on your way."

"Thanks! And I hope you can join me at the cabin next year to try your luck on bass and Northerns. They're not steelhead, but they're a lot of fun, nonetheless." He turned to the rest of the group and added, "And I trust you all to verify that I'd have made that invitation even if I hadn't known about the access to good steelhead water!"

"Sure, Marty!" they all laughed. Then Anna spoke up: "Much as I'd like to see him twist in the wind a bit, I do have to admit that we've all enjoyed his hospitality 'up North, at the lake,' even though none of us fishes. But if you're a fly fisherman, Chris, I'm sure you'll love it. Don't miss the opportunity if you have the time next summer."

The party went on until about 8. Chris had the opportunity to get to know all of his colleagues, as well as their spouses. Anna and Tony realized that their children were starting to get cranky, and decided that they'd better get them home and to bed before they had a serious meltdown. The others followed their lead, but only after they'd helped Marty put away the tables and chairs, and loaded all the dishes in the dishwasher.

As they started for the door, Chris asked Marty, "Is it okay if I leave my car here overnight? After a couple glasses of your home brew, as well as some wine, I don't think it's a good idea for me to drive. Besides, I can use the exercise after all that great food."

"I noticed you enjoyed the bars," Marcia laughed.

"Several times—unfortunately. If it's okay to leave my car, I'll come back and pick it up in the morning."

"That's fine," Marty said. "But you don't have to walk. Someone can give you a ride."

"Sure, we'd be happy to drop you off," Marcia said. "Jerry's the 'designated driver' tonight, so you don't need to worry about riding with someone else who's had too much to drink."

"You don't want to run afoul of the local constabulary," Jerry added. "And I don't mean just with DUI. That's always something to avoid—which is why we always have a designated driver. I'm glad to see you share the same view. But the local police don't have a particularly kind view of the College. If you ever get stopped for anything—broken tail light, forgetting to signal a turn, speeding, anything at all—DO NOT try to talk your way out of it by telling the cop that you're a professor at NNC. That will only make it worse."

"Why's that—'town-gown' problems?"

"That's an understatement," Marcia said. "And it starts at the top. The local police chief, Carl van den Hoek, and Hank hate each other. And as in many college towns, a fairly large percentage of the nuisance calls that the local police have to handle involve students—especially if they're wandering home from a bar at closing time. On Friday or Saturday nights, there's 'the great migration,' with students walking back to campus from bars in town. That's the good news—the College is close enough to downtown that it's rare for any of them to drink and drive. But the bad news is, sometimes the walk home is a little too long in relation to bladder capacity. So the police get calls about students peeing in someone's yard, or walking through someone's gardens looking for a shortcut home."

"Apparently that's one of the things that started the bad blood between Carl and Hank," Jerry said. "Someone called to report that a couple were doing some pretty heavy-duty groping in their back yard. When the cops arrived, they still had their clothes on, but in another few minutes, they'd probably have been 'caught in the act.' But since he still had his pants on, the guy tried to high-tail it over the fence (leaving his girlfriend to deal with the cops by herself, like the true gentleman that he was). In the process, he managed to break down the fence, but he didn't get out of the yard before the police grabbed him. The homeowner said he wouldn't file charges if the kid paid for the damage, but he wouldn't cooperate. He claimed he hadn't been doing anything wrong, and that the fence was already broken—even though there were two police officers who witnessed him knock it down. Not to mention that he was trespassing. The kid's old man was a prominent donor to the College, and he wouldn't believe that his beloved little Junior would ever do anything wrong. It had to be a case of 'false identification' and 'police harassment.' Instead of helping the property owners get their money, Hank sided with the student (and his wealthy father). Unfortunately for the student, the fence he broke belonged to a local attorney. In the end, he got his money. He also put up a new fence to keep anyone out in the future, and put motion-sensor lights in the back yard. And he made sure that everyone knew that Hank had tried to protect the little brat, which added to the bad publicity for the College. That's one of the key reasons Carl dislikes Hank so much. He has no respect for him."

"But it goes deeper than that," Marcia added. "Apparently one evening at the country club, Hank tried to get a little too friendly with Carl's wife. She didn't like it. Carl liked it even less. Hank maintained it was all a misunderstanding, to which Carl reportedly replied, 'How can you misunderstand somebody's hand on your ass?' Combine that with the number of student-related incidents that the police have to deal with in New Leiden, and you can see why the police don't have a high opinion of NNC. So, the bottom line is, if you're ever stopped by the police, smile, say 'Yes sir,' or 'Yes, ma'am,' hand them your driver's license, and don't say that you're from NNC. It won't win you any favors if you do."

By this point, everyone was out the door. Chris put his casserole dish in his car, and stopped to say a final goodbye to everyone before he started home.

"Thank you all for coming," Marty said. "And for the help cleaning up." He turned to Chris. "I hope that with the flurry of social activity at the beginning of the semester, you don't come to expect it every week. Our next departmental event will be our annual Christmas dinner, and there will be a campus-wide reception about the same time. At least you've had a chance to get to know your colleagues in a non-academic setting. Occasionally one of them will join the others you've met for coffee, too. While none of them is as outspoken on most issues as I am, I think I can safely say that if it comes down to a confrontation with anyone else on campus, they'll all have your back unless you're arguing for something completely off the wall."

As the last people were starting toward their cars, Marty called out from the porch, "Good luck, everyone. I hope we all have a productive and uneventful year. With a presidential search in the offing, who knows what lies ahead! I'm told that the ancient Chinese had a curse: 'May you live in interesting times.' Here's wishing all of us an 'uninteresting' year ahead."

8
"The Kant Man Isn't In"

Thursday, September 19

AFTER THE PARTY AT MARTY'S, Chris spent most of the next week grading papers. He'd just gotten those back to the students, when he got a new batch of *die Quellen* essays. When he finished grading them, he felt like he could finally catch his breath. It had been a few weeks since he'd gone to the CUB to join the Marty's "*Kaffee Klatsch.*" Today, his desk was cleared of papers, and the first exam in his history class wasn't until next week. So he decided to treat himself to a cinnamon roll, and see what new pearls of wisdom he could pick up from the group.

When he got to the coffee shop, he saw that an extra table had been added to accommodate a larger group that morning. In addition to the "regulars," he recognized a few people he'd met at the Langbroeks' party, as well as some new faces. There was an empty seat between Johanna and Dirk, so he tried to slip into it without disrupting the flow of conversation. When there was a lull, Johanna asked, "Have all y'all met Chris?" The man on the other side of her immediately turned to him and said, "No, I haven't had the pleasure. I'm Pieter van Rijn, from Philosophy. Technically, it's the Department of Philosophy and Religious Studies, but I only handle the philosophy part." He laughed, "I'm usually better known as 'Annika's husband.' When you've been here a while, you'll understand why—she's a lot more visible than I am.""That's a polite way of putting it," Dirk said. "Since she's Hank's Executive Assistant, she has to deal with all the problems he creates. It's kind of like working with a lightning rod strapped to her back." Johanna added, "Another reason we don't see as much of Pieter as we do of Annika is that he spends most of his free time at the shooting range. He's a champion marksman—he's won quite a few state and regional tournaments. He almost made the US Olympic team a few years ago."

"I didn't expect to get as far as I did in that competition," Pieter said. "While it may seem like I spend a lot of time practicing, I would need a lot more to make that cut. But I also have to work for a living, not to mention helping Annika raise the kids."

Across the table from Chris was an older woman Chris didn't recognize. Her gray hair was tied back in a bun. Her blue eyes sparkled behind her wire-rimmed glasses. She was sitting next to Marty, who started to introduce her to Chris. She reached across the table to shake his hand. "Good morning," she said quietly. 'I'm Zoe van den Berg. Classics.'"

Johanna laughed: "Notice how she worded that. A few years ago, she'd have said that she was 'from the Classics Department.' Now she IS the Classics Department." Chris noticed that Johanna's drawl was clearly in evidence this morning; she almost stretched "is" into two syllables.

"It's another one of those departments that Hank doesn't think is necessary," Zoe explained. "If it were up to him, we'd have Biology and Chemistry for the pre-med students, and Computer Science and Business for everyone else. That would be the College. He'd like to get rid of all of the language programs, but especially the 'dead languages,' Greek and Latin. When the other member of my department left a few years ago, Hank wouldn't let me hire a replacement. I'm sure Marty's told you that your department is in the same boat with us. I tried to argue that if I had another member in my department, we could help out with *die Quellen*. Although that's a sacred cow with him, even that wouldn't work."

Several people added their opinions about Hank's staffing policies. When there was another lull in the conversation, Chris asked Pieter, "Since you're in Philosophy, could you tell me who might be able to answer a fairly basic question about Kant?"

"I can probably help you, as long as the question isn't TOO complicated," Pieter replied. "What do you want to know?"

"In my Nineteenth Century Europe class next week, I plan to talk briefly about philosophy in the first half of the century. What I picked up in an Intellectual History course in grad school will probably cover it. But I wasn't clear on a couple of points about Kant. I went over to Calvin Hall and stopped by your department yesterday, but that didn't get me anywhere."

"Who'd you talk to?"

"I can't remember his name, but he looked like he was probably a senior member of the department. Not a younger one, at any rate. I asked him if he could answer a question about Kant. That was apparently a mistake."

"Why? What'd he say?"

"He said, 'I'm sorry, the Kant man isn't in.'"

"WHAT?" Pieter burst out laughing. "That's probably the dumbest thing I've ever heard coming from Calvin Hall—and that's saying something! There IS no 'Kant man' in our department! I'm probably the closest thing to it, since I teach the courses in medieval, early modern, and contemporary philosophy. Except for the Religious Studies faculty, I'm about the only one in the building whose specialty isn't Ethics. That's why I teach most of the general philosophy courses. So, although it's something of a stretch, compared to them, I guess I'm the closest thing in the department you'll find to a 'Kant man.' But if you really want an authoritative answer about Kant, you should talk to Annika."

Chris looked a bit confused. "Is Annika a philosopher, too?"

Marty laughed. "No offense to Pieter, but she's probably the best philosopher in the family. From what I hear, she's the best shot, too."

"No offense taken. You won't get any argument from me on either account. If she had the time to devote to it, she'd win far more shooting competitions than I do. In the last few years, she's really developed her skills in biathlon. She's always been a good cross-country skier. I can't keep up with her over any distance. And as Marty just reminded us all," Pieter laughed, "she's a better shot than I am, too. A few years ago, we were watching the Winter Olympics, and they showed a little of the women's biathlon competition. I looked at her and said, 'You could do that!' She agreed. That winter, she helped organize a local club, and she's been active in it ever since. She's won several regional competitions. I'll be the first to admit that she's a better shot, better skier, and—if she had time to get back into it—a better philosopher than I am."

"But she doesn't teach?" Chris asked.

"No, she's still ABD. When I got the job here, she hoped she'd be able to finish her dissertation in the first year or so, and then piece something together by teaching a few classes here and at Chartwell. If nothing else, we thought she'd be teaching *die Quellen*. It wouldn't have been much of a commute to Chartwell, since our house is out in the country, almost half way to Edison. But after she was here a few months, the job opened up in Hank's office. It seemed like a good idea at the time. Unfortunately, she quickly found out that she wasn't going to have any time to work on her dissertation, especially before the kids started to school."

"How much does she have left to finish?" Marty asked.

"Not all that much. I think she could probably get it done if she had six months to work on it without significant interruption. But that's never going to happen as long as she's working for Hank. Maybe his replacement will be a little more flexible. She'd also like to get back into the classroom, at least part-time. She's volunteered to teach in *die Quellen*, but Hank says he can't spare her from his office, even for only an hour a day, three days a week. It's just another example of how Hank likes to control everything."

Everyone at the table nodded in agreement. Then Pieter added, "I'm sure she'd love to help you out with a Kant question. But PLEASE . . . don't call her at the office! Hank insists that everyone 'stick to business' when they're at work. He doesn't mind sending her off to the Bean Bag to get him his morning latte, but he'd have a cow if she were to answer an academic question in the office. And he wouldn't look too kindly on you, either, if he knew who was asking her the question. Why don't you call her at home this evening? Our number's in the campus directory. I'll let her know that you'll be calling. I'm sure she'll enjoy the opportunity to talk about Kant for a few minutes. And any insights she gives you will be far more than you'd ever get from any of my colleagues."

Dirk agreed: "When I first came here, the philosophers were all would-be Logical Positivists. A couple of them acted like they were going to get Wittgenstein or Russell to join the department. Unfortunately, both of them were already dead. But when the Faculty created *die Quellen*, they also added a requirement for an interdisciplinary course focusing on ethics. Students are supposed to take that in their senior year—sort of a bookend for *die Quellen*."

"For Philosophy and Religious Studies, that was a 'cash cow,'" Marty added. "Enrollments had been dwindling in philosophy classes. Back in the 60's and 70's, they had to offer at least one course on existentialism every semester, and they were always full. But that didn't last too long. With the new requirement, they didn't need to worry about losing any faculty positions. They just had to shift their focus to ethics and aesthetics. Unlike *die Quellen*, those classes were all pretty much within their areas of interest and expertise. They weren't straight 'philosophy,' but they were still courses they knew something about, and thus enjoyed teaching. And they didn't have to grade as many papers as they would have in *die Quellen.* As the older faculty retired, most of the new hires have specialized in ethics. Pieter's a notable exception."

"The ethics course isn't too bad," Pieter replied. "It's team taught, so sometimes you run the risk of getting paired up with a colleague from another department who doesn't put as much into it as you do, but that's rare. And it's only one class every year."

"We don't have that luxury," Marty grumbled. "For us, it's *die Quellen,* every semester."

Pieter laughed, "I agree with you—it's definitely better than having to teach in 'SOWS.'"

Marty snapped, "Dammit Pieter, I wish you wouldn't use that term, especially within earshot of Chris. You know damned well that if someone from my department called it that, the *Quellen* Thought Police would be on our case immediately."

"What's SOWS?" Chris asked.

"Forget you ever heard that term," Marty barked. "And DON'T EVER USE IT!"

Pieter apologized, "I'm sorry Marty. I should have known better." Then he turned to Chris and explained, "When *die Quellen* was named, they gave it the subtitle of 'Sources of Western Society.' Some people were touting it as if it were the final barricade against the barbarians—like it was the only thing left to preserve the foundations of Western Civilization. But a writer on the student paper quickly picked up on the acronym: SOWS. She joked that the course was intended to 'make silk purses out of SOWS ears.' That quickly became a campus-wide joke. When the title was changed to 'Sources of World Society,' the acronym—and the joke—still fit. But the 'true believers,' who were—and still are—die-hard supporters of *die Quellen,* didn't see the humor. Marty's right—forget you ever heard that term. You don't want to piss off the *Quellen* Thought Police."

"Oh, come on now!" sighed Walt Braaten. The turn in the conversation had caught his attention. "Thought Police? Where do you come up with that idea?"

Johanna leaned over to Chris and whispered, "If ya know what's good for ya, stay quiet!"

He looked at her, as if asking for clarification.

"I'm not kiddin'! Keep your head down and your mouth shut! I know what's going to happen next. You'll be a lot better off if ya don't get drawn into it!"

Dirk agreed. "Remember that thunderstorm we had a few weeks ago?"

Chris nodded.

"Well, you just heard the first rumblings of another one on the horizon. There's no telling how severe it'll be, but you definitely don't want to get caught in the middle of it."

Chris didn't fully understand what was taking place. But he could immediately sense that it wasn't something he wanted to be a part of. As he looked around the table, he saw that almost everyone else was trying to stay out of the line of fire, too.

Marty almost growled at Walt. "You wouldn't know, because you've never said anything that's critical of the course. You know damned well the English Department— and Hank, whose ear they have—won't tolerate any criticism of their beloved course. Think about the Tenure and Hiring Practices Committee."

"What about it?" Walt asked. "That committee gets elected by the faculty, with new people coming on every year. And they only serve a three year term. Tenure isn't decided by the English Department."

"Take a look at who's been on that committee for the last 10 years—or longer. There is ALWAYS someone from English—sometimes two. And there are always a couple of their buddies with them who've drunk the *Quellen* Kool-aid. Anyone who dares to criticize that precious course too much will jeopardize their chances for tenure or promotion. My promotion to Full Professor was delayed a year because three of the 'true believers' didn't think my record merited promotion. Hell, I've published more than the three of them put together. And you can't blame my student evaluations or service record. No, it was simply because I don't like having to teach the course, year in and year out. And I'm not afraid to say it."

"There he goes again!" sighed Walt. "And we have to listen to you bitch about it, year in and year out."

"There's a simple solution to that, Walt," Marty growled. "Get me out of *die Quellen*, and I promise: as long as I don't have to teach that course, you will never hear me complain about it again. But until that happens, I'm going to continue to try to get people to look at 'the Emperor's new clothes'—to get them to see what the course is really like, instead of what some 'true believer' tells them it is."

The intensity of their argument continued to increase. Walt offered every argument Marty had ever heard about the course. But since he'd heard them so many times, Marty had a response for each one. When Marty accused him of simply parroting the views of Hank and the English Department, Walt countered, "The speaker at last year's fall convocation said it was exactly the kind of course that American higher education really needs now. What he was describing fit *die Quellen* perfectly."

"Rule number one for people on the college speakers' circuit: always tell the audience what they want to hear. Find out what's important to the person signing the check, and you can't go wrong," Marty laughed.

"It's just because you don't like the people in the English Department."

"Now, I obviously don't agree with my colleagues from English, on many things—especially *die Quellen*. But I respect their views. They've been in the trenches. But Hank and people like you can't tell me what I should think about it, or that I should keep my feelings to myself. If you or some of your colleagues from Business taught in the course, you'd probably have a different opinion of it."

"We'd love to, but we have to meet the demands of our students. They need all of our courses offered regularly."

"So, what are our majors—chopped liver?"

"I don't know what you're always whining about. Most of the campus thinks your department is privileged to be teaching in the college's signature course."

"Privileged? To be required to teach a course that we don't want to teach, to students who don't want to take it? How can anyone consider that 'privileged'?"

"The course is planned for you by a committee, so you don't have any prep work. You have guaranteed enrollments. You don't need to worry about classes being cancelled, and possibly having your salary cut as a result."

"Reading all those goofy texts they assign isn't prep work? And when was the last time you heard of a history course being cancelled—with the exception of some of Johansson's? We could easily offer extra sections of our introductory courses every semester, and they'd all be full."

After Walt made a few more comments about how "great" the course was, Marty responded, "If it's such a great course, why can it only be staffed under duress?"

"What do you mean, 'under duress'?"

"We have no choice in the matter. A third of our teaching load is specifically designated for *die Quellen*. And I'm not just talking about History. It's the same for English. Bill Kaufman only gets to teach his creative writing class once every other year. Students are clamoring to get into it every time he offers it, and he can't come close to satisfying demand. He could fill at least one section of it every semester, and be teaching more students per class than he does in *die Quellen*—remember, it's capped at twenty students, and our departmental classes have a cap of twenty-five. And most of us always let one or two more in. But no, he has to teach a section of *die Quellen* every semester. We're wasting a fabulous resource there."

Johanna waved both arms and whistled, and then put her hands in a "T" shape and shouted, "Time out!"

Both Marty and Walt looked at her in surprise. They each started to say something, but when they saw the look in her eyes, they thought better of it, and sat back in their chairs.

Johanna looked each them in the eye and said calmly, "Walt, I agree with you—up to a point. We'd all prefer not to have to listen to Marty complain about having to teach *die Quellen*. But at the same time, ya gotta admit, he's got a point, too."

Again, Walt and Marty both started to speak, but her look cautioned them not to. They both nodded for her to continue.

"Walt, you're just one of many people who believe that *die Quellen* is wonderful. And most of ya say that you'd love to teach it, if only . . . ." She looked around the table. "Y'all can fill in the blank. If only: you didn't have to teach your majors; you didn't need to spend that time on research; you were really prepared to teach that course. And Marty's right that he and the rest of the historians— and even a few members of the English Department— could say the same thing. But they don't have a choice." She looked around the table again, and continued, "I think all y'all would admit: when it comes right down to it, if Hank somehow came up with a way to cover your classes so that all y'all could teach *die Quellen*, y'all really wouldn't do it. I think all of us are happy the way things are right now—most of us don't really care what happens with that class, as long as we don't have to teach it."

Walt started to disagree, but then shook his head. "You're probably right about that," he admitted.

"But I just had an epiphany. As I was listening to the two of you just now—or to be more precise, trying NOT to listen—it hit me: There's another reason why Hank loves the course."

"What's that?" Marty asked hesitantly.

"Think about it. I'm sure that Hank believes what he says about *die Quellen*—to the extent that he believes in anything besides self-aggrandizement. He has this nice façade of supporting 'the college's signature course,' and testimonials from the alums who were 'enlightened and inspired.' But there's somethin' more important in it for him. If he's got faculty arguin' about whether or not it's a good course, or who should or shouldn't teach it, he's got what he really loves: a disunited faculty. If animosities build up among us, it's difficult for us to present a united front against anythin' he wants to do. If we didn't have the salary scale, he'd be dolin' out money to create 'haves' and 'have not's' who were always at each other's throats."

Before Johanna could say anything more, Casey van Pelt came running up to the table. He was so excited that he looked like he might explode. "I'm sorry to interrupt, but I've got something you're all going to want to hear."

"No problem, Casey," Marty said. "Johanna just brought a sensible end to an unfortunate disagreement. We're ready to move on to something more productive. What have you got?"

"Well, let's put it this way, Marty: if you're looking for something to do in retirement, there's a vacancy in a president's office down in Iowa. I'll give you three guesses for which one—and the first two don't count."

"You've got to be shitting me!—sorry for the 'French,' Johanna!—you've got to be kidding me! Rothman?"

"None other," Casey beamed.

"What happened? I thought he was just put on probation."

"He was. But after that young vet stood up to him, a lot of other people started coming out of the woodwork. Rothman had been bullying people all over the campus, just like he did here. And everyone was afraid to say anything. Then the word spread about the incident that got him put on probation. That gave a lot of others the courage to say something. They figured that if that young vet was brave enough to stand up to Rothman's bullying, they could, too. The Board of Regents got so many complaints that they called an emergency meeting. They met for less than half an hour, and fired him. They said his behavior was 'not appropriate for the most visible member of the college community.' As you might expect, he blustered that he was going to sue them for breach of contract. But they pointed out that his contract had several clauses about 'appropriate behavior.' Any ONE of those would've been sufficient to fire him. If he wanted to sue, he could go ahead—it was his own money that he'd be wasting. Basically they told him to leave immediately, and not let the door hit his ass on the way out. His salary will be paid for the rest of the year, but he was to have his desk cleared out before the end of the week."

At first, Marty was speechless. So was everyone else at the table. Walt took the opportunity to excuse himself: "On that note, I think I'd better be heading back to my office. I'm sorry I hit a raw nerve, Marty. We'll probably never agree about *die Quellen*, but I'll try to be a little more careful with what I say about it in the future."

"Thanks, Walt. I'm sorry to have blown up at you. Maybe with our new dean, and a new president coming in next year, we'll get some changes. I know that would improve the morale of my department! But for the time being, I'm just going to savor this news. It's going to take me a while to process that—it's hard to believe that someone finally put a stop to Rothman's bullying. It's not often that Regents, or Trustees, or whatever a school wants to call them, do much to a president besides pat him on the back and give him more money." He turned to Casey: "But I thought you said earlier that they'd threatened him with a six month suspension."

"Well," Casey said, "he'd apparently pissed most of them off by trying to bring about too many changes, and doing it too quickly. And the number of complaints they got in the last few weeks convinced them that they didn't want him around at all. So they just skipped the suspension and fired his ass!"

Dirk cleared his throat. "Any idiot should know that at a conservative school like Zwingli, they're not going to like radical changes."

Marty chuckled, "Obviously Rothman wasn't just 'any idiot.'"

The table erupted in laughter. After it died down, several people excused themselves, and went back to their offices. Marty was almost the last to leave. Just as he was starting to get up, Zoe caught his attention.

"Before you go," she said shyly, "could I ask you for some advice, Marty?"

"Sure, what's up? But I say that with a caveat: you've just seen an example of how highly my opinions are valued."

"Don't worry about Walt," she said. "He still hasn't figured out that Hank rarely knows what he's saying. But it's Hank that I want to talk to you about."

"I'm hardly an expert on dealing with Hank. What's he done this time?"

"As you know, for several years, Hank has been blocking my efforts to get a second Classics professor. And as I was telling your new colleague earlier—Chris, isn't it?—Hank's told me numerous times that if I retire, he'll close down Classics, and give my position to another department."

"Sure—we're both in the same boat. I can think of several departments that are already salivating over the possibility of getting our positions. Has he been threatening you with that again?"

"No—the exact opposite. He called me into his office yesterday, and told me that he'd reconsidered. He's authorizing me to start a search for a second Classicist. That's a relief in one sense. Even if he doesn't replace me when I retire, if we've hired another Classicist, the department won't be any worse off than we are now."

"Then what's the problem?"

"Well, for starters, I don't trust him."

"I'm sorry, Zoe, but you've got to get in line for that," he laughed.

"That's true, but I'm especially suspicious of this."

"I can't blame you. But is there something in particular, other than the fact that he's reversing his position? That is odd, of course—he rarely backs down from any decision, especially when it comes to faculty positions."

"For the past several years, when I've made my annual request for a new faculty line, I've given him a job description outlining what I think we need."

"Which I'm sure he's never read."

"Until now," she said. "When he told me I could go ahead and start a search, he gave me the job description that he'd approved."

"Was it what you'd asked for?"

"More or less. It included most of the things I'd given him. But it also added a few very specialized qualifications that I wouldn't expect to find in an average pool of applicants."

"He's obviously got a candidate in mind," Marty snorted.

"That's what I thought, too."

"But he can't just handpick a new prof. There has to be a search committee. If he doesn't follow standard procedures, and violates Affirmative Action guidelines, the Feds will cut us off from financial aid and faculty grants. Without federal grants, the Science division would be running on fumes. He wouldn't risk that."

"Oh, he's got a search committee all right!" She named off the people that he had appointed.

"With the exception of you and Monica Schutte, that reads like a 'Brown-Noser Hall of Fame,'" Marty laughed.

"And at first, he wasn't even going to include me on the committee!"

"You're kidding!"

"I wish I were. But I told him that he had to have someone on the committee from the department involved. And in a one-person department, I was the only option.

That was something I wouldn't back down from. So he reluctantly added me. Monica's supposed to chair the committee. I don't have any complaints about that—no one's going to question her credibility."

"She almost never says anything at Faculty Assembly. So he probably figures she'll just go along with what everyone else says. But he's sorely mistaken if he thinks she'll rubber stamp everything he gives her. She's the fourth generation of her family to teach here. Her great-grandfather was one of the first faculty members hired by the College, and her mother was one of the first women on the NNC faculty. She's not going to do anything that she doesn't think is in line with the school's founding principles."

"I agree—but she and I could be outvoted by the others. Some of them will do anything he tells them. They'd never cross him."

"Human Relations has a detailed procedure manual for faculty searches. If you see anything that deviates from that, no matter how minor, be sure to bring it to their attention."

"I plan to. But I'm just trying to figure out what he's up to."

"For starters, when you get an application that fits the job description 'to a T,' you'll know who his candidate is. And beyond that, in the immortal words of 'Deep Throat,' 'Follow the money!'"

*   *   *   *   *

HANK HUNG UP THE PHONE, and got up from his desk. He walked over to the window, and watched the football team on the practice field. He shook his head in disgust, and went to Annika's desk.

"That was Paul Rothman," he said. "The stupid son of a bitch just got himself fired."

"Fired? I thought you said he was going to be on probation."

211

"That's what he thought, too. But he'd apparently made a lot of enemies on campus, and not any friends, especially not among the Board of Regents, where it really counts. I told him, over and over again: 'Make sure you've got a loyal Board before you start building your own legacy.' But did he listen to me? Of course not! So when that little flunky from the grounds crew started whining about how badly he was treated, everybody Rothman ever looked at crosswise came out of the woodwork."

"So what's he going to do now?" To herself, she thought, *"It serves the son of a bitch right!"* It was difficult for her to hide a smile.

"That's what he called me for. He wanted to know what I thought he should do. He wondered if he should start applying for openings at other schools," Hank snorted.

"That doesn't sound very realistic."

"Exactly what I told him. He'd be wasting his time to try that. As far as any self-respecting college is concerned, he's toxic right now. If he'd been trying to get out of there and move to a bigger school before this all blew up, they'd probably have given him glowing reviews, just in hopes of getting rid of him. But after they've fired him, he doesn't have a chance."

"What alternatives does he have?" Again, to herself she thought, *"None, I hope."*

"Not many. I told him that if he didn't want to sell insurance or used cars, he'd have to be creative. For starters, I suggested he check with some of the for-profit schools. He'd probably fit in at one of those. If he's lucky, he might find some kind of administrative position, at least on a part-time basis. He has the administrative credentials for that, and maybe he can convince them that it was more about the school than it was about him. That's what I'd try to do, anyway—put a decent spin on it. But for now, I told him to just lie low for a few weeks and put this behind him. They're going to keep paying him through the end of the academic year, so he's got a little time."

Annika shook her head. "It doesn't sound like a good situation." What she was really thinking was, *"Of course you'd put a 'spin' on it. Why can't our Trustees figure out that you're as bad as Rothman, and throw you out, too?"*

"On a more pleasant topic, I've been talking to Mike Nagel. His colleagues in Institutional Advancement are starting to set up a bunch of alumni events throughout the rest of the year. They want to use my retirement to bring in some more donations. Since we just finished a major capital campaign, he doesn't want to start something big too soon. But he thinks that if Hannah and I attend a bunch of alumni gatherings, sort of like a 'farewell tour,' that might be an effective fundraiser."

Annika forced herself to smile, and said, "Oh, draw on the good feelings the alumni have about you as a basis for more giving." She swallowed hard, and added, "That sounds like a great idea."

"That's what I thought, too. I discussed it with Mike, and he thinks there are too many events for us to cover together, so Hannah and I are going to divide them up. She'll visit about a third of them, and I'll cover the rest."

"Is she up to taking on so much fundraising by herself?"

"We talked it over last night, and she said she thought she'd probably need someone to help her. I suggested we see if Gene Graandsma could go with her."

Annika looked at him in surprise. "Gene Graandsma? Why him?"

"As head of the Board of Trustees, he'd add the necessary touch of 'gravitas.' And he's somebody I don't have to worry about with Hanna."

"Whatever you say." *"But I wouldn't trust Gene that far,"* she thought.

"Whenever I'm anywhere close to the Cities, or flying in and out of there, I'll stay in our condo."

"The College's condo, don't you mean?"

"NO! It's OUR condo."

"But the College pays for it."

"Sure—it's part of my 'non-salary compensation.' It obviously benefits the College if I can use it when I'm on college business. But it's ours. And when I retire, that goes with me."

Annika was happy she was looking away from him at the moment. He would not have been happy with the way she rolled her eyes at that comment.

"Oh, are you planning to move to the Cities when you retire?"

"At least part time. I'm working on a couple of options that will get us out of Minnesota in the winter. With our grandkids all living near the Cities, it will be nice to have somewhere convenient to stay when we visit them."

"You're not going to stay in New Leiden?"

Hank laughed. "You've got to be kidding! I'm sure as hell getting out of this podunk burg as soon as I can next spring! My replacement should take over July 1, so of course we'll want to give his family time to move into the President's house as soon as possible." He made an exaggerated "wink-wink." Then he added, "That will give me a good excuse to get out of here as soon as I can after graduation." He smiled at her smugly, as if he'd just sneaked a handful of cookies out of a cookie jar.

"You and Hanna will be missed," Annika replied. And she thought to herself, *"Like you miss a bad tooth after it's been pulled."*

9
Summerfield Meadows

Wednesday, October 23

LIKE MOST OF HIS STUDENTS, Chris was looking forward to Fall Break. By the time it finally arrived, he felt like he'd just finished boot camp. The workload in his history course wasn't any different than he'd had before. But he was still overwhelmed by the constant influx of papers in *die Quellen*. It seemed like he barely got one set graded in time to start another one. There had also been a midterm exam on the Friday before Fall Break. He had initially planned to start grading those right away. After he mentioned that to Marty, though, he changed his plans. Marty convinced him that the break wasn't just for students; faculty needed some time off, too. He suggested that Chris drive down to the Twin Cities for a couple of days. He was going to do the same thing, and spend a few days relaxing with his grandchildren.

Chris took advantage of NNC's special rate at a hotel near the airport, and used the hotel shuttle and the light rail to get around Minneapolis. On Saturday, he went to a couple of movies that weren't going to make it to New Leiden's small theater complex. Then he enjoyed the first of several ethnic restaurants that he planned to visit over the next few days. They were all too "exotic" to be found in New Leiden. He spent part of Sunday wandering through the Mall of America. There he found a few Vikings, Wild, and Timberwolves sweatshirts for his nieces and nephews. He was pleased that he'd been able to get most of his Christmas shopping taken care of, and it wasn't even November yet. Chris went back to the hotel and enjoyed the pool and hot tub for a while, before watching part of the Vikings game on television. He would have watched all of it, but he slept through most of the second and third quarters. At this rate, he'd be refreshed and ready to take on that stack of exams by the time he got back to his apartment Wednesday afternoon.

Chris wasn't the only one who left town for the break. And of the faculty who had remained in town, only a few of them bothered going to their offices. Most of the people on campus were administrators, plus skeleton crews in the CUB and the athletic complex. It was the way Hank enjoyed the campus most—so he wouldn't have to pretend to be friendly with all the people he normally ran into on campus. He'd scheduled a meeting with Sarah for 11:00 on Wednesday. Since it was mid-term break, he told her he wanted to review her performance in the first half of the semester. She was looking forward to that meeting with considerable trepidation.

About 10:30 that morning, Hank heard the phone ring in the outer office, and then Elke buzzed him on his intercom. "President Thompson for you on line one."

Annika heard Elke's voice, and quickly stuck her heard around the door. "Remember: it's Charles—for God's sake, don't call him Chuck!"

Hank grumbled, and reached for the phone. "Charles! It's great to hear from you. What can I do for you this fine morning?" He thought to himself, *"What's that son of a bitch up to now? He probably just wants to gloat about that Summerfield money."*

"Good morning, Hank. I'm sure this is a sensitive subject, but I need to talk to you about the Summerfield property."

"You're right—it is a sensitive subject. I hope you're not calling just to rub my nose in that."

"Not at all, Hank. I don't know what you did to piss off their son, but I'll always be grateful for whatever it was. But Rich hasn't told me any of the details, so I certainly won't dwell on that."

"So why are you calling, then?"

"Well, there's been an interesting development with that land. Even though Rich made the decision that it should go to Chartwell, his parents don't want to see NNC completely excluded. So they've come up with a plan that I think you'll like."

Hank squirmed a bit in his chair. He was sure he wasn't going to like anything that Charles Thompson was eager to tell him. But there was no way he could avoid asking, "Oh, what's that?"

"They agree with Rich that Chartwell can do whatever it wants with most of the land."

"I thought you weren't going to rub my nose in it," Hank said to himself.

"But they still have such fond feelings for both schools that they want to do something that will benefit each of them."

"Really? What's that?"

"They've told Rich that they want part of the land set aside for a housing development—'Summerfield Meadows.' They'll take care of putting in the sewer system, water, underground power and utilities—the whole nine yards."

"And how does this benefit NNC—or Chartwell, for that matter?"

"They want to sell lots to faculty and staff from both colleges, almost for a song. Do you know what lots are selling for around here these days."

"Last I heard, anywhere from $30,000 to $50,000. What will they want for them?"

"Just $3000 per lot! But they have some very specific restrictions. For example, they want to make sure somebody doesn't just buy one, and then turn around and sell it at market value for a tidy profit. So they'll have some restrictions on re-sale to eliminate 'flipping.' That sounds reasonable to me. In addition to making the lots available for such a low price, they want to build some amenities for the families who build houses there—a small community center, with a pool, baseball and soccer fields.

If a lot of younger faculty build houses out there, there'll be a ton of kids in no time."

"Why would faculty want to move way out there? And what if someone else wants to buy one of those lots— someone who's not on the faculty at either college?"

"Way out of town? The place that they're talking about is only about 6 miles from either of our campuses. And the Summerfields are even willing to subsidize a bus system between New Leiden and Edison, so faculty wouldn't have to drive to school every day. With that, both of us would get some good PR about how 'green' our faculty are. The Summerfields hope that all of this will help promote interaction between the two schools. I'm sure others will be attracted to the place, too, even if they aren't affiliated with either college. They could buy lots if they wanted to, but not until faculty and staff have 'first dibs.' After an initial sign-up period for people from both colleges, outsiders would then have a chance to buy anything that's left. They'd have to pay more for the lots, but it would still be less than regular market value. But I think most of the lots would be grabbed up pretty quickly by people from both colleges—it's not going to be that big a development."

"Sounds nice, but I'm not sure that many of our faculty would be interested."

"Why the Hell not? Ours are already champing at the bit to get signed up."

"You know how important the idea of the 'intellectual commons' is to our academic community. It's not just the 'shared inquiry' on campus, but the whole idea of living and working together, sharing the life of the mind. That would be difficult if they weren't living in New Leiden."

"Spare me the fundraising bullshit, Hank! You can do whatever you want, but I hope you'll let your faculty know about this. The Summerfields are being extremely generous here, so I hope you're not just going to cut off your nose to spite your face—or more precisely, punish your faculty just because you're bitter that Rich

Summerfield decided that Chartwell should get his parents' land."

"Why are you so hot on the idea—this means that Chartwell's going to be getting less money from the land than you would otherwise."

"Look at it this way: even with this chunk of land set aside, we'll still be getting more than we would have if the whole thing had been split with NNC. Because we were so supportive of this, we obviously won some extra points with Rich."

"Okay, here it comes. I'm afraid to ask," Hank thought. He tried to sound as enthusiastic as possible. "How's that, Charles?"

"Well, we had an initial brainstorming session about this, and we came up with some ways to fine tune his parents' initial idea—the bus system, for example. He said that he'd been afraid we would be obstructive, and just poo-poo his parents' idea in hopes of getting all the land. But since we were so cooperative, he decided to make an extra donation to Chartwell. He's going to fund an endowed chair in our Computer Science Department."

"Congratulations, Charles!" What he was really thinking was, *"You lucky bastard!"* Then he added, "Sure, this sounds good, but I'm not sure how interested our faculty will be."

"This will be a wonderful opportunity, Hank, especially for younger faculty. I know yours don't make any more than our faculty do. Look at it this way: it's one way to help them financially without having to come up with more money for salaries!"

"Sure—sounds like a good deal. I'll pass the word along on campus, and if there's any interest, I'll have somebody get in contact with your office to set up some kind of arrangements to handle this. Thanks for letting me know."

"My pleasure, Hank. I'll be looking forward to hearing from someone soon. On a different topic, I assume we have the standard bet on for the NNC/Chartwell football game—a case of steaks? That batch last year was particularly good, so I'm looking forward to them again this year."

"Of course the bet's still on! I've got a feeling Harry Westbrook's finally 'turned the corner' with this team. I can already taste those steaks!"

When he hung up, Hank grumbled, "Shit—we don't have a chance. Losing every year is bad enough, without having to see the smirk on that bastard's face when I have to pay off that damned bet."

Annika had just come into the room. She asked, "Then why do you keep making the bet every year?"

"Because there's no way I can get out of it without looking like I'm afraid we'll lose every year—which we will, as long as that damned Westbrook is still coaching here. If he doesn't do something dramatic pretty soon, he's toast."

"What did President Thompson want, besides the football bet?"

"Just one more thing to rub my nose in. He's cooked something up with that Summerfield guy."

"The one who was going to give us half of his parents' land?" "*. . . before you screwed everything up,*" she added to herself.

"Yeah, that one. Apparently his parents feel bad about him screwing us out of what they were going to give us, so the son and Thompson now have something else to humiliate us."

"What's that?" she asked. What she wanted to say was, *"You're the one who screwed that deal up! You're lucky they'll even talk to you."*

"He says they're planning to start some kind of housing development on part of their land. They'll put in all the utilities, build a community center, and sell the lots to faculty from both colleges for only $3000 each."

"Wow! That sounds like a fantastic deal to me! What's wrong with that?"

"I don't want to see our faculty taking charity from Chartwell! Besides, how can we maintain our ideal of the 'intellectual commons' if a lot of our faculty live out of town—particularly if they're living with a bunch of Chartwell faculty. What would that do to the strong sense of community that we pride ourselves on here at NNC?"

"Hank, this isn't an alumni reception! You're not going to convince me with the usual clichés that you dole out to potential donors. This sounds like something that could really help our faculty—especially younger ones. Most of them have trouble coming up with enough money to buy a house at today's prices. $3000 for a lot? That's amazing! Faculty will love the idea."

"Well they're not going to hear about it from me!"

"What do you mean? You can't be serious! You can't keep people from taking advantage of something like this!"

"Oh, I can't stop them, of course. If they hear about it, they can go ahead on their own. But I'm sure as Hell not going to do anything to facilitate this. It's not the kind of thing the College should be involved in. We can't interfere with the Law of Supply and Demand!"

Annika stared at him, and shook her head. She thought, *"Do you really believe the crap that's spewing out of your mouth? It doesn't make any sense! You screw up one of the best potential donations the College has ever been offered, and then you want to compound it by trying to sweep a great deal for faculty under the carpet."*

She held her breath for a few seconds, counted to ten, and then said, "Whatever you think is best. But it's almost time for your meeting with Dean Christiansen. Do you want me to go get you a latte before she gets here?" She turned toward the door to her office, so he wouldn't see her face, which she could feel was beginning to turn red. Somehow, she managed to keep her hands from shaking enough for him to notice.

"Sure, that would be great. If she gets here before you come back, just bring it into my office."

She left his office as quickly as she could, closed the door, and stepped behind her desk. She grabbed the back of her chair, and held it until she was sure her hands wouldn't shake if she released her grip. She took a couple more deep breaths, and then went to fetch Hank's latte. As she stepped into the hall, she saw Sarah coming toward her. Sarah said hello, and started to say something else, but she stopped herself when she saw the look on Annika's face. Annika put her finger to her lips and shook her head to show that she didn't want to talk. Then she moved her arms in a swimming motion. Sarah nodded in agreement and pointed to her watch, indicating that they would meet at the pool at noon.

When that was set, Annika finally spoke, loudly enough for anyone in the hall—or Hank's office, if he were listening—to hear: "Good morning, Sarah. I'm on my way to the Bean Bag to get Hank his morning latte. Would you like me to bring something back for you, too?"

Sarah looked puzzled, but she figured she should go along with whatever Annika was up to. She answered in an equally loud voice, "That's very kind of you! Just a small, drip coffee would be great! Thank you very much!"

Sarah stepped into the outer room of the President's office, and stopped in front of Elke's desk. "I'm scheduled to meet with Hank. Is he free yet?"

"I'm sorry, he's just finishing something up. He'll be with you in a minute, I'm sure. Please have a seat."

Sarah sat down to wait. She'd been expecting this. Every time she'd been scheduled to meet with Hank, he'd kept her waiting for at least five minutes. She figured it was just part of his effort to "control" everything, including her.

She was still sitting in Elke's office when Annika returned from the Bean Bag. "Are you still waiting for Hank?" Annika took another deep breath, and handed Sarah her cup of coffee. "Let me take this latte to Hank, and see what's taking him so long."

She knocked on Hank's door, and waited for him to answer. None of the office phone lines was lit up, but he might be using his cell phone. When she knocked a second time, he finally answered, "Come in!"

She opened the door, and saw that he was staring intently at his computer. He clicked the mouse to minimize the application he was using, and stood up to take his latte from her. "Is Sarah here yet?"

"Of course! She's been waiting for you for almost ten minutes. What have you been doing?"

"Sorry—I got involved in a project on my computer, and lost track of the time. Can you please send her in?

To herself, she thought, *"Glad you like the latte. You're welcome! – oh, that's right, you didn't say thank you, did you, you ungrateful SOB?"* But she managed to force a smile, and said, "I'll be happy to."

When Sarah came into his office, if she was upset at having to wait for Hank, she didn't show it. Hank moved a chair for her to sit in, and then returned to his own chair behind his desk. Although he had a couch and other chairs in the office, whenever possible, he liked to talk to people across the expanse of his large desk. He thought it added to his "gravitas."

"I hope you've enjoyed Fall Break," he said, once he'd gotten settled. "Did you have a chance to get out of town?" He sipped his latte, and looked at her over the top of his cup.

"No, I thought I'd take advantage of the quiet campus, and get caught up on a number of things I haven't been able to work on without interruption. There are so many committee meetings that I have to attend every week, that it's hard to start any larger projects. I devoted all day Monday and most of yesterday to getting one of those taken care of. It's a relief to finally get it out of the way. Besides, Owen's working on a project, so he wouldn't have been able to join me if I'd wanted to go somewhere. Since he's working in his home office, he's there when I get home. With nothing going on around campus this week, we've had the evenings to ourselves this week. So we're getting caught up on movies and tv programs that we've been recording for the last few months."

"How's that home office thing working out? Does he actually get anything done? I always thought people who wanted to work at home just wanted to get up late and sit at their computers in their pajamas. I wouldn't think anybody could get a lot done outside a regular office."

Sarah could feel her grip tightening on her coffee cup. She was afraid she might crush it and spill coffee all over herself. She set it on the desk, and tried to look relaxed as she took a deep breath. *"Ignore that,"* she told herself. *"He's just trying to bait you. If you react, he'll use that to his advantage."*

"Oh, no," she smiled. "He finds the arrangement very productive." For good measure, she added, "His work takes him into the Cities every couple weeks, so he keeps in regular contact with his colleagues there. They have a good idea of what he's been doing all the time. If he were slacking off, they'd know it right away. And whenever I've had to spend evenings or part of a weekend here on campus, he's spent that time in his own office. He's probably spending more time 'at work' now than he did when he went into the office every day. And it's a lot more productive for him to be at his desk at home than to be sitting in traffic on I-494 or 35W in Minneapolis."

"Oh, I'm sure it is. I wasn't trying to imply that he wasn't working hard since you moved here."

"Like Hell you weren't," she thought. But she smiled, and said, "Of course not. I didn't get that impression at all."

"So, tell me: what are your impressions after your first half of a semester here? How would you rate your performance so far?"

"Well, it's only been a few months, though it seems a lot longer. I was afraid I'd have trouble getting a handle on everything. You had everything arranged for me pretty clearly, which has been a blessing. I really appreciate that." She thought to herself, *"God, I can't believe I'm being such a kiss-up. I hope he can't see my nose growing—I feel like Pinocchio!"*

"That's great. I'm glad I could help you get started on the right foot. I remember when I first started as a Dean. I wasn't given anything to give me a sense of direction. I had to figure it all out by myself. I vowed that I would never leave someone in that position if I could help it. I'm glad I've been able to make the way smoother for you."

Hank rambled on for another five minutes, reminiscing about his "climb to the top." Sarah thought that she should have counted the number of times he said "I," but she realized that she'd have quickly lost track. Besides, she was having enough trouble following his conversation as it was. That took all of her powers of concentration.

Finally, he stopped himself. "I'm sorry, you didn't come in here to listen to me ramble on about myself."

"Oh, no, it's been very enlightening. I had no idea you had such an interesting academic career." She was sure her nose had just grown another inch.

Hank seemed to puff himself up in his chair. "Well, thank you! I was afraid I might have been boring you. But let's get back to how you've been adjusting to life at NNC. Are you running into any problems?"

"Not so far. I seem to be developing a decent working relationship with the faculty, at least the ones on the committees I meet with every week."

"That's the least of your worries. I wouldn't spend any time fretting about how well you get along with the faculty. That's not something to worry about. Just focus on establishing control—make sure they know you're in charge. Spending time 'building bridges' to the faculty is the last thing you need to do. Just make sure you show them who's in control. Have you had a chance to read anything about managerial success? I've found quite a few books that provide some useful guidelines. I'll be happy to loan you some if you'd like."

"That would be great. I probably won't have a chance to devote much time to that until Christmas break, but if you wouldn't mind loaning me one or two, I'd be very grateful."

"I've got some good ones that you should find really helpful, especially as you try to establish yourself in relation to the faculty. If you're not careful, they'll be walking all over you before you know it. And if you can't maintain control over the faculty, you won't get any support from the Trustees. They need to see that you can maintain a sense of order. Otherwise they'll have faculty whining to them every time they turn around. The last thing they want is to be bothered by faculty complaints. I'm sure my replacement will tell you the same thing when he gets into this office."

"Or she," Sarah interjected.

"Oh, sure, . . . or she." Hank laughed again. "That's not very likely. I wouldn't be betting on that horse. With you as Dean, I'm pretty sure the Trustees won't be hiring a woman president, too. I pretty much eliminated that possibility when I hired you."

"What do you mean by that?"

"The faculty have been whining for years that we need more women in our administration. When I hired Mary de Groet as VP for Finance, I thought that might shut them up, but there was still a lot of squawking. Then the search committee for Dean—your position—came up with three women as finalists. Since you were hired, it seems pretty clear that my replacement won't be a woman, too."

Sarah wasn't sure how to respond to that. She kept reminding herself that in only about eight months, Hank would be gone. But right now, she wasn't sure she would last that long. She managed a smile, and said, "I look forward to reading some of the books you recommend. But as I mentioned, I probably won't be able to get to them until Christmas break. Is there anything else you need from me today? I know that you were working on something before I came in, so I don't want to take up more of your time."

"No, that'll be all. Thanks for coming in. I'll keep checking with you as the semester goes along. As always, if you need any advice, just let me know. I'll bring a couple of books when I come in tomorrow, and drop them off at your office. I'm sure you'll find them helpful."

Sarah got up and walked out of the office. As she passed by Annika's desk, she didn't say anything, but tapped her watch. Annika nodded. She could see that Hank was watching Sarah as she left, so she said, "It's great to see you again, Sarah. I hope you enjoy what's left of Fall Break."

Hank seemed satisfied with that brief exchange, so he went back to his desk, and reloaded the application that he'd been using on his computer.

Sarah took her briefcase back to her office, and then went immediately to the pool. She changed quickly, and had already swum half a dozen laps before she heard Annika dive into the lane next to hers. She swam a few more laps, and finally felt the tension from her meeting with Hank slowly start to disappear. For good measure, she swam a couple more, and then went to shower. She had just gotten dressed when Annika came in from the pool.

"Give me just a minute to shower and get dressed. Then we need to talk!"

A few minutes later, Annika came over to the bench where Sarah was sitting. Annika was still drying her hair, but otherwise she was ready to return to work.

"How was your meeting with Hank?" Annika asked.

"Worse than I'd expected. I was afraid he might have some complaints about what I've been doing, but there wasn't anything like that at all. But I had to listen to him drone on about his brilliant career, and then suffer through one of the most blatant examples of sexism that I've ever encountered."

"Usually a meeting with Hank ends up being more about Hank than about the supposed subject of the meeting."

"I've noticed that a little before, but today was the worst I've seen. His pronunciation of the English language definitely doesn't include the 'silent I,' does it?"

Annika laughed. "That pretty much sums him up. 'I-yi-yi.' He's his own favorite topic of conversation. But what sexist avenue did he go down today. He didn't make a pass at you, did he?"

"No. Is that usually a problem with him?"

"Never to the point of being proved. He usually brushes it off as being a 'misunderstanding.' At least that's what he told me when I objected to something he said, which sounded to me like he was making a pass at me."

"What did you do about it?"

"There wasn't much I could do. He said I'd misinterpreted something he said, so I had to smile and accept that. But I managed to avoid the problem in the future."

"How'd you do that?"

"I told him that it was good that it was just a misunderstanding, because Pieter is very protective and insanely jealous—the first part's true, but I made up the second part. Then I pointed out that he's also a champion marksman, and it would be a clear shot from the top floor of the field house to Hank's desk. It's less than 100 yards away, so it's easily within the effective range of a 22 long rifle, especially in the hands of someone who's as good a shot as Pieter is. I told Hank that I was afraid that if Pieter thought he'd made a pass at me, he might set himself up in the field house and wait until Hank sat down in his desk, and plug him right there. Pieter would never do something like that, but it seemed to put the fear of God into Hank. There have been no 'misunderstandings' since."

"But Hank's desk isn't in front of the window."

"Not anymore!" Annika laughed. "When I came to the office the next day, he had Max Cuypers and some of his

Buildings and Grounds staff rearranging the furniture. Since then, his desk has been over to the side of the room, with his back against a bare wall. But what did he say to you today?"

"He basically said that I'd been hired so that the Trustees wouldn't hire a woman to replace him. Not me in particular, but a female dean, at any rate."

"I've heard him say something like that myself. I've been trying to figure out how to tell you about that, but I never could find a good time. Don't take it personally. As you say, he'd have been happy with any woman as dean, if that would help assure that the College didn't get a female president."

"Do you think that would've been likely, anyway? I get the impression the Trustees are a pretty conservative bunch."

"Most of them are. But I think the majority of them would also give a qualified female candidate serious attention. Hank's gotten most of them behind him, because he's been successful as a fundraiser, and he keeps a pretty tight rein on most of the budget—at least the parts that don't affect him personally. Still, he knows he can't push them too far. Most of them are alums, who won't go along with anything they think might hurt the college or tarnish its image. A few years ago, he was suggesting that they let the school be taken over by a for-profit outfit. That didn't sit well with any of them."

"That's good to hear. But you obviously wanted to talk to me about something besides my meeting with Hank. What's going on?"

"Did he happen to mention 'Summerfield Meadows?'" Annika asked.

"No. What's that? I've never heard of it. I assume it has something to do with the land deal he screwed up."

"Correct! Apparently, the Summerfields feel so strongly about both Chartwell and NNC that they want to do something for both colleges, even after Hank pissed off their son, Rich. So Rich met with President Thompson, and told him that they want to use part of the land for a housing development. They're calling it 'Summerfield Meadows.' They'll put in the streets and utilities, and even a small community center and playfields. And they'll sell lots to faculty for only $3000. That's about 10% of the going rate—or less!"

"That sounds like a fantastic plan. So what's the problem?"

"Hank feels that they're just rubbing his nose in his earlier screw-up. He said he doesn't want our faculty taking 'charity' from Chartwell. And then he threw in every cliché he could about our 'love of the intellectual commons,' 'shared inquiry,' and the like. He admitted that he couldn't prevent our faculty from participating, but he said he wouldn't have anything to do with it, and he wouldn't tell them anything about it."

"My God, that man is petty—even worse than I thought! Talk about childish! He can't keep something like that secret for long."

"Maybe he figures that if the idea's really popular at Chartwell, all the lots will be bought up before any of our faculty have a chance to get in on the deal. But how can we let people know? If he thinks I leaked any information about this, he'll make my last eight months with him a living Hell—probably even fire me. And since he didn't mention it to you, he'll think you don't know anything at all about it. If you say something to him, he'll figure out that it came from me, and I'll be just as bad off as if I'd told the faculty myself."

"Let me take care of it. I think I can get the word out without implicating either one of us. And I'll manage to look surprised when I hear about it."

As usual, Sarah and Annika left separately. They didn't want Hank to see them walking back to their offices together. That was particularly important today, because he'd be furious if he thought Sarah had learned about the Summerfield Meadows proposal.

When she was back in her office, Sarah opened her private e-mail account. She always avoided using her NNC e-mail for personal matters anyway, but she definitely thought that was necessary today. Instead of her name, the user id was simply "Planck" at a free e-mail service. She quickly wrote a message to Marty:

> *If you're back from Fall Break, how about joining me for pizza about 6:00 this evening at Snuffy's? I'll even buy the wine—you can't beat that!*
>
> *The first one there gets the back booth?*
>
> *Planck*

She clicked "send," and crossed her fingers that Marty wasn't still in the Cities. Classes resumed the next day, but he could easily have dinner with his grandchildren and come home later in the evening.

A few minutes later, the computer chimed to alert her to a new e-mail message. She laughed aloud when she read his reply:

> *Planck:*
>
> *Sounds great to me—I've been having "Snuffy's withdrawal" for a couple of weeks.*
>
> *Since Heisenberg won't be with us, I've made sure there's no uncertainty: I called to reserve the back booth at 6.*
>
> *Marty*

She chuckled to herself, "So much for my worry that he might not know who'd sent the message, and just chucked it into 'trash.'"

When she got to Snuffy's a couple minutes before 6, she saw his car in the parking lot. She walked to the back booth. He was already making himself comfortable, pouring them each a glass of wine.

"Ah, Professor Planck, I presume! Since you said you were paying for the wine, I thought we should splurge: I ordered a carafe of the house Chianti. There's still half an hour left of Happy Hour, so it'll set you back about six bucks," he laughed.

Sarah slid into the booth opposite Marty, and took one of the glasses from him. "Cheers," she said, and clinked his glass. "To historians who know something about modern physics."

"Not much, I must confess. But whenever I teach the History of Modern Europe survey, I cover the revolution in science in the late nineteenth and early twentieth century: Curie's work with radiation, Einstein's Theory of Relativity, Planck and Quantum Physics, Heisenberg's Uncertainty Principle, and the like. Since you're the only physicist I've ever dined with at Snuffy's, it didn't take Sherlock Holmes to figure out who'd sent me the message."

The waitress came to take their order. After she'd left, Marty asked, "What's going on? I suspect there's more to this invitation than just the chance to share a carafe of cheap wine—though I've never been known to turn that down."

"You figured that out pretty well, too. You warned me that it wouldn't be easy working with Hank. You were right. I keep telling myself that it's only for the rest of this academic year. But sometimes I think it'll be a miracle if I don't strangle him in his office."

"If you haven't figured this out already, you'd probably have to get in line to do that. What'd he do this time?"

"That's where it gets tricky. For a number of reasons, I don't want to say too much about it, because it would get someone else in serious trouble."

"Let me guess—Annika, right?"

She nodded. "You're on a roll today: exactly! Let's just say that I'm looking for someone to poke his finger in Hank's eye—figuratively, of course."

"Where do I sign up?" Marty laughed. "Of course, that's something else that most people around here would get in line for."

"I want to be very careful how I phrase this, because no one is supposed to know about it. If it's handled the wrong way, Hank will be furious. And he'll make life miserable for Annika."

"Well, if you can't tell me anything, how am I supposed to do something? You've got me confused on this one."

"Just bear with me. Do you have much interaction with your colleagues at Chartwell?"

"A little. We sponsor a symposium every spring. It alternates between campuses. They'll be hosting it this year."

"Okay—then wouldn't it be about time for you to be checking with them to see how the arrangements are going for this year's symposium? To see if they need any help with anything?"

"They usually take care of everything themselves, like we do. But sure, if there's a reason I should get in touch with them, that's as good an excuse as any."

"Great! Now, hopefully they'll mention something about this, but if they don't, ask them about 'Summerfield Meadows.' But be careful how you do it. I'm not even supposed to know about it. You definitely aren't—nor is anyone else on the Faculty. As I say, I hope your colleagues at Chartwell will bring it up. But if they don't, see if you can coax a little information about it out of them."

"And what am I supposed to do with the information if they do tell me about it?"

"That depends. If Hank makes an announcement about it at the Faculty Assembly meeting next Monday, then you don't need to do anything. But if he doesn't, it might be a good time for someone to ask—if they've heard about it from someone at Chartwell, of course, and not from Annika or me."

Marty smiled, and said, "Heard about what?"

Sarah was about to say "Summerfield Meadows," but she saw the gleam in his eye. "Exactly!" she laughed. "I don't know anything about it either!"

*   *   *   *   *

Monday, October 28

THE FACULTY ASSEMBLY was going along comfortably on Monday afternoon. There were a few new course proposals that were generally straightforward. But they still brought the usual range of comments from a handful of faculty members who felt obligated to comment on every item of the agenda. Francine Reim, one of the senior members of the English Department, asked several pointed questions about the methodology to be used in a new Psychology course. Dirk leaned over to Chris and whispered, "Ah, her record continues! She has to speak at every meeting. I like to think of her as the Cal Ripken, Jr., of our faculty. I'm sure she holds the record for consecutive meetings with her name mentioned in the minutes!"

Throughout most of the meeting, Chris noticed that many of the faculty spent the time reading their e-mail or browsing the internet. When an agenda item seemed to affect their department, they looked up from their laptops, and occasionally commented. But most of the time, they were intently working on their computers. Dirk noticed him watching one of their colleagues down the aisle, who looked like she was checking her Facebook account. "She's probably blogging about how boring this meeting is," Dirk said softly. "If a student did that in one of her classes, she'd raise holy Hell! But I guess she thinks it's okay for her to do it here. She used to sit and knit through every meeting, which I found just as annoying. Marty once threatened to bring his fly tying vise to a meeting, just to see what the knitters would do. But he never followed through on that. I always wondered how they'd have reacted."

Marty was sitting on the opposite side of the room. He'd come in just before the meeting started, and sat alone. If there was a chance that he might be a lightning rod for Hank's anger if he spoke up today, he didn't want any of his friends to be collateral damage.

After the course proposals were reviewed, there was a brief discussion of a department's proposed changes in its requirements for a major. That ran into difficulties at the outset, so it was sent back to the Curriculum Committee for some fine-tuning. The Assembly found itself in the unusual position of having finished the agenda before the allotted time had expired. Hank, who had looked bored throughout the meeting, kept peeking at his watch. He was obviously eager to adjourn the meeting and get back to his office. He asked if there were any announcements. A few faculty members announced forthcoming events sponsored by their departments. *"To which no one else on campus would ever be interested in going,"* Hank thought. After the last announcement, he looked at his watch again, and asked, "Is there any other business before we adjourn?"

He was about to strike the gavel for adjournment, when Marty raised his hand. "I have a question, if I may." Hank looked at him suspiciously. Sarah kept her eyes on Hank; she studiously avoided looking in Marty's direction. Hank looked irritated, but she was sure he would look worse in a few minutes.

After Hank nodded for him to proceed, Marty stood up so everyone could hear him. "As you know, the History Department co-sponsors an annual symposium with Chartwell every spring."

The mention of "Chartwell" immediately caught Hank's attention. He looked at Marty and said, "I thought you said you had a question. Could you please ask it?"

"I'm getting there," Marty said. "I just thought it would be useful for people to know the background of this. Last week, I had a phone conversation with my counterpart at Chartwell, to organize our planning for the spring symposium. In the course of the conversation, he asked me what our faculty thought of the plans for 'Summerfield Meadows.' I told him I'd never heard of it, so I asked him to explain it. He said that President Thompson had announced it last week. I thought you might be doing that today, but it doesn't look that way. So I'm curious: when will you be making the announcement to the NNC faculty and staff?"

Hank looked like he'd been hit with a sledge hammer. He was completely caught off guard. He stammered a bit, coughed, and drank half a bottle of water before he spoke. He looked at Sarah, who somehow managed to look just as confused by Marty's question as the rest of the faculty were. "Well, . . . er . . . the project you're referring to is . . . uh . . . pretty complex, Marty. I've . . . uh . . . got my staff working on a news release, which I plan to send out early next week. I thought that Chartwell was going to do the same, but apparently they jumped the gun. Looking at the agenda for this meeting, I didn't see how I could give it sufficient attention—though it looks like I was wrong about that today. I'm sorry for leaving this hanging, Marty, but I'm sure you'll understand that I want to give everyone the full information at once. Please be assured that all of you will have a full report about this exciting project next week. I'm sure it's something that many of you will be interested in. Let me just leave it at that."

Marty smiled. "Thanks, Hank! I'm sure the information I got only scratches the surface. I can appreciate how complex it must be to organize something like this. Considering the quality of the staff in your office, and the Dean's, I have no doubt that we'll have all the information we need as soon as you can possibly get it to us. Thank you." He thought to himself, *"The slippery bastard. He didn't even know where to start, but before he was through, he'd even convinced himself that he'd been planning to tell us all about it."*

Hank adjourned the meeting, and Sarah joined him as he headed back to his office. "Is this a new project in cooperation with Chartwell?" she asked. "If you need any assistance from my office, I hope you won't hesitate to let me know."

"What? . . . Oh, sure. Annika will be the point person on this, so I'll have her get in touch with you. After she gets the information to your office, if you could help her draft a news release, that would be very helpful. I'm leaving town this evening, and I won't be back until the beginning of next week. If you and Annika can have something ready for me to send out when I get back, that would be great."

Sarah turned into her own office, and then stopped to watch as Hank continue down the hall to his own. After he left town that evening, she would call Annika, but for now, she knew it was best to pretend that she didn't know anything about what had just happened.

When Hank got back to his office, he told Annika to join him—"IMMEDIATELY!" She could tell he was upset. Although she guessed it might have something to do with Summerfield Meadows, she didn't know how that could have come up at the Faculty Assembly meeting.

"How did the Faculty Assembly go?" she asked.

"Same crap as usual. I don't know why I have to waste my time listening to faculty discussing course proposals. It's almost like listening to them trying to figure out how many angels can dance on the head of a pin. And then that damned Dykstra brought up the Summerfield Meadows project. He can't keep his big nose out of anything."

"How did he know about that? You didn't tell anyone on campus, did you?" She held her breath.

"No, he's been talking to his counterpart at Chartwell, planning that stupid symposium they host every spring— another waste of time and money. Who in Hell needs another history symposium? But apparently Thompson told the Chartwell faculty about the plans for Summerfield Meadows, and this guy blabbed to Marty. Once he got wind of it, you might as well have just broadcast it to the whole campus."

"You didn't really expect it to remain a secret, did you?"

"No, but if they'd gotten started on it before our faculty knew anything about it, most of the lots would have probably been sold. But now we've got to get involved— ASAP. As you know, I'm leaving town this evening, and won't be back until early next week. I need you to contact Thompson's executive assistant, and get the full details from her. Then you need to get together with Sarah and write up a news release for me to send out as soon as I'm back on campus. That damned Dykstra! He really takes the cake!"

"Yeah, he sure does." Fortunately, she was already headed back to her desk, so Hank couldn't see the smile on her face, which stretched from ear to ear.

10
Fourth and Long

Monday, November 18

AFTER ANNIKA GOT THE DETAILS from President Thompson's Executive Assistant, she and Sarah were able to put together a news release about Summerfield Meadows rather quickly. The three of them also worked out a system to administer sales of the lots in the planned subdivision. Everything was to be in place so sales could begin in early January. There was considerable interest on both campuses, especially among younger faculty. So they expected the lots would sell quickly once they became available. Hank still wasn't happy with the idea, but he tried to convince everyone that he was a big supporter. By having Sarah and Annika work out the details, he didn't need to work directly with anyone at Chartwell, or with Rich Summerfield. That was fine with him.

The Chartwell/NNC football game had been the previous Saturday. Chartwell took an early lead, but the Flying Dutch mounted a spirited comeback. As the clock was winding down at the end of the fourth quarter, NNC was down by four points. They had driven the ball inside the Chartwell 10 yard line. After a short run, followed by two penalties and a couple of incomplete passes, it was fourth and goal from the 18-yard line. With ten seconds left on the clock, the quarterback found a receiver open in the end zone. If the referees had called a penalty on a blatant case of pass interference, NNC might have won. They would at least have had a chance to run another play or two. Instead, the Flying Dutch gave up the ball on downs, and ended their season with only one victory. For most NNC fans, a win over Chartwell would have salvaged the season. But even that wouldn't have been enough to satisfy Hank. Long before this loss, he'd made up his mind.

When Hank got to his office Monday morning, he was ready to call Bill Logan and tell him to fire Harry Westbrook. But Harry had already seen the writing on the wall. Sunday afternoon, he'd called Bill to tell him that he was resigning. He hoped that by "falling on his sword," he could spare his staff any retribution. He was wrong. Hank wanted to clean house. Bill had left a message for Hank, asking him to call as soon as he got to his office. When he called Bill back, Hank left no room for doubt. "I want them all gone. Harry and all of the assistant coaches need to pack their bags and get the Hell out of here."

"But this is Division III," Bill pleaded. "The assistant coaches also teach most of our 'life skills' and 'wellness' courses. Most of them have been here for ten or fifteen years. This isn't Division I, where most assistant coaches go with a head coach to a new job."

"That's part of the problem around here! All of these assistants have helped create an environment where the players don't think they can win. We have to change all of that. All of them have to go! And nothing you can say will change my mind. So get on with it! But if you don't want to, I can easily find a new AD, too!"

Word of Hank's decision to fire all of the assistants spread quickly around campus. Most of the regular members of the *"Kaffee Klatsch"* had already heard about it before they got to the CUB for coffee. That did nothing to improve their general opinions about Hank. Instead, it simply confirmed their worst views of him.

Marty, of course, didn't hesitate to share his opinions: "If he cared half as much about the academic atmosphere around here as he does about the football team, we might really be as good as he tells everyone we are. This year, one of the offensive linemen has a good chance of getting a Fulbright, and a wide receiver made it to the interview stage for a Rhodes. But that's not as important to Hank as winning games."

Johanna nodded in agreement. "And it's not like the Athletic Department makes any money off football. People who go to our games will keep goin', whether we win or lose. It's just somethin' they do on Saturday afternoons."

"That's not how Hank sees it, I'm sure." Ed replied. "I bet he thinks that if we were winning more games, we'd fill the stadium, and that would somehow start a positive cash flow. Then he'd have to start a fundraiser to expand the stadium—which is the last thing we need. I don't care how many games we win a year, we'll never come close to filling our stadium as it is. Fortunately, we'll never have to listen to him try to make that argument. This change of coaches should be the last time he meddles in the athletic program before he retires. With any luck, his replacement won't be so hung up on the football team's record."

"Speaking of which," Marty asked, "has anyone heard anything about how the search for a new president is going?"

"Only what was included in the Trustees' initial press release," Dirk said. "They're playing their cards pretty close to their vest."

Johanna laughed, "From what I've heard, part of that is to keep Hank from stickin' his nose into the process. He did manage to get a couple of his 'Golden Children' appointed to the search committee. But apparently somebody must have figured out that he was hoping to influence the committee. They've been making sure no one leaks any information—to Hank, or to anyone else."

"Annika's on the committee, too," Ed said. "It probably makes sense to have her involved. But Hank probably thinks that's to his advantage. I'm sure he thinks she'll be his direct pipeline of information."

"My guess is that he'll be disappointed there," Marty replied. "I'm sure he expects her to tell him whatever he wants to know, and to make sure the search goes the way he wants. But he shouldn't make the mistake of equating her loyalty to the College, or her respect for his office, with blind loyalty to him. From what I've seen, she's not likely to confuse those. And she definitely won't do something that she doesn't think is in the best interests of NNC. If the Trustees say they don't want any leaks, she'll do her best to make sure there aren't any. For someone who never attended NNC, she has more loyalty to the place than most alums."

"That's the good news," Dirk said. "But the bad news is that the Trustees probably want to keep everything secret until they announce who the successful candidate is. That's the way a lot of schools have been running searches lately. The Faculty Assembly needs to take a firm stand: we need to meet the finalists, and they need to come to campus for question and answer sessions. We can't let them just stick us with someone they pick in secret. If they do that, they'll doom faculty/administration relations 'from the get-go.'"

"It seems to be a trend around the country," Marty grumbled. "Regents, or Trustees, or whatever you want to call them, argue that if they make public any information about potential candidates, it would jeopardize their positions on their home campus. If they weren't selected, then their positions would be compromised, and they wouldn't be able to continue working effectively. It might even cost them their jobs, if they have overly sensitive Regents who are concerned about 'loyalty.' So, they contend, most potentially good candidates would get scared off, and we'd be stuck with a dud."

"I can understand that, up to a point," Dirk said. "But at the same time, a lot of candidates use a search to bolster their own positions back home. They never really have any intention of taking a job, but they let their schools know that someone else wants them. Then they use that as leverage to get more money. They stay there for a few more years, and try the same thing again. After a while, though, the Trustees may start to get wise. If they're not careful, the Trustees will call their bluff, and they'll have to take a job that's not what they really wanted. But if they're lucky, when they do get ready to leave, their old schools will still want them enough to make one more, higher offer to get them to stay. Then they use that to squeeze more money out of the new place. It's a vicious cycle."

Marty agreed: "All of that works fine for someone at the Dean's level or above. They have a golden aura about them, at least as far as Trustees are concerned. But for Trustees—and Deans or Presidents—faculty are a dime a dozen. When's the last time anyone ever saw Trustees offer a faculty member more money to stay somewhere? That almost never happens. Instead, if someone threatens to leave a faculty position, Trustees usually see that as a chance to bring in a younger prof, with a lower salary. You'd think that what's good for the goose would be good for the gander, too. But not when it involves how Trustees treat administrators. Faculty are expendable. Administrators are a precious commodity."

Dirk nodded in agreement. "Hank froze faculty positions over a decade ago. Even when he was trying to push for continually larger enrollments, he announced in no uncertain terms that there would be no new faculty positions added. And he's stuck to that. But how many new administrative positions has he added? When 'sustainability' became the hot buzz-word among college presidents, Hank had to add an 'Office for Sustainability Concerns.' But one 'Sustainability Coordinator' wasn't enough; now he has two assistants, plus an additional secretary. And the work that used to be accomplished by the Dean and one Associate Dean is now spread out to a second Associate Dean and three Assistant Deans. I'm surprised he hasn't created a few 'Deputy Assistant Deans,' or some such nonsense. But meanwhile, instead of the two Administrative Assistants we had for the departments in Macalester, now there's only one, and she's responsible for Philosophy and Religious Studies, too. Hank cuts low paid positions to make way for more administrators."

"But when 'sustainability' is no longer the hot ticket," Johanna said, "that office can be replaced by somethin' else. If he'd added tenure-line faculty positions, once they got tenure, he'd be stuck with 'em. Hank likes the flexibility of hirin' and firin' as the mood strikes 'im."

Dirk picked up his cup and napkin, wiping off the table in front of him. "On that cheery note, I've got to get back to my office. One of my students turned in a paper that I forwarded on to the Student Honors Council. The Chair of the Council wants to talk to me about it before they meet with the student."

Chris, who had been a silent witness to the preceding conversation, held out his hand to stop Dirk. "Is there a problem with it?"

"Oh, it's a great paper!" Dirk laughed. "So great that someone else already got it published."

"What gave it away?" Ed asked.

"For starters, the student who turned it in isn't the world's best writer. The two shorter papers he wrote earlier in the semester got a D+ and a very generous C-. His midterm wasn't written any better, either. So now he turns in a twenty-page research paper, when the assignment was for ten to 15 pages. And it was very well written. I gave it a B+, only because it didn't have a clear thesis. I was about to enter that in the grade book, when the other grades sort of flashed me a warning. So I randomly picked a sentence out of the paper, and did an internet search. In two or three seconds, I had a link to the paper. Not surprisingly, it had been published in one of the journals I'd listed as a good resource for their first two papers."

"So, what's the Chair of the Council need to talk to you about? Seems pretty cut and dried to me," Ed asked.

Dirk laughed. "I think they're trying to figure out why I was only going to give it a B+, when it was good enough to publication."

"How are you going to answer that one?" Marty chuckled. "You're going to scare away anyone who ever thought of taking one of your classes."

"Oh, that's easy! That's the reason he didn't have a thesis: he simply deleted the first page. He may have figured that he'd make enough typos in transcribing it that I wouldn't notice how much better it was written than everything else he'd submitted to me. But he—or more likely someone he hired to transcribe it—didn't make many typos. Most of it was probably just 'cut and paste' from the article on-line. Even if he had, that wouldn't have hidden it from me. On his other papers, spelling was the least of his problems."

Johanna shook her head. "I never cease to be amazed at how naïve students think we are."

"There are obviously a few exceptions," Marty said, "but most of the students I've caught cheating aren't spending their free time at Mensa meetings. A couple of years ago, Johansson had a student in History 102 turn in a book review. It was more appropriate for my section of 101, which I'd taught the previous semester, than it was for 102. But, if you were generous, the period it covered probably fit the early part of his class as much as it did the end of mine. Since it was a good book, he decided to let that go—until he got to the second page."

"What was the problem there," Chris asked.

"Well, the title page had the student's name—something like Frank Johnson—and 'History 102.' But the 'header' on every subsequent page read, 'Jim Smith, History 101.' He called me to ask if Jim Smith had taken 101 from me—which he had. And that reminded me that he'd turned in a review of that book. When he told me about the paper he had in his hand, we checked the campus directory. Lo and behold, they lived in the same dorm! Imagine that! They were both called before the Honors Council, and they both maintained that Jim was innocent. Frank said he'd been using Jim's computer for something else and saw the paper, and decided to help himself. Frank wound up on disciplinary probation, and they cautioned Jim that they'd be watching him to make sure that similar problems didn't recur."

Dirk shook his head. "It would be bad enough if it were just the students. But the same kind of crap happens with their profs." He looked at Chris and said, "I know we've already told you about the problem we had a few years ago, when one of el Deano's Golden Children tried to fake having her Ph.D. And she almost got away with it."

"And don't let anybody try to tell you that it's a recent phenomenon," Marty grumbled. "When I was in grad school, the Chair of another department left 'under a cloud.' A few years later, I finally heard the story from my Chair. The guy was only an associate professor, and he needed to publish at least one more article to be eligible for Full. He could tell that the administration was starting to up the ante in terms of requirements for tenure and promotion, so he figured he'd better get an article published as soon as possible if he wanted to make full professor."

"So what did he do, lift part of someone else's paper?" Chris asked.

"Worse than that," Marty laughed. "The Dean got a call from the editor of a journal in this guy's field. He said there were 'problems' with it, and suggested that the Dean have a committee look at it. The Dean gave it to a committee of other department chairs. It took them less than five minutes to resolve the issue—the idiot had submitted a previously published article in its entirety! Since it had been published in a different journal, I guess he figured that no one would ever notice. This was pre-internet, so it wasn't just a simple matter of doing a quick on-line search."

"I can't believe someone would cheat that blatantly!" Chris said.

"Oh, that's just part of it. When they confronted him, can you guess what he gave as an excuse?"

"I wouldn't even know where to start," Dirk said. The others nodded in agreement.

"Okay, now remember, this is a department chair. Theoretically, he was one of the academic officials at a major state university. When they asked him to explain what had happened, he said, 'Oh, that's simple. My secretary forgot to put the quotation marks at the beginning and at the end.'"

"Ya HAVE to be makin' that up," Johanna laughed. "No one could be that blatant!"

"I kid you not! That was his excuse. Of course, they didn't buy it. He was out the door at the end of the semester. His academic career, such as it was, was over. But he landed on his feet, as they often do."

"How so?" Chris asked.

"He'd been very active in local politics, and his state representative got him appointed to some cushy board at the state capital. I think he was probably earning a lot more money there than he had as a department chair."

"Okay, that's it," Dirk said. "On THAT cheery note, I need to get out of here! I assume I'll see most of you before Thanksgiving, but if I don't, have a great Turkey Day!"

The rest of the group started clearing the cups and dishes, too. As they started back to Macalester, Marty turned to Chris. "Speaking of Thanksgiving, I've been meaning to ask: do you have any plans for the holiday? Since we have classes on Monday and Tuesday, it doesn't give you much time to fly to Seattle. If you don't have any plans, I'd love to have you join me for Thanksgiving dinner. All of my family will be coming, and my daughter and daughter-in-law have given me strict instructions that they're in charge of dinner. So I can assure you that the meal will be much better than it would be if I were the cook."

"That would be great!" Chris said. "I hadn't figured out what I was going to do, but I'm sure anything I'd come up with couldn't compare to a family Thanksgiving dinner. Are you sure your family won't mind?"

"Not at all. In fact, one of them suggested it. My son, who's an NNC alum, was asking me about 'Johansson's replacement.' When I mentioned that you weren't married, he suggested that I invite you to join us. He remembers what it was like the first year he was in law school, when he wasn't able to come home for Thanksgiving. Just a word of warning: my grandkids can sometimes be a bit 'lively.' They're not wild or out of control, but like any kids, they can create a bit of noise from time to time."

"That's not a problem. It'll be like having my nieces and nephews around. I'm looking forward to it. Is there anything I can bring?"

"My daughter-in-law was very specific about that—she and my daughter are in charge of dinner. So I wouldn't want to get in their way on that account. If you'd like to bring a bottle of wine, that would be great. That Washington wine you brought to the department picnic was a big hit."

"That's easy to arrange! I'm looking forward to meeting your family!"

"Great – why don't you plan on coming by around 1 or 1:30. We generally watch a little football, but just so you know, the rule in the house is that the tv is off while we're enjoying dinner."

"That's not an issue for me. I don't follow pro football that closely, unless the Seahawks are playing—and they're usually not in the Thanksgiving Day mix."

Chris turned toward Macalester, but Marty kept heading in the direction of the Carroll Center. "I wish I could walk back to the office with you, Chris, but I have a meeting with the Dean. I got a cryptic message from Mary de Smet, her new secretary, informing me that 'Dean Christiansen would like to talk to you about next year's staffing for *die Quellen*.' No other details. I'm afraid the honeymoon may be over with our new dean."

"You can't be sure, Marty. She's been fair about everything she's done so far, hasn't she? Maybe she will be regarding *die Quellen*, too."

"One can only hope. Wish me luck!"

*   *   *   *   *

MARTY WAS A LITTLE EARLY for his appointment, so he made a stop in the men's room on the way. Just to make sure he didn't run into Hank in the process, he used the rest room on the first floor. When he got to Sarah's office, he was still a few minutes ahead of schedule. Since Mary had been hired after Sarah arrived on campus, he had only seen her at Department Chair meetings. He hadn't really met her yet. So he quickly introduced himself to her, and then took a seat. Based on his previous experience with deans, he expected to be cooling his heels for fifteen or twenty minutes before he finally got to talk to Sarah, and then he'd probably get the bum's rush before her next appointment. So he was pleasantly surprised by what happened next. He hadn't really gotten settled, and was just starting to reach for a copy of the alumni magazine on a nearby table when Mary said, "Dr. Dykstra, Dean Christiansen can see you now. Please go into her office."

Marty smiled, but thought to himself, *"Okay, how bad can it be? She can't expect us to teach more sections of* die Quellen *than we already do. Even Rothman saw he had to back off that one."*

Sarah got up from her desk and shook his hand. She closed the door behind him as she pointed to one of the vacant chairs set around a small table. She took a seat across the table, rather than returning to her chair behind the desk. She offered him coffee, but since his stomach was still sloshing from the *Kaffee Klatsch*, he declined. She poured herself a cup from the carafe on the table.

"Okay, let's get this over with, without the chit-chat," he thought.

Sarah took a sip of her coffee, and set the cup back on the table. She picked up a stack of papers, which Marty recognized. They were the departmental staffing proposals for the coming year. His was somewhere in the pile. At least it wasn't the one on top, with red marks all over it.

"I've been trying to get a handle on staffing for next year," she said. "Everything in your department seems to fit pretty well. But I have some staffing issues with *die Quellen.*"

Marty was about to say something, but thought he should see where she was going with this conversation. So he simply asked, "What kinds of issues? That's usually all worked out by *die Quellen's* director. It doesn't matter who the director is, the procedure is always the same: we just get a memo telling us what sections we're teaching. End of discussion."

"Well, it's a little more complicated this year. I had a meeting with Hannelore van Leuven yesterday." Sarah pointed to the staffing form on the top of the pages, with all the red marks. "She proposed a list of German courses for next year that is essentially a re-hash of what she'd done every year for the past decade. Unfortunately, her enrollments in the upper division courses have never gotten to double digits. Most years, she's lucky if she gets five or six, which I consider a minimum for any course to be offered."

Marty held his breath. Based on previous confrontations with Hannelore, he wasn't sure he liked where this was heading.

"Hannelore likes things 'a certain way,' you might say," he replied. "When Dirk was secretary of the Faculty Assembly, she called him to let him know that she didn't think his minutes were complete enough. She said she'd be happy to loan him her notes from the meetings, so he could provide a more accurate record of what was said. He declined the offer. She wasn't pleased." He paused for a minute, took a deep breath, and asked, "How did you respond to her proposal?"

"I told her that she was going to have to come up with some new courses that would draw students, or else teach a section of *die Quellen* every semester. I'm sure you can figure out what she suggested."

"Let me guess: she wants to teach a course in German history, right? She's proposed that to us several times in the past, and every time, the department has voted unanimously not to allow that to happen."

"That's interesting. She told me that she wasn't sure you'd go along with the idea, but wanted to bring it up to me first. Okay, that's one strike against her. She said she had the equivalent of a master's in history from Germany, so she was qualified to teach history for you."

Once again, Marty stopped himself before he said what he was really thinking. He had the feeling it was best to let Sarah continue on her own without him possibly messing things up worse than they probably were already.

"Just so you know, Marty, I told her I didn't think it was a very good idea."

Marty straightened up in his seat. *"Did I just hear what I thought I heard?"*

"First of all, we have a history department where everyone has gone through a selection process, and as much as possible, given the nature of searches, you have the people who best fit the needs of the department. Isn't there someone in your department who can teach German history?"

"Sure—both Chris and I can. My classes would cover earlier periods: Reformation, Thirty Years War, Enlightenment, that sort of thing. I know that when he was teaching in Oregon, Chris taught a course on Hitler and Nazi Germany, and I'm sure he could cover Germany and postwar Europe as well."

"That's what I thought. Hannelore thought it was deplorable that a department of your size doesn't teach German history. I looked at the schedule of what you've all taught over the last five years, and it doesn't look like you teach many specialized, upper division courses at all!

251

But I also see that you spend 1/3 of your time teaching *die Quellen*. Right?"

At first, Marty was speechless. *"I still don't believe what I'm hearing. Should I pinch myself to see if I'm dreaming?"*

When he didn't reply immediately, Sarah repeated, "Right, Marty?"

"Yes, that's right. I'm sorry--that's something I've been saying for at least ten years, but nobody ever listened to me."

"Well, it doesn't seem like rocket science to me. I told Hannelore that it didn't make any sense to me to have her teach German history instead of *die Quellen*, and then have an historian unable to teach German history BECAUSE he's teaching *die Quellen*. As long as I'm in charge, we're going to have our classes taught by members of the appropriate department."

"And how did Hannelore react to that?" Marty asked cautiously.

"She didn't seem very pleased. But I told her that Hank had stressed to me how much of an honor it is for people to be able to teach in a course that's central to the very essence of this college. I reminded her about the 'intellectual commons' and 'shared inquiry,' and how important those are to Hank. So she should consider herself lucky to have that opportunity. I don't think she was convinced, but that's the way it's going to be."

Marty smiled, but he was still afraid to say anything.

"I don't watch a lot of football," she added, "but I know enough to recognize an end run when I see one." She paused a moment, and then asked, "Don't you have anything to say? You've been remarkably quiet."

"Would 'Hallelujah and Amen' be appropriate?" Marty laughed.

"I wouldn't go that far," Sarah said, "but I was sure you'd appreciate the news. The problem is, now I have another potential issue as it relates to your department."

"What's that?"

"Think about it. The way I turned down her request, I've pretty much locked your department into teaching German history next year. I know you're a popular teacher, but I suspect that a course on Hitler and Nazi Germany would probably attract more students than one of your early modern classes, right?"

"I hate to admit it, but I don't think there's any question."

"And since the classes you proposed for him to teach next year are part of a regular rotation, the only way Chris could teach German history would be to do that instead of a section of *die Quellen*."

"Everyone who teaches *die Quellen* has always had to teach both semesters, unless they have a sabbatical. With rare exceptions (and NEVER an historian), no one has ever been allowed to teach just one semester."

"Well, that's something that will be changing soon," Sarah said bluntly.

"If that's the case, I'm sure Chris would prefer to teach German history instead of a section of *die Quellen*."

"That's where the problem comes. How will the rest of your department react if 'the new guy' gets out of something they've had to teach every year? Will that pose problems for him when it comes time for Third Year Review or Tenure evaluation?"

Marty thought for a moment. "I don't think it would be a problem for anyone, since it's only one section, and on a one-time basis—particularly considering the fact that none of them wants Hannelore to ever teach a class with a History designation." He paused a moment, and then smiled. "I'm sure they would all be agreeable . . . particularly if they knew they might find themselves with a similar schedule change sometime in the near future."

Sarah laughed. "Somehow I knew you'd see it that way. Why don't you run it by your department—but do it without Chris there, in case there are any objections. Don't put him in an awkward position. And make sure they know it's my idea. If they're all agreeable, we'll change your department schedule accordingly. And tell them that I'm looking at ways to make this a more common option for all of them."

"I'm sure there will be no objections—especially about the last part! I'll bring it up at our meeting this week, and let you know as soon as I've talked to all of them."

"This obviously brings up a bigger question."

Marty was afraid to ask, but finally brought himself to say, "What's that?"

"What's the 'special magic' with *die Quellen* supposed to be, anyway? I've been trying to figure that out ever since I got here last summer."

Marty hesitated for a moment before he replied, "Well, I'm probably not the person to ask. It's well known that I don't hold a majority opinion about the course."

"I know—that's why I want to hear what you have to say. Everyone else around here does nothing but sing its praises. Hank makes it sound like it was dropped from the heavens on golden tablets. Even Hannelore was going on and on about how great the course is—at least until I told her that she'd be teaching it next year. I guess I must have been absent when they passed out the magic Kool Aid."

Marty just about choked when she mentioned "golden tablets," and it was all he could do to keep from bursting out laughing when she got to the "Kool Aid." After a brief chuckle slipped out, he composed himself, and tried to answer her question seriously.

"When you get right down to it, the problem is essentially 'Athens vs. Jerusalem.'"

"What in the Hell is that supposed to mean?"

"I'm sorry, that's something from my history background. When I started grad school, I was stressing out over my first exam in a graduate history class. One of my friends said, 'What are you worried about? There's really only one question.' I had no idea what he was talking about. So he looked at me and said, 'No matter how you word it, it all comes down to Athens vs.

Jerusalem.' I was just as confused as you are right now. So I asked him to explain what he was talking about."

"I'd appreciate it if you could do the same for me," she laughed.

"If you wanted the 'long version,' I would start out by talking about how the early Christian scholar Tertullian asked the question, 'What has Athens to do with Jerusalem?'"

"I think I'd probably prefer the 'short version.'"

"That's what I figured. Essentially, it's 'faith vs. reason,' or as applied to the question at hand, 'idea vs. reality.' Tertullian was arguing that religion and philosophy—or scholarship—are incompatible."

"Okay, so Athens represents philosophy, and Jerusalem stands for religion. And that's supposed to be the answer to every question? I don't follow the logic there."

"Well, I admit, my friend was often given to hyperbole. But to a certain extent, I agree with him. If you look at it as 'idea vs. reality,' it probably makes more sense. Ideas tend to take on a life of their own. People believe in them, even when there are specific examples—facts—that show that they're not necessarily correct. Look at how people view the issue of climate change, or how they evaluate presidents or other political leaders. No amount of evidence will convince a Tea Party member that the Obama administration ever did anything good, or that a Republican president might have ever contributed to the deficit."

"And that's what you think is going on with *die Quellen?*"

"Sure. Most of the campus is convinced that it's the greatest course ever taught. They heard someone say it's central to the very being of NNC, and they believe it. But they've never had anything to do with it themselves. Have you read the external review that was conducted about five years ago?"

"Yes . . . I was going to ask you about that"

"Well, you're one step ahead of most people, including your predecessor and Hank."

"It had some good things to say about the program, but there were some fairly harsh criticisms, too. How could they overlook those?"

"They simply 'cherry-picked.' I have no doubt that they skimmed through it, and read what they wanted to see. At the same time, they just ignored what they didn't agree with. It was like it wasn't even there. So despite the negative elements of that evaluation, everyone keeps saying this is such a great course that we can't ever change it. Hank even brags about how glowing the evaluation was."

"That's something I don't understand. Hank told me he's been insistent on one key point: that whatever changes the Faculty make with the curriculum, they can't change *die Quellen*. But it HAS changed, quite a bit, from what I see. That's mentioned right at the beginning of the evaluation. It doesn't look anything at all like the way it was originally taught."

"You'll never convince very many people of that. It's been 'refined,' or 'improved,' but never 'changed.' That's the difference between Idea and Reality. And I can tell you from bitter experience, you could talk until you're blue in the face, and no one would ever listen to anything besides their idea of it. There've been several attempts to make some changes, but every time, after a year or so, everyone who likes it as it is starts throwing their hands in the air. They run around screaming that they can't deal with the new changes, and it reverts back to the old model. The only changes that have stuck have been things that make it even more comfortable for humanities faculty. If anyone from my department complains about that, they're criticized for not being supportive of the program that their department signed onto thirty years ago. Of course, I've been bitching about the course for so long that no one listens to anything I have to say about it."

"I'm sure you're familiar with Margaret Mead, the anthropologist," Sarah said. "She argued that if you want to bring change in a society, you have to do it in one fell swoop. If you try to do it in small, incremental steps, institutional inertia will prevent any real change from ever taking hold."

"I know my colleagues in the Anthro department don't necessarily agree with Mead any more, but I think she was right on that point. My grad school friend had a corollary to 'Athens vs. Jerusalem': 'continuity vs. change.' Societies—or institutions—don't like change. Most individuals don't, either. Look at NNC: faculty who don't have any Dutch background think 'there's too much Dutch stuff around here,' while someone like me thinks that what little there is, is almost all superficial. How much do we hang onto our heritage, and how much do we let go as we get farther from our roots?"

"I don't have any Dutch heritage, but I recognize how important that is to the College. Hank seems to as well. . . . Why are you making that face?"

"When it serves as a way to get a big donation, or to get him an award from the Dutch government, he's 'Mr. Netherlands.' But about ten years ago, a local group wanted to start a campaign to establish a 'Dutch Heritage Center' on campus. Hank blocked it—he said we shouldn't be catering to any individual constituency at the exclusion of others. We needed to be 'more inclusive.'"

"But he seemed excited about the new Dutch Studies Center when he announced in August."

"Sure, because someone was making a big donation for it. I'm sure that he lobbied for an 'unrestricted gift,' but knowing the van der Kellens, I'm sure they wouldn't give money for anything but a Center for Dutch Studies. So to get their money, he was happy to be the leading advocate of their cause, at least temporarily. Notice that he also managed to get his name associated with it, too."

"The College obviously has had to change, as the founding generation died off, and their children and grandchildren became more assimilated. I can't imagine that it would've survived if it hadn't adapted to changing times."

"Absolutely! He lost the support of a few of the more conservative alums when he said that beer and wine could be served at functions in the CUB—though not at student events. But most of them didn't have a problem with that. And the catering service now makes a bundle by hosting wedding receptions and other events where most people like to enjoy 'an adult beverage.' Societies become stagnant if they don't evolve gradually. Colleges are a kind of society. If they don't maintain some dynamic growth, and continue to develop, they'll fall into a kind of intellectual dry rot. The problem is, how do you resolve the tension between continuity and change? And to get back to my original point, how do you reconcile Idea and Reality? "

"I guess it's my job to figure out how to find that balance at NNC," Sarah sighed. "I don't know what kind of change will come to *die Quellen*, but I'm convinced that it's not sustainable with the current structure—especially regarding staffing. To meet our budgetary needs, Hank says we need to increase enrollments. That means we'll need to have more people teaching in *die Quellen*. I'm not sure yet how we'll accomplish that. But I can tell you with certainty that next year, there will be a senior-level German prof teaching in the course, and one member of the History Department will be teaching only one section of it. It's up to your department to decide whether that will be you or Chris. Let me know as soon as you've figured that out. Thanks for coming in this morning, Marty."

There were dozens of things that Marty was thinking as a reply, but he thought it would be best not to push his luck. It was clear that as far as Sarah was concerned, the meeting was over. He got up, shook her hand, and said, "Thank you! I have to say, this has been the most amazing meeting I've ever had in this office. I'll be very interested to see what ideas you come up with. I'll get back to you about the German history course as soon as we have our next department meeting."

When he got out in the hall, he stopped, looked to make sure no one was looking, and then pinched himself. Having confirmed that he wasn't dreaming, he went down the stairs, rather than walking past Hank's office to the elevator. It had been too good a morning to risk ruining with a chance meeting with Hank.

*   *   *   *   *

WHILE MARTY HAD BEEN MEETING WITH SARAH, Hank had been having a good morning, too. But his was more tangible.

About the same time that Marty was starting down the stairs, Hank was just finishing a phone call. He hung up the phone, pumped both hands in the air, and shouted, "YES!"

His outburst prompted Annika to poke her head around the corner. "What's going on? Did you and Mike Nagel just land a big donation?"

"No, nothing like that, at least for the College. But for me, it comes pretty close!"

"What do you mean?" she asked hesitantly. She wasn't sure she wanted to hear his answer.

"That was Dale McCutcheon. We've known each other since we were both deans together in our first administrative positions. He was Dean of Sciences, and I was Dean of Humanities and Social Sciences. We started at the same time, and quickly became friends. We've kept in touch ever since then."

"Is he the one you and Hannah vacation with sometimes?"

"Yeah—they have a cabin in Michigan's Upper Peninsula. We don't go there every year, but fairly often. He was president of a college in Ohio, about like NNC. He retired last year, and has been working on a project that's about to take off."

"What kind of project?" She thought to herself, *"Do I dare ask? It's sure to be some kind of scam that's going to make Hank even more money."*

"He's starting an outfit called 'Academic Executive Seminars.' He just finalized a lease on a conference center in the Phoenix area, right next to a golf course. He'll run seminars for deans, provosts, college presidents, that type of thing."

"And this is good news for you . . . how?"

"Duh!—what do you expect? I'm going to be his partner. As the founder, he'll be the organization's President, and I'll be the Executive Vice-President. We'll live down there through the winter, and then clear out in the summer. Nobody's going to sign up for an executive seminar in Phoenix in the summer!"

"So, who's going to sign up for these seminars? Can you generate enough business to make a go of it?"

"No problem. Both of us have enough contacts in the Upper Midwest to get it started, and as soon as word spreads, it will take off from there."

"You're sure about that? There's enough of a market to cover expenses?"

Hank laughed. "Of course there is. Right now, most people send their new deans or presidents to seminars at Harvard. But once they've done that, they're looking for something else. Think about it—if you're freezing your ass off at a small school up in North Dakota or Wisconsin, wouldn't you like to go to an administrative seminar in Phoenix? Academic sessions in the morning, and a round of golf in the afternoon. Decent food and accommodations that are comfortable, but not excessively plush, a chance to network with peers, learn from experienced professionals, all that good stuff."

"And colleges will pay for all of that? Most of them are tightening belts and still trying to deal with the recession. How likely is a Board of Trustees going to be to foot the bill for something like that?"

"Oh, you are naïve, aren't you? They'd never send faculty to something like that. But they always want their top administrators to be up on all of the newest trends in recruitment, marketing, fundraising, infrastructure, and anything else you can think of. We'll also host meetings for Regents or Trustees—you know, 'retreats'—so they can get away from the hassles of their campuses and focus on the issues at hand. And alumni offices are always looking for ways to 'engage' their constituents. Hosting a 'senior learning seminar' at our site will draw a lot of interest. They can have one of their faculty lead a short seminar on some topic of interest: ecology, sustainability, ethics in government—whatever the current 'hot topic' might be. And if it's associated with something called 'Academic Executive Seminars,' it will sound a lot more serious than going to a place with a name like 'Whispering Palms Resort.' They can get out of a frigid Midwest winter and expand their intellectual horizons."

"And play golf?"

"Of course. There's a lot of networking and follow-up from sessions that takes place on a golf course."

"If it's such a lucrative deal, why is the conference center available so conveniently?"

"That's the good part. Dale's brother-in-law lives down there, and he's a real estate attorney. Dale asked him to keep his eyes open for something like this. The previous occupants had a good business going, but got too greedy. They used some 'creative accounting,' and got involved in running professional training in areas where they didn't have the necessary certification. State bar associations and medical associations get really touchy about those things. So between the IRS and the state licensing boards, they went out of business. Dale's brother-in-law heard about it, and called him right away. Dale just signed the lease papers yesterday."

"So, let me guess, you already have your legal counsel in place? Dale's brother-in-law, right?"

"Of course. But except for occasional issues like our incorporation application, there's not a lot for him to do. That's the nice thing about executive seminars for academics: we don't have to worry about running afoul of accreditation boards. If we put together seminars that deal with the current hot topics in academia, we'll have an eager clientele. We're not doing anything shady or underhanded. We'll have well-run seminars, balanced off with the chance for some relaxation on the golf course in the afternoon. There are plenty of specialists we can contract to give the actual seminars: education profs, management specialists—all of whom welcome the chance to pick up a little money on the side. They're happy, the people who attend are happy. We'll be filling a need in the marketplace."

"If you have other people running the seminars, what do you and Dale contribute to this enterprise?"

"Why, leadership, of course! We'll provide the 'vision.' We have the contacts to recruit the first few groups, and it will take off from there. In a year or two, we hope to branch off to develop an 'executive search' service."

"Head-hunters?"

"Sure. Nobody conducts a presidential search these days without using a head-hunter. It's the same with most dean searches, too. And with the contacts that we'll develop with our seminars, we should be able to break into that market pretty easily."

"Well, good luck! At least you know you'll have something to keep you busy when you retire." To herself, she thought, *"And good riddance! I'll be sure to let your successor know what quality to expect from your seminars!"*

"Thanks! Say, will you keep your ears tuned for a call from Hannah? She and Gene just took off for a visit to several alumni gatherings this week, and she said she'd call me when they got to Duluth this afternoon."

"Where else are they going? Someplace warmer than Duluth, I hope."

"Not much warmer. They're sticking to Minnesota and Wisconsin this trip. After Thanksgiving, she and I will be going to Arizona to an alumni meeting in Tucson. We'll probably stop by Phoenix to meet with Dale and his wife, and check out the new conference center. And then we'll be back here in time for the Christmas music program. If it's like the last one, I think I'd rather stay in Arizona."

"You told the Music Department that you wanted them to really expand the program, which they're doing!"

"I know, but they don't have to pick all that esoteric, modern crap. When I have to sit in the front row for every performance, I don't want to listen to something that's bound to put me to sleep."

"Okay, I'll let you know when Hannah calls." As she went back to her desk, she shook her head and thought, *"I still don't see how he can be so relaxed about her traveling around with Gene on so many trips. I don't have a good feeling about that."*

*   *   *   *   *

HANNAH CALLED HANK'S OFFICE ABOUT 4:30, and Annika answered. "We'd hoped to get here earlier, but there was some traffic backed up coming into Duluth. And since it's November, it's no surprise that we ran into some snow near the Iron Range. But we're checked into our rooms. Tell Hank I'll call him when we get back from the alumni dinner."

After they had a chance to freshen up and change clothes, Hannah and Gene met in the lobby and drove to the alumni event. Although there was a cash bar at the reception, both of them stayed with soft drinks, since some of the older, more conservative alumni had never come to grips with the idea of alcohol being associated with NNC. They did each allow themselves a glass of wine with dinner, which they used to toast the officers of the local alumni chapter. Hannah said a few words on behalf of Hank, expressing his regret at being unable to attend all of the alumni gatherings that had been scheduled in his honor that fall. Gene gave a report from the Board of Trustees. He thanked everyone for their contributions to the most recent fund drive, and gave a PowerPoint presentation highlighting the latest construction projects on campus. He gave them a good-natured 'warning' that the new president would undoubtedly be starting a new capital campaign. And after giving a brief overview of the status of the search process currently underway, he assured them that the future of NNC looked bright. He distributed a few pledge envelopes, and got a reasonably good response. Mike Nagel would be pleased.

They got back to their rooms at the hotel about 9:30. Hannah called Hank and gave him a report about the alumni gathering. "You didn't miss anything," she laughed. "There were the standard questions, the usual complaints about wanting to make sure they know where their money goes, and finally the local alumni rep raised a toast in honor of your leadership. Consider yourself lucky not to have been here."

"Thanks for covering it for me. And thank Gene, too. I really appreciate it."

"We're supposed to meet for breakfast at 7:30, so we can get an early start on the road to Wisconsin. I'll be sure to tell him then."

Gene had kicked off his shoes and had turned on Monday Night Football. He was thinking about heading down to the bar to get a beer, when he heard a knock on the door. He was about to open the door to the hallway, when he realized the knock was on the door to the adjoining room. When he opened it, Hannah was holding a bottle of wine and two glasses.

"I didn't think you'd ever get off the phone with Hank," he said. "I thought I was going to have to go down to the bar to get a drink. I'm glad you thought to bring this along."

"Since we really couldn't have more than a glass of wine at an alumni dinner, and it probably wouldn't look good for us to be seen sitting in a lobby bar together, this seemed like the logical alternative. Here's a corkscrew—would you please do the honors?"

Gene sat down on the couch and Hannah sat next to him. "Hank said to be sure to thank you for helping with these alumni events. So, on his behalf, thank you!"

"It's my pleasure." He raised his glass, and said, "To a productive and enjoyable trip!"

Hannah clinked his glass with hers, and took a sip of wine. "Cheers! Remember, we're supposed to meet for breakfast at 7:30 in the morning."

"I know. Shall I phone you or nudge you?"

"What do you think?" she asked, as she raised her glass for another toast.

11
Little Pitchers

Thursday, November 28—Thanksgiving

CHRIS GOT TO MARTY'S HOUSE about 1:15. He'd stopped by a florist's Wednesday afternoon, so he arrived at Marty's with a Thanksgiving floral arrangement, as well as two bottles of Washington wine. He wasn't sure if people would prefer red or white with turkey dinner, so he brought a bottle of each. With both hands full, he wasn't sure how he'd manage to ring the doorbell. But as he started up the front steps, the door opened.

"Here, let me help you with some of that! You must be Chris. Dad's been saying great things about you. I'm Mike, by the way." He took the flowers, and extended his right hand to shake Chris's. "Dad's out back with Erica— my 11-year-old. The last time I checked, it sounded like he was teaching her how to shoot a hook shot. If you want to stick your head out there and let him know you're here, the door's straight ahead. Otherwise, you can take off your coat and make yourself comfortable until they come in."

"It's a little chilly for basketball outdoors, isn't it?" Chris asked.

"You obviously haven't lived in Minnesota very long, have you?" a tall, blond woman laughed as she came out of the kitchen. "If it's not cold enough to put down ice for hockey, you can still play basketball. Usually by Thanksgiving, it's a little cold to play basketball outside. But this year, Erica's in luck. She's just starting to play on an organized team at school, and she's been dying to have her Grandpa teach her more than she's learning there. He keeps trying to tell her that he only played a couple years of college ball, but as far as she's concerned, he's a member of the NBA Hall of Fame." After she finished wiping her hands on a dishtowel, she reached across the table and shook Chris's hand. "I'm Karen, Mike's wife. If you do go outside, be forewarned: she'll probably recruit you for some instruction, too."

"Uh-oh," Chris laughed. "It sounds like Marty's been telling stories about my alleged basketball career."

"Not too much," Mike said, "but as far as Erica is concerned right now, anyone who's ever played basketball for a college team pretty much walks on water. She's convinced herself that she's going to go to college on a basketball scholarship. Dad's doing his best to convince her to focus on an academic scholarship first. If she gets a basketball scholarship, too, he would love that. But the odds are much higher of her making it on grades. And if she goes to a Division III school, like NNC, there are no athletic scholarships. She's a bright kid, and I think Dad's already got her pegged for a Rhodes Scholarship—not that he's biased, or anything," he laughed

Chris stepped out behind the house, to where Marty and Erica were working on the fundamentals of a hook shot. When Chris said "Hi," Erica sent a quick bounce pass in his direction. "Let's see what you've got from 3-point range!"

"It looks like my reputation is on the line!" Chris laughed. He dribbled the ball a couple of times to get the feel of it, and arched a jump shot toward the basket. It landed in the center of the net, and—*swish!*—dropped through with almost no sound.

"Woo-hoo! Nothin' but net, from downtown! Awesome!" Erica screamed. "You're right, Grandpa! I bet you WILL beat Chartwell this year!"

Marty laughed, "I think we found our cheer squad for the NNC-Chartwell faculty game." He turned to Erica and said, "I think we'd better call it a day, honey. I'm starting to get cold, and I don't want to put Chris's reputation on the line by making him try to duplicate that first shot of his."

Marty picked up the ball and walked Erica back to the house. When they got to Chris, he made a more formal introduction, and then ushered them into the house. As they came through the door, another woman in her late 30's came out of the kitchen. "Hi! I'm Liese. I hear you've already met my little brother, Mike," she laughed, grinning in the direction of her brother, who was coming up the stairs from the basement. He made a face at her as he carried a container of food into the kitchen. "As you can see, he'll always behave like a little brother. I'm glad you could join us today."

She was followed by a young boy, about four years old. "Eddie, please say hello to Mr. van Zant," she told him. At first, he looked cautiously around his mother. But with a little coaxing, he stepped up to Chris and held out his hand. "How do you do, Mr. van Zant. My name is Edward Cunningham. But you can call me Eddie." Then he looked at his mother and said, "That's my Mom. She's a teacher, so she knows everything! Her name's really Elizabeth, but nobody ever calls her that. You can call her Liese. That's Dutch. It was my great-grandma's name. If you'll excuse me, I'm working on a project for Grandpa downstairs. Thank you for joining us today." With that, he turned on his heel, and made a beeline for the basement stairs.

Liese blushed, and laughed, "Please excuse Eddie. He's the youngest of five grandchildren, and sometimes he has to prove that he's as grown up as the rest of them—which usually isn't saying much. Right now, he's upset because we won't let him start playing on an organized hockey team for another year. There's a '6 and under Mites league,' but we'd like him to get a little more size before he starts playing in a league. He probably wouldn't mind it as much if we could get the rink set up in our back yard. But it hasn't been cold enough yet. So he sees his brother and sister, as well as the neighbor kids, going to their hockey practices at the community rink, and he feels left out. Once he's out skating in the back yard, he won't notice it as much. But this year, he has to wait, while his cousin is blessed with weather warm enough to play basketball outside with Grandpa on Thanksgiving! Most years that isn't the case. Fortunately, Dad found something to keep Eddie busy downstairs—I don't know what it is, but Dad promised me it doesn't involve saws or nails. So if it's something that keeps Eddie occupied, I'm not worried about him."

"What's Eddie up to now? He was just in the kitchen with me a second ago!" A man in his early 40's came out of the kitchen and put his arm around Liese.

"Just being the grown-up host," Liese laughed. "Chris, this is my husband, Jerry Cunningham. He's responsible for the rampant case of 'hockey fever' in our family. He played hockey in college, and he's a coach on both of our kids' teams. Both of them have practices tomorrow. Fortunately they're not until tomorrow evening, so we don't have to go back home until after lunch."

"His brother and sister BOTH play hockey?" Chris asked. "Are there that many girls who play hockey?"

Jerry laughed. "You're new to Minnesota, aren't you? When Tom, our oldest, started out, there weren't any teams for girls near where we lived, so he had a couple of girls on his 'Mites' team the first year or so. But two years later, when Kristy started playing, there were enough girls for two 'Mites' teams in her age group. It was the same in the other school districts in our area, so they have enough teams for a decent-sized league. And ALL of those girls want to go to the U of M and play for the Golden Gophers!"

Mike came out of the kitchen with a tray of wine glasses, and a couple bottles of wine. "Instead of standing around here, why don't we go into the living room. I think Tom's already got a ballgame on. Chris, Dad told me great things about that Washington wine that you brought, so we'll save that for dinner. For now, I've opened some of what we brought from the Cities. Or if you'd prefer beer, I'm sure Dad has some of his home brew chilled up.

Without even looking, I can also say with confidence that he'll have some Heineken in the 'fridge, too."

"I'm game for some home brew," Chris said. "What I had the last time I was here was pretty impressive!"

Marty stuck his head around the kitchen door. "Did I hear that somebody wants to join me with some of my home brew? Go on into the living room, and I'll bring some right out."

When they got to the living room, the television was on, with a football game well underway. The four most comfortable seats in the room were occupied by Marty's grandchildren. They were sprawled across all of the couches and armchairs, with no space left for anyone else. Eddie obviously had more important things occupying him downstairs. Mike cleared his throat, and they all ignored him. He did it again, more loudly, and got a glimmer of attention. "Ahem!!" he tried again. "Please notice that we have a guest with us today, so please mind your manners! You four are all welcome to join the rest of us and watch the games this afternoon. But the four of you can't take up all the space! If you wanna watch the game up here, you're goin' t' have to share some space. And remember, Grandpa put a flat screen in the family room, too! So if you'd rather not watch it with us old fogies, you can go down there. We'll make sure that there are plenty of snacks there, too."

Tom got up from the couch and said, "Uncle Mike, you probably think it was the food that sealed the deal. But you had me with the bit about having to watch the game with you 'old fogies.' I'm heading downstairs—just don't forget the food," he chuckled.

On his way out the door, Tom stopped to introduce himself to Chris, and then introduced his sister Kristy. As they followed Tom and Kristy, Erica did the same for her brother, Karl. "You'll have to forgive Karl," she said. "He's a soccer player, and his season just ended. He doesn't play any winter sports, so he'll be moping around until practices start again in the spring. But in Minnesota, you never know when that might be," she laughed.

After the children had left, Chris was about to comment on how mature and polite they had all been. But Mike spoke first: "Chris, can we hire you to come live with us? Before you say anything about how polite they all are, let me assure you, that's not their normal behavior. They're fine whenever Dad wants them to do something, but if it's just their parents, you'd think we had them slaving away on a chain gang."

"I think everyone says that about their kids," Chris laughed. "My brothers and sister all swear that they want to trade kids with their friends, because they always behave better around other people than they do at home."

Marty had just come in the room with a small pitcher of home brew, and a couple of empty glasses. "As ye sow, so shall ye reap!" he laughed. "Someday you'll all realize that grandchildren are God's way of giving grandparents some sweet revenge!"

He turned to Chris and said, "They all bitch and moan about all the things their kids do—or won't do, when it comes to things around the house. All I can do is look at them and say, 'Obviously the apples didn't fall very far from the trees!' As I warned you, it can get a little lively here when all the grandkids are around. To change the subject, did you say you wanted some home brew? This batch wasn't quite ready in time for the department picnic. It's a little darker than what you tried last time, but don't worry—it's not too heavy. It's a German Bock."

Liese brought in a tray of snacks, and after everyone filled their plates, they settled in to watch football for a while. About 2:30, Karen called Mike and Jerry into the kitchen to help with some final preparations. By 3:00 they had finally gotten everyone seated in the dining room. They'd put several tables together, so everyone was able to sit in the same room. Marty circulated with the bottles of wine that Chris had brought, and after saying a Thanksgiving prayer, he asked everyone to join him in a toast: "To family and friends, new and old! We all have a great deal to be thankful for again this year!"

After everyone had clinked glasses with the people near them (Eddie being the most enthusiastic of the group), Mike asked, "Speaking of old friends, how's Klaas doing? I thought he might be joining us today."

"Oh, he's doing fine. He's like the Eveready Bunny! I invited him to join us. But with the mild weather we've been having, his kids were able to take him down to the Cities for a few days. That doesn't usually happen at this time of the year, so he's happy as a clam! The weather's supposed to be good through the weekend, so he's going to stay with them until Sunday. This will probably be the last time he gets down there until spring. Since he doesn't drive any more—thank God!—it usually has to work out for them to be able to drive up here and back on the same day. With good weather, that's not a problem. But at his age, they don't want to start out on the road if there's any risk of getting caught in a winter storm. He asked me to be sure to say 'hi' to all of you."

Marty turned to Chris and explained, "His kids were afraid they'd have to pry his car keys out of his hands, but as it turned out, that wasn't a problem. One day he called his son and said, 'There are too many crazy people on the road these days, and I shouldn't add to the number.' One of his granddaughters was having trouble with her car, and couldn't afford to buy a new one, so he gave her his." He turned to Mike and said, "This will come as no surprise to you, Mike: he wanted to make sure none of his other grandchildren felt excluded. He looked up the retail value of the car, and gave that amount to each of the others."

"Considering the way he babied his cars," Mike said, "I'm sure she couldn't have bought another one of that quality for anywhere near 'book value.'"

Marty laughed, "From what I understand, she's still driving it. He told me that whenever he sees her, she assures him that she keeps it serviced regularly, and it still runs 'like a brand new one.'"

"Why doesn't he move closer to them?" Liese asked. "Don't all his kids live in the Cities, or at least in the suburbs?"

"They've tried to get him to do that for years. He used to say that all his friends lived here, and he didn't want to move away from them to live in a retirement center with a bunch of strangers. But by now, almost all of his friends have passed away. A few moved to Arizona or Florida, and I think most of them are gone, too. Now he just says he's more comfortable here. When it's nice weather, he still goes out for a daily walk. Along the way, he usually stops by the cemetery, and spends some time at Henrietta's grave." He turned to Chris and explained, "Henrietta was his wife. She died about ten years ago, after they'd been married over sixty years."

Marty turned back to Liese, and added, "He told me that he's afraid that if he moves closer to his kids, they're getting old enough that they might retire soon and move away, and he'd be left even more isolated than he is here. At least in New Leiden, he still has some friends who drop by to see him fairly regularly. And most importantly, he has all the memories of his life here. He's also afraid that if he moved down there, he'd be an imposition on them. He doesn't want them disrupting their lives to keep him occupied, and the alternative could easily be that they might leave him alone, and he wouldn't see them any more than he does now. So every few weeks, one of them either brings their family up here to spend the weekend with him, or more often than not, takes him down there for a few days. They've apparently given up trying to persuade him to move.

By now, platters of turkey, mashed potatoes, dressing, and other Thanksgiving standards were circulating around the table. Conversation died down for a while, as everyone enjoyed the meal.

Mike looked at the food Chris was putting on his plate and smiled. "Has Dad told you about his infamous Thanksgiving dinner when he was in grad school?"

"No—am I missing out on something I should know about?"

Marty laughed, "Not too much—just a reminder that sometimes trying to do something nice for someone can come back and bite you on the rear."

"Okay, you've got my curiosity up," Chris said. "What's the story of your 'infamous Thanksgiving dinner'—if no one else minds hearing it again?"

"Not at all," Jerry said. "We've all heard it many times, but we always enjoy it. It's become part of our family tradition. I don't think Thanksgiving would be complete without hearing about it."

Marty shook his head, and then chuckled, "Okay, if you insist. But remember: I'm not the one who brought it up!"

"We're all ears," Mike laughed.

"Okay, I was in grad school. Annette and I were planning to go her parents' house for Thanksgiving, but there was a major storm front moving in, with blizzard conditions expected. Everyone agreed we should stay put. So we bought a small turkey, and planned to have dinner by ourselves. But then I found out that one of the new graduate students in my department was going to be all alone for the holiday, too. I didn't know him at all, but from what little I'd seen, he didn't seem to have many friends in the department. So we invited him to join us. He came over a little early, and planted himself in front of the tv set. Turns out he was a big Dallas Cowboys fan. He was also quite religious. We quickly found that out when he informed us that the Cowboys were so successful at the time because their coach, Tom Landry, was 'such a good Christian.' With my usual diplomacy, I told him that I thought God probably had more important things to deal with than pro football teams. That pretty much set the tone for the rest of the afternoon."

"You can't stop there, Dad!" Liese said. "You haven't gotten to the dinner yet. That was one Mom never forgot."

"I've been trying to forget it for over 40 years," Marty laughed. "Okay, so I invited him to join us at the table, and turned off the tv. He apparently thought he was going to be eating off a tv tray while he watched the rest of the game, but Annette explained to him in no uncertain terms that we didn't do things like that in our household—as you've noticed here. So he sat up to the table, and I said a table prayer—like I did today. He let me know that it wasn't up to his religious standards. Then Annette started bringing everything out of the kitchen: turkey, dressing, mashed potatoes, gravy, sweet potatoes, her special green bean/sour cream casserole, homemade rolls, cranberries and cranberry sauce, pickles and olives—the whole nine yards. He took the platter of meat and said, 'I'm a picky eater.' He helped himself to a drumstick, a spoonful of mashed potatoes, and a couple of rolls, and then proceeded to drown the whole plate in gravy. That was all he ate. Annette had made pumpkin pie, but he said that was too spicy for him."

"You left out the part about the wine," Erica said. "Come on Grandpa, you have to tell the whole story."

Marty laughed, and picked up his wine glass and twirled it in his fingers. "I poured Annette a glass of wine, and offered to do the same for him. But instead of simply declining the offer politely, he gave me a sermon on the evils of intemperance. Apparently the only time wine had ever crossed his lips was once by accident, at an interfaith communion service. And he still had never forgiven the pastor who 'deceived' him, supposedly in an attempt to lead him down the slippery slope to a life of drunken debauchery. I told him I respected his views, and I would never try to force anyone to drink alcohol when they didn't want to. But I certainly intended to enjoy it with my wife. I'd bought a big jug of it, since I thought three of us would be sharing it. Of course, jug wine was about all a TA salary would accommodate, anyway. He quickly put Annette and me in the mood to polish off the whole thing ourselves."

"But you didn't kick him out, did you Grandpa?" Eddie asked.

"No, Eddie, I didn't. I thought that one rude person in the house was enough for the day, so I made a point of being as polite as I possibly could. As soon as we finished eating, I went into the living room and turned the tv on again. Then we watched the rest of the Cowboys game. Fortunately, by that time it was already midway through the fourth quarter. As soon as the game was over, I thanked him for joining us, and handed him his coat.

"As far as I know," Marty continued, "that was one of only three dinners that he was ever invited to during his entire graduate career: the first one, the last one, and the only one. I hadn't planned to tell anybody about it, but he went back to the grad center and started complaining about how Annette and I had tried to force all those 'weird' foods on him, not to mention trying to ply him with demon rum—or at least its evil cousin, wine. By the time I got to my office Monday, word had spread, and everyone wanted to know what had really happened. Most of my fellow grad students had enjoyed some of Annette's cooking at one point or another—either at our house or at departmental pot luck dinners—so they knew she wasn't one who went in for 'weird' recipes. After I told a couple people what had actually happened, word spread pretty quickly. Several people had been planning to follow our example, and invite him to join them for dinner over Christmas break. But after our experience, those plans were all scuttled immediately. No one EVER invited him to dinner again. So that's the story of my 'infamous Thanksgiving dinner.' Is everyone happy now? If so, can somebody please pass me some turkey?"

Eddie replied, "Thanks Grandpa! I always like to hear that story. It was nice of you and Grandma to invite that man for dinner. And it was nice of you to keep being polite to him. Mommy says that's what manners are for. But I'm sure glad you don't ever invite him to join us here!"

Marty laughed, "I'm glad you recognize that manners are important, Eddie. But don't worry: even though I always try to be polite, even when there are times when I would really like to do something else, I can promise you that I will never, ever be so polite that I would invite that man to dinner again."

By this time, the turkey had made its way around the table, and everyone's attention went back to eating.

Eventually Mike asked Chris, "So, how have you enjoyed your first year at NNC thus far?"

"It's been great! Fortunately, Marty arranged for me to have a light schedule this fall. With only two more weeks left in the semester, the end is in sight!"

"And how are you enjoying teaching *die Quellen*," Liese asked, with a wry smile. "Or shouldn't I ask?"

Chris thought for a moment, and then said, "That's been a rather unusual experience."

"Very diplomatically put," Marty said. "I think we should leave it at that for now."

"What about you, Dad?" Mike asked. "Is 'the end in sight' for you in the near future? I keep waiting to hear that you're going to retire." He nodded down the table toward Erica and said, "I know someone who'd love to have you as her assistant basketball coach."

"I'm glad you asked that question," Marty laughed. "Hank announced that he's retiring at the end of this academic year. As soon as he's out the door, I'll tell the Dean that I'm planning to retire at the end of next year. But I don't trust the son of a bitch enough to make that announcement before he actually leaves."

"Dad!! Watch your mouth—little pitchers have big ears, remember!" Liese scolded him.

"That's right, Grandpa," Eddie said with a very serious look on his face. "Even if he is a son of a bitch, you shouldn't call him that. It might hurt his feelings."

When the laughter died down, Marty looked at Eddie and said, "Thank you for reminding me of that, Eddie. I'll try to be more careful in the future. I certainly don't want to hurt anyone's feelings."

Karen and Liese asked if anyone wanted dessert right away, or if they'd prefer to wait a while. To their surprise, even the children claimed to be too full to eat dessert yet. Eddie probably expressed it best: "If I have dessert now, I'll only be able to eat a small piece of pie. I want to wait, so I can have a BIG ONE!"

Mike refilled a few of the wine glasses, and then he and Jerry sent everyone back to the living room, or in the case of the kids, downstairs to the family room. "Mike and I are going to take care of the dishes," Jerry said, "so why don't the rest of you take your wine into the living room and relax. Marty: just make sure that you keep your glass on the table—we don't want you to fall asleep with it in your hand and spill it all over your easy chair."

Marty turned to Chris, and shook his head. "I'm the Rodney Dangerfield of this family: I just don't get no respect, no respect at all."

After they'd gotten settled in comfortable chairs, Chris asked Marty, "I'm curious: did you always plan to be a history teacher? Did you start out as a history major?"

"Quite the contrary," Marty laughed. "I'd had a bad experience with a high school history class, so history was the last thing I wanted to take when I registered for my first college courses. But by the time it was my time to register, most of the classes I wanted were already full. I had to find one more class, or I'd have been in trouble. In those days, if you didn't take a full load every semester, you'd lose your student deferment, and you'd get drafted. The only class that had an opening in it was Klaas's section of History 101."

"So, if not history, what were you planning to major in?"

"I was going to be a German teacher. I'd taken three years of German in high school—much to the chagrin of my father. After what his cousins experienced in World War II, he hated all things German. But I had a great teacher in high school, and loved it. So that's how I started out."

"How'd you end up in history, then?"

"Well, a lot depends on who your teacher is. Klaas made history 'come alive' for me. And that was in sharp contrast to my experience in German."

"Which was . . . ?"

Marty laughed. "I think my first college German prof did her student teaching in the SS! She'd look at the class and say something like, 'Vee haff ziss rule, und zer ahr forty-sree exzeptions. You vill learn ziss rule, und ze exzeptions!' I also quickly realized that the upper division classes would all be lit courses. Don't get me wrong—I love literature. But I've never enjoyed lit classes, where you sit around trying to figure out what an author 'really means' by some recurring motif. 'What's the significance of the color red in Toni Morrison's *Beloved*?' That kind of thing. The classes that I started taking in the History Department were such a sharp contrast to that experience that it was an easy choice to make."

"How about your Dutch history specialty? When'd you start in that direction?"

Marty laughed again. "For obvious reasons, I thought I'd probably concentrate on Germany. I had a good foundation with the language, and it seemed logical."

"So, how'd you wind up with a Dutch focus?"

"I thought that if I would eventually go to graduate school, I'd probably need a second language. Although my parents spoke Dutch, my knowledge of it was very limited. So partly for academic reasons, and partly for 'cultural heritage,' I signed up for Dutch 101 in my sophomore year."

"Don't believe him, Chris," Liese laughed. "It's all because of his beard."

"There has to be a story there," said Chris. "What's your beard have to do with you becoming a Dutch historian?"

"That's a bit of an oversimplification, but there is some truth to it," Marty chuckled. "I'd played on the basketball team my first two years in college. Although I didn't start as a freshman, I still made the varsity, and played quite a bit. In my sophomore year, I started at forward. Then, in the summer between my sophomore and junior years, I decided to grow a beard—which I've had ever since, by the way. Our coach was something of a Neanderthal, who had his crew-cut trimmed at least once a week. When basketball practice started in October, I showed up the first day and he looked at me and growled, 'Dykstra, either that beard goes, or you do.' There were no scholarships involved—we're talking Division III basketball, after all. I figured that if I wanted to play basketball, there were still intramurals. And somehow I'd gotten it in my head that girls liked my beard. So it wasn't a tough decision. I handed him the ball, and went into the locker room to change."

Marty took a sip of his wine, and continued. "When I left the gym, just on the spur of the moment, I went to the Study Abroad Office. I asked if there was any way I could still get into a program to study in Europe spring semester. A few of the other Dutch-heritage colleges around the country had just formed a consortium offering a semester program in the Netherlands. Unfortunately, the application deadline had just passed. Our Study Abroad Director hadn't been able to get any NNC students to sign up for that program, so he called them up, and asked if they would take one more student, even though I'd missed the deadline. My grades weren't as good as I'd have liked at that point, but I had more than the minimum g.p.a., and they still had a few spaces left. The timing was right in other ways, too."

"What do you mean?" Chris asked.

"As I mentioned earlier, in those days, you had to earn a full load of credits every semester—at least if you were male. Otherwise, you'd lose your student deferment, and they'd draft you. Usually a semester abroad didn't transfer back as a full load. So unless you wanted to live dangerously, studying overseas wasn't an option for most men. But that fall, they started the draft lottery. My number was 327, so there wasn't much chance that I'd get drafted. The next thing I knew, it was spring semester, and I was on a plane to Amsterdam. It was the best thing that ever happened to me. I'd been trying to figure out how to get 'over the hump' academically—it seemed like I could never get more than a B+. When I came back from that semester in the Netherlands, all the pieces seemed to fit together. I got A's in all but one of my classes my senior year. And I'd have never gotten an A from the guy who gave me a B+, no matter what I did."

"Why's that?"

"He had me pegged as a 'B+ student.' If he saw my name on a paper or exam, I don't think he even needed to read it—he 'knew' it would be a B+. I think that to this day, if he were still alive, I could write a manuscript that was awarded a Pulitzer in history, and if he saw my name on it, he'd still give it a B+. That's one reason why I've always insisted that my students write exams in 'Blue Books'—so I can turn the covers over before I grade them, and not know whose exam it is until I'm done."

Liese laughed, "He only had trouble with one more 'B+ prof'—isn't that right Dad?"

"I try to forget that," he laughed. "In one of my first graduate classes, the entire grade was based on a research paper. If we didn't like the grade, we could re-submit the paper as many times as we wanted, until we were happy with the grade."

"That sounds like a pretty good deal," Chris said.

"In theory, it was. But when he gave me a B+, I asked if I could re-submit the paper. He said there was no point. 'You've written an A paper on a B+ topic.' A topic which he had approved, by the way."

"Ouch!"

"That's what I thought—no, actually I had some choicer words than that. But I've always taken some satisfaction from the fact that he didn't get tenure. I did. I find some poetic justice there."

"So what did you specialize in when you were in grad school? Obviously something beyond 'B+ topics," Chris laughed.

"By that time, I really wanted to focus on Dutch history. But there wasn't anyone in my graduate department who knew anything about that, so my major field was theoretically German history. I was able to work in a lot of Dutch issues on the side. That way, I could do what I really wanted to, while keeping my major professor happy in the process. I managed to get a Fulbright to spend a year studying and doing research in the Netherlands. And that had a special bonus: I met Annette. She was finishing her degree, and when I came back to the US, she came to get her Master's degree. We got married the next year."

"How did you end up back at NNC? That must have been another case of good timing."

"It was. When I finished my degree, I had a couple of temporary jobs—sabbatical replacements, like you had out in Oregon. And then there was an opening here that fit my qualifications. As a bonus, Annette was able to teach Dutch here. It took her a few years, but she was finally able to finish her Ph.D., too.

"There's a bit of irony about my position," Marty continued. "I replaced the guy who'd had me pegged as a B+ student. I never asked anyone directly, but I always got the impression that he wasn't very pleased when they hired me. After I was here a few years, when Klaas retired, I took over his Dutch history classes. And now, or at least in a couple years, I hope to have you do the same."

Karen came into the room, and tried to catch everyone's attention. "Okay, we're ready to serve some dessert. We have three kinds of pie: pumpkin, cherry, and pecan. You can have a piece of any or all, and you have your choice of either whipped cream or ice cream. Eddie already has his name on a piece of cherry pie a la mode, but there's plenty left for everyone."

While everyone was enjoying their dessert, Liese asked, "Chris, are you going to the Christmas music extravaganza next week?"

"I have a couple of students in the choir, and one's in the orchestra. So I thought I should go and show them I'm interested in what they do outside of class."

"That's a good idea, Chris," Marty said. "I hope somebody warned you that you'll invariably have a few students who will have problems getting any assignments in on time in the coming week. I forgot to tell you about that."

"They mentioned that in the first orientation session for *die Quellen*. Somebody started to talk about that in the general new faculty orientation, too, but the new music faculty had apparently been briefed about it. They said that 'the Christmas music program is an important component of our co-curricular activities, and it is not incompatible with our academic mission,' or something along those lines. It sounded like a canned response to me."

"That's an understatement. Ever since this current incarnation of the Christmas program took shape about ten or twelve years ago, you might as well just write off the last two weeks of class, at least in terms of any assignments. But if Hank had his way, it would be even worse?"

"How so? What's Hank have to do with the music program?"

"It goes back to his paranoia about all the Lutheran colleges in the Upper Midwest. As we get close to Christmas, public television and radio will be carrying performances from all of their various Christmas musical programs. Some of them are pretty elaborate—more than a thousand students participating, with three or four choral ensembles, symphony orchestras, bell choirs, you name it. Every time Hank sees those, all he really sees are dollar signs. He figures we should have a Christmas program like theirs"

"Is the Music Department really that big here?"

"You've cut to the quick, Chris," Marty laughed. "As you know, the Reformed Church's musical tradition is nothing like what the Lutherans have. Even though NNC doesn't have any direct affiliation with the Reformed Church, the Church still has a big influence in Dutch culture. Music isn't that big a part of it—at least not as much as it is for Lutherans, especially Norwegian Lutherans. But even though Hank is supposedly so tuned into Dutch culture—remember, he got an award from the Dutch government for all of his 'contributions'—he hasn't figured that out. There are only a couple hundred students involved in our music ensembles—orchestra and choirs combined. That's a fraction of what the Lutheran schools have participating. They can almost fill their auditoriums up with just the performers' relatives. So while they have sell-out crowds at four or five performances, we only present ours three times—and to large numbers of empty seats every time."

"If there are only a couple hundred students involved, what's the problem for the rest of the campus?"

"As you mentioned, you have some students participating. Given all the time they have to spend at rehearsals before next Friday, they won't have any time to do anything else. Everything else is supposed to take a back seat to it. As you can imagine, the Music Department likes all the attention. If you talk to most of our colleagues over in Oberlin Hall, you'd think we had a conservatory on campus. And they hope that if they start a tradition of a huge Christmas extravaganza, Hank will add more Music faculty. Don't get me wrong—given the size of our orchestra and choir, the students do a great job. But with all the support from Hank, and with dreams of even more to come, the Music Department has started to go off the deep end the last few years. I go every year to support my students, just like you're planning to do. But some of the stuff they've been performing the last few years has gotten pretty esoteric. In this part of the world, where the local population doesn't necessarily have the greatest sophistication when it comes to music, that's not a recipe for bringing in bigger crowds every year. But now it's 'the focal point of our holiday tradition,' as Hank describes it, so I don't expect to see changes in it any time soon. On some of the weirder choral pieces, the only enjoyable part is the fact that Hank sits in the front row, and it's always an effort for him to stay awake through the entire performance. Watching that is almost entertaining by itself. One of these years, Hannah's going to crack one of his ribs when she nudges him to stay awake."

Liese turned to Marty and asked, "Does the College still have that big Christmas dinner for faculty and staff. I remember Mom always enjoyed going to that every year."

Marty shook his head. "I'm afraid that's gone the way of the dodo bird and the passenger pigeon. That's another piece of our supposed 'community' that's fallen by the wayside. To a certain extent, I can understand, because there are just too many faculty and staff to have the kind of sit-down dinner we used to have. But that's not the real reason for the changes."

"No? . . . what's that?" Liese asked.

"Finances, of course. After they moved away from the sit-down dinner, they had a very nice event, with buffet stations set up throughout the CUB. For cost reasons, that eventually gave way to 'hearty hors d'oeuvres,' and a couple years ago, it became just a dessert. But we could all understand the financial issue. This year, it's a luncheon buffet."

"That sounds like an improvement over 'just a dessert.'"

"It would be, except that this year, it's only for faculty and staff—not their spouses. They told emeriti that they could bring their spouses, but faculty can't. The argument there was that emeriti would be making a special trip to campus for it. But with faculty spouses, that would involve an extra trip for each family. So for 'conservation' and 'sustainability' reasons, they decided not to include spouses."

"Oh, of course," Liese laughed. "Because it's such a long commute for anyone living in New Leiden! That definitely makes sense," she said bitterly.

"I'm always amazed how people like Hank go on and on about how important the idea of 'community' is at NNC, and whenever they can save a few dollars somewhere, that's one of the first things thrown under the bus," Marty grumbled. "The meal isn't the real point of the whole thing. While there are a few people who would do just about anything for a free meal, I think most people are like me. The dessert last year was a nice event. I think most of us would've been happy with a 'community' Christmas gathering at which all they served were cookies, tea, and coffee. That would've been a nice way to bring everyone together and thank them for what they do to keep the College running. That's especially the case for the staff."

"Why didn't they just do that, Dad?" Liese asked.

"Because this way, Hank and Hannah don't have to pretend to be nice to as many people. They stand there in a receiving line, with plastic smiles stuck on their faces. Hannah stands just behind Hank and smiles, and holds out a limp hand for the coldest 'dead-fish' handshake you can imagine."

"I remember Mom complaining about that. Hannah hasn't gotten any better at socializing?"

"Ha!" Marty laughed. "If anything, she's worse" Marty looked around to make sure there weren't any "little pitchers" in the vicinity, and said, "As your grandfather used to say, 'She thinks her shit don't stink – but her farts give her away.'"

"Dad!!" Liese shrieked. Then she turned to Chris, "Please ignore him! Sometimes he can't help himself. I think he prides himself on his crude analogies, especially when he can quote someone like Grandpa and try to pass the blame on to him. And I'm not convinced Grandpa actually said half the stuff Dad credits him with—or blames him for. At least he saved that one until Eddie wasn't around. I can just imagine having to hear that one repeated over and over on the way back to the Cities tomorrow!"

"But as I said," Marty continued, "the main argument is financial. Hank just sent another memo to department chairs, telling us how important it is to 'tighten our belts.' And then the next day, there was a news release about how he was creating another new Assistant Dean position, as well as an addition to the Sustainability Office's staff. There always seems to be enough money lying around for more administrators."

Liese laughed. "I'm sure it will come as no surprise to you, Chris, but we've been hearing him complain about that since we were Eddie's age."

"Guilty as charged," Marty said, "and even before you were around to hear me. But I've also been right for over forty years! The only difference is, it's gotten worse under Hank. On the one hand, he's pinching pennies wherever he can. Then he turns around and blows money on the latest shiny object that's caught his attention, like the wind mill. Last year, he insisted that staff remain at work until 4:30 on Christmas Eve. If they wanted to leave any earlier, they were supposed to take annual leave time. It didn't matter to him that a number of churches in town had services starting at 4:00."

"Meanwhile," Marty continued, "he and Hannah had already left town for the holidays. Most of the staff supervisors just turned a blind eye, and let people go home earlier, but a few followed his orders to the letter. If they thought he'd reward them for their loyalty somehow, they were sadly mistaken. By the time he got back from Christmas break, he'd forgotten all about it. A couple of supervisors tried to snitch on another office, where everyone had gone home around 3:00, and he told them not to bother him with petty administrative details—he said that was up to the individual supervisor. That whole fiasco didn't win him any points among the staff, I can assure you. There was even a poster stuck up in the CUB, with Hank's face superimposed on a picture of the Grinch. Fortunately someone took that down before he came back to campus. If he'd seen that, he'd have been furious."

By the time the next ballgame started, Karen and Liese had set up a table with fixings for sandwiches. After another round of food, Chris finally told Marty that he should head for home. With the time difference, it was just about the right time to call his family in Washington.

"Do you mind if I leave my car here again, Marty? I've had enough of your brew and the wine that I'm not going to drive."

"You don't have to walk," Marty said. "Someone can give you a ride home."

"From what everyone's been telling me, I don't think there will be many more days when it will be warm enough for me to walk," Chris laughed. "I'd better take advantage of this opportunity. Besides, with all the food that Karen and Liese kept sending in my direction, I definitely need to try to walk it off. But thanks, anyway. I'll walk over tomorrow and pick it up."

"Be sure to stick your head in when you come to get your car. If you're here anywhere close to noon, those leftovers will be back on the table again."

Chris went downstairs and said goodbye to the kids, and then did the same with their parents when he came back upstairs. Marty brought him his coat, and walked him out to the porch.

"Before you leave, Chris, there's something I've been meaning to ask you."

"Sure, what's that Marty?"

"You know that new development that Hank announced, Summerfield Meadows?"

"Sure, that sounds like a great deal!"

"It definitely is. I hope you'll take advantage of it. Even if you won't be in a position to build any time soon, you should at least get one of the lots. I can't imagine that you'll ever have that kind of opportunity again—ever! Now, I'm not trying to pry into your personal finances, but if you're not in a position to come up with the money to buy one of those lots, I wanted to let you know that I would be happy to loan you the money—all, or any part of it."

"That's very generous of you Marty, but you shouldn't do something like that for me!"

"Think of it this way: if I were to loan you the money, even for less interest than you would pay for a mortgage loan from your bank, I'd be getting paid some interest on my money. As it is now, if my money is sitting in a savings account, the amount of interest I get every year barely pays for the postage when the bank sends me monthly statements. So it wouldn't be any kind of sacrifice on my part. I just don't want you to miss out on the opportunity to get one of those lots."

"When you put it that way, it sounds like a good deal for both of us! I was able to put away a pretty good percentage of my salary in Oregon, so I think I can cover most of it. But if it looks like I might be a little short, I promise you, I won't let the deal go by because I don't have it all myself. I'll be sure to let you know."

"Please do. In the meantime, good luck with the rest of the semester! You've almost got the first one behind you. Only one more, and you'll be working for a new president. I don't know about you, but I can hardly wait! Now, be careful on your way home. The temperature is supposed to drop below freezing, so keep an eye out for ice patches. We'll see you when you come back for your car tomorrow!"

Marty watched Chris walk down the street, and he turned to go back into the house. Just as he opened the door, Eddie came running up to him.

"Grandpa, I finished the project you gave me. Is there anything else I can help you with?"

"I'm sure there is, Eddie. Why don't we go see? But first, I think I hear a couple pieces of pie calling our names."

"I don't hear anything, Grandpa. Are you sure? Remember, Mommy said I had big ears."

"Oh, they're not as big as mine, Eddie. And I just put new batteries in my hearing aids. So trust me—they're calling our names, all right."

"Grandpa—why does Mommy think I'm a pitcher? I wanna play shortstop. I don't wanna pitch."

Marty laughed. "I thought you wanted to play hockey."

"I do—but I wanna play baseball in the summer, too."

"Well, don't worry about what your Mom says. I don't think she knows that much about baseball. You play whatever position you want to play. She'll be happy with whatever you want to do."

He put his hand on Eddie's shoulder, and they went off in search of the pie.

12

A New Year Begins

Monday, January 6

CHRIS HEARD THE ANNOUNCEMENT for his flight, and got in line to board. He'd been told the flight would be almost full, but he knew it would have been even harder to get a seat the previous week, with people returning to Europe after spending the holidays in the US. By waiting until today, he'd been able to get a cheaper ticket. But that meant he was competing for space with student groups leaving for J-term courses in Europe. At least he'd been able to get an aisle seat. With the plane's configuration, there would only be one person between him and the window, without a third passenger squeezed in between them.

He watched as they processed the "passengers needing extra time to board." There were several families with small children, who acted like they were already tired of the flight. *"With my luck, I'll probably have one of those kids behind me kicking my seat, and another in front of me, peeking over the seat at me the whole trip,"* he said to himself. *"Or if I'm really cursed, they'll be next to me."* One of the children was already crying, and he could hear her screams all the way down the jetway to the plane. He was sure what seat that family would be near: his.

When he finally got to his seat, he was relieved to see that there were no children near him. He put his carry-on in the compartment above his seat. After taking out a folder with some assorted reading materials, he slid his briefcase under the seat in front of him. Once they were in the air, he'd take out his computer and do some work. He wanted to be well prepared for what he'd be doing in the archives in Utrecht. With jetlag, he wouldn't be as sharp as he'd like to be when he got there. He sat down and leafed through his folder until he found an article that he'd planned to read over break. He'd just gotten started reading it when a young woman stopped next to him in the aisle. She put her carry-on in the bin next to his, and pointed toward the seat next to him.

"I'm sorry to bother you," she said with a smile, "but I have the window seat."

When he stood up to let her get to her seat, he couldn't help but notice her height, as her eyes were at the same level as his. They were also the most brilliant blue that he'd ever seen. He suddenly realized that he was staring at her, and quickly looked away. "Here," he said, "let me hold your computer case while you get seated."

They both settled into their seats and buckled their seatbelts. Chris picked up his folder, and found the spot in the article where he'd left off. Before he read another sentence, she interrupted him.

"Excuse me," she said, "but I couldn't help but notice the logo on the outside of your folder. Are you an alum of NNC?"

"Not an alum—I teach there. Are you a 'Flying Dutch' alum?"

"No, but I recognized the logo. I teach art history at Chartwell, so I guess we're almost neighbors. At least we're from the same part of the state." Then she laughed, "Yes, the dreaded Chartwell! Just don't call me 'Chuck.'"

Chris blushed, and said, "Don't worry! From what I understand, that's a particular 'hot button item' for our president. He wouldn't take kindly to any faculty making references to the 'Chuck Fartwell' slogan that the students seem to like so much—except to condemn it, of course. As a new, untenured assistant prof, you won't hear me using the term. What's the reaction on your campus."

"Well, at first, I think President Thompson was offended by it. He usually doesn't like foul language, or things that hint at it, like 'Chuck Fartwell.' Although his name is Charles, he definitely doesn't like to be called Chuck, as he reportedly has to keep reminding your president. That probably contributed to his reaction. But when he heard that President van Daam was so upset by it, he suddenly became an advocate for free speech—at least at NNC. So by now, I think we've heard all the clichés: 'You know how college kids can be'; 'Sometimes you need to let students do stupid things, it's all part of the learning process'—stuff like that. I'm sure he'd change his tune if it were our students doing it. But for now, as long as it's something that irritates President van Daam, anyway, I think he almost enjoys it."

"I'm sorry, I should've introduced myself. I'm Chris van Zant."

She reached over and shook his hand. "Mariah Cunningham. And before you ask: yes, my parents were fans of 'Paint Your Wagon.' My dad loves the song, 'They Call the Wind Mariah.' So when I was born, it seemed obvious to both of them that it should be my name. I can't really complain, though. It could be a lot worse—especially if they were intent on picking a name from a musical. So, what do you teach, Chris?"

"European history—specifically Dutch."

"Is that why you're on this flight? Is it a research trip? If you're a brand new faculty member, I can't imagine that you'd be leading a J-term course already."

"You're right, I'm headed for an archive in Utrecht. I probably won't be leading any J-term groups for another year or two. But my department chair asked me to put together a proposal for next year, or maybe the year after. What about you? Are you leading a group of students on a J-term class?" He looked around to see if there were any students near them wearing Chartwell sweatshirts.

"No, I did that last year—'The Art of Renaissance Italy.' And I really had a good experience—except for one or two little student behavior episodes that I'd prefer never to repeat. I'll probably do it again in a couple years. But right now, I'm doing some 'field research' for a class I'll be teaching next fall. I'm on my way to visit some museums. I'll go to a few in Germany and France first, and then I'll finish up in Amsterdam. There are also several others scattered around the Netherlands that I hope to see."

"An art history class? What's the focus? The Dutch Masters, van Gogh?"

Mariah laughed. "That would be a logical conclusion! But actually, it's not for an art history class at all, except in a peripheral way. Chartwell has a Museum Studies program. Most of the faculty who teach in it are from the History Department. But there are a couple of us from other departments—specifically, one from Anthro, and me. I often get students in my art history classes who'd like to work in a museum someday. So I'm a logical addition to that program. Next fall, I'll be teaching a course on 'Art Collection Management.' So for the next couple of weeks, I'll be visiting museums to get some good examples of how their collections are displayed. I expect I'll find a few examples of how NOT to do it, too. First, I'm going to some of the 'big names,' in Berlin, Munich, and Paris. I'll finish up at the van Gogh Museum and the Rijksmuseum in Amsterdam."

"Wow—that's quite a whirl-wind itinerary!"

"I know, but I've got a rail pass, and a few nights, I'll be in sleeper cars on the train. The first couple of weeks will be pretty hectic. But the last week or so, when I'm in the Netherlands, the schedule won't be quite as bad. Besides the big museums, I'm going to visit a few smaller ones, too. Realistically, most of our students will only get to really big ones as tourists, at least until they get some experience. A number of the smaller ones I'll be visiting are in the Netherlands. Did you say you're going to Utrecht? That's one of the places I'm planning to visit, too. There are several small museums that look pretty interesting, at least from their websites."

"I'll be spending about three weeks there. There's a small archive where I've worked before. It has some newly released documents I need to see in order to finish an article I've been working on. Have you been to Utrecht before?"

"No—I've never been to the Netherlands! This'll be my first visit."

Chris wasn't sure if he should say what he was thinking. But a quick glance showed him that she didn't have any rings on her left hand. That didn't guarantee that she was "unattached," but it gave him the courage to ask, "When are you going to be in Utrecht? Depending on when you'll be there, and how far I've been able to get with those documents, I'd be happy to show you the highlights of the city—that is, if your schedule at the museums leaves you any free time."

"I'm supposed to get there on the 22rd or the 23th—either Tuesday or Wednesday evening. I'm scheduled to fly home from Amsterdam on the 30th—the following Thursday. When are you going home?"

"My flight leaves Amsterdam on the morning of the 28th. I'll probably go there from Utrecht the day before and spend the night there."

"My plan is to spend a couple of days in Utrecht before I go someplace for most of the weekend. I haven't decided where yet. I'll stay in Amsterdam from Sunday night until I leave on Thursday. Have you spent a lot of time in Utrecht, besides in the archive where you'll be working?"

"I lived there for a year as a Fulbright student. I can give you some good suggestions on some student hangouts that have pretty good food, so you can stretch your budget a little. "

"I'd love that. It would be even more fun if you could show them to me yourself."

Chris felt himself starting to blush, but he thought to himself, *"In for a penny, in for a pound!"* He dug into his briefcase and pulled out a business card, which he handed to her. "That sounds like a great plan! My e-mail address is on the card. Let's keep in touch, and we can work out the details about when you'll be getting there. After a couple of days in the archive, I should have a good idea of how much free time I might have when you're in town, and we can plan accordingly."

"Great! Let me give you my address, too—do you have something I can write on? My cards are in the overhead."

Chris handed her his folder, and she wrote her e-mail address on the inside cover.

"I can't wait," she said. "I've never been to the Netherlands before, and I'd love to see at least a little of it with someone who knows what they're looking at!"

By this time, the plane was about ready to pull away from the terminal. Their conversation was briefly silenced while the flight attendants went through the standard pre-departure safety information. Before they were airborne, Chris and Mariah had resumed their conversation, and it was only briefly interrupted again by beverage and food service. Chris never did get back to the article in his folder. Instead, he had what was probably the longest, and most enjoyable, conversation of his life. After they landed in Amsterdam and retrieved their luggage, he helped her get to the train for Berlin.

She climbed on board the train, and he handed up her suitcase. "Thanks for your help, Chris! There will be a couple of nights when I won't have e-mail service, but I'll be sure to keep in touch so that we can coordinate my visit to Utrecht. In the meantime, good luck with your research! I hope you get far enough along with it so that you can show me the highlights of Utrecht!"

"Thanks! I look forward to your visit." He thought to himself, *"If I needed any motivation to get that work done quickly, I don't anymore! There's no way in Hell that I won't be finished by the time she gets to Utrecht!"*

*   *   *   *   *

Thursday, January 23
MARTY SET HIS NOTEBOOK DOWN on his desk. He glanced at the calendar and smiled. It was nearly the end of the third week of January Term. There was only one week left,

and then, after a few days of break, the new semester would be starting. He didn't really dislike J-term. But it always seemed artificial to him. With three hours of class every day, it didn't have the normal rhythm of a regular semester. And no matter what he assigned, students always thought it was too much for a J-term course. Besides, there wasn't enough time for students to complete a decent research paper, and the assignments they did complete often seemed half-hearted. He'd be happy when spring semester began. He'd already set a countdown calendar on his computer, counting the days until Hank officially retired. And he smiled every time he looked at it, because he was sure Hank would be leaving town as soon after Commencement as possible. However many days the countdown calendar showed, he was sure Hank wouldn't actually be around that long—he'd undoubtedly be gone before his official "last day in office."

Just as he sat down at his computer to check his e-mail, it chimed to let him know he had a new message. He opened his in-box, and saw that he had several. The newest one was from Chris. He'd been sending weekly updates, and it sounded like the trip was going well. The latest message was no exception:

> *Hi Marty!*
>
> *As I mentioned earlier, the staff at the archive have been fantastic! When I got here, they had all of the newly released documents waiting for me. They have a new digital scanner, so I was able to scan everything and send it to my e-mail account. Then I downloaded all of the files to my computer, so I have them together with all of the other material I got when I was here before. Don't worry—it's all backed up! I've put one copy on a thumb drive, and everything is also automatically backed up "in the cloud." Just to be on the safe side, I also copied the new documents onto a CD, which I mailed back to my campus address. If you*

get a chance, could you look in my departmental mailbox to see if it's there yet?

I probably seem paranoid, but my major professor taught me to be extra careful. In the late '60s, he spent a sabbatical year in Germany. At the end of the year, he sent a steamer trunk back home to Washington. Among other things, it included all of the notes he'd taken in an archive in East Germany. It's been almost 40 years, and the trunk still hasn't arrived. He never finished that research project. I'm not taking any chances.

I was able to get all of the documents copied on my first two days here. The archive has a nice reading room, and there's a coffee shop and cafeteria in the basement. Technically, they're for staff, but they let visiting scholars have access to them, too. So rather than try to make do with a small table and poor lighting in the room at my friends' house, I've come over here every day to work on my article. The documents were even more valuable than I'd hoped, and they fit perfectly with what I'd already been working on.

I'm happy to report that I finished the first draft of my article yesterday! I'm going to "let it sit" for a few days, before I go over it again with a fine-tooth comb. And then I'll give it another once-over when I'm back home. Last fall, you said you'd be willing to read my article when I got it finished. If you're still willing, I hope to have it polished enough to give to you by the start of spring semester.

My flight back to MSP is next Tuesday, so if the weather cooperates and the shuttle is on schedule, I should be back in New Leiden that night. I'll stop by your office when I'm back on campus—probably Thursday. In the meantime, I hope your J-term class is going well.

See you next week!
Chris

Marty smiled as he closed his e-mail. *"That's great news,"* he thought. *"If he can get that article published, that's one less thing to worry about for tenure."* On Monday, Marty had seen the department's student evaluations from fall semester, and Chris had gotten rave reviews, in *die Quellen* as well as in his history course. Although serving on the "Prestigious Scholarships Committee" wouldn't be enough by itself to satisfy the "service" component of his tenure review, Marty would make sure he got on a campus-wide committee next year. He'd already spoken to the chair of the "Committee on Committees," who promised him she'd slot Chris for a committee assignment. *"Great news indeed! I think this calls for a cinnamon roll and coffee!"*

He bundled himself into his heavy winter coat, and walked over to the CUB. Before he left the building, he checked Chris' mailbox. He was happy to see that a padded envelope with Dutch postage was on the top of his stack of mail. When he got back from coffee, he'd send him an e-mail to let him know it had arrived.

The thermometer outside Marty's office window read 5°, but there was a wind blowing that had been picking up speed since it left northern Alberta. The wind chill made it feel like it was -20°, if not colder. He quickly realized that he'd probably end up extending his coffee break through lunch, so he wouldn't have to make a second trip to the CUB.

He hadn't expected to find many of his *Kaffee Klatsch* group in the CUB, and he was right. Chris was obviously in the Netherlands, having flown out of MSP almost three weeks earlier. Alf was leading a J-term group in Costa Rica, studying "Birds of Central America." While he knew Alf would give them a rigorous academic program, he also knew they would all return with suntans that would be the envy of most of the campus. Dirk had been invited to present a paper at a conference in Florence. Since he hadn't been scheduled to teach a J-term class, Karen had accompanied him, and they were spending a couple weeks exploring Tuscany. There would undoubtedly be some new Italian specialties at the next event she catered.

When he walked into the coffee shop, it took a couple of minutes for the fog on his glasses to dissipate. When he could finally see clearly, he saw that Zoe was waving to him and pointing to an empty seat next to her. He got himself a cup of coffee and a cinnamon roll, and joined her.

"What's up?" he asked. "You look like you have news about something, but I suppose it's not necessarily good, if it concerns the search in your department."

"I don't know yet if it's good or bad. But I have no doubt that I know who Hank's 'ringer' is in our applicant pool. Does the name McCutcheon mean anything to you?"

"Not that I can think of. It doesn't ring any bells for me. Should it?"

"Well, you told me that when we got an application that fit Hank's customized job description 'to a t,' we'd know who he'd be pushing for the position."

"I assume you've found him—or her—then?"

"Almost to the letter. A young guy named Thomas McCutcheon. I was curious, so I googled 'McCutcheon' to see what I could find."

"What'd you come up with."

"Well, not surprisingly, there are hundreds of possibilities. But I think it's pretty obvious what the connection is. There's a Ryan McCutcheon, who just retired as president of a small college in Ohio."

"Let me guess—he knows Hank somehow."

"Bingo! According to the bio on the college website, it looks like he and Hank climbed the greasy pole together. They were deans at the same school: he was Dean of Sciences when Hank was in Humanities and Social Sciences. I did a little more snooping around, and the 'word on the street' is that the two of them have remained friends ever since. Hank and Hannah even vacation with the McCutcheons sometimes. So he's obviously known our candidate since he was a boy."

"If he built the job description around him, I assume there's no question that Thomas meets all the qualifications."

"That's the problem, at least from his perspective. The job description specifies that 'the successful candidate must have completed all of the requirements for the Ph.D. by August 1.' According to at least one of his references, that doesn't seem likely. The recommendations are all positive, but it sounds like it would be overly optimistic to expect him to finish his dissertation before next year."

"Well, that should settle things, shouldn't it?"

"One would hope so. But with Hank, who knows?"

"I know he likes to play fast and loose with the rules sometimes, but how would he get around that requirement."

"I don't know, but I wouldn't put anything past him. This could be his parting shot as he walks out the door. Who knows what he and this McCutcheon have lined up. I'm sure the father would be very grateful to Hank if his son were to land a tenure-line faculty position in this job market."

"How's the rest of the pool look? Are there any good candidates?"

"As you might expect, there are a few whose credentials are only tangentially related to the job description. They're applying out of desperation, hoping that we don't come up with any really qualified applicants, so we'll take a look at them."

"That's par for the course. There's usually a handful that you can weed out right at the beginning of any search."

"But there are several who look really good. Obviously, this McCutcheon fellow fits the job description. He should, if it was written specifically for him. But in addition to not having finished his degree, he's weak in terms of experience, except as a TA. It doesn't look like he's ever taught his own course. There's a young woman who's on a temporary appointment at a small college in Pennsylvania who looks very sharp. She fits the job description almost as well as the guy it was designed for, and she has full-time teaching experience, as well as her Ph.D. in hand. She sent a summary of her course evaluations, and they're all glowing. I think we'd be lucky if we could hire her."

"You'll be especially lucky if you can get her past 'President Gatekeeper.' I hope Hank doesn't screw around with this."

Zoe noticed that more people were filling in the seats near their end of the table, and thought it would be best to change the subject. She didn't want Hank to know that she'd figured out what he was doing with the Classics position. It wasn't that she distrusted anyone at the table; she knew that Marty wouldn't tell anyone. But if someone else heard about it, they might add it to their list of complaints about Hank. And who knew where that might lead? Even if Hank did mess with the search, she wasn't sure there was anything they could do about it. So there was no point in getting anyone riled up—for now, at any rate.

Terry and Johanna both arrived at the same time and sat down next to Marty and Zoe. Marty suddenly realized that while he'd been talking to Zoe, the table had filled up. Except for the few who were out of the country, it looked like most of the *Kaffee Klatsch* was there now. Considering the time, he guessed that he wasn't the only one who'd be staying through to lunch.

"Has anybody heard from Dirk lately?" Johanna asked. "With the weather we have here right now, I half expect a message telling us that they've decided to stay in Italy."

Ed laughed, "I wouldn't blame them at all. As much as Dirk likes Italian wine, I'm sure he'd love to stay and move from one winery to the next, with an occasional stopover at a cooking school for Karen to fine-tune her skills."

"I got an e-mail from him yesterday," Marty said. "They're coming home this weekend. It sounds like they're having a great time. No threats of not returning, though. He's not close enough to retirement for that. Now, if I were in his shoes, I might be tempted."

"How about Chris?" Marianna asked. "How's his research trip going, Marty?"

"I got a message from him just before I came over here. It sounds like the archive was a gold mine for him. And he's even had time to work on his article—enough to get a draft finished. It sounds like he made enough progress that he can even take a few days to enjoy the Netherlands before he comes back next week."

Terry looked around the table and asked, "Would anybody mind if I changed the subject to something more serious?"

"Not at all," Marianna said. "What's up?"

"First of all, I have to qualify this by saying that I'm not sure if it's true or not. But if it is, I think we need to all be prepared to take a stand at the next Faculty Assembly. I've heard a rumor that Hank's been talking to the City about the traffic light."

"Oh, Christ, not that again!" Johanna groaned. "How many times do we have to go through that?"

Terry nodded. "Well, apparently the Mayor was complaining to Hank again, and Chief van den Hoek says he's tired of having to deal with all the townspeople who gripe about the traffic jams it creates."

"Traffic jams?" Ed laughed. "In New Leiden? How long do they last—ten minutes? People around here don't even know what a real traffic jam is. When I was in grad school in California, I'd spend more time in a traffic jam just getting to campus than these folks spend in their cars in a month."

"I agree," Terry said. "But they argue that the whole problem is the bottleneck caused by the traffic light on campus. If they could eliminate it, or at least adjust the timing of the damned thing, they could get rid of the bottleneck."

Bill cleared his throat. "To quote George, in *Who's Afraid of Virginia Wolff,* 'I will not give up Berlin!'"

Ed shook his head in confusion. "I appreciate you adding a literary dimension to our conversation, Bill. But just what in the Hell is that supposed to mean?"

"The Faculty Assembly is always going on and on about 'shared governance.' Even Hank makes a token nod to it every once in a while—though usually in a way to show that it's really all a sham these days. What has happened to 'shared governance' around this place? What, if anything, is left of it?"

Marty nodded in agreement. "I've been around here longer than most people (though thankfully not everyone). When I first came here, the Faculty Assembly really did play a role in setting policies and running the place. These days, about the only thing we do at Faculty Assembly meetings is approve course proposals. And since some of our colleagues are so determined to put every aspect of the curriculum under their microscope, we spend so much time parsing course descriptions that we don't do anything else. That's all taken care of by professional administrators."

"So, what happened?" Johanna asked. "Why doesn't the Faculty Assembly do anythin' significant anymore?"

Marty looked around the table and sighed, "Because we gave all our power away."

"What do you mean, 'we gave it away'?" Marianna asked.

"It's simple. For the faculty to really run things efficiently (if that's possible—which of course may be questionable), they have to spend time in committees. And everyone knows how much we hate to serve on committees. How many Division or Faculty Assembly meetings have you been in when somebody got nominated to serve on a committee simply because they weren't there? Then everybody laughs about it! We keep watering down the value of committee service. So a class of managerial *condottieri* was created—administrative mercenaries. They move around the country, going from school to school as they climb the greasy pole. Rather than listen to faculty argue *ad infinitum* about whether or not the third paragraph of a new administrative policy should have a semi-colon in it, presidents and deans found it much easier to work with professional administrators. They were able to sell the power-grab by telling us that they were sparing us the drudgework that we didn't like to do. We could spend more time on teaching and research. And of course, those same deans and presidents then argued that since we were freed up to do more research, we had to be expected to publish more. Which meant that we'd have less time to do administrative stuff, so they'd have to hire more administrators. It's a vicious cycle, with the end result being that 'shared governance' now means we have responsibility for approving courses, and maybe every decade or so wasting a couple more years coming up with another new curriculum. Meanwhile, the administration takes care of everything else."

"And to restate my question," Ed said, "what in the Hell does this have to do with Berlin—or the stoplight, for that matter?"

Bill laughed, "My apologies, Ed! I forgot that you tend to be more literal than I am. As Marty just explained, over the years, the Faculty's power has been dramatically reduced. Our teeth have been pulled, if you will. If it were up to Hank, there wouldn't even be a Faculty Assembly, and there wouldn't be tenured faculty, either. He'd like to be able to hire and fire us 'as the market demands.' But Marty didn't mention the one thing that the Faculty still have control over here at NNC: the traffic light on campus."

"I still don't see the issue," Ed said.

"I'm sorry," Bill said, "I forgot that you joined the Faculty after this came up the last time. When the College was founded, the planners, in their infinite wisdom, thought there should be a grand thoroughfare through the middle of campus. And with the originality for which the founders of colleges are almost universally renowned, they called it 'Campus Avenue.' At that time, the campus was on the outskirts of town. But New Leiden gradually expanded to encircle, and move far beyond, the campus. As a result, Campus Avenue became a main connecting route between 'downtown' and the housing developments that sprang up after World War II. At the same time, what light industry there is around here expanded on the opposite side of town."

"So everyone who lives out beyond the campus has to take Campus Avenue to get downtown, or to work on the other side of town?" Ed asked.

"Exactly! But long before all that developed, the College wanted to show that it was progressive, and keeping up with modern technology. The rest of the town still only had stop signs, but the campus was going to have an electric stop light! And not just a blinking light. The faculty—as the incorporated entity, the NNC Faculty Association—paid for it. And they made an agreement with the city that they would maintain it. Today, that's the main crossing that students use to get from their dorms to the rest of campus—to their classes, the gym, the cafeteria, the CUB—everything. So for decades, the stoplight has been set to accommodate pedestrian traffic. Students just walk up, push a button, and traffic gets stopped on demand. Meanwhile, city traffic has continued to increase. It all comes to a stand-still at the bottleneck created by the only stoplight on Campus Avenue."

"That all makes sense. But I'm still waiting for you to take me to Berlin," Ed said.

"I'm getting there," Bill laughed. "The city would like to take over control of the stoplight. That way, they could adjust its timing to fit the ebb and flow of traffic across town, especially at rush hours. But no one in town seems to remember that it was the faculty who installed—and still control—the light. Hank's not about to admit that he doesn't control everything. He would love to accommodate them—he figures it's one of the few ways that he can score some points with the city fathers, and maybe even improve relations with Chief van den Hoek. But any faculty who are familiar with the issue, and the way 'shared governance' has evolved over the last few decades, recognize that this is the last vestige of faculty power here. If we give this up, then we'll only be left with approving course proposals at Faculty Assembly meetings—until they do away with that, too. So, to put it in dramatic terms, it's the barricade on which we'll make our final stand. Or, like the US during the Berlin Blockade, and George in *Who's Afraid of Virginia Woolf*, 'I will not give up Berlin!'"

"It seems like there must be some way that we could maintain control of the stoplight, and still ease the bottleneck on Campus Avenue," Ed said.

"Sure there is. But not by having Hank tell us to turn control of it over to the city. I'm pretty sure that if the city simply asked the faculty—not Hank, but the faculty—if they'd help alleviate the bottleneck by adjusting the timing of the light to accommodate traffic, most of us would agree. But they've never asked the faculty—only Hank. Everyone in town assumes that he runs the show. And since he thinks he does, too, he doesn't bother to tell them that it's the faculty who are technically in control of the light, not the College itself."

Marty added, "Hell, for starters, the city and the College could build a pedestrian walkway over Campus Avenue. That would make it a lot easier for students to cross over to campus, and they could easily adjust the timing of the light any way they wanted, without any impact on the students. But that would just be one more thing that Hank would say the College 'can't afford.' He can afford to hire more administrators, but not do anything productive for the College. They might even be able to get some financial support from the state, since Campus

Avenue carries so much traffic now. But as long as Hank keeps trying to hand over control of the light to the City, nothing's going to happen."

"Thanks," Ed said. "That all makes sense. I'll join you on the barricade, and like you, 'I will not give up Berlin!'"

*   *   *   *   *

HANK HUNG UP THE PHONE, and got up from his desk. He looked out his window, and watched the snow blowing around the terrace. Then he went out to Annika's desk. "That was Rothman again."

"Is he still looking for a job? I hope he's not thinking he can come back here."

"No, the lucky bastard's landed on his feet—not a perfect landing, but better than what he probably deserves."

"What's he found? I can't imagine another college would hire him, at least not this soon. As you said, he has to be pretty toxic as far as most decent-quality schools are concerned."

"He took my suggestion, and contacted a couple for-profit schools. One in the Chicago area hired him to be their 'Assistant Director for Curriculum Development.'"

"That's quite a come-down from being a college president."

"Sure, but it also beats unemployment! I get the feeling that everyone in their administration is at least an Assistant Director of something or other. It obviously doesn't pay all that well, because he's also going to be teaching English comp courses at a local community college. Paula will definitely be making more money than he will be."

"What's she got lined up?"

"He told me she was going to open her own interior design studio, but she got hired by some big design outfit based in the Chicago. Apparently she used to work for the woman who runs it, and she offered to make Paula a VP."

308

"How's Paul taking that—I can't imagine him being very comfortable with her making more money than he does."

"He doesn't have much choice in the matter. Knowing Paula, I'm sure she's never going to let him forget that he managed to get himself fired. She had to give up her career when he started climbing the greasy pole, so she probably figures it's her turn now. I'm sure she won't screw things up like he did. If he knows what's good for him, he'll smile and tell her how proud of her he is. If he can't manage that, he'll probably be sent packing before too long."

Annika thought to herself, *"I wouldn't blame her. He always treated her as the 'little woman,' who couldn't possibly think for herself."*

He started back to his desk, but then he turned back to her and said, "I need you to set up a meeting with the Financial Concerns Committee."

"Can you give me some information, so that I can tell them what it's about?"

"Looking ahead at next year's budget, they're going to have to help us do some more belt-tightening. When I met with them last fall, I told them that it was not financially sustainable for the College to pick up the extra insurance for retirees who are on Medicare, and especially not for their spouses."

"I thought that idea didn't go anywhere."

"It didn't. I thought all those old farts would put their loyalty to the College ahead of their individual self-interest. But the Association of Retired Professors showed up and basically said, 'We have a contract, and we have an attorney.'"

"I thought the Financial Concerns Committee said that wouldn't save much money. What's it cost per month for each retiree on our group policy? I thought they said it was only $20 or $30 a month, for each person. That doesn't sound very 'unsustainable.'"

"You're starting to sound like that goddamned committee! It's the principle of the thing. People need to put the long-term interests of the College ahead of their own short-term gain."

"You're going to have a tough time selling that to the Committee. What else are you thinking of."

"At a minimum, we need to start charging for parking around here?"

"Parking fees—on this campus?"

"Sure—if these people were working in the Cities, they'd be paying hundreds—probably thousands—of dollars a year to park in a lot downtown."

"They'd also have much bigger salaries. And if they didn't want to pay for parking downtown, they could take the light rail or bus."

"Again, it's the principle of the thing. Everyone needs to help tighten our belts and share in the effort to help the College through this financial crisis. The NNC community needs to join together in this shared sacrifice."

"And let me guess," Annika said to herself. *"I'm sure your parking fees would come out of some special fund, just like your insurance does. It's really easy for you to talk about 'shared sacrifice.'"*

*   *   *   *   *

Thursday, January 30

CHRIS'S FLIGHT HAD BEEN ON TIME on Tuesday, and he'd connected with the shuttle to New Leiden. He got home late Tuesday night. He slept in Wednesday, did his laundry, and then helped his downstairs neighbor shovel snow off the driveway. He called Marty to let him know he'd be going up to campus on Thursday. They planned to meet after Marty's class, and go have coffee.

No matter what he'd been doing since he left Amsterdam, all he could think about was the preceding week. Mariah had arrived in Utrecht late Tuesday evening. He met her for breakfast at her hotel Wednesday morning, and then went with her to visit several museums. In between museum visits, they stopped for coffee once, and again for lunch. In the afternoon, after they'd left the third museum of the day, he gave her his "25-cent tour" of some of the highlights of the city. They had dinner at a student-oriented restaurant near the University, and stopped at a pub near her hotel to listen to some jazz.

They repeated much of the same routine on Thursday. Before he left to pick her up at her hotel again, he sent Marty an e-mail, giving him a progress report on his research trip. He met Mariah at her hotel again, and resumed her museum visits. They went to the last two on her list, and then had coffee and pastry at a small café across the square from her hotel. Just as they were leaving the café, there was a flash of lightning, and thunder rattled the windows around the square. When the first few drops of rain started to fall, they ducked under an awning outside a shop, in hopes of waiting out the rain. They were next to a small florist's shop, so Chris stepped in and bought a pink carnation. When he handed it to Mariah, she didn't say a word.

"Damn!" he thought. *"I've really stepped in it this time. So much for my romantic moves!"*

They walked down the street, looking in store windows, staying under awnings to keep out of the rain. She still hadn't said anything. But at least she still had the flower, which she was keeping close to her chest. He didn't know if that was because she really liked it or just didn't want it crushed by a passerby. The sun peeked out behind a cloud, and Chris saw that the rain shower had passed.

"It looks like it's stopped raining. Would you like to go someplace near the university and find some lunch."

She looked at the nearby shops and laughed. "I've got a better idea. Are you up for a picnic?"

"That sounds great to me! We're surrounded by all the key ingredients—there's a cheese shop, a bakery, and a pastry shop for dessert. It looks like the meat market over there has some great smoked meats, too—salami, ham, you name it."

"I noticed there was a small wine shop on the corner. That would make it complete."

After they bought their lunch supplies and visited the wine shop, they started off to look for a dry place to eat their lunch. Suddenly Chris stopped. "Damn!" he said.

"What is it?" Mariah asked.

"I forgot to get a corkscrew! I have one where I'm staying, but it would take us at least half an hour to get there. I'd better go back to the wine shop and buy one."

"I've got one in my suitcase. We can stop by the room and pick it up—no problem!"

As they started across the square to her hotel, there was another clap of thunder, followed by more rain. They made it to the hotel before the rain got too heavy, but it was clear that an outdoor picnic was no longer such a great idea.

"Hey, don't worry about it," she laughed. "We've got all the fixin's—we just need someplace dry to eat. My room has two chairs and a table. There's even a radio, so we can have some music to accompany our meal. Now that's first class!"

When they got to her room, she found her corkscrew and handed it to him. "Here—you can do the honors. I'll get some glasses, and find some napkins. After you open the wine, why don't you put the food on the table?"

She turned on the radio, and found a station playing classical music. When she came back with the glasses, she had an extra one, holding the carnation.

"Thanks for the lovely flower!"

"You're welcome!" he laughed. "I wasn't sure if I'd done something wrong, since you didn't say anything."

"I'm sorry! I was just so touched—I wasn't expecting it. As I said, it's lovely!"

He poured them each a glass of wine, and raised a toast. "To new friends!"

"To new friends!" she laughed.

They clinked their glasses together, and then each took a sip. "MMM! Nice! What kind is it," she asked.

"It's an Argentinian Malbec," he said.

"I don't know much about wine. I've never heard of that kind. Do you know a lot about wine?"

Chris laughed. "Not much at all. One of my colleagues at NNC served me some of this last fall. I'd never heard of it before then. When I saw it today, it was the obvious choice. I had no idea what most of the others in that shop were. In grad school, if the wine had a cork in it, it was generally beyond my budget. But I'm familiar with some of the better known wineries in Washington—at least by name. Wait a minute, let me try that again." He puffed himself up a bit, and feigned a "sophisticated" accent. "Ah, yes, an Argentinian Malbec. One of my favorites. This is a particularly good year. It has such a firm texture, with hints of plums, blackberries, and a slight overtone of oak." He laughed. "I don't suppose that was very convincing."

"Your first answer was just fine!" she said, and clinked his glass again.

He smiled across their glasses, and noticed her eyes again. "You have the brightest blue eyes I've ever seen," he said.

She blushed, but managed to say "Thanks."

Chris thought to himself, *"I'm not sure I should do this, but what the Hell! An impromptu picnic, a bottle of wine. It can't get too much more romantic than this."*

He set down his glass, and reached across the table and took her hand. *"Here goes nothing!"* he thought, and leaned across the table and kissed her. She set her glass next to his, they both stood up, and she put her arms around his neck.

They didn't get around to eating their picnic lunch until later in the afternoon. That evening, they ventured out briefly for dinner. He asked her if she wanted to go back to the pub to listen to jazz again, or maybe find another club.

She shook her head. "I think I'd rather listen to classical music on the radio," so they went back to her hotel.

The next morning, he joined her for breakfast again, but this time he didn't have to travel across town to get there. When they went downstairs to breakfast, he took a deep breath and asked, "What are your plans now? You said you were going to travel for a few days before you go to Amsterdam. Where do you think you'll go? Maybe I could join you," he said hesitantly.

"I was originally planning to go to one of the small towns along the coast. But with the weather we've been having, that doesn't seem like such a good idea. I haven't been able to see much of Utrecht outside of the museums, so I thought maybe I could stay here over the weekend. I can check down at the front desk to see if I can keep this room for a couple more days."

"In that case, I have a better idea," he said nervously. "Jan and Trina, the friends I'm staying with, flew to the States last Saturday. They're letting me stay at their place until I leave for Amsterdam. If you don't want to pay for a hotel room for the next few nights, I'd love to have you join me."

"I think that's a wonderful idea—but only if you let me reciprocate. I have a hotel room reserved in Amsterdam starting Sunday night. Why don't we go to Amsterdam together on Sunday, and you can stay with me until you fly home on Tuesday. It makes more sense to share the cost of that room for a couple nights than to both pay for separate rooms. Something tells me we wouldn't have much need for a second room," she laughed.

Monday morning in Amsterdam, they visited the Rijksmuseum and the van Gogh Museum, and did some sightseeing in the afternoon, but they spent more time looking into each other's eyes than they did looking at museum exhibits. Chris found a restaurant featuring Indonesian "Rijsttafel" for dinner, and then they spent the rest of the night and part of the next morning saying goodbye. Rather than deal with the congestion at the airport, she saw him off at the train station. They made plans to meet for dinner in New Leiden Saturday night. All the way home, Chris could think of nothing else.

When he got to his office Thursday morning, he picked up his mail. Marty had sent him a message confirming that the disk with his newly copied files had arrived, so he picked that up and took it to his office. Before he left Utrecht, he'd saved a copy of his paper to his "cloud" back up, and he made an extra copy of that as soon as he got to his office. He wasn't taking any chances that he might lose it.

When he heard Marty come back from his class, he went down to his office. "Welcome back!" Marty said, and reached out to shake his hand. "Let's hear about your trip! It sounds like it was really productive. I'm looking forward to reading your article."

"Yeah, it was great. As I told you in my e-mail, the staff at the archive were very helpful, so that gave me a lot of time to get a draft of the article finished."

"And how was Utrecht? I hope you had a chance to do something besides work in the archive."

"Oh, sure," Chris said dreamily. "I had a great time."

The tone of Chris's voice caught Marty's attention. He looked carefully at him, and exclaimed, "Oh, my God! The man's fallen in love!"

Chris blushed. "What do you mean? Does it show?"

"Does it show?" Marty laughed. "As my dad used to say, 'you've got that sick calf look about you.' So, who is it? How'd you meet her? Is she from Utrecht, or an American? Tell me all about it!"

"No, she's not Dutch. You're not going to believe this: she teaches at Chartwell! She sat next to me on the plane to Amsterdam, and I promised I'd show her the highlights of Utrecht."

"It appears that you did!" Marty laughed. "Did she come back on the same flight, too?"

"No, she gets back to MSP this afternoon. But she's coming for dinner Saturday!"

"Well, I'm not going to say anything more. When things settle down a bit, and your relationship has a chance to develop, I look forward to meeting her. But for now, let's go over to the CUB. I think this definitely deserves a cinnamon roll in celebration! And don't worry—I won't tell anyone else about it. I'll leave that up to you when you think the time is right—maybe you can bring her to a college function so we can all have a chance to meet her. I must say, it sounds like your trip was definitely a great investment of college funds—academically as well as personally! But knowing Hank, I'm sure that if he found out about it, he'd probably want you to pay him a match-maker's fee!"

13
Back to the Day in Question

Friday, February 21—Late Morning

HANK SAT AT HIS COMPUTER, drumming his fingers. It was past 11:00, and he was still struggling to put the finishing touches on his presentation to the Board of Trustees the next morning. He'd gone over several key points with Gene Graandsma before Gene and Hannah had left on another round of Alumni Association meetings. He knew what he wanted to say, but he couldn't quite figure out the best way to put it. Normally Annika wrote most of his presentations, but this time, there were a couple of sections he didn't want to leave to her. He was sure that when she found out about them, she'd be furious. *"But that's her problem,"* he thought. *"I have to look out for my own long-term interests."*

Annika poked her head into his office. "Is Gene supposed to get back today? Are you planning to go over the Board's agenda with him before the meeting?"

"Their flight's supposed to get in this afternoon. If the weather cooperates, they'll be here this evening. I thought I could review everything with him over dinner. Speaking of flights: can you take care of the registration for me for that Liberal Arts College Presidents Association Conference in Las Vegas next month, and see what kinds of flights you can line up for me?"

"Will Hannah be going with you?"

"No, she and Gene are going to be swanning around at a couple of Alumni Association events in Iowa and Illinois."

"I still don't think it's such a good idea for Hannah to be doing so much traveling with him."

"Why not? What could possibly happen? It's Gene, for Christ's sake!"

"What's that supposed to mean? Don't you think something could happen between Gene and Hannah?"

"Hah! Gene and Hannah? That's a laugh!"

"What makes you say that?"

"Doesn't Gene strike you as being a little 'light in the loafers'?"

"You think Gene Graandsma is gay?"

"Don't you?"

"Hardly! I have a pretty refined 'gay-dar,' and Gene's never shown up on that," she laughed.

"Oh, come on. Look at how he dresses: pink shirts, flowered ties."

"He's stylish. Both he and Demi have a good sense of clothing styles, and keep up on what's in fashion."

"He does just about everything but 'swish.' I'm surprised he hasn't opened a florist shop to keep himself busy while Demi runs the exercise studios. I've never been able to figure out why somebody with Demi's looks is hooked up with a limp wristed guy like Gene."

"You're misreading Gene's mannerisms. Trust me. I'm the voice of experience: the Graandsmas are the only couple who've both tried to make a pass at me."

"You have to be imagining things. I'm sure it was a misunderstanding. You said the same thing about me."

Annika looked him straight in the eye and said, "Let's not go down that road again, okay? Trust me, they both made passes at me."

"Why would you think Demi would ever make a pass at you?"

"You really have no idea, do you?"

"Idea of what?"

"Let me put it this way: Demi puts the B in LGBTQ."

"WHAT? You're making that up!"

"Not at all. She's 'bi.' She apparently has a great time with Gene, but every once in a while she reportedly likes to 'expand her horizons.' If the rumors are correct, when she goes on business trips, she even likes to hook up with 'three-somes.' Sometimes it's two other women, sometimes one of them is male."

"Why would Gene put up with that?"

"First of all, it's her money that funds their life style. If he complained, he'd be out on the street, with no immediate source of income. But apparently she doesn't mind if he messes around, too—though he's strictly hetero, from what I hear. I guess they both enjoy an 'open marriage.'"

"No, I still don't believe it—about either one of them!"

"Believe what you want. I'm just telling you what seems to be the common understanding of people who know them. Now, if you'll excuse me, I'm going to take an early lunch. It sounds like we're going to get a doozy of a storm this afternoon, and I need to get a practice round in at the biathlon track before we get socked in. With the Board meeting, I might not get another chance this weekend. The only thing left on your agenda this morning is your meeting with Zoe van den Berg and Monica Schutte. And you said you didn't need me—no, didn't WANT me—to be here for that. Elke can cover anything until I get back. If you need any assistance with the last part of your presentation for the Trustees, I can help you then."

"Don't worry about my presentation. I can take care of it on my own."

After Annika left, Hank went back to his desk. He took out a notepad, and scribbled a note for himself, which he put with the others on the corner of his desk. He planned to get all of those taken care of before he went home that evening.

After he'd been at his computer for about fifteen minutes, Elke knocked on his door.

"Excuse me: Zoe van den Berg and Monica Schutte are here for their meeting."

"Thanks, Elke! Please show them in." To himself, he groaned, *What a pair to draw to – add somebody like*

319

Francine Reim to their little group, and you'd have the start of a Shakespeare play. I'm sure they'd qualify as a coven." He clicked his mouse to minimize the application he'd been using, and picked up the file on his desk. It included the application materials for the top two candidates for the Classics position, as well as the search committee's recommendation. When they entered his office, he rose from his desk, shook their hands, and showed them to the chairs in front of his desk. Then he went back behind his desk and sat in his "Presidential Chair."

"I've been looking at your committee files," he said. "It looks like you had some excellent candidates. And your recommendation is . . . ?"

Monica couldn't disguise the irritation in her voice. "As it states clearly in our executive summary, the committee unanimously supports Mary Anne Fischer. She is, without doubt, the superior candidate. She's completed her Ph.D., she has full-time teaching experience, and she already has a journal article that's currently out for review."

"I see that. But I can't support that recommendation."

"What!?! She's the committee's unanimous choice."

"Well, I think the committee has made a bad choice. As I said, I can't support it. I don't think she would be a good fit in the NNC community."

Zoe cleared her throat. "And who, may I ask, would you suggest we hire instead?"

"In reviewing the other candidates, I'm convinced that this other applicant, Thomas McCutcheon, would be a much better fit here. Looking at his background, the type of schools he's attended, his research focus—all of that fits the job description perfectly. Yes, I think Tommy would fit into the NNC community perfectly."

"Tommy??" Monica asked incredulously.

"Oh, you know me, Monica—I'm not much for formalities. I'm sure he would prefer to be called Tommy rather than Thomas."

Monica stared at him in disbelief. "Let me tell you why I think you're making a mistake: First of all, Fischer is clearly better qualified. She's completed her degree. She has experience. She's about to have an article published in a scholarly journal. And 'Tommy' has been a Teaching Assistant. He hasn't even finished his Ph.D. yet! That's a specific requirement for the position. If you give him the job over someone who already has her degree, you'll not only be violating the hiring guidelines established for the College. You'll undoubtedly be opening up the College for a potential lawsuit."

"That's not a problem. In reviewing the budget projections for the coming year, it's clear that the College can't afford to add a new tenure-line faculty position in the coming year. It'll have to be delayed until next year. And I'm sure that by that time, our candidate will be 'Dr. McCutcheon.' So there will be no problems hiring him."

"No problems? The whole process stinks to high Heaven! 'There's something rotten in Denmark!' If Fischer finds out that you've delayed the hire to accommodate another candidate who's not currently qualified, I wouldn't blame her for suing you."

Hank slammed his hand down on his desk. "THIS IS NOT A MATTER FOR DISCUSSION! I CANNOT SUPPORT THE COMMITTEE'S RECOMMENDA-TION! I TOLD YOU THAT! YOU'RE NOT LISTENING TO ME! YOUR COMMITTEE CLEARLY DIDN'T DO A GOOD ENOUGH JOB VETTING THE CANDIDATES!" He paused for a breath. "You can go through all the motions you want to, but I have to look at the future of the College. It's clear to me that one candidate will best fit in with the NNC Community, and that's Tommy McCutcheon. You need to look at the best interests of the College as we move forward in the twenty-first century!"

Monica stood up, and looked Hank straight in the eye: "I don't have to sit here and be treated like this. How dare you yell at me!" She started toward the door.

"You can't just get up and walk away from me!" Hanks yelled.

"The Hell I can't! Just watch me! I'm the fourth generation of my family to teach here. My children are alums, and I expect my grandchildren will be, too. My family was here before you were born, and we'll be here long after you're gone. You think you'll just walk out the door in June scot-free. You think that if she sues, she'll be suing the College, and not you. Well, if I were you, I wouldn't be so sure! I know that if it were me, I wouldn't just be suing the College. I'd be suing your ass, too. Don't forget: that file you have on your desk is just a copy. The originals have been filed with the Human Relations Office. If she decides to sue, which I hope she does, her lawyers will subpoena that file as soon as they can. I don't know if you realize it, but the way you've messed with other searches, you probably don't have any allies in HR, either. So don't expect them to conveniently 'misplace' that file. And even if they did, I think you're smart enough to know that there are a couple other copies floating around, too."

Zoe stood up to follow Monica. "And think about this, Hank," she said. "Let's say 'Tommy' does come. You'll be gone. When he goes through Third Year Review and Tenure evaluation, you won't be here anymore to pull strings for him—to protect him. And if you've pissed off his Department Chair as well as one of the most respected members of the faculty, how's he going to get tenure? But of course, you won't have to worry about that, will you? You'll be comfortable in some retirement village. And when his father calls and asks you, 'Why didn't you grease the skids for my kid's tenure, Hank?' you'll just hold up your hands and say, 'What could I do? I'm not there to keep the faculty in line anymore.'"

As she was about to walk out the door, Monica stopped, turned around, and looked him straight in the eye. She said, with a very precise, clipped cadence, "If she does decide to sue, which I hope she does, don't expect me to speak on your behalf. I'll be a witness for the plaintiff!"

She and Zoe then walked out the door, and Monica slammed it behind them.

They walked down the hall, and went into Sarah's office. Monica stopped at Mary de Smet's desk. "Is the Dean available? We need to talk to her if she has a few minutes. I'm sorry this is such short notice."

"I think so. She has a dentist appointment later, so she didn't want to schedule anything this morning that might make her late for that. Let me check with her." Mary went back to Sarah's office and returned a minute or two later. "She says to go on into her office. She has about half an hour before she needs to leave for the dentist."

When they stepped into her office, Sarah could tell that they were both upset. Monica, in particular, looked like steam was about to shoot out of her ears.

"What's going on? Is there something I can help you with?"

Monica described their meeting with Hank, and Sarah shook her head. "That's amazing! I've been warned that he sometimes plays fast and loose with the rules, but this takes the cake! It's worse than anything I've ever heard of before—here, or anywhere else, for that matter. I'm not sure there's anything I can do about it, though. If Hank's made up his mind, he's not likely to change it—especially if a female faculty member, or even a dean, asks him. But this explains one thing, at least."

"What's that?" Monica asked.

"I knew there was something wrong with the way he ran that search. Normally the Dean is supposed to be in charge of faculty hires. Hank usually doesn't want to busy himself with details like that. Most of the time, it's hard enough to get him to meet all of the candidates. But this time, he said he wanted to handle everything. He said it was important because the van der Kellens had established the new Center for Dutch Studies, and his own name was going to be on the endowed chair. I tried to set it up like a normal search, but he wouldn't hear of it. I doubt that he'll listen to me any more now than he did then."

Zoe nodded in agreement. "We're not expecting you to be able to change his mind. That would be asking for a miracle. But we wanted to make sure you knew what Hank was doing—and we didn't want you to be blindsided if the other candidate decides to sue."

"I'll talk to him, but I won't hold out much hope that it will have any impact. I can't do it until Monday, though. He's getting ready for the Board of Trustees meeting tomorrow. I'll be there, too, but he's pretty much told me that he expects me to sit quietly in the back and let him run things. I asked him if he needed any help getting ready today, and he told me that he wanted to do it himself. Annika told me that he didn't even want her to help him finish his presentation to the Trustees, which is quite out of the ordinary. She usually has to write almost everything he says. I don't know what he's cooking up, but if it's anything like this, I'm not looking forward to finding out. I'll get in touch with you both after I talk to him next week. But as I said, I'm not optimistic."

"We understand," Monica said. "But we appreciate your willingness to make the effort. Thanks for your time." Sarah showed the two of them to the door, and closed it after they left. *"What in the Hell did I get myself into here?"* she thought. *"Every time he does something and I think it can't get any worse, he pulls another stunt. How's he going to top this one? I don't know how I'm going to make it until he leaves this summer!"*

*   *   *   *   *

AFTER MONICA AND ZOE HAD LEFT HIS OFFICE, Hank picked up the phone. He flipped open the folder that the search committee had put together, and found Thomas McCutcheon's file. He dialed the cell number, but he was immediately transferred to his voice mail. Although he was still furious at Monica and Zoe, he kept his voice calm when he left a message: "Tommy, this is Hank van Daam. I just met with the head of the search committee and the

Chair of the Classics Department. Give me a call when you have a chance, so we can talk about it. I'll be tied up with a Board of Trustees meeting all weekend, so if you can't get back to me this afternoon, please call me Monday morning."

He hung up, and went back to his computer. He opened the application he'd been using earlier, and after he calmed down a little, he went back to his Trustees presentation. About 12:30, he went over to the CUB to get some lunch. After the meeting with Monica and Zoe, he wasn't in the mood to make small talk with any other faculty members. To avoid that, he grabbed a sandwich and took it back to his office. He'd just finished eating when Elke knocked on his door.

"Yes—what is it?" he growled.

"There are a couple representatives from the Staff Association here to see you."

"Do they have an appointment? I didn't see anything about a meeting with them today. What do they want?

"They apologized about that. It's apparently something that just came up. I told them I wasn't sure you had time to see them, but they said it would only take a few minutes. So I said I'd check with you."

"Oh, Hell—I'm not making much progress on this damned report right now anyway. One more interruption won't make much difference. Send them in—but warn them: I can only spare a few minutes."

Elke ushered the two staff representatives into his office, and Hank got up from his desk. He turned on his classic "just call me Hank" smile, shook their hands, and pointed to the seats where Zoe and Monica had been earlier. He went back to his seat behind the desk. "What can I do for you today?" he asked.

Marie de Beer spoke first. A member of the custodial staff, she was currently the President of the Staff Association. "Have you heard the weather alert? There's been a severe winter storm warning issued for most of central Minnesota. We're supposed to be right in the middle of it."

"So? What am I supposed to do about it?"

Henry Steenwyk, the College's head electrician, shook his head. "Chief van den Hoek issued a couple of bulletins this morning, telling everyone to stock up on food, and stay off the streets this afternoon except for 'essential travel.' Before we get all the snow, there's going to be an ice storm. Schools are going to let out early, so that all the buses can be back to the garage before the ice storm hits."

"The College doesn't follow the schedule of the public schools," Hank snarled. "We're a residential campus! Our students don't need to worry about busses and traffic. They can easily walk back to their dorms."

"But faculty and staff can't," Maria replied. "And anyone with kids is going to want to get home to make sure they've made it home and are okay in the storm. If NNC doesn't send people home early, there are going to be a lot of people driving later in the day, when Chief van den Hoek is trying to keep the streets clear of non-essential traffic."

"Let's put it this way," Henry added. "The Police Chief has issued an order to stay off the streets. The State Police have announced there will be a 'No Towing' order this evening. If anyone drives, and goes off the road, they'll be stuck—in dangerously cold weather. And if someone ends up getting hurt as a result, and it happens because the College wouldn't cooperate with the police order and let them go home early, the lawyers in town will be salivating. I shudder to think of the lawsuits that would come out of that. It could cost the College millions."

"I think this whole thing is being blown out of proportion. It's winter—in Minnesota! It's just a storm, for cryin' out loud! We get 'em every winter."

"There are storms, and there are STORMS," Maria replied. "From what the National Weather Service is predicting, this may be one of the worst in ten or fifteen years, or longer. Look at it from this perspective: you're retiring at the end of the academic year, right?"

"Right—what's that have to do with anything?"

"It's kind of like a bad waitress in a cheap restaurant. She ignores you through most of the meal, screws up a couple of orders, and essentially grunts and growls at you if you ask her to bring you what you really wanted. But just before you're finished, and you're about ready to pay up without leaving a tip, she's suddenly at your beck and call. She refills your coffee or soft drink. She gives you a little extra ice cream on the piece of pie that she recommended for you. She even helps you put on your coat. And by the time you finally leave, you have such a good feeling about her that you leave an extra large tip."

Hank's face started to turn red. He obviously didn't like her analogy.

Maria noticed his reaction, and added quickly, "Don't get me wrong—I'm not comparing you to a bad waitress. But the same principle applies to a great president, too."

"How so? What's that have to do with my retirement, much less whether or not we shut down the College early today?"

"It's all about the 'van Daam Legacy,'" she smiled. "It doesn't matter how many great things you've done over the course of your entire career. What most people will think of when they hear your name will be what you've done this year. This is your last semester here. It'll put the final stamp on your legacy. If you make everyone stay on campus until after the storm hits, you'll be remembered as the president who didn't have any concern for his staff and faculty. And if someone gets hurt as a result, you'll be the guy who was responsible for that—including any law suits that come out of it."

Henry added: "But if you send everyone home early, you'll be remembered as the president who put the welfare of his personnel ahead of simply following routine. You'll have helped mend some of the town-gown animosities by responding immediately and positively to Chief van den

Hoek's safety bulletins. Cooperation with local authorities always looks good," he smiled.

"And I suppose you want all the staff to be sent home with full pay for the day."

"That's the way it usually works in emergencies like this," Henry replied.

Maria looked at Henry, and then spoke up again. "From what I understand about him, I bet Chief van den Hoek would just love to have a reason to complain about you, and to make you look bad. But if you get everyone home and off the streets, he'll have to commend you and the College for your concerns for community safety. I'm sure that will drive him nuts!"

Hank thought to himself, *"Hell, if you put it like that, it sounds like a damned good idea. Anything that might make that son of a bitch uncomfortable is fine with me!"*

He looked at Maria and Henry and said, "Okay, tell Elke that I want her to send out an e-mail and a phone message to everyone on campus—that's what we got that fancy emergency communication system for, isn't it? The notice should say something like this: . . ." He thought a minute, and then continued: "'In the interests of safety, everyone should leave campus as soon as possible to avoid the impending storm. Except for personnel who are essential to the core operations of the College, everyone should plan to leave before 3:00.' Or words to that effect. Does that satisfy you?"

"That's exactly what we hoped to hear from you," Maria replied. "Thank you for your cooperation, and for your concern for the welfare of the staff and faculty."

"I still think it's a lot of fuss about nothing. But there probably isn't anything I can do about that without making myself look bad. Enjoy your afternoon off," he grumbled.

Monica and Henry stopped at Elke's desk and gave her the information that Hank wanted sent out. In a few minutes, a recorded phone message and an e-mail had been sent out to all faculty, staff and students. The campus would start emptying out almost immediately.

After they got in the elevator, Henry turned to Monica. "Well done! The part about 'the van Daam Legacy' was brilliant. The appeal to financial concerns certainly wasn't going anywhere. And I was worried when you started talking about the bad waitress in a cheap restaurant—fortunately you spun that so he didn't take it personally. I wasn't sure he was going to agree before you brought up his 'Legacy.'"

"From what I've seen over the years, there's only one thing that Hank's really concerned about. And it isn't the College, and definitely not us peons who work for him."

"What's that?"

"Simple: it's Hank. It's like the old line about conflict of interest: 'if it's in my interest, there's no conflict.' Hank cares about Hank. If something benefits him or can make him look good, he's all for it. If he doesn't see any benefit for himself, he's not interested. The 'van Daam Legacy' is well established. It can be summed up in one five-letter word."

"And that is?"

"Greed!"

"Well, I'm just glad that that he agreed to let everyone go home early. When the storm hits this afternoon, I plan to be home, indoors with my family, with a fire roaring in the Franklin stove. I'm sure I'll have to be outside with the snow blower most of tomorrow. But today, I'm just going to lie low. I don't want to have to venture out on the streets in a blizzard."

Shortly after Maria and Henry had left, Annika returned to her office. She had obviously stopped by the gym for a shower and to change out of her biathlon gear. She poked her head into Hank's office to let him know she was back.

"Don't expect to find anyone on campus for much longer," Hank grumbled.

"Why's that?"

"Everybody's freaking out about this storm. The Weather Service is predicting an ice storm first, and then heavy snowfall. The Police Department is asking everyone to stay off the streets except for essential travel. They want the streets clear so that emergency vehicles can get around. So I've had Elke send out a message on the emergency communication system. I told everyone to leave as soon as they can. So when you get finished with all the arrangements for tomorrow's Board of Trustees meeting, you should head out, too."

"I think that was a very wise move on your part. I'm sure the faculty and staff will all appreciate it. And it can't hurt relations with the city, either."

"That's what I thought, too"

Annika went back to her office, and thought to herself, *"Yeah, but where'd you get the idea? I can't believe you thought of it yourself—not something that might benefit College personnel."*

A few minutes later, she came back into Hank's office. "I'm looking at flights for you for that conference you talked about. When you go to Las Vegas, do you need to stop in Phoenix? Or is your friend taking care of getting the retreat center organized."

"That's a good idea. I'll call him over the weekend, and let him know I'll be stopping on my way back. I need to call him about something else, anyway"

"How are plans for 'Academic Executive Seminars' coming along, anyway? You haven't said anything about that for a while."

"McCutcheon's taking care of everything for now. I can't officially be part of the AES staff until July 1, after I'm retired here. I also won't be made VP until I invest my share of the 'seed money.' I can't do that until the insurance policy reaches maturity at the end of June."

"What insurance policy?"

"For as long as I've been President, the College has been paying for a life insurance policy for me. When I live to the end of my term in office, there will be a $2 million payout, split evenly between the College and me. A big chunk of my share will immediately be invested in AES."

Annika whistled. "That must be one Hell of an insurance policy!"

"If I didn't make it to June 30," he said, "Hannah and the College would each get $5 million."

"Doesn't that make you feel a little uneasy?"

"What?"

"If you serve out your term in office, Hannah shares $1 million with you, and the College gets its own million. But if something were to happen to you, they'd each get $5 million. If I were you, I'd be very careful whenever I stepped out into a crosswalk."

"Don't be ridiculous!   Now, if you're through besmirching the motives of the College and my wife, I have work to do. I still have to finish my presentation to the board."

"I could've had that done for you this morning, you know. I had most of it written for you yesterday. I'd have written the rest of it, too, if you'd just told me what you wanted me to include."

"Sure, but this is something I want to take care of myself. Gene gave me some very good ideas about how to word the section about the sabbatical."

"Sabbatical? Whose? Why are the Trustees dealing with sabbaticals at this time of the year? They usually do that at their fall meeting."

"This one's a little different. It's mine?"

"Yours?   How can you get a sabbatical?   You're retiring! For a sabbatical, you have to come back for at least a year. And you have to have some kind of research project."

"As I said, this one's different. It will give me the opportunity to reflect on my term in office as President, and make recommendations to the Board about ways in which the Office of President can be strengthened."

"But you're going to be running seminars for AES! How can you have time to 'reflect' when you're doing that?"

"Oh, that'll be easy. Besides, the Board thinks it's essential for hiring a new replacement. More and more schools are offering their presidents a sabbatical when they retire. If NNC doesn't, they won't be able to hire the quality of president that the College deserves. Speaking of which, how's the search for my replacement coming along?"

"You know I can't talk to you about that! The Chair of the Search Committee is scheduled to talk to the Board about it tomorrow."

"I know. But they told me I can't be there when he does."

"Good. You have no business being there. Let's just say that 'the search is still in its formative stages.' That's all you'll get out of me. And don't think I haven't noticed that you changed the subject. The whole idea of giving a 'sabbatical' to someone who is retiring makes no sense. Especially when that person has been telling everyone on campus that they need to help with the 'belt tightening' to deal with the financial crisis. The retirees, whose insurance you said was too expensive for the College to cover, will go nuts when they hear about this."

"I'll be gone by the time they do. The Board doesn't release personal financial information."

"And the Board supports it?"

"Gene says they will. As I said, if NNC doesn't follow the example of what other schools are doing, quality candidates won't be interested in coming here. That will be in my report to the Board tomorrow. Now—after you get all the arrangements finalized for the Board meeting tomorrow, let me know when you leave. Then I'll see you back here first thing in the morning."

Annika wasn't able to leave as quickly as she'd hoped. And as the day dragged on for her, she became more and more anxious about the weather conditions. Just before 3:00, the ice storm started. The snow followed around 4. By 6:00, Annika was finally gone, and Hank's was the only car left in the parking lot by the CUB. He was finally getting the wording of his Board report the way he wanted it. Hannah was stuck in the Cities, so he had nothing better to do than finish the report. He figured he'd be home by 7:00—7:30 at the latest.

But by 7:30, Hank was lying on the terrace outside his office, buried under a growing pile of snow.

14

The Morning After

FRANK O'LEARY LOOKED AT HIS WATCH. It was almost 7:30. "Have the next of kin been notified yet?" he asked.

"Nobody's been notified, except BCA," Carl replied. "Hannah, Hank's wife—widow, I guess I should say now—is on her way from the Cities. She got stuck there in the storm last night. She hoped to get on the road early this morning, but she was delayed by an accident on I-94. I talked to her a little while ago. She said she hoped to be here by about 10:30 or so."

"Did you tell her about her husband?"

"No. He disappeared last night, and no one knew where he was. She called this morning, just after we found him. Rather than tell her on the phone, I thought we should wait to do it in person."

"How many people know about this, then?"

"Right now, only a handful of people know anything. Besides my desk sergeant, who called the BCA, there's Officer van Klees—she's the one who's been taking all the pictures. Tom and Max here were the ones who uncovered the body. And then there's Denny Bakken, the student who found it in the first place."

"What was he doing up here so early in the morning?"

"See that streak of red snow over there? The kid was clearing the terrace with a snow blower. Hank was always very insistent that the terrace be cleared of snow before he got to his office. And that was especially important today—there's a Board of Trustees meeting this weekend. Denny started clearing the snow when it was still dark, but even then, he could tell when the blower

334

started spitting out bloody snow. He ran and got his supervisor, Max, who was having coffee with Tom. They were trying to figure out where Hank might be hiding out. When Denny told them what he'd seen, they came straight up here. They uncovered the body—Tom tried to disturb as little as possible, but he thought they needed to find the source of the blood as quickly as possible. If it was Hank under the snow, they hoped there might be a chance that he was still alive—however unlikely that might have been. Obviously, he wasn't. The kid was pretty shaken up."

"Where is he now?"

"Tom took him to his office. He gave him a blanket, and told him to try to take a nap on the couch. I'm not sure he'll be able to manage that."

"I'd like to talk to him as soon as I can. I see you've got the terrace closed off—is that his office in there?"

Carl nodded.

"Block it off, too. I don't want anyone else up here or in the office until the crime scene team gets here from Bemidji. I've heard the highway's only one-lane in a few spots, but at least it's open all the way from Bemidji. When his widow gets here, we'll have to break her the bad news. And as soon as we can, I'll need to interview her, too."

"I've been trying to reach the Dean," Carl said. "I just left a message on her voice mail. She's second in command, so she should know what's happened, too. When Hannah gets here, I'd really appreciate it if you could be the one to break her the bad news. It's not that I don't want to do it—Hank and I butted heads on a number of issues. If I were to be the one who told her that Hank is dead, that would probably upset her even more."

"That's probably a good idea. Keep trying to reach the Dean, too, and when you do, ask her to come see me right away. Right now, I'd like to talk to Denny. Is there someplace quiet where I can interview him?"

"Sure. Tom can take you down to his office, and you can talk to him there. If you give me your cell number, I can let you know when I get in touch with the Dean. I'll have somebody keep an eye out for your crime scene team, too. When they get here, I'll have them brought straight up here."

Frank looked around. "We obviously can't use Hank's office until the forensics team gets through with it. But there's no sense in everybody standing around and freezing their asses off out here. Can you see if there's a room where we can wait until they get here? Does one of you have a pass key?"

Max laughed. "You're talkin' to the right guys, Frank. Between me and Tom, we've got keys to unlock every door on campus. There's a conference room at the other end of the hall. We'll wait for you there until you get back."

"We should probably make that our center of operations. Will that work?"

"Whatever you need," Max said.

Tom led Frank to his office. On the way, Frank asked, "I assume you have some kind of student counseling service on campus, right?"

"Sure, and there's always a counselor available—24/7. While you're talking to Denny, I'll give them a call, and ask them to have somebody available to talk to him after you've interviewed him."

"Thanks. I was hoping you could arrange something like that. I'm sure he's pretty shaken up by what he found this morning."

As Frank expected, Denny hadn't been able to sleep. He was sitting on the edge of the couch with his hands between his knees, rocking nervously. Tom introduced him to Frank, who said, "I'm glad to meet you, Denny. I only wish it hadn't been in these circumstances. You must have been out there pretty early this morning. You've got to be getting hungry by now, aren't you?"

Denny nodded. "Normally I'd have eaten breakfast in the cafeteria by now. I was going to go there right after I cleared the terrace and put down some ice melt. But I'm not sure I want to go there now. I probably shouldn't be talking to anybody about this, right?" Although he wasn't crying, Frank and Tom could see that he had been, and it didn't look like he'd be able to keep himself under control himself much longer.

Tom put his hand on Denny's shoulder. "Denny, Frank needs to talk to you—to have you describe what you saw this morning. After he's done, I'll arrange to have someone get you something to eat." He handed Frank one of his business cards. "When you've finished interviewing him, give me a call, and I'll take it from there."

Frank took out a recorder, and turned it on. "Denny, I'd like you to tell me everything you can about what you saw this morning. I'm going to record our conversation, so that I can have a clear record of everything you tell me. Just try to forget that it's there, and answer my questions as completely as possible."

He asked Denny to describe what he'd seen that morning. "Besides the dark snow," he said, "what else made you think there was somebody under the snow?"

"The phone beeped."

"That startled me, too," Frank said. "And that was after they'd already brushed some of the snow away and we knew what was there."

Denny finished telling how he'd taken Max and Tom up to the terrace, and how they uncovered the body. Then Tom had brought Denny back to his office, which was where Frank met him.

"Thanks, Denny. I really appreciate the fact that you didn't try digging in that snow yourself. You did the right thing by getting Max and Tom to go up there with you. Sometimes, after we describe something, we think of things later, even if we think we've covered everything we've seen. If that happens to you, and you come up with something else that you think I should know, don't hesitate to call me." He handed him a business card. "My phone number's on here, as well as my e-mail address. If you think of anything—anything at all—don't hesitate to let me know. Now, I'm going back up to the third floor of the Carroll Center. We'll be working in the conference room. Let me call Tom, and have him get you something to eat."

Tom arrived a few minutes later. "Denny, I hope you don't mind, but I just called the Counseling Service. You had a pretty traumatic experience this morning, and Frank and I thought it would be good for you to talk to someone about it—besides us, that is."

"Thanks. That's probably a good idea. But I've never talked to a counselor before."

"Don't worry," Tom said. "There's nothing to be concerned about. I know the staff in the Counseling Staff pretty well. Our offices interact quite a bit. They're a great bunch of people. Sometimes it helps to have someone to talk to when you're dealing with significant developments in your life. And I think this definitely qualifies as a significant development! Let's go over to the CUB and get you something to eat—I asked to have the counselor meet us there. On a weekday, they'd have probably gotten there by now. But since it's Saturday, there's a skeleton staff on campus. So they have to do a little shifting of responsibilities. As soon as they can free up somebody, they'll be there."

When they got to the CUB, Tom bought Denny's breakfast, and found an empty meeting room where he could eat without being disturbed. Denny seemed to relax a little as they talked, and he showed that he definitely hadn't lost his appetite. As he was finishing his last piece of toast, Wanda Petri, Head of Counselling Services, stepped up to their table.

"I'm sorry it took so long for me to get here, Tom. You know how it is on Saturdays—especially with all the snow from last night's storm. So tell me, what's going on?"

Tom explained what had happened. Wanda put her hand to her mouth and sat down slowly. "Oh . . . my . . . God! This is terrible! Are you sure it's Hank?"

"No doubt at all," Tom said. "It's definitely Hank. But please, this is in the STRICTEST confidence. You can't say anything about it to ANYONE! Hannah doesn't know yet. She's on her way back from the Cities. Carl van den Hoek is trying to get in touch with the Dean, but when we came down here, he still hadn't talked to her yet."

"Of course. What do you want me to do?"

Tom looked at Denny and said, "Unfortunately, Denny was the one who came across the body. We thought it would be a good idea for him to talk to someone from your office, so that you can help him deal with what he's been through this morning. I'll leave him in your capable hands, and get back upstairs. Frank—the BCA Agent who's running everything now—asked me to take some donuts upstairs for everyone working there, so I'd better get a move on."

"That sounds good to me," Wanda replied. "Will that be okay with you, Denny?"

He nodded. Once again, he looked like he might start crying, but he took a sip of coffee, and swallowed hard. "Thanks!"

Tom left Denny with Wanda, and loaded a tray with pastries. Then he started back upstairs, where he rejoined Frank, Max, and Carl. Just as he got back to the terrace, Carl's phone rang. It was Sarah, returning his call. "You left a message saying that there was something urgent. What's going on? There's a Board of Trustees meeting right after lunch, and I'd like to get to my office by 10:00 to get ready for it. But I'm happy to help you any way I can before then."

"There's no easy way to say this, Sarah, so I'll be direct. But before I say anything, I need you to promise me that you won't say anything to anyone about it until we tell you it's okay."

"Sure—of course, whatever you say. What's going on?"

"This morning, just before dawn, a student worker found Hank in the snow outside his office."

"What? . . . Hank? . . . In the snow? . . . Is he going to be okay?"

"I'm sorry, Sarah, I should've been more precise. Hank was found DEAD outside his office."

"How? . . . What happened? . . . Are you sure it's Hank?"

"We don't know what happened. But we're positive it's Hank. There's a BCA forensic crime scene team on their way down from Bemidji. Hopefully they'll be able to figure out what happened. I'm just trying to make sure that no one from around here screws anything up. But here's the problem—why I need you not to say anything about this yet: Hannah's on her way home from the Cities."

"Let me guess: she doesn't know yet, does she?"

"Unfortunately, that's correct. The BCA agent here is going to talk to her as soon as she arrives. But it wouldn't hurt to have a woman here for 'moral support' when she gets the news. How soon can you get over here?" Carl asked. "Hannah thought she'd be here around 10:30."

"I didn't get your call right away because I was in the shower. I took my leisurely time getting dressed, and when I went into the kitchen, I saw the message light blinking. That's the bad news. The good news is, I saw it as I was about to head out the door. The neighbor kid just finished clearing my driveway, so I'll be able to get out of the garage. I should be there in 10 minutes, if the streets are cleared between here and campus. Where will I find you?"

"Max opened the conference room on the top floor of the Carroll Center. We're all waiting here until the crime scene team gets here from Bemidji, which should be pretty soon."

"Great—that's just across the hall from my office. I'll see you there."

Just after Carl finished talking to Sarah, he got a call on his portable radio. One of the officers waiting down in the parking lot said that the forensics team had arrived. They were unloading their gear from their van, and with the help of some of the New Leiden police, they'd be upstairs in a few minutes.

About five minutes later, the elevator opened. A man and a woman, both dressed in heavy winter coats, stepped out carrying a case in each hand. They were followed by two of Carl's staff, who were carrying other pieces of equipment.

Frank recognized them immediately. "I see the Norwegian cavalry has arrived!" he laughed. "I appreciate that you could get down here so quickly. They must have gotten the roads pretty well cleared this morning."

The man took off his hat, and nodded, "There were still a few spots where the snow hadn't been completely cleared, and we had to wait a little for one-lane traffic. But generally, it was clear, and traffic moved very well." He pointed toward his colleague and laughed, "And with Dale Earnhardt, Jr., here at the wheel, we made good time. According to the traffic reports we heard on the radio, there was apparently a big mess down in St. Paul. It sounded like that had traffic tied up for quite a while. We were lucky—we didn't run into anything like that."

Frank turned to Carl and the others in the room. "Let me introduce my two colleagues from BCA Forensics: Torstein Haugen, and Solveig Nygaard. As I said, the 'Norwegian cavalry,'" he laughed.

"Stuff it, Frank," Solveig growled. "Let's get to work. We didn't drag ourselves all the way down here to make polite conversation."

Frank put his hands in front of him in defense, and said, "I'm sorry. If I'd realized you'd gotten up on the wrong side of the bed this morning, I'd have been more careful," he laughed.

Solveig flipped him the bird. "What do you have for us this morning, Frank? And let me guess: whatever it is won't be inside this lovely, warm building, will it?"

"You're right there," he said. "There's a body stuck in the snow outside on the terrace. You'll need to go over that as soon as you can. But the guy's office is right down the hall. While I'm checking out his computer and phone,

one of you can check out the rest of his office while the other one finishes on the terrace."

"Dibs!" Solveig yelled. "Torstein, I'm obviously the person best qualified to check out the office. The stuff outside is bound to be more complicated—much more appropriate for your expertise."

Torstein groaned, "I don't know how you figure that— but if we divide things up that way, I'm sure as Hell not letting you drive back. My knuckles are still white from the trip down here. You know, you <u>could</u> have taken a few more minutes to get here. You didn't have to try to set a new land speed record." He turned to Frank and groaned, "I think she actually touched down a couple times on the curves, though it felt like we were airborne most of the way."

"But Frank wanted us here right away . . . didn't you Frank? And we had to make up for the time we lost in the one-lane sections."

"I'm not getting in the middle of that!" Frank laughed. "But before either one of you gets started on anything in here, you should both get outside right away. The staff from the Medical Examiner's Office will be here soon. Before they take the body up to their office in Bemidji, you need to process everything around it. I'd like to get them back on the road as quickly as possible. On the way out to the terrace, I can introduce everyone here."

As they started outside, Frank said, "This is Carl van den Hoek. He's Chief of the New Leiden Police Department. Apparently he and the deceased were not on the best of terms, so he thought it was a good idea to call BCA before his staff did anything, and let us take care of everything from start to finish, rather than wait to call us in after they'd done the initial work."

"Good thinking, Carl," Solveig said. "Let me guess: small town politics, right? The slightest screw-up, and you might be out of your job before you know it."

"That pretty much captures the essence," Carl said. "Because we don't know the cause of death, BCA would eventually be involved anyway. And since I didn't have the best of relationships with Hank, I wanted to make sure nothing got messed up—or if it did, none of my staff would be to blame."

Frank cleared his throat. "Not that anyone from BCA would ever mess anything up, right Torstein."

"Not us, at any rate," Torstein laughed. "I know my saying this doesn't fit the traditional 'Norwegian modesty,' but Solveig and I make one Hell of a team. We've been able to clear up a number of cases that weren't going anywhere after somebody else overlooked some basic evidence before BCA got involved."

"Thanks, Torstein," Frank said. "I have no doubt that you'll get this one cleared up right away, too." He turned to Carl and explained, "Despite how it might have sounded inside, I actually get along well with the two of them. I hate to say it within earshot of them, but they're the best team I've ever worked with."

As they stepped out onto the terrace, Frank said, "Be careful walking out here. There was an ice storm before the snow hit, so everything has a nice glaze on it. The student who was clearing the terrace was going to spread some ice-melt out here, but that got interrupted, for obvious reasons." He looked around him and said, "Let's continue with introductions. Carl, can you do the honors for your staff member here?"

"Sure. Solveig and Torstein, this is Laura van Klees. She's probably the most important member of my staff right now, at least from your perspective. I've had her taking pictures of everything out there, from just about every possible angle. She can copy all of them for you whenever you'd like."

"Thanks, Carl!" Solveig said. "Laura, while we're checking things out here, can you copy the photos onto a USB drive? Then, as soon as I get my computer set up, I can put all of them on my hard drive." She turned to Torstein: "What do you say—shall we get to it?"

Laura went back inside, and started downloading the photos. As she was waiting for them all to be copied to the drive, the elevator bell rang, and Annika stepped into the hall. She saw that the door to the conference room was open, and walked down to investigate. When she came into the room, she saw Laura and asked, "What's going on? We have a Board of Trustees meeting starting at 1:00! I have to get this conference room ready!"

"I think you'd better talk to Chief van den Hoek. Can you come with me?" She turned and led Annika outside.

Carl walked up to her, and put his hand on her arm. "Good morning, Annika. I'm afraid I have some bad news for you."

"What do you mean?"

"Early this morning, Denny Haugen was clearing the snow off the terrace, and he found Hank in the snow."

"What? Is Hank okay?"

"Christ," Carl grumbled. "I'm going to have to learn to get this right. I should have said, Denny found Hank's body in the snow. He's dead."

"WHAT? How did that happen? WHEN did it happen?"

"We don't know how—or when—yet. That's why these people are here. They're from the Bureau of Criminal Apprehension. I've handed the case over to them. Hopefully they'll be able to give us some answers."

Just then, Sarah walked out onto the terrace. When she saw Annika, she walked over to her and put her arm around her. "Carl called me a little while ago, and asked me to come in."

"Why didn't you call me and let me know?" Annika asked.

"They didn't want word of this to leak out yet. Hannah's still on the way back from the Cities."

"She doesn't know yet?"

"No—the BCA Agent in charge will break the news to her as soon as she arrives."

"When's she supposed to get here?"

"Any time now. She's traveling with Gene Graandsma, so when he gets here, we'll have to contact the rest of the Trustees. They'll probably want to cancel the Board meeting. But they'll probably need to have a brief meeting to figure out what to do in response to this. We'll have to find somewhere else for them to meet. As you undoubtedly saw inside, the BCA staff have set up shop in the conference room on this floor. It's the obvious place for them to use, since they'll have easy access to his office and the terrace from there. Can you find another room for the Trustees?"

"Sure. I'll open the meeting room on the second floor. It's not quite as big, but it's adequate. I'll get on that right away. We scheduled coffee and pastries for the meeting, so I'll tell the food service to take it there."

Carl overheard the conversation and stopped her before she could leave. "If I remember correctly, your office is just outside Hank's, isn't it?"

"Yes. Why?"

"Well, until the BCA crime scene team has a chance to check out Hank's office, they'll need to keep that whole office complex off limits to everyone. That includes your office too, I'm afraid."

Before Annika could protest, Sarah said, "Why don't you use mine? Mary won't be in today, so you can use her desk and computer. Except for specific files on your own computer, you should be able to access just about anything else you might need from there." She handed Annika her office keys and said, "Here, can you open it up please? And if you don't mind, could you turn on my computer, too? I'll log on when I get inside. As soon as you can, please call Terry Daalmans and ask him to get up here right away. Don't give him any details—just tell him it's an emergency. And I want HIM, and not anyone else from the Public Information Office. As soon as we've been able to tell Hannah what happened, we'll need to get some press releases out right away. He can get started drafting those before she gets here. "

Torstein and Solveig had been examining Hank from just about every angle. Solveig had her camera out, and was taking pictures of the body and its surroundings. She noticed Carl looking at her and said, "I know Laura said she got pictures of everything. But it doesn't hurt to have too many, especially as we're getting the rest of the snow cleared away from the body. Torstein is just about done checking it out. Who uncovered the body?"

Carl pointed to Tom and Max, whom he hadn't had a chance to introduce yet. "After a student found the blood, they brushed off enough snow to find the body. I hope they didn't mess things up too badly."

"Not at all! I was just going to say that I wanted to thank whoever did it. Obviously, some things had to be disturbed, just to find out what was under the snow. I was holding my breath when we came out here, expecting to see everything messed up. But they did a great job!"

A few minutes later, Laura came outside with the USB drive. She took it to Solveig: "Here are all of the photos I took this morning. If you need anything else, just let me know."

"Thanks! I can only think of one thing right now. When we came in, I saw you were all enjoying some pastries. The next time somebody comes upstairs, could you ask them to bring a couple cups of coffee along—black, no sugar? Torstein and I would be very grateful."

By the time they'd finished processing everything around the body, the Medical Examiner's staff had arrived. Solveig and Torstein had them remove the body to transport it to Bemidji. Then they expanded their focus to the rest of the terrace. Laura brought them out some donuts, and one of her colleagues brought some coffee. "If you need more after you finish this, they've cranked up a coffee pot in there. So when you feel like slipping in out of the cold, there's plenty more where this came from."

A few minutes later, Carl's portable radio crackled. "Chief, an SUV just pulled into the parking lot. It looks like it's Mrs. van Daam. She's with some guy in a suit. I assume that's the President of the Board of Trustees you were expecting."

"Keep them there! We'll be right down!"

Carl turned to Frank and said, "Given my history with Hank, I think I should stay in the background."

Frank agreed. "In fact, Carl, why don't you stay up here for a few minutes, and then come down and join us in a little bit. Tom and Sarah can go with me, and if Hannah needs any kind of 'official' confirmation of what we know so far, we can provide it. Can I assume Tom's in Hannah's good graces? Since she doesn't know me, that would make things go a little smoother."

Carl nodded in agreement.

Sarah, Frank, and Tom took the elevator to the ground floor of the Carroll Center, and then walked over to the parking lot by the CUB. Hannah was talking to a pair of police officers there, and was obviously upset with them.

When she saw Sarah and Tom, she hurried over to them. Having no idea who Frank might be, she ignored him, and confronted Sarah. Gene followed close behind her.

"Where's Hank? I've been trying to call him since last night, and he won't answer—no matter what number I call. I asked those policemen over there, and they said they weren't authorized to say anything. Say anything about what? What the Hell's going on around here?" She finally noticed Frank and asked, "And who's he?"

Sarah reached out and put her hand on Hannah's arm. "Hannah, this is Frank O'Leary. He's with the Minnesota Bureau of Criminal Apprehension."

"Why is he here? Has Hank done something wrong? He hasn't broken any laws, has he?"

Sarah took a deep breath. "There's no easy way to tell you this, Hannah. . . . You need to listen to Mr. O'Leary."

"Listen to him? About what?"

Frank tried to make his voice sound as comforting as possible. "Just before sunrise, President van Daam was found dead outside his office?"

"What? You've got to be mistaken! Hank can't be dead!"

"No. Unfortunately, it's the sad truth."

"Oh my God! What happened? With BCA here, does that mean you think someone killed him? Who would want to do something like that?"

Frank stepped closer, and said, "That's what we're trying to find out, Mrs. van Daam. We have a crime scene team upstairs right now. As soon as we know something, we'll let you know immediately."

"Is Hank still up there? Can I see him?"

Tom shook his head. "The Medical Examiner's staff just took the body to their regional office in Bemidji. They need to determine the cause of death. As soon as they're finished, they'll release the body. If you'd like, I can contact the funeral home and let them know what's happening. That way, whenever you're ready, they can help you with the arrangements. In the meantime, why don't you go home? I'll make sure they call you the minute the Medical Examiner's finished."

Just then, Carl walked into the parking lot. When Hannah saw him, she pointed at him and said, "He's not having anything to do with this, I hope!"

Frank shook his head. "Only in a peripheral way. As soon as he learned what had happened to your husband, he alerted our office. Fortunately, I was staying here in town—I got stuck here in the storm last night. He's put his staff at our disposal, but BCA is in charge of the investigation."

Carl came over to Hannah and said, "Hannah, I know Hank and I had our differences, but I want you to know that I'll do everything I can to help find out what happened to him. We have BCA staff here, so I know everything is in good hands. If we can be of assistance to you in any way, please let me know."

She relaxed a little, and held out her hand. "Thanks, Carl. I'm sorry I snapped at you. That was unnecessary. I really appreciate you getting the BCA here so quickly. I'm sure you'll do whatever you can to help. Thank you."

Gene Graandsma stepped next to Hannah and put his arm around her shoulder. "Let me take you home, Hannah. I can run you over to the funeral home as soon as they call."

Sarah held up her hand. "Before you do that, Gene, I need to talk to you briefly. No one on the Board of Trustees knows anything about this yet. The police didn't release any information until they could tell Hannah. We didn't want her to hear it from someone else by accident. Given the circumstances, I assume you'll probably want to postpone the Board meeting. But I'm sure you'll want to meet briefly to deal with some of the immediate repercussions of this, and I know there are a couple items that have to be taken care of today. Do you want me to call the other Board members and let them know what's happened? The BCA staff are using the conference room on the third floor, where you usually meet. Annika's setting something up in the meeting room on the second floor. We can let the Trustees know about Hank, and tell them that they should go there when they get to campus."

"Thanks! I'll take Hannah home and try to get her to rest a little. If I'm not out of the meeting by the time the Medical Examiner releases the body, maybe you could get someone to go with her to the funeral home to talk about arrangements?"

Sarah looked at Tom, who very subtly shook his head to indicate that it wasn't something he thought he should do. She knew Carl wasn't an option. "Gene, if you can't do it, it might be a good idea to have a woman go with her. She might find that more comfortable than if someone like Tom or Max went along."

Frank said, "We have no idea how long it might take the Medical Examiner. If you can't do it, I think Sarah's idea of having another woman with Hannah is a good one. Carl, do you think you could spare Officer van Klees?"

"That sounds fine—it definitely wouldn't be a problem from our perspective. With Solveig and Torstein in charge of everything up there now, she'll probably be looking for something to keep her busy." He turned to Gene and Hannah and asked, "Would you like her to go along with the two of you now, and stay with Hannah until it's time to go to the funeral home?"

"No," Hannah said. "I'll be okay. Gene can take me home now. Why don't you have the funeral director call Officer van Klees when he needs me to come by? Then she can call me when she's on the way over to pick me up. If the meeting's over before then, Gene can take me. Otherwise, she and I can go together while he's still here on campus."

*　　*　　*　　*　　*

TERRY DAALMANS HADN'T BEEN VERY HAPPY about having to come to the office on Saturday, especially when Annika wouldn't tell him why they needed him. When she told him that the Dean insisted that it had to be him personally, and no one else from his office, he figured it had to be something important. But with the Board of Trustees meeting that day, it could have been just about anything.

When Sarah told him about Hank, Terry went straight to his office and drafted a news release. He came back and showed it to Sarah, who immediately approved it. Now that Hannah had been informed, Sarah wanted him to get the news out as quickly as possible. In addition to posting it on the College's website, he sent it to the local newspaper and radio stations, as well as the regional television affiliates and press wire services. He was sure that news would also spread quickly by word of mouth. He was right.

After Marty had gotten his driveway cleared, he decided to do some grocery shopping. On Friday, he thought he had enough food stockpiled to last out the storm, but Saturday morning he'd realized that his milk was long past its "use by" date. And he needed some fresh salad ingredients. One of his New Year's resolutions had been to "eat healthier," so he'd been trying to eat more salads. The previous evening, he'd finished off one salad bag. When he opened the other one in the vegetable drawer, he discovered that the lettuce was already turning brown.

It was just after 11:00 when he drove to Dick's Market. He was pleasantly surprised by the way the city had already cleared the main streets. He could see that most of the side streets still weren't plowed, but it looked like those would be taken care of soon. When he got to the parking lot at Dick's, he could see he wasn't the only one who was out to replenish his grocery supplies. The lot was almost full.

He'd just found the last item on his shopping list and was heading toward the check-out counter when he saw Chris. More accurately, he almost ran into him. Chris wasn't paying much attention to anything but the young woman with him. The two of them were holding hands, and staring dreamily into each other's eyes. They were almost totally oblivious to anything or anyone else.

Marty cleared his throat. "Ahem. . . . Good morning, Chris! It's great to see you this morning." He smiled broadly at both of them and asked, "Am I in luck? Is this the day I get to meet the woman who's been taking up so much of your time lately?"

They both blushed, and Chris said, "Of course! I'm sorry, Marty. I didn't see you. Let me introduce you: this is Mariah Cunningham. As I told you, she teaches art history at Chartwell. Mariah, this is my department chair, Marty Dykstra."

"It's a pleasure to meet you, Marty. Chris has told me a great deal about you. It's wonderful that you've been so supportive of him since he got here last summer."

"I'm pleased to meet you, too, Mariah. How was the road from Edison this morning?"

Mariah was already blushing, but now she turned bright red. Marty realized that he must have said something he shouldn't have.

Although he didn't turn quite as red as Mariah, Chris was blushing, too. But he at least managed to say something: "Well, we don't really know. Mariah drove over here yesterday. When the storm hit, she wasn't able to go back. So she had to stay at my place."

Marty tried to control his smile, but he knew he couldn't hide it completely. "That sounds like a wise idea. I hear the roads were really bad last night. It would have been dangerous to try to drive back. You definitely made the right choice. I'm sure the two of you could find plenty of things to keep you busy."

Chris was trying to think of something to say that wouldn't embarrass Mariah even more, when he saw the store manager coming their way.

"Good morning, Bob," Marty said. "Have you met my colleague Chris, and his friend Mariah? Chris, this is Bob van Klees. He's an NNC alum, and more significantly, a former student of mine. But before he could leave town after graduation, he fell in love with a local girl, and settled down here. She's one of 'New Leiden's finest.' And Bob's the manager here at Dick's. How's Officer Laura doing, by the way?"

Bob looked quickly at Chris and Mariah, and hurriedly said, "Pleased to meet the two of you." Then he turned to Marty. "Have you heard the news about Hank van Daam? Laura just called me. There's supposed to be something on the news any minute."

"What are you talking about?" Marty asked. "What's Hank done now? Especially something newsworthy? Don't tell me he's decided not to retire!"

"No, nothing like that. Laura said that someone found him dead on the terrace outside his office this morning. There are apparently several people from the BCA here already."

Marty shook his head. "I guess you can always count on me to say something inappropriate—especially if it involves Hank."

"Pardon my ignorance, but what's the BCA?" Chris asked.

"Bureau of Criminal Apprehension," Marty said. "It's the primary law enforcement investigation unit in Minnesota." He turned to Bob and asked, "Did Laura give you any more details?"

"No, just that the BCA folks are in charge, and they're going over everything to try to find out what happened. When I saw you, I figured you probably hadn't heard yet, since I'd just gotten the call from Laura. That's about as close to the source as you can get. They kept a tight lid on it this morning until they could tell Mrs. van Daam. I'm going to my office and see if there's anything on the radio about it." He started to leave, and then turned to Chris and Mariah. "I'm sorry—I just got caught up in telling Marty this terrible news. I'm pleased to meet you both. I hope we have a chance to meet again under more pleasant circumstances. Please come back again soon."

Mariah took her phone out of her pocket. "If they've just sent out a news release, I'm sure no one at Chartwell has heard about this yet. Someone should let President Thompson know. I'll call my department chair, and then she can get the word to him."

About fifteen minutes later, Sarah's phone rang. "Sarah Christiansen speaking. May I help you?"

"Dean Christiansen, this is Charles Thompson . . . at Chartwell. I've just heard the most terrible news about Hank. Is it true? One of our department heads got a call from one of her junior faculty members, who said she'd heard it from an 'authoritative source.' But apparently that was while she was in a grocery store in New Leiden. With that many 'degrees of separation,' I thought I should get in touch with you to see if it's true."

"Unfortunately, it is. We just put out a news release. We don't have much information at this point, other than that he was found dead outside his office early this morning. When the BCA finishes its investigation, we hope to know what happened. I'll let you know as soon as we have any more details. And at the risk of sounding like one of Hank's clichés, please call me Sarah."

"Thanks, Sarah. I'll appreciate getting more information when you have it. In the meantime, I assume you'll want to postpone tonight's games."

"Oh, Christ! I forgot all about the damned basketball games! Yes, we definitely need to postpone them! Thanks for reminding me! If you can put out the word at Chartwell, I'll make sure everyone here knows. Our Public Information Office will let the local media know about it, too. When things settle down a little, we can have our athletic directors figure out a good time to reschedule them. Thanks for calling!"

As soon as she hung up, she called Terry Daalmens, as well as Tom Logan, and asked them to work out all the details involved in postponing the games. She went to Mary's desk, where Annika was just hanging up the phone. "I've managed to contact all of the Trustees," Annika said. "A couple of them seemed pretty shaken up by the news. I understand that they'll need to meet, at least briefly. But I hope nobody expects them to accomplish a great deal today."

"They'll have to deal with a couple of issues," Sarah replied. "First, they'll need to figure out what to do about an interim president, and how this will affect the search for Hank's replacement. But they also need to approve tenure and promotion candidates at this meeting—the College By-laws are very specific about that. Candidates have to be informed before March 1, and the Board probably won't be able to schedule another meeting before then. Fortunately, here's nothing controversial on that list this year. It's pretty much a 'slam dunk.' It shouldn't take more than a few minutes. Other than those few items, I can't imagine that the meeting will last very long."

GENE DROVE HANNAH HOME, and after he helped her inside, he brought in her bags. While he was doing that, she started a pot of coffee. She took a package of cookies out of the freezer.

When Gene came into the kitchen, he could see that she'd been crying. "Are you okay?"

"Not really," she said. "I've got to figure out what I'm going to do about my finances. Hank tapped into quite a bit of our savings to buy his way into what was supposed to be a lucrative 'academic seminars center' with one of his cronies. I'm sure I'll get that money back eventually, but until that gets up and running, most of the money is already committed to remodeling their retreat center and that kind of thing. I'll have to move out of this place. I can move to the condo in the Cities temporarily, but I don't know how I'll keep up the payments on that." She went over to the coffee maker and filled their cups.

"You're joking, right?" Gene asked.

"Hell no, I'm not joking! Hank was in charge of everything financial. He wouldn't let me have any say in any of it."

"So . . . you don't know about the life insurance?"

"What life insurance?"

"Oh, you sweet, naïve little thing, you! When he started here, Hank talked the College into taking out a life insurance policy for him."

"For how much?"

"Well, if he'd lived until June 30, he and the College would've each gotten $1 million."

"$1 million? You're kidding me! Hank never told me about that. But he didn't live until June 30. So what's that mean for me now?"

Gene smiled at her. He walked over and took her hands. He kissed her on the forehead and said, "Unless that idiot did something stupid, like committing suicide, it means that you'll be the beneficiary of $5 million. The College will get an equal amount."

Hannah sat down on a stool next to the counter. "FIVE million? FIVE? MILLION? Holy shit! I had absolutely no idea!"

"I don't think you'll need to worry much about finances," Gene laughed.

"I guess not. Hell, I could probably just live off the interest on money like that."

"If you were as cheap as Hank was, maybe. I'd suggest you get a good financial counsellor, and find something that will bring you a nice, safe, but productive yield on your investments. You don't want to piss it all away, but you shouldn't live like a tight-wad, either. Enjoy yourself!"

"You know, sometimes Hank could be a real pain in the ass. But I think that from now on, or at least after that insurance money arrives, I'll only have warm, fuzzy feelings about the man."

She put her arms around his neck and gave him a big, passionate kiss. "How'd you like to help me spend some of my money?"

"I was hoping you'd say something like that," he laughed.

15

CSI: New Leiden

Saturday, February 22

ABOUT NOON, FRANK SUGGESTED they take a brief lunch break. Tom led them to the CUB, where they chose a variety of sandwiches and salads. They found a small room off the main dining area, where they could eat in private. When they returned to the third floor of the Carroll Center, they stopped on the way to go back out to where Hank's body had been found. They were about halfway along the terrace, when Frank stopped, and pointed out to the football field. "What was going on out there? Obviously it was something before the storm hit. See those shapes in the snow? It looks like somebody was messing around out there before that last layer of snow got dumped on it. Were students building snow forts? Maybe getting ready for a snowball fight? Look at the sides of some of those lines—where the snow couldn't build up. It looks like there's orange paint or something on some of them."

Tom looked where he was pointing, and said, "I saw some students running around out there for a while, just before the worst part of the storm hit. After I heard a couple blasts of thunder, it got quiet. They probably headed for some place warmer and dryer—and with lightning in the air, safer. I'm not sure what they were up to, but I'll try to find out. I'll put the word out to the head residents in the dorms, and see if they can find out who was out there, and what they were doing. And I'll go down there myself and check out the orange stuff. Maybe I can figure out what that's from."

"Make sure the students know we don't think any of them did anything wrong! Tell 'em we're just trying to find any clues that might help us understand what happened to President van Daam. They'll have all heard the news by now, I'm sure. If a group of students was out there, you know damned well somebody was taking pictures—they probably took dozens of 'selfies' there, no matter what they were doing. If we knew who they were, we'd probably find the pictures plastered all over Facebook. Those might help us get an idea about what was going on last night. Odds are, they probably weren't out there when he died. But maybe we'll get lucky and find a clue. Right now, we need to try all the angles we have. Can you have somebody send out a message to students across campus? Ask if any students took photos out on that field last night. If so, could they please send them to my e-mail address? Again, please stress that we don't think anybody did anything wrong out there. Nobody's going to get into trouble. We just want their help."

"Sure, I'll have someone do that right away!" Tom said. "I'll also get someone to set you up with guest access to our campus wi-fi. That way you'll be able to use your own computers up here to access your e-mail or the internet without any problems."

Torstein turned to Frank and Solveig, and nodded towards Hank's office. "If you two are going to check out his computer and the rest of his office, you'd better get cracking. I can take care of the rest of this out here. When I get done out here, I'll come in and help with the office. Tom, can you let them in there?"

Frank nodded. "Thanks, Torstein! Hopefully you won't have to stay out in the cold too long. Solveig: I can get started on the computer while you go through the rest of the office. I have a couple other things to take care of first, not the least of which is a trip to the men's room. But I'll join you as soon as I can."

"No hurry. I can help you out with the computer, too, if I can get everything else checked out quickly."

Solveig and Tom went back to the conference room, and she removed her coat and hat. She took her camera out of her briefcase, and followed Tom to Hank's office. "When Annika comes back up, can you please send her in here? She might be able to help me make sense of some things that won't necessarily be obvious to me."

When Tom left, Solveig started taking pictures of everything: the top of Hank's desk, his closet, even the view out his window. Next, she sat down in his chair and carefully started looking at everything on his desk, as well as the contents of his desk drawers. Then she checked his phone. She could see that he had answered a call just before 6:00. Caller id showed that it was from "Pieter van Rijn." She made a note of that. There were no more calls registered on the phone until 7:45. After that, there were several calls from a different number. She picked up Hank's cell phone, which was in the baggie full of items that Torstein had removed from Hank's pockets. She checked his contacts list, and found the number that had been calling him after 7:45: "Hannah's Cell – ICE." She'd called his cell as many times as she'd called his office number. *"Ooh, I bet she wasn't happy,"* she thought. She saw that there were also a couple of other calls from an on-campus number. She cross-checked it with the number she'd been given for Tom's office. *"Bingo!"*

She heard Frank come in the office. "Found anything interesting?" he asked?

"Not much," she said. "Annika's husband talked to him just before 6. There was no more phone activity until 7:45, and he didn't answer ANY of the calls that came in from that point on. So we have a window for when it might have happened: sometime between 6:00 and 7:45. Denny didn't find him until after 6 this morning. No wonder Hank was already cold and stiff!"

They looked up when they heard a knock on the door. It was Annika. "Tom said you wanted to see me? Is there something I can help you with?"

"We just have a couple of questions," Frank said. "Maybe you can help us with them."

"Sure—fire away!"

"According to his phone log, he got a phone call from your husband's number just before 6:00."

"That's right. I'd told him I was going to be home about 5:30, and with the storm, he was worried about me when I wasn't home yet. And he was pissed at Hank as a result."

"Was there a problem? What caused the delay?"

"To put it simply: Hank. He was working on his presentation for the Board of Trustees meeting today, and he had me taking care of some last minute details. With the storm, everyone on campus was supposed to leave by 3. But Hank didn't think anyone really needed to worry about the storm."

"From the looks of things, that's pretty ironic," Solveig said.

"You can say that again! He was all bluster about how he wasn't afraid of any 'little ol' storm.' I told him I'd put my money on Mother Nature." She waited a moment for Solveig to ask her something else, and then said, "What else did you need? I should probably check to see how Sarah's doing with the Trustees. Their meeting's about to start."

"Did your husband call you from a land line or cell phone?" Frank asked.

"If the phone log shows just his name, then it was his cell. Our home number displays both of our names on caller id."

"Will he be coming to campus today?"

"He wasn't planning to, but I could ask him. May I ask why?"

"I'd like to talk to him about that conversation he had with Hank. And just to cover all bases, I'd like to take a look at the call log on his cell. Could you ask him to bring it up here sometime today?"

"Sure. That shouldn't be a problem. Is there anything else? I really should get to the meeting room."

"Just one more quick question," Frank said. "I just tried to look at Hank's computer, but it had timed out. I need a password to get into it. In the front of his top drawer, Solveig found a piece of paper with this on it: 'User=Pres@nieuwnedcol.edu, PW=HvD12345!' Can I assume that's his password?"

"Probably. I wouldn't be surprised. He didn't have a lot of sophistication when it came to computers—especially passwords. If IT didn't require that we change passwords every six months, I'm sure his would've been something really basic, like 'Password' or '123456.' Adding the exclamation mark is more sophistication than I'd have expected from him. If that doesn't work, we can get somebody from Tech Services to come over and unlock it for you. They can override the lock-outs on all of the College computers. With some of our less computer-savvy faculty, we'd have all kinds of problems if they couldn't do that."

Frank tapped a key on the computer, and the log-in page appeared. He entered the userid and password Solveig had found in the desk. The computer made a few grinding sounds, and then the screen opened to the desktop.

"Bingo!" Frank cried. "I'll dig around in here for a while. If I have any questions, where can I find you?"

"As I said, I have to go down to the second floor for a minute to make sure everything's okay for the Trustees. But after that, I'll be in the Dean's office—right across from the conference room. When do you think I'll be able to get back into my office? It's the one right through that door."

"I think you should be able to use your office by tomorrow sometime—if we're lucky, maybe even late this afternoon. To speed things up, would you mind giving me the password to your computer? I could have you turn it on for me, but if I did that, I'd have to be standing over you to make sure you didn't do anything on the computer."

Annika jerked in surprise.

"I'm sorry," Frank assured her. "It's not that I think you've done anything. But at this stage of the investigation, we have to make sure that nothing's done in here that's not under our immediate control."

"Don't worry. I understand. Since I turned the computer off around 5:30, I can't imagine that you'll find anything related to Hank's disappearance after Pieter talked to him. Despite the IT staff's admonitions about 'never give your password to anyone,' I'm not worried that you'll do terrible things with my computer." She jotted down her userid and password on a note pad. "Just promise me that you'll tear this up when you're done with my computer. I shouldn't be down at the Trustees meeting very long. After that, you can find me in the Dean's office."

Frank turned his attention back to Hank's computer. He ran a quick diagnostic check, which showed that there had been periodic activity on his word processing program throughout the afternoon, but the last time any files had been updated was shortly after 6:30. He went to Annika's computer to run the same program. "Solveig, I've just finished the initial diagnostic check on Hank's computer," he said. "If you have a minute, while I'm checking Annika's with the same program, can you go over his and see what he was doing besides the word processing document he was working on?—e-mail, web surfing, anything."

About an hour later, Solveig went to the door from Hank's office to the terrace, and called out to Torstein: "You look like you need a break. Why don't you join us in the conference room? But you need to go the long way around—I've taken some samples of material on the carpet by the door. Depending what that turns up, I might want to look at it again. I don't want you bringing anything in from outside that might contaminate it."

Torstein raised his left hand in a mock salute. "Yes, ma'am! I'll meet you in the conference room."

When she got as far as Sarah's office, she stuck her head in and called out to Annika: "Can you join us in the conference room? I have a couple more questions you might be able to help us with."

"Sure—I'll be right there."

By the time Torstein came in, Solveig was already there, together with Frank, Tom, and Annika.

"We're still looking at everything," Frank said. "But Solveig wanted to bring us up to date on what she's found so far." He looked at Torstein and laughed, "I think she may have felt a little guilty about Torstein being stuck out on the terrace."

Frank's computer chimed, indicating that he'd just gotten an e-mail message. He nodded toward the computer. "I'm happy to say, whatever Tom sent out to the students, we're getting a good response. It looks like that's another photo coming in. The students who were out on the football field have sent me about a dozen photos so far. Hopefully we'll see something in them that might help us figure this out." He turned to Solveig: "Okay, what do you have from Hank's office so far?"

"Well, there's the obvious stuff that Tom saw when he was looking for Hank last night. His suit jacket and raincoat are in the closet, with no indication that they'd been worn out in the storm. His keys are on the desk. His phone shows that he took a call from Annika's husband just before 6:00. She said that he'd talked to Hank about then. He was pissed because she hadn't been able to leave the office before the storm hit. Can't say that I'd blame him!"

"Anything else on the desk?" Frank asked.

"There was a personnel file—apparently they're hiring a new Classics prof. Besides that, there were a couple of notes—at least one of which ties into what I found on his computer."

"What are those about?"

"The first one just has the word 'Sabbatical' on it. And he was working on a document on his computer called 'Trustees-2-22.doc.'" She turned to Frank and said, "That's the one you said had been accessed about 6:30."

To the rest of the group she said, "I assume that's what he was planning to present to the Trustees this afternoon. It included a couple of paragraphs that basically said, 'Thank you for the sabbatical.' I don't know much about academics, but I thought that was something a prof was given to go do research somewhere else."

She could see that Annika stiffened when she said "sabbatical." "That's right," Annika said, very bitterly. "A sabbatical gives someone a chance to focus intensely on a research project. The way it works here, a faculty member can have a semester off at full pay, or a full year at three-quarters of their annual salary. Regardless of whether it's for a semester or a year, the faculty member needs to return to teach at the College for at least a year after their sabbatical."

The elevator chimed, and Sarah stepped into the hall. When she saw the group gathered in the conference room, she went to join them.

She looked at Annika and said, "The Trustees voted on tenure and promotion without any questions. As I expected, that didn't take very long. Then they decided that they wanted to go into 'executive session,' so I had to leave. What's going on up here? Has anyone figured out what happened?"

"Not yet," Frank said. "Solveig's just telling us what she's found in Hank's office so far."

Solveig turned to Annika. "Okay, to get back to Hank's note, and what he was going to say to the Trustees. Why would he be thanking them for a sabbatical?"

"That's a good question," Annika grunted. "I asked him pretty much the same question yesterday afternoon. He gave me a song and dance about how important it would be for them to give him a 'sabbatical' if they wanted to hire a good replacement." When she said "sabbatical," she made quotation marks in the air with her fingers. "He said that a lot of other schools have been giving their presidents 'sabbaticals' when they retired, and if we wanted good candidates, the College needed to do the same for him.

Referring to it as a 'sabbatical' was ridiculous! He should've called it what it really would have been: a 'golden parachute.'"

"Okay, that clears up that point," Solveig said. "The rest of the presentation for the Trustees is pretty straightforward. It was also obviously written by somebody other than the person who wrote the part about the sabbatical—somebody who actually knows how to write well."

Annika smiled and waved her hand. "That would be me. I usually wrote most of his presentations. But he didn't want me to have anything to do with the last part of this one. I guess he thought I'd be upset by the 'sabbatical' proposal—and he was right. We had a disagreement about that yesterday afternoon."

"That's what I figured," Solveig said. "That's the way it usually works. I'm convinced that when a lot of supervisors say they're 'too busy' to write something, and pass it along to one of their underlings, what they really mean is that they can't write it well themselves. Either that, or they're too lazy to do it."

"Thanks for the editorial," Frank laughed. "Now, what else do you have?"

"There was a note stuck in his appointment calendar." She looked at Annika and Sarah and asked, "Do you have an idea what this means? It's kind of in short-hand—like you might use in a text message: 'ck 2 c if Demi G can accmpny 2 Vegas.' I assume that means something like, 'Check to see if Demi G can accompany to Vegas.' Any ideas?"

Annika immediately blushed. "I can't believe it! Sure, I have a pretty good idea what that means."

"Dare I ask?" Sarah said. "That has to be Gene's wife, right?

Annika nodded, and explained to the others, "Demi G is Gene Graandsma's wife. She just came up in a discussion yesterday?"

"In what connection," Solveig asked.

365

"This is a little embarrassing."

"We're trying to figure out how the guy died," Solveig assured her. "He can't be embarrassed by anything anymore, so you shouldn't worry about it, either. Whatever you tell us stays here." She chuckled, "Sort of like 'what happens in Vegas stays in Vegas.' Talk about irony!"

"I think that's exactly what he had in mind," Annika said. "I was telling him that I didn't think it was such a good idea that Hannah was traveling with Gene Graandsma as much as she has been lately. In the course of that conversation, I mentioned that Gene's wife, Demi, 'puts the B in LGBTQ.' That's exactly the way I said it."

"So . . . then he wanted to see if she could travel with him?"

"Apparently so. I told him that she had a reputation for liking to find people to set up 'threesomes' when she traveled—sometimes with women, sometimes mixed company."

"Let me guess: is she tall, blonde, attractive, and 'well built'?"

"All of the above. You can also add that she looks very athletic. She runs a chain of exercise studios, so she's in great shape."

"Okay," Solveig said. "That explains something else in his computer."

"What do you mean?" Frank asked.

"Well, let's put it this way: he was probably a fan of Dylan's album, 'Blonde on Blonde.'"

"I hate to repeat myself," Frank said impatiently, "but what the Hell do you mean?"

"He apparently liked blondes," Solveig said.

Annika blushed again.

"Not just blondes—blondes with big tits. . . . and he especially liked blondes with big tits doing things with other big titted blondes."

The word "embarrassed" would not have adequately described Annika at that point. If there had been a hole to crawl into, she would have hidden there.

"You mean he had porn on his computer?" Frank asked.

"Not really hard-core stuff," Solveig said. "But a lot of pictures of 'blonde on blonde,' if you know what I mean—with a few redheads and brunettes thrown in for good measure."

"How come I didn't come across that?" Frank asked. "Don't get me wrong, I'm not disappointed—just curious how I could miss something like that."

"Don't feel bad—I almost missed it, too. He had a neat little app on his computer. It looks like he could sit there and watch all the fun activities, and then with one click, he could minimize it so no one would have any idea what he was doing on his computer. To open the app again, he just had to type in an access code using a special calculator app. I noticed he had a couple calculator apps on his computer, which made me curious. I've read about high school students hiding stuff on their cell phones like that." She looked at Torstein and chuckled, "I could probably get you that app for your computer if you'd like, Torstein. We're too late for Valentine's Day, but isn't your birthday coming up soon?"

Now it was Torstein's turn to flip her the bird. "Very funny! I'll pass on that one! Was there anything else on his computer that we should know about, now that you've enlightened us about his recreational interests?"

"No, it looks like the only things he was working on yesterday afternoon were his talk to the Trustees, and 'Debbie does Barbie.'"

Frank's computer chimed that he'd gotten another message. After he checked his inbox, he said, "Okay, I'm still getting photos from students. I think we've gotten enough by now to start laying them out in some kind of order. Let's check the timestamp on them, and set them up chronologically. Sarah: can we use a printer in your office to print these?"

Annika was still shaken by what Solveig had found in Hank's computer, but she managed to say, "We can do it at Mary's computer. Come on, I'll help you get everything set up. Just promise me I won't have to see anything from Hank's computer."

"It's a deal," Solveig said.

The Medical Examiner's office called Carl just before 3:00, to let him know they were sending him the report in an e-mail. Also, Hank's body was ready to be released to his family, so Carl had Laura take Hannah to the funeral home so she could make arrangements to have the body brought back from Bemidji.

Carl used the computer at Mary's desk to download and print several copies of the Medical Examiner's report. He gave them to Frank, and asked Tom to get Solveig and Torstein. He knocked on Sarah's door, and asked her if she could join them all in the conference room. Max had been called away to deal with a maintenance problem in one of the dorms, but otherwise, everyone who had met earlier was there. "Okay, everybody. Please read this over," Frank said, "and then let's talk about it. We've been at this for several hours. Why don't we go over to the CUB and discuss this over a fresh cup of coffee. I think a brief change of scenery would do us a lot of good. Sarah, I know you'll probably have to get back to the meeting soon. But if you could join us for at least a few minutes, it might be easier for you to brief the Trustees. Tom, do you think we could use that side room again, so we can be by ourselves?"

"Sure—I'll call over there right now and make sure it's open for us."

Sarah looked at the report. "Thanks! I'd appreciate your insights. Looking at this, I'm not sure how much of it I'll understand on my own. I may be a scientist, but I don't have any experience with medical terminology. I'd appreciate any help you can give me to translate it."

As they started toward the elevator, Frank turned to Solveig, "I don't think I've seen you since the wedding. How was your honeymoon? Where'd you go?"

"Cancun—we had a fabulous time!" She smiled, "As you can see, I still have a little of my tan left."

Frank turned to the others and explained, "Solveig just got married in December. The twenty-first, wasn't it."

Torstein laughed, "The Winter's Solstice! A honeymoon seems like an appropriate way to spend the longest night of the year."

Solveig jabbed her elbow into his ribs, but smiled and said, "Torstein's just jealous. He's still a bachelor, and has to spend HIS nights alone."

Frank said, "Well, all kidding aside, it was a beautiful wedding."

"Thanks, Frank, I'm glad you enjoyed it."

"And they had one Hell of a reception! I can't say I enjoyed the morning after as much, though! What was that Norwegian firewater that your dad kept making me drink?"

"You mean the Aquavit? Nobody MADE you drink it! Every time he came around with a bottle, your glass was empty. And you always held it out for a refill. You should have gone easy on that stuff! Especially if you're not used to it."

"That's what my wife kept telling me—that night, and the next day as well. I didn't get any sympathy from her, I can assure you."

"Well, I'm glad you enjoyed the reception, anyway—despite the after-effects," she laughed.

When they got to the coffee shop, Tom reminded them where to find beverages, cookies, and pastries. When they'd all found something to their liking, they got in line in front of the cashier. Sarah waved her hands to stop their conversation for a moment. "I'm sure you have a per diem to cover this—except for Tom and Carl, that is. But for the brief time that I'm in charge around here, I think it's appropriate that my office pick up the tab. I'll follow all of you through the line. You can just point to me, and tell them that I'm paying."

Tom whispered to Frank: "The Dean's paying? That's something that Hank was never accused of doing! I'm sorry—I shouldn't speak ill of the dead. But he was one cheap son of a bitch!"

Since it was Saturday afternoon, there were only a few people in the CUB, and they would have had their choice of the small rooms off the main area even without Tom's call. But on his request, the cafeteria staff had opened a room that was tucked into a corner, so they could meet without anyone even noticing they were there. Frank looked around the table and said, "Torstein and Solveig: since Sarah will have to get back for the Trustees meeting soon, can one of you give her a brief summary of what this report says?"

Solveig had just taken a bite of a muffin, and while she was trying to chew it so she could swallow, Torstein spoke up first. He looked at the report again and said, "Well, basically, he suffered significant loss of blood from the scalp laceration—an artery at the back of his head was severed. In addition, he had a severe blow to the base of his skull, which would have knocked him out. Neither of those was necessarily fatal. He might have been able to stop the flow of blood, or at least slowed it enough to get help to stop it. He had his cell phone with him, so he could've called for some assistance—911, or campus security. But when he was knocked out, that obviously wasn't an option. Likewise, the blow itself wasn't enough to kill him. Although he was unconscious, without the bleeding, he'd have probably 'come to' fairly soon. Again, he could have called someone for help. There's always the chance that the concussive force of the blow might have caused him to stop breathing. But if that had happened, he'd have died more quickly. His heart would have stopped beating, and he wouldn't have lost so much blood. When he was knocked out, there was nothing to stop the bleeding. The final *coup de grace* was asphyxiation. Quite simply put, the snow smothered him. Although it was heavy, there wasn't so much of it that he couldn't have dug himself out—if he'd been conscious, that is. But after he was knocked out, he probably never regained consciousness."

"So, are you saying he bled to death, or was asphyxiated?" Sarah asked.

"If they had to specify a single cause of death, it would be asphyxiation. But at the same time, the combination of blood loss while being knocked out was one he couldn't have survived without assistance. If someone had found him immediately after this all happened, it might have been another story. He'd have had a concussion, at least. If there had been some internal, cerebral bleeding, that might have had some serious after effects. But the report doesn't indicate that as being an issue. By the time the kid found him, he was already cold and stiff—sorry to be so blunt about it. And that's about it. Frank said that they've got the kid talking to a counsellor."

"His name's Denny," Frank said. "Denny Bakken—one of your fellow Norwegians, I guess. Seems like a nice kid. Too bad he had to be the one who found Hank."

Torstein nodded. "Can you make sure somebody lets him know that there was nothing—I mean absolutely nothing—that he could have done that would have helped the guy? The last thing Denny needs to do is to start thinking that he might have been able to do something to save Hank's life. We just appreciate the fact that he had the good sense not to mess anything up."

"Thanks for clarifying all of this for me," Sarah said. "I'll relay that to the Trustees. And I'll pass your comments about Denny along to the Counselling Service. Now, I hate to eat and run, but I have to get back to the meeting. If you come up with anything else, please let me know right away."

After Sarah left, they talked about the report for a few minutes, until they'd all finished their coffee. Then Solveig said, "If I'd wanted to just sit around a table and

371

talk, I could've done that at home with my husband. No offense, but that would've been a lot more to my liking. Torstein and I need to get finished up and drive back to our lab pretty soon."

About half an hour later, Sarah was on her way back from the Trustees meeting, just as Max stepped out of the elevator. They both went to the conference room, where they found everyone looking at photos. "A water pipe broke in one of the dorms. We finally got everythin' cleaned up." He pointed toward the photos on the main conference table. "I heard that you were askin' students to send ya photos. Several kids in the dorm were talkin' about it. It looks like you're getting' a good response."

"Yeah," Frank said. "But we still don't know what the Hell they were doing."

"Ask, and it shall be given," Max laughed.

"You mean you know?" Carl asked. "Out with it!"

"While I was in the dorm checkin' the damage from the broken pipe, I overheard some students talkin' about it. They were tryin' to leave a message out on the field that would be seen by everyone goin' to the basketball games with Chartwell College tonight."

"Which have been postponed, by the way," Sarah said.

"So I heard," Max continued. "They'd just gotten started when the 'thunder snow' hit, so they scrambled back to their dorms. They'd only finished a few letters."

"What was the message?" Solveig asked.

"Let me guess," Annika groaned. "Chuck Fartwell?"

Torstein thought about it for a minute, and then laughed. "Chartwell College. Chuck Fartwell. Ha! You can always count on college students! They may not know how to spell, but they can always figure out how to change a few letters around and get something to 'titter' about, and maybe cause embarrassment to their elders."

"You sound like the voice of experience," Solveig laughed.

"Not me personally, just as an innocent bystander."

"There has to be a good story here," Solveig said. "Out with it."

"Okay, you asked for it—but don't blame me if you get offended."

"Since when am I easily offended?" she asked.

"But you can't guarantee the same for everyone else here"

Sarah spoke up: "My dad was in the Navy. I promise you, you can't offend me. And I'm sure it won't compare to what Solveig found on Hank's computer. Let's hear it!"

"I guess you've got a point there. Okay: my freshman year, a group of women on campus organized a 'synchronized swimming' club. They scheduled their big extravaganza for Mom's Weekend. Unfortunately, they made the mistake of calling it 'Ripples in Rhythm.' They put up posters all over campus."

"Oh, no!" Solveig groaned. "And somebody changed the letters. And I'm sure I know what they changed."

"You guessed it—a guy in my dorm went around campus and replaced the first 'R' with an 'N' on every poster. He was very creative—he duplicated the font style, color, size—everything. From a distance, you couldn't really tell that the posters had been altered. His efforts were not well received by the administration, as you might guess. He spent the next two semesters on probation. The president wanted him kicked out altogether. I'm sure 'Chuck Fartwell' isn't a favorite of the administration here, either. Am I right?"

Annika nodded. "A few students showed up at the Chartwell/NNC basketball games last year wearing 'Chuck Fartwell' t-shirts. Hank went ballistic."

"Just the reaction to encourage more such behavior, right?"

"Correct. If he saw that last night, he'd have been furious."

"That brings up an interesting point," Solveig said. "I'm curious about the layout of his office. His desk is tucked way over in the corner. Yet, there's a beautiful view of the campus out that big window. Considering what he spent his time doing on his computer, I can understand that he'd want the monitor set so that no one could see what he was doing—either someone out on the terrace, or anyone coming into his office. But you'd think he'd like to take advantage of that view somehow."

Max shook his head. "I've always been struck by his paranoid attitude toward the staff. He didn't like the possibility that anyone might look in at him from outside. And he didn't wanna be disturbed by custodial staff if he was workin' late. They had strict orders that if his door was closed, he was to be left alone. "

Tom nodded in agreement. "When I went looking for him last night, I was afraid to knock on his door. If I'd disturbed 'an important project,' he'd have chewed my ass. Of course, now we have a better idea of what some of his 'important projects' were."

"There's another reason his desk is in the corner," Annika said. "I'm sure you'll hear about it before too long, so you might as well hear it from me."

"What's that?" Solveig asked.

"When I first started working for Hank, I complained when he made a pass at me. He said that I'd 'misunderstood' him—that he would never make a pass at a woman. He repeatedly said he'd never do anything like that. But the word around town is that there were a lot of similar 'misunderstandings.'"

"I can confirm that!" Carl grumbled. "My wife didn't like it when he put his hand on her ass. As with Annika, he claimed it was just a 'misunderstanding.'"

Annika continued. "When it happened to me, he claimed his feelings were hurt. 'How could you accuse me of such a thing?' he whined. I told him I'd accept his explanation, but if there were ever another 'misunderstanding,' I'd tell Pieter. I reminded him that Pieter is an excellent marksman, and that the top floor of the Field House was easily within range of a small-bore rifle."

"Sort of like the 'Texas Book Depository,' right here in New Leiden, huh?" Torstein said.

"Exactly! Pieter would never think of doing anything like that. Although he's an accomplished marksman, he doesn't even hunt—all he shoots are targets. But Hank didn't know that."

"That explains why Hank had me bring a crew up here to rearrange his office furniture," Max laughed. "I always wondered 'bout that. His predecessors always liked the view, but he wanted to be tucked over in the corner."

There was a knock at the door, and everyone turned to see one of the Trustees standing in the doorway. "Sarah, would you mind coming back down to the Board Meeting. There are a few things we need to discuss with you."

She excused herself, and the others went back to work. Solveig and Torstein returned to Hank's office, and Frank stayed in the conference room, working with the photos he'd just received. A few minutes later, Pieter stepped out of the elevator. He found Annika at Mary's desk, and she took him across the hall to meet Frank.

"Annika called and told me about Hank. She also said you wanted to talk to me about my phone call last night. From what she told me, it sounds like I may have been one of the last people to talk to him."

"As near as we can tell, you were the last one," Frank said. "Can you tell us about the call? What did you talk about?"

After Pieter had summarized the phone call, Frank asked to look at his phone. His phone log showed over a dozen calls to Annika's number. When he compared it to Annika's phone log for the same period, hers was empty.

"Why are there so many calls to you on his phone, but none of them show up on yours? Why'd you turn it off? If you were heading home in a storm, I'd think you'd want your phone on."

"Oh, it was on, alright. But there's a dead spot about half way between here and our house. And I was stuck there because some idiot lost control and got stuck, backing up traffic in both directions. If I'd known that was going to happen, I'd have taken the long way home. It usually takes about fifteen minutes longer than the road I usually drive, but there's cell phone service the whole way."

"Were you home the whole time, Pieter?" Solveig asked.

"Except for about ten minutes, I was. When she hadn't come home, and I couldn't reach her, I decided I should go look for her. But when I got out in the storm and realized how bad the roads were, I thought the better of it, and turned around and came back home."

"Was there anyone there with you?"

"No, our kids were staying overnight with some friends last night. Sort of a 'blizzard party,' holed up with videos and popcorn."

"What time did you finally get home, Annika?" Solveig asked.

"It was almost 7:30."

"So there was about an hour and a half when neither of you had any contact with each other."

"That's right," Annika said. "And in my case, I was cut off from contact from everyone."

"So obviously no one can vouch for your whereabouts during that time—either of you?"

"I guess you can put it that way," Annika said. "There were people in the other cars who were waiting behind the stuck cars, and the students who finally got them going again, but no one saw me outside of my car. Why do you ask?"

"Just routine," Solveig assured them. "We're just trying to explore every possible angle."

Frank asked them both a few more questions, and when he was finished, Annika went back to Mary's desk, and Pieter left to pick up their children.

A little later in the afternoon, Solveig and Torstein went back to the conference room for another cup of coffee.

Frank had gotten a couple more student photos, and he'd arranged them on the main table with the others.

"How's it going, Frank?" Solveig asked.

He shrugged. "So-so. The pictures we've gotten thus far don't really show anything up here on the terrace. Most of them are facing in other directions."

Annika heard them talking, and came across the hall to join them. "How are you coming with my office, Solveig?"

"I was just going to tell you," Solveig replied. "We're done with your office—including your computer. Frank ran a quick diagnostic on it, and it shows exactly what you said: it was turned off just before 5:30, and wasn't turned back on until today. I ran another check on it myself, just like I did with Hank's. It confirmed what Frank found. You can go back there whenever you want to. But for the time being, Hank's office is still off limits. There are still a couple things we might have to look at again tomorrow."

"Thanks. I've been able to do most things at Mary's computer, but there are a few files I need from mine. I was just going to pour myself a cup of coffee—can I get you one?"

"That'd be great," Solveig said. "A cup of coffee is the reason Torstein and I are back here—that, and before we leave, see if we can help Frank figure out the jig-saw puzzle of the photos the students have been sending him."

Sarah came up the stairs, and joined the others.

"How's the meeting going?" Annika asked. "I didn't think they'd meet this long."

"Neither did I," Sarah replied. "But there were some things they thought they had to take care of today. They just adjourned. They'll schedule a special meeting sometime next month. I have to say, the meeting didn't go exactly as I'd expected it to."

"In what way?"

"Well, as I DID anticipate, they decided to abort the search for Hank's successor. They want everything to settle down before they start a new administration. That all makes sense."

"So, what didn't you expect?"

"They named an Interim President."

"So quickly? Who'd they appoint?"

Sarah spread her arms out and shrugged, "Unfortunately, I think, yours truly."

"What do you mean, 'unfortunately'?" Annika said. "I think you're the obvious choice."

"But I haven't even been here a year!"

"And if they brought someone in from outside, they'd be brand new. You've had over a semester to get the feel of the place. And besides . . . this keeps everything 'in house.'"

"What do you mean by that?"

Annika laughed. "It's simple. I'm sure they don't want to be surprised by anything Hank was doing. I'm not suggesting he was doing anything illegal, but some of his dealings were starting to sound a little shady. He was clearly trying to make sure that he walked out of here with as much money in his pockets as he possibly could. With you in charge, anything like that could be kept 'within the NNC family.' From what I know of the Board, they wouldn't just sweep something under the rug if it were illegal. But they also don't want any dirty laundry hung out for all the world to see. You're a known entity here. You'll bring stability."

Sarah shook her head. "I'm glad you have confidence in me. The person who really knows what goes on around here is you, Annika. So I'm glad that you'll be my Executive Assistant. I hope you don't have any plans to quit on me any time soon."

"Not if you think you need me. I figured that when a new president got on board, there would also be a new Executive Assistant. Then I could think about doing something different for a change. But I'll be happy to stay on as long as you want me to."

Frank cleared his throat. "It sounds like you consider this something of a dubious honor, Sarah. But as an outsider, I agree with Annika. From what little I've seen around here today, you seem like the kind of person who can give the place some stability until everything gets sorted out. With any luck, we'll even be able to clear out of Hank's office by Monday afternoon—maybe even earlier, if we get lucky—so you can start thinking about moving down there whenever you're ready."

Max nodded, "I agree. I think you're a great choice for Interim President. I assume you'll wanna wait a week or two before you move into that office. But when you're ready, just call my office, and we'll get people up here to move everything down the hall for you."

"I'm still not convinced," Sarah laughed. "But the Trustees made it clear that I don't have much choice in the matter. They feel that they need an Interim President immediately, and they don't have the time to find someone from outside. So . . . I guess I'm stuck with it until they can start a search for the new president. Hopefully they can get that taken care of next fall. Maybe we can have one in here by next January. I'll keep my fingers crossed!"

"Who are they going to have serve as Interim Dean until you come back from the President's Office," Tom asked.

Sarah groaned. "That's another problem. At this point, they don't think that's necessary. They said I won't have to do all the fundraising that Hank was involved in, at least this semester. So they think I can cover both offices through the spring, and then they'll appoint an Interim Dean this summer."

"In that case," Max said, "I'll call Henry Steenwyk over at the Electrical Shop. He can have one of his phone techs set up the phone in your office so that you can access Annika's. That way, until you get moved into the President's Office, you'll have an intercom, and she'll be able to transfer calls to you without any problems."

Frank pointed to the collection of pictures on the table. "Now that you have the perspective of a President . . ."

"INTERIM President!"

"Whatever! But we could use a fresh set of eyes on these pictures. The good news is, most of them were taken around 6:30. That's within our general time-frame for whatever happened to Hank. But the bad news is, we don't really have any pictures looking up in this direction."

Sarah walked around the table, occasionally stopping to pick up a photo to examine it more carefully. "I see what you mean. But what about this couple—they show up in quite a few photos, and in several of them, they're taking 'selfies' from an angle that looks like it would put this building in the background. That's what you're looking for, isn't it? Have they sent you anything yet?"

"I see what you're saying, but I don't think we've gotten anything from them. There's nothing here that shows the angle that would come out of any of those pictures."

Torsten picked up a couple of the photos. "From the looks of it, those two weren't too interested in what everyone else was doing in the snow. It doesn't look like they ever let go of one another. They're pretty cuddly in most of them. Maybe they don't want anyone to see pictures of them being so affectionate—maybe Mom and Dad don't know about their relationship, he has a girlfriend back home, or something like that."

Annika looked at the pictures in Torstein's hand. "I know her! That's Nancy van Wageningen. She used to be a work-study student in Pieter's department. She's on the women's basketball team."

"Could you contact her and see if they could send us some of their photos. You can promise them that no one outside of this group will be looking at them."

"Sure. I'll be right back."

Annika came back a few minutes later, and said, "No luck—at least for now. Her roommate said that Nancy's parents are in town, and she's gone shopping with them.

Then they're going out to dinner. They came for the basketball game—she's not a starter, but she gets quite a bit of playing time. The parents were already on the road when the games were cancelled. They didn't find out until they got to town. Since they had a motel room reserved, they decided to stay overnight and spend the afternoon and evening with her—shopping and dinner: the kind of stuff they wouldn't have been able to do with her today if the game hadn't been cancelled. I asked her roommate to have Nancy call me when she gets back."

Solveig looked at everyone and said, "I don't think we're going to make much more progress here until we get some more photos. Torstein and I are going to take everything we've collected back to our office. But I'd like to see what those photos might tell us. I think the more pairs of eyes we can get on those, the better off we'll be. I hope we can be back here by late tomorrow morning—early afternoon at the latest."

After Solveig and Torstein loaded up their gear and left, Frank and the others stayed in the conference room for a while. Finally Frank suggested that everyone else leave. They would meet again in the morning, hopefully with more photos, as well as a fresh perspective. As the others were going out the door, Frank asked, "Do any of you have any suggestions for places to eat? I've got a little more work to do in Hank's office, but then I'll be ready to find some dinner."

"It depends on what kind of food you want," Tom said. "There's a decent Chinese restaurant out near the city limits—just be sure to order off the a la carte section, and not the standard 'Combination A'-type dinners. Those are pretty ho-hum. There's a sports bar downtown that has great burgers. And if you're looking for pizza, or a limited choice of fairly decent Italian food, Snuffy's Italian Garden is a local favorite. Once you decide where you want to go, give me a call, and I can give you directions. "

"Thanks! If you don't have any other plans for the evening, why don't you join me?"

"I'd love to! I was supposed to be at the basketball games tonight. My wife's not a big sports fan, so she made plans to play bridge. With the games cancelled, I'm on my own for the evening. I'd love to join you. Give me a call when you're ready, and I can swing by your hotel and pick you up."

*   *   *   *   *

Sunday, February 23

FRANK WAS BACK ON CAMPUS just before 9:30 a.m. He'd called Tom before he left the hotel, so there was a member of the campus security staff waiting to unlock the door to Hank's office for him. She told Frank that Tom would be joining him soon, and that Sarah and Annika were both in the Dean's Office. Frank decided to go there first.

When he knocked on the door, Annika looked up and smiled. "Good morning! You should've gotten some photos from Nancy van Wageningen by now," she said. "I talked to her last night, and she said she and her boyfriend both had a bunch of pictures, and that they'd send them to you right away. She'd been with her parents most of the day, and hadn't heard about our request for photos."

"I haven't had a chance to check my e-mail yet. I'll go across the hall and do that. After I print them off here on Mary's printer, why don't you and Sarah join me, and see if we can figure out anything this morning."

"Have you ever thought about getting a Smart Phone?" Annika laughed. "If you had one, you could have checked them out over breakfast."

"Don't you start, too! My wife's been on my case about that for longer than I care to remember. Much as I hate to admit it, this is probably the convincing argument."

Solveig and Torstein returned from Bemidji just before 11:00, and the entire group got together in the conference room. Carl and Laura were the last to arrive. In addition to the pictures Nancy van Wageningen had sent, Frank had gotten some more from a few other students, too. Some of

382

those also had good angles that showed the terrace outside Hank's office. But nothing seemed to provide any clues related to Hank's death. Since nothing was happening in the conference room, Sarah and Annika went back to their desks to work on details left from the Trustees meeting.

About 11:30, the group in the conference room heard a knock on the door. Frank looked up to see Denny standing there, nervously twisting his stocking cap in his hands. Frank went over to him and put his hand on his shoulder.

"Good morning, Denny! You look like something's bothering you. What's the matter?"

"Well, you said that if I thought of anything, I should let you know. You're probably going to think this is stupid, but I got to thinking about something last night. It's probably nothing, but I thought I should tell you about it. I kept going over it in my head all night."

"I'm sure it's not 'stupid,' Denny. Sometimes even the smallest details can hold the answer to a mystery. And right now, we're still looking for that kind of special detail. Stay right here a minute! I'm going to get Torstein and Solveig. I'd like 'em to hear whatever it is that you want to tell me."

When the three of them returned, they took Denny out into the hall. "Good morning, Denny," Torstein said. "Frank says you thought of something that might help us figure this out. What's that?"

"It's probably nothing."

"You can let us decide that," Solveig said. "We'd love to hear anything you think might help us."

"Can we go out on the terrace? Maybe I'm remembering things wrong. It would help me if I could have a look at the terrace again."

"Sure," Frank said. "Just give us a second to get our coats on. After the storm, the temperature just kept dropping. It was cold enough yesterday, but it's at least ten degrees colder this morning."

When they got outside, Denny looked around and nodded. "Yeah, it's like I remembered it. I was right."

"Right about what?" Solveig asked.

"Icicles."

"Icicles? What about them?"

"Where are they?" Denny asked. "When I got back to my dorm yesterday, the area alongside the building— under the eaves—was roped off, with big yellow signs warning people, 'Beware: Danger of Falling Icicles.'"

"Sure. That's common with the kind of weather changes there were around here the last few days."

"But look down the terrace. There aren't any icicles. Just a few broken pieces hanging from the ivy. When I was blowing snow yesterday, I didn't have to worry about icicles falling on me—there weren't any. But the blower was grinding up pieces of them that were buried in the snow. Let's take a look at the section I didn't get to after we found Hank."

The four of them walked to the end of the terrace. There were quite a few tracks in the deep snow, where Torstein had been walking while he was taking photos. But there was still a lot of untracked snow in the area.

Denny stepped in some of the tracks Torstein had made the day before, until he got to a deep mound of snow directly below the edge of the roof. He reached into the snow, dug around a moment, and brought out a chunk of ice. It was about two inches in diameter, and about eight inches long. It tapered gradually from a fairly smooth, rounded top, to a ragged end that suggested it had been part of a much longer piece. Embedded in the rounded end were several strands of fiber. They looked like they'd been broken off from something else, too.

"What are those?" Frank asked.

Solveig took the piece of ice from Denny, and after she looked at it carefully, she handed it to Torstein. "Ivy," she said. "The icicle was obviously forming in the ivy, and when it got too heavy, it broke off. If you look along the edge of the overhang, you can see where sections of the ivy have come loose. There are strands of it hanging all the way along the terrace."

"I noticed that yesterday when I was taking pictures," Torstein said, "but I didn't think anything of it then. Let's go back in and look at them. I also want to take another glance at the pictures the students have been sending you, Frank. This might give us that 'different perspective' that you were hoping for."

Torstein turned to Denny. "Thank you! We don't know yet what this means, but it gives us a fresh perspective. Maybe some other things will fall into focus now."

"You're welcome! I wasn't sure it would be anything worth bothering you for, but I thought it would be better to tell you about it, and let you decide. I'd better get going, and let you get back to work." He turned and slowly started back inside.

"Not so fast!" Solveig said. "Can you join us for a donut? I noticed that Tom brought some goodies to the conference room, and Annika has the coffee maker going. You might be able to give us a fresh perspective on what we've been working on in there, too."

Denny's spirits immediately picked up. "Really? Thanks! I'd love that. Everything you're doing here seems so interesting. It would be great to watch you at work for a little while."

When they got back inside, Frank checked his computer again, and found there were several new photos. While Solveig and Torstein got Denny a donut and coffee, he printed off the latest images, and took them to the table. He asked Annika and Sarah to join them.

Sarah was surprised to see Denny there. Frank explained, "Denny thought of something he'd forgotten yesterday. Solveig and Torstein think it might help give us a different perspective on the photos we've been looking at. I'll let them explain."

Frank handed Solveig the photos he'd just gotten from the printer, and she arranged them with the others on the table. "Remember, we've checked the time-stamp on these, and we've arranged them chronologically. We'd like everyone to look at them again, but this time, we'd like you to look for just one thing: icicles. Just concentrate on the photos that show the terrace."

Carl was the first to speak up. "Okay, this one here was taken at 6:27. There are icicles all the way along the terrace. It looks like there are a few that have broken off, but it's a pretty solid line."

Solveig turned to Frank. "Can you call that one up on your computer? I'd like to blow that up a little to check some details."

A few minutes later, Frank had set his computer up on the conference table, and they were looking at the picture. As she zoomed in on the terrace, Solveig said, "I won't be able to enlarge it too much without losing all of the detail. This is about the best resolution we can get. But I think this is good enough."

"Good enough for what?" Sarah asked.

"Look at where there are gaps in the icicles. Unless I'm mistaken, you can barely see strands of ivy hanging down there. They obviously gave way after the icicles picked up too much weight. Look above them—some of the snow slid off the roof. That probably loaded up the ivy to the point where it couldn't hold the weight of the ice anymore."

"What's the deal with all the ivy around here, anyway?" Torstein asked. "I wasn't surprised to see it on some of the older brick buildings. But on the concrete facing of this building? That seems like it's a bit over the top, isn't it?"

Max laughed. "You coulda never convinced Hank o' that. He wanted ivy everywhere! I tried to tell him that it was goin' to play Hell with the building surfaces—especially on the bricks. We'll probably have to go in and redo the mortar on most of the old brick buildings in a couple o' years. But he insisted that he wanted to see 'the halls of ivy.' That was his idea of what a college should look like."

Solveig pointed to some other photos on the table. "Look at these as we move along chronologically. There are a few bare patches on the roof, and underneath those, some of the icicles have disappeared. "

"Look at this one that Nancy van Wageningen sent me this morning," Frank said. "Does that look like there's someone outside Hank's office?"

Solveig loaded the photo on Frank's computer, and enlarged it. "It's hard to tell, because it's dark under the overhang. But it sure looks like somebody's there."

She tried enlarging the photo again, but all the detail was lost as the pixels expanded. She clicked back to the view she'd just been looking at. Torstein bent over her shoulder and pointed at the screen. "It may just be my imagination," he said, "but I think that looks like somebody in a white shirt. He's close enough to the door that he could be just coming out or going in."

"Since we found Hank outside, my guess would be the former," Solveig said. "The carpet didn't show any signs of someone tracking snow inside. When was that photo taken?"

"The time-stamp says 6:34."

"And there's a solid line of icicles in front of Hank's office in that photo."

"Here's one from 6:41. You can't see anyone on the terrace anymore. And look at the icicles—there's a big gap in front of Hank's office."

The next photo had been taken at 6:43. "Look at this one," Solveig said. "It must have been scary to be out there in that!" She pointed to a photo in which the sky was brightly illuminated. "It's pretty much a white-out in the distance, but through the snow, you can just make out a bolt of lightning in the left side of the picture. There must have been a pretty good blast of thunder with that one."

Torstein picked up the last photo. "This one was taken at 6:46. You can barely make out the clock tower in this one, and that coincides with the time-stamp on the photo. Look at the roof over the terrace. Almost all of the snow is gone. And there are only a couple of icicles left—they're barely hanging from a few strands of ivy."

Frank looked at the photos again, and turned to Torstein and Solveig. "So, what do you make of all of this."

"There's no way to know exactly what happened, but I've got a theory," Torstein said. "Let me bring my computer over here, and show you some pictures that Solveig and I took when we were outside yesterday. I started on a preliminary report last night, but there were still too many missing pieces to warrant giving you anything yet, Frank. But I think those pieces have been fit into place—thanks to Denny's observation."

He loaded up a photo app, and started going through some of the pictures he'd taken the day before, as well as the ones they'd gotten from Laura. He turned to Denny and said, "A couple of these are going to show Hank. Are you going to be okay with that?"

Denny took a deep breath and said, "I saw the real thing. The image of him lying there is probably going to stay with me forever. I don't think looking at pictures of him is going to make much difference. If it starts to bother me, I'll go outside."

Torstein's first few photos showed the terrace. "As Denny just pointed out, notice: there aren't any icicles. But there are some broken strands of ivy all the way along there." He scrolled ahead to some pictures of the snow near where they'd found Hank. "I didn't think anything about this yesterday, but if you look at the places where Tom and Max brushed away the snow to get to Hank, there are pieces of ice in the snow. That's what happened to the icicles. When the snow slid off the roof, it took the icicles with it."

"Okay, so what caused the snow to slide off?" Sarah asked.

"It could be any number of things," Solveig said. "If Hank slammed the door behind him when he came out onto the terrace, that might have triggered some of it to slide. That lightning was so close that the thunder must have rattled everything. That would've jostled the roof enough to loosen the snow there, too. And the bell tower is just above the terrace. You can see from the pictures that there was snow on the roof at 6:41. But by 6:46, most of it had slid off. It probably wasn't any one of those things, but a combination of all of them. What seems clear now is that by 6:46, Hank was under that pile of snow."

Torstein scrolled to another set of his pictures. "Okay, Denny, these are the ones I was talking about. If you'd prefer to go outside, please feel free to do so."

"No, go ahead. I'll be okay."

"Here's the contusion at the base of Hank's skull. I checked the railing. In a spot near where Denny found him, I saw this." He switched to another image, and enlarged it. The snow had been dusted off the railing, and he had focused on the ice underneath it. "Remember how icy it was under the snow yesterday? Friday afternoon's ice storm left nearly a quarter inch of ice, and then the snow covered that up. I brushed the snow off a big section of the railing, and here's what I found." The enlarged photo showed a section of the railing where the ice was cracked. "Something hit this part of the railing and cracked the ice—it's the only place I found any cracks like this. Now, look here!" He brought up another picture, and zoomed in on it. "Right there, at the edge of that crack. Do you see that?"

"It looks like a couple strands of hair," Denny said.

"Right you are, Denny! Good eyes! And those strands of hair are the same color as Hank's. Whoever did his hair could probably give us the specific shade, as well as the brand of coloring. I didn't notice any gray in his hair, except at the roots. There are also splotches of blood in that same section—probably from the scalp laceration. I've ordered a DNA test on them. We'll know for certain if the hair and blood are his when I get the results."

"So, what do you think happened out there?" Annika asked.

"This is just my theory. As I said, there's probably no way we'll ever know for certain. But here's what I think happened. Imagine this scenario: First of all, those kids are running around out on the football field. And they're trying to leave a message that everyone could see."

"Chuck Fartwell," Solveig laughed.

"Something that Hank hated, right?"

Annika nodded.

"So, Hank sees 'em out there, figures out what they're doin', and goes out on the terrace to yell at 'em—to give 'em Hell and get 'em to stop. He's probably hopping mad, and he slams the door behind him. Before he can yell at the students down below, he walks right into the path of a falling icicle."

"What are the odds of that happening? Isn't that pretty far-fetched?" Carl asked.

"Definitely pretty long odds! I'm sure he would've liked to have won with those odds on that trip he was planning to Vegas. He could've come home a rich man. But every year, more than a dozen people in the US die from some kind of accident related to icicles. There's no reason he couldn't be one of them. And that's a national average—it's a helluva lot more likely to happen here than in Arizona or Florida."

"Okay, so let's accept, for the time being, that he got hit by an icicle. What happened then?"

"When he gets hit, it catches him by surprise—and it hurts like Hell! He puts his hand to his head and feels a lot of blood. There's a severed artery, remember? When I checked his body, his hand was covered with blood, and it hadn't been lying in a pool of it. Maybe he hears something else out there—probably other icicles falling. He turns to see what it is, and slips on the ice. On the way down, he hits his head on the railing, and it cold-cocks him. The thunder rolls, and the clock chimes. Then the rest of the snow sides off the roof and buries him—splat! Loss of blood. Asphyxiation. He never regains consciousness. If Denny hadn't been clearing the terrace, he might have been there until the spring thaw."

Max spoke up: "Yesterday, Solveig was talkin' about a couple of ironies surrounding his death. You can add this to your list."

"What do you mean?"

"The ivy. I tried to talk him out of plantin' all of that goddamned ivy around campus. It's creatin' a nightmare for building maintenance. But now you're sayin' that the ivy couldn't carry the weight of the icicles and the snow. If he hadn't insisted on all of that ivy, he might not have gotten hit by an icicle."

"I'm still having trouble accepting the idea that he was killed by an icicle," Carl said.

"An icicle, a balcony railing, and a heavy pile of snow that smothered him," Torstein reminded him. "We'll know a little more when we get the results of the DNA tests on those hairs, but I suspect they'll just confirm my theory. There's nothing to suggest that there was anyone else out on the terrace Friday night."

"It's kind of like Ralphie," Solveig said.

"Ralphie? Ralphie who? What the Hell are you talking about?" Carl asked.

"Haven't you ever seen 'A Christmas Story'? You know, the movie about the kid with the BB gun—'You'll shoot your eye out, kid!'"

"Sure, we watch it with our kids every Christmas. It's a tradition in our family."

"In mine, too," Solveig replied. "Remember what his Mom says near the end? 'Be careful, Ralphie. Those icicles have been known to kill people.' I agree with Torstein. I think that's what happened to Hank."

16
Aftermath

Monday, February 24

SARAH WAS WORKING at her own desk. Frank had told her that BCA was through with Hank's office, and she could move into it whenever she wanted to. But she thought she'd wait at least a few weeks. She asked Mary to go through Hank's desk and sort out any personal items. After what Solveig had found in Hank's computer, she wanted to spare Annika any further embarrassment. Together with the coats in his closet, she'd give his other personal effects to Hannah after the funeral. That was scheduled for Thursday afternoon. Sarah announced that classes would be canceled, and any faculty or staff who wanted to attend the funeral would be given time off to do so. She got the impression that a lot of people didn't really want to attend, but they were planning on going just to avoid embarrassing the College. If the only people who attended were those who liked him, it would have been a very sparse turnout.

Henry Steenwyk's staff had gotten her phone set up so she could access Hank's line, as well as use it as an intercom to talk to Annika. It probably would have been more convenient to have Annika work at Mary's desk. But she and Annika agreed that they shouldn't disrupt Mary's routine any more than necessary. Without an Interim Dean, things would soon be chaotic enough in that office the way it was. They didn't want to add to the confusion.

Sarah's phone rang, and she picked it up. It was Annika: "There's a fellow on the line named Tommy McCutcheon. He said that he's returning Hank's call from

Friday afternoon. Hank left a message for him, saying that he wanted to talk to him about the Classics position."

"Okay, put the call through. And then can you bring me that personnel file that was on Hank's desk? That probably has the details I need to know about this." She thought to herself, *"This has to be Hank's 'ringer' that Zoe and Monica were complaining about."*

She pushed the button for the other line. "This is Sarah Christiansen. How may I help you?"

"This is Tommy McCutcheon. Hank—I mean President van Daam—left a message on my voice mail on Friday. He said he wanted to talk to me about the Classics position I applied for. Can you connect me with him, please?"

"I'm sorry, but there was a terrible accident Friday evening. President van Daam was killed."

"You can't be serious!"

"I'm afraid I am. The funeral will be Thursday afternoon."

"And what is your position at the College?"

"Until Saturday, I was Dean. Now, because of this tragedy, I'm Interim President."

"This is still so hard to believe. I'll have to call my father and let him know."

"Your father? Did he know President van Daam?"

"Yes, they've known each other since they were deans together. I hope this doesn't sound insensitive, but you don't have any idea what he wanted to talk to me about, do you?—why he called me on Friday?"

"I'm sorry, I haven't been involved with that search. Let me check with Human Resources, and I can have someone from their staff call you back. I assume your number is in your application materials?"

"Yes, it is. Thank you very much!"

Just as she was hanging up the phone, Annika brought her the file. She read the recommendation from the search committee, and then glanced at the application materials for the two candidates. Then she called Monica Schutte.

"Monica Schutte speaking. How may I help you?"

"Good morning, Monica! This is Sarah Christiansen."

"Good morning President Christiansen," she laughed.

"I'd still prefer Sarah, if you don't mind."

"I'm sorry, Sarah. Please ignore my weak sense of humor—especially regarding the tragedy you're having to deal with. That must be a nightmare! What can I help you with?"

"I need a little information from you regarding the search you're chairing in Classics. I just got a call from one of the candidates, who said Hank tried to call him on Friday. This has to be the guy you and Zoe were talking about."

"Thomas McCutcheon?"

Sarah noticed how her voice had taken on an icy tone when she said his name.

"That's right. He said Hank left a message for him. Hank apparently told him that he'd met with you and Zoe, and he wanted him to call him back today."

"That's all he said? Hank didn't tell him about the outcome of the search—or at least of our meeting?"

"Apparently not. And in looking through the application materials, I can't figure out why Hank would've called him. The other candidate—Mary Anne Fischer—is obviously a far better candidate, as you clearly pointed out in your recommendation. So obviously, Hank was really going to follow through with this."

"Zoe and I met with Hank, alright." Sarah was struck by the bitterness in Monica's voice. "As we told you Friday, he told us that he was rejecting our recommendation, and hiring 'Tommy.' He was even going to delay the appointment a year so he could complete his Ph.D. and meet the minimum qualifications. I tried to point out why he was wrong, and he started pounding the table and yelling at me. At that point, I walked out. I don't have to take that kind of crap. That's when we stopped at your office, to let you know what was going on."

"Well, 'Tommy' mentioned that his dad and Hank went back a long way. I was afraid there might be something funny going on, but I wouldn't have expected Hank to do something that far out of line. I know you told me what he'd said, but I was still naïve enough to think you might have been exaggerating. I stand corrected."

"So, what are you going to do now?"

"Let me think for a minute. The only thing in the file, besides the application materials, is the memo from your committee, recommending that the College offer the position to Dr. Fischer. Did Hank give you anything in writing that he was overriding that recommendation?"

"No, nothing. He just yelled at us."

"And he apparently didn't say anything about it in the message he left for young Mr. McCutcheon, either." She thought for a minute, and then said, "Hang up the phone, please. I'm going to call you right back. But the conversation we just had never happened."

Sarah redialed Monica's number, and when she answered, Monica sounded a little confused. "Good morning, Monica! This is Sarah Christiansen."

"Good morning, Sarah. How can I help you this morning?" She wasn't sure what else to say.

"I'm trying to land on my feet here, clearing up some of the loose ends that Hank left unfinished before his tragic death. I just got a call from one of the candidates for the Classics position, asking about the status of the search. I have the memo you sent to Hank, recommending that we hire Mary Anne Fischer. I'm just calling to confirm that she is your committee's first choice. Is that right?"

Monica smiled. "Yes, that's right. In fact, she was our unanimous choice."

"That's all I wanted to know! I'll have Human Resources notify all of the candidates right away. They'll send a letter to all of the unsuccessful applicants. But since he called this morning, I'll have them give Mr. McCutcheon a call right away. If you'd like to call Dr. Fischer and give her the news unofficially, I'm sure she'll be happy to hear from you. If you do, tell her that official confirmation will be coming from HR as soon as possible."

"I would love to do that. I'll call her right now. And I'll let Zoe know, too. She'll be ecstatic! And thank you!"

"I always enjoy giving people good news. And being able to hire a great candidate is definitely good news. You'd better call her right away, to make sure she doesn't accept an offer from another school! From the quick glance I had at her application, she looks like someone we definitely want to come here."

As soon as she ended her call with Monica, she called Helen Kerkman, the Director of Human Resources. When Sarah identified herself, Helen said, "Oh, my God, Sarah! I just heard the terrible news about Hank this morning. I'm pleased that the Board of Trustees named you Interim President. If there's anything I can do to help you, please don't hesitate to ask me."

"I was hoping you'd say that! As a matter of fact, there is something I need your help with. I see Monica sent you her recommendation about the Classics search."

"I just got it Friday. It looks like the candidate they recommended fit what they wanted really well. But I didn't hear anything from Hank, so I didn't have the go-ahead to notify the applicants."

"That's why I'm calling. I'll send the paperwork over right away, with my approval of the committee's recommendation. I've asked Monica to call Dr. Fischer informally, and to let her know that she'd be hearing from your office soon."

"Sure, we'll contact her as soon as I have the forms from you."

"I'll have Mary run them right over to you. I know you normally just send out a letter to the unsuccessful candidates. But one of them called this morning. Apparently Hank tried to call him on Friday, and left a message for him to call back this morning."

"Why would Hank be calling one of the candidates—especially not the one the search committee recommended?"

Sarah closed her eyes and crossed her fingers. "I was wondering that, too. Hank didn't give him any indication of why he called, other than that it regarded the search. When he called back this morning, Annika transferred his call to me. I hadn't seen the personnel file yet, so I told him I'd get in touch with your office, and that you'd call him back. Would you mind doing that for me?"

"I'll be happy to. Which one is it?"

"Thomas McCutcheon. His phone number is in the file. Thanks, Helen! I really appreciate your help."

"Think nothing of it. That's what you pay me for!"

When she ended the call, Sarah set the file back on her desk. She thought to herself, *"Okay, Hank, how many more fires am I going to have to put out for you?"*

*　　*　　*　　*　　*

Thursday, February 27

HANK'S FUNERAL ON THURSDAY AFTERNOON was well attended. Like most of the other people there, Sarah would have preferred to be somewhere else. But she realized that she had no choice, particularly after Hannah asked her to give the eulogy. Her talk was relatively brief, and full of clichés and platitudes, though she tried not to overdo it. She talked about Hank's "vision," his "love for the College," and his "strong feelings for his Dutch heritage." She didn't say anything specific that she could be questioned about later, and most of the clichés she used had come from Hank's own speeches. Since Annika had helped him write almost all of them, it was easy for her to find the key phrases. Later that day Marty told her, "I thought you gave a great eulogy, Sarah. My only problem was that I don't think I knew the guy you were talking about," he laughed. "It almost made me think I liked him. I have to confess: I never would've been able to pull that off. In all seriousness, I don't think Hannah could have picked a better person to give the eulogy. You did it with taste and dignity, even if you had to be rather vague."

There was a reception in the church basement, and afterward, Hannah came up to Sarah to thank her. "What a wonderful eulogy! Thank you, Sarah. You've given me such a marvelous gift today. It really helped me deal with the grief I was bearing throughout the service. Again, thank you!"

"It was the least I could do. Hank was such a big presence around here that it will be difficult for anyone to fill that void easily."

"How kind of you to say that! Speaking of 'filling voids,' if I can change the subject for a moment: do you need me to move out of the President's Residence immediately? It might take me a couple weeks to get everything sorted out."

"NO! Of course not! There's no need for me to move there. I'm the Interim President, and when they select a new president, I'll go back to being Dean. It would make no sense for me to move into that house now, and then move back into ours again later. Besides, you need to take time to go through everything at your own pace. I wouldn't think of rushing you! By the way, how's everything going for you?"

Sarah noticed that Gene Graandsma had not left Hannah's side since he had walked her from the car into the funeral. Demi, however, was nowhere to be seen.

"Oh, everything seems to be going as well as can be expected. Gene's been helping me with a lot of things. I don't know what I'd do without his assistance. And the folks at Health and Benefits Office on campus have been a great help! They got me all the necessary forms to submit for his life insurance, and they told me that should be coming through in a couple of weeks."

"Have you given any thought about where you'll live? Are you going to stay here in New Leiden?"

"Oh, no, I don't think so. Our children—I guess I need to say 'my children' now—live in the Cities, so I'll probably spend a lot of time there. But I've never really liked the cold winters in the Upper Midwest. I'll probably spend my winters someplace warm. And I can use our condo whenever I want to go to the Cities to see the grandchildren."

"That sounds like a great idea, Hannah. Just remember, if there's any way that the College can be of assistance, please let me know."

Something about the word "condo" struck a chord with Sarah. She made a mental note to check on that later. She shook hands with Hannah and Gene, and returned to her office. *"Why do I have this nagging feeling that it's going to be a long spring?"* she asked herself.

*   *   *   *   *

Thursday, April 24

IN THE WEEKS FOLLOWING HANK'S FUNERAL, Sarah kept coming across different parts of Hank's "legacy." None of it was illegal. But several things he had done seemed to her to be at least ethically questionable. So far, she'd been lucky. As had been the case with the Classics position, she'd been able to resolve the various problems that had come up without causing any potential problems for the College.

The NNC-Chartwell basketball games were rescheduled. As Hank had feared, the men's team lost badly, but the Flying Dutch women won. The next day, the faculty played their annual charity game. The Flying Dutch were trailing by two points with less than ten seconds to go. Talmadge Sumner took a pass near the basket, and he looked like he was about to make one of his signature hook shots. When two defenders moved to cover him, he passed the ball to Chris, who was just outside the three-point line, now undefended. Chris released a high-arching jump shot that hit the rim, bounced off the

399

backboard, and rolled around the rim twice before going in. The NNC fans were ecstatic. Most of the Chartwell fans were confused to see their art historian cheering louder than anyone else in the gym.

During spring break, in late March, Sarah moved into the President's Office. She refused to refer to it as "Hank's office." As she told Annika, "it was here long before Hank came on the scene, and it will be here long after we're both gone. It's the President's Office, and that's it!"

About 8:30 that morning, Annika was sitting at her desk when Chris knocked on her door. "Come in, Chris. Can I help you with something?"

He shifted his weight back and forth from one foot to the other, and said quietly, "Are you still the person who's handling the lots at Summerfield Meadows?"

"Yes, I am—at least for the time being. Is there a problem? We have a number of people on a waiting list, so if you need to back out of the purchase, that shouldn't be a problem."

"No, I want to keep my lot. I hope to be able to start building a house in a year or so."

"Then what can I help you with?"

"I was wondering what the procedure might be for switching lots with someone."

"Well, as you know, the Summerfields don't want to have two isolated groups of faculty, with NNC families in one area, and Chartwell folks in another."

"No, that's not an issue. It's just that I know someone at Chartwell who would like to switch lots with the person who has the one next to mine."

Annika smiled at him. "That wouldn't happen to be the young art historian at Chartwell, would it?"

Chris immediately blushed.

She laughed, "I got a call from my counterpart at Chartwell this morning, saying that she'd gotten a similar query—from their art historian. So, tell me: why would she want to switch her lot on the hillside, with a great view, for the one next to yours."

"Because it's flat," he said.

"Because it's flat? Why would she want to trade a nice view lot for the flat one next to yours?"

She could see that Chris was starting to squirm.

"Hockey," he said softly.

"Does this young art historian play hockey?"

"She played left wing on her college team, all four years."

"A lot wouldn't be big enough for her to set up a hockey rink. And besides, where would she live? These are residential lots, remember?"

Chris was searching for an appropriate answer when she laughed, "Let me guess: she's looking for someplace to set up a rink when she has children, and they're old enough to skate, right?"

Chris nodded.

"So . . . how do you fit into this picture?"

Before he could come up with an answer, she broke out laughing. "I'm sorry—I shouldn't have been so cruel. I think it's really sweet! I've seen you together around town, and you make a lovely couple. When I got the call from my colleague at Chartwell, it was pretty easy to put two and two together. Does this mean that wedding bells are in the offing?"

Chris blushed, and nodded. "But please don't tell anyone yet. We're planning to get married in August. I haven't had a chance to tell Marty or anyone else yet, so I'd appreciate it if you kept it quiet."

"My lips are sealed. And don't worry: I think we can figure out how to switch her lot for the one next to yours. But what about basketball? What if these hypothetical kids want to play basketball like their dad?"

"Isn't that what a driveway's for? My lot's flat, and I know just where I'll put a hoop and backboard."

"Sounds good to me! Just let me know when I can start spreading your good news."

"Thanks a lot, Annika. I'll let you know as soon as I've had a chance to tell Marty."

A few minutes later, Sarah opened the door to her office, and asked Annika to join her. "Charles Thompson asked me to call Rich Summerfield about something related to Summerfield Meadows. He thought it might help smooth over some of the damage Hank left if I were the one to call. Since you've been working with the housing development, I thought it would be a good idea to have you listen in on the conversation. If I have any questions, you can be my backup."

"More Summerfield Meadows business today? Twice in one day . . . that's unusual."

"What else have you been doing with it?"

"I'll fill you in later."

"Let me guess: does it have anything to do with Chris van Zant and his friend at Chartwell?"

"No comment," Annika laughed, "other than to say that he somehow thinks they've been able to keep it a secret."

Sarah dialed Rich Summerfield's number, and reached his secretary. "This is President Sarah Christiansen at Nieuw Nederland College. Could I speak to Rich Summerfield, please?"

The secretary put her on hold, and a minute or so later, Rich Summerfield came on the line.

"This is Rich Summerfield. How can I help you President Christiansen? Just assure me that you don't want to name something at the housing development after Hank van Daam!"

"I can assure you, that's never going to come up. But please, can we dispense with formalities? Please call me Sarah. I also have Annika van Rijn here with me. Since she's been working with the lots and other logistical aspects of the development, I thought she could answer any questions you might have about what we've been doing so far. She has a great deal more hands-on experience with it than I do at this point. If you don't mind, I'll switch to the speaker phone so she can be part of the conversation."

"Sure, that would be fine. But how can you be so sure about the naming thing? When a college president dies in office, it seems like half a campus gets renamed in his honor, at least anywhere I've seen it happen."

"That's not on my agenda. At the first Faculty Assembly meeting after Hank died, someone wanted to change the name of one of the main classroom buildings to the 'Henrik "Hank" van Daam Center for Academic Excellence.' It was obviously one of Hank's toadies."

"You're kidding me! What was the response?"

"Someone else asked that we take a straw poll, with written ballots. So I asked, 'how many would like to rename something in his honor, and if so, what?"

"What did they say?"

"Three said 'yes.' One, of course, wanted that 'Center for Academic Excellence' named after Hank, one suggested the athletic center, and another thought the recycling center would be appropriate, because of his 'concern for green issues.' Everyone else said 'no.' But some of those voting 'no' nonetheless proposed name changes, too. A couple of them suggested the garbage compactor, and half a dozen of them thought we should have the 'Hank van Daam sewage treatment plant.' So, I think I'm safe to say you don't have to worry about that."

Rich laughed. "Okay, that brought a smile to my face. So what do you need to talk to me about this morning, Sarah?"

"Charles Thompson suggested that I call you to get your approval on something we've been discussing. We think it fits the spirit of what you had in mind for Summerfield Meadows, but we didn't want to go ahead with the planning until we ran it by you first."

"Well, I'm always willing to listen. Fire away!"

"We've been talking about trying to increase the cooperation between the two colleges, and one obvious place to start seems to be our drama programs. We'd like to start a summer theater festival, with faculty from both colleges serving as directors, and the casts drawn as equally as possible from the two student bodies."

"Sounds like a great idea. But how does that affect Summerfield Meadows?"

"That's where we want to make sure you approve of our plan before we take it any further. We were hoping that you wouldn't have any objections to our using the community center as a venue for the theater festival. We could put up temporary lighting, and bring additional chairs over from both campuses as necessary."

"Let me get this straight: you want to jury rig the community center, and monopolize it for part of the summer to run a theater festival?"

"That's essentially it, yes."

He thought about it for a few minutes, and then said, "I'm sorry. I don't think that would work."

"But I'm sure the technical staff on both campuses could get the place set up as a decent venue for student plays, and get everything put back to its original condition by the end of the summer."

"No, you don't understand what I'm saying. I don't think that would work. A jury-rigged community center isn't going to give your students a decent experience with theater."

Sarah was about to say something, when Annika waved her to be quiet. She held her finger to her lips, and quietly whispered, "Shhh! Let him talk."

"When I was in college," he continued, "I worked on the stage crew for several plays. I had no interest in acting, but I loved the technical stuff backstage—especially lighting and sound. Those are some of my favorite memories of college. I don't think someone can get an experience like that in a 'make-do,' temporary set-up in a one-story community center."

Annika motioned for Sarah to say something. "I know, those are my thoughts, too. But neither Chartwell nor NNC has a very good theater. And if we had the festival on either one of our campuses, students from the other one would always feel like they were at a disadvantage."

"I agree—100%. That's why we need a theater at Summerfield Meadows."

"I beg your pardon?" Sarah couldn't believe what she was hearing.

"I'll tell you what: why don't you have the drama faculty at both campuses jointly draw up a proposal for a theater festival, as well as other cooperative work throughout the academic year, and then send it to me. I'd also like to see what they think is necessary for a decent theater complex—and I don't mean something that's just 'adequate.' It has to hold at least 300 or 400 people. If I'm going to build a theater, I want something with a full proscenium, where the crew can lift sets and curtains up above the stage, and have professional quality lighting and sound."

"Theater complex?" Sarah asked.

"That's right! I want to see a proposal that includes a smaller venue for 'theater in the round' productions. If they can get me a rough outline of what they want in the next month, I can get an architect to draw up some plans, and we can break ground before classes start in the fall. Does that sound okay to you?"

"It sounds wonderful!" Sarah said.

"And what else are the two schools working on together. I hope they can go beyond this theater project."

Sarah said, "Since Annika's been working most closely with it, I'll let her summarize some of the things that have been going on."

"Good morning, Mr. Summerfield," Annika said, with as cheery a voice as she could muster. "I think there are several other things that will be starting up before fall semester begins. But the one that comes to mind immediately is a very creative project between our history department and the museum studies program at Chartwell. Apparently two professors have put their heads together, and they've been spending most of their spare time working on a collaborative project. They're establishing new levels of inter-departmental cooperation. We're expecting great things to come out of that kind of effort."

Sarah could barely keep from laughing.

"That's great to hear! I'm sorry that the College had to go through the trauma of Hank's death, but it sounds like you've got things headed in a very positive direction. Thanks for calling—send me that theater proposal as soon as you can, and we'll get my staff working on the building plans right away."

"It was a pleasure talking to you," Sarah said. "I look forward to meeting you the next time you're visiting in the area."

When she finished the call, she turned to Anika and said, "Did I really hear him correctly? He wants to build a 'theater complex'? Holy shit! I've got to call Charles and let him know about this! I'm sure he didn't expect this when he asked me to call Summerfield!"

* * * * *

JUST BEFORE 10:00, Marty came into the President's Office, and stopped at Elke's desk. "I got a message that President Christiansen wanted to talk to me about 'staffing.' I thought that was all settled last fall."

"That's all I know, Marty. Please go in. She's expecting you."

He briefly said hello to Annika as he passed her desk, and knocked on Sarah's door.

Sarah got up from her desk—now situated so that she could look out over the campus—and met him at the door. "Come in, Marty. Let's use the two chairs by the coffee table. They're the most comfortable in the office, as far as I'm concerned. Would you like Elke to bring you some coffee?"

"No, I'm fine, thanks. I'm supposed to meet Chris and some others at the CUB after I leave here, and I'll probably end up drinking too much coffee there. I probably shouldn't get a head start. How are you holding up under the rigors of holding down two jobs?"

"It's pretty much all I thought it would be, and maybe a little worse. If they'd give me an Acting Dean, that would help. Or better yet, get me out of this office and back down the hall. Unfortunately, that's not going to happen."

"I've heard some rumors to that effect. Are they true?"

"The Board of Trustees have told me that they don't want to do a search for a new president. They want me to stay on permanently. Apparently a group of faculty more or less demanded it."

"When are they going to announce that?"

"A news release is going out this afternoon. But at this point, you're free to tell anyone about it. I have to ask: did you have anything to do with that, Marty?"

He held up his hands to declare his innocence. "Not me! I didn't have anything to do with it! I will admit to having been asked my opinion, and giving it, and I'm pleased to hear that everyone else seems to agree. But that's the extent of my involvement"

"I'm glad to hear that, because I didn't want to bring this next thing up if it might look like it was a *quid pro quo*."

"What do you mean?

"I'd like you to teach a reduced load next year. Two classes in the fall, and one in the spring."

"But that only leaves one history class, and two sections of *die Quellen*."

"No, we're about to enter a new era, Marty. And it's the twilight era for *die Quellen*. Maybe Hannelore would describe it in Wagnerian terms: '*die Götterdämmerung*'— the 'Twilight of the Gods.' I'm sure the English department looks at it that way."

"Okay, don't hold me in suspense. What are you talking about?"

"I've appointed a committee to come up with a proposal for a new 'common course' to replace *die Quellen*."

"How will the Board of Trustees react to that? Most of them seem to have accepted the myth of 'shared inquiry,' with *die Quellen* as the foundation of the 'intellectual commons.'"

"This may come as a shock to you, Marty, but it was their idea. With a little nudging from me, I must confess."

"How did you manage that?"

"At the Trustees meeting last month, I scheduled some time for them to meet with a group of students to get their opinions about the course."

"Whenever that's been tried in the past, the students were all hand-picked. They all toed the party line, and sang its praises better than the College Choir."

"I anticipated that. These students were chosen at random—forty students, representing all four classes. There were obviously a few who loved the course, but the majority told a very different story. When I suggested that we develop a new course, one that would make better use of the College's resources, the Trustees gave me the green light."

"The 'Margaret Mead Method,' I take it. How are you going to manage all of that?"

"For starters, there will be a large group, with a representative from every department. Then the members of that group will divide into several working committees. It'll be their responsibility to figure out all the details and come up with a final proposal from the whole group."

"You mentioned English—if you don't mind my asking, how did our friends there react to that?"

"Oh, they sent a delegation to see me. I think there are smaller groups representing entire countries at the UN. They said that because of the role that English and History have traditionally played in *die Quellen*, they felt that they needed to have more than one representative on this committee. They also didn't seem to like it that I had appointed Bill Kaufman to represent their department."

"What did you say to that?"

"I told them that I appreciated all the fine work they had done in *die Quellen* throughout its existence. That course brought the College a long way. But now, we needed to move forward vigorously as we progress in the twenty-first century, and that requires that we come up with something completely new. For starters, every department has to be invested in this. In my opinion, if this course is to be truly central to the mission of the college, everyone needs to teach in it sometime. As far as I'm concerned, once we get this course up and running, one of the requirements for tenure and promotion, including promotion to full professor, with be that faculty will have to have taught in the course. Otherwise, no tenure, no promotion. It's going to take some creativity. For one thing, we've got to come up with an alternative to *die Quellen* for our college-wide writing course. That's why I picked Bill. I'm sure many of his colleagues in English would prefer that we simply hire more faculty in that department, and have them teach English comp to all of our students. But that's not going to happen. I don't know how this is going to work out in the end, but I know we're not going to continue on with *die Quellen*, at least as it now exists."

"Good luck! It'll be interesting to see what they come up with. But back to your original point—why do you want me to teach a reduced load next year? What am I supposed to teach?"

"I'm talking about three history classes—the ones you're already scheduled for. I just want to shuffle the schedule a little. I think you've spent enough time 'toiling in the vineyard' of *die Quellen*. You've already told me that you want to retire after next year. I can assure you that your request for a replacement will be approved. This close to retirement, you're not going to have another sabbatical. I'd like to see your last year here be with a lighter load. I checked what we worked out as your schedule for next year. You're supposed to have two lecture classes in the fall, and your senior research seminar in the spring, right?"

"Yes, that's the way I remember it."

"What about teaching the two classes in the fall on Tuesdays and Thursdays. And from what you've done in the past, I see you normally have the seminar in a three-hour block on one day, right?"

Marty nodded. *"Where's this going,"* he thought.

"How about teaching the seminar on Tuesday afternoons?"

"What would I do the rest of my time?"

"I've heard through the grape-vine that you've been working on a college history for quite a few years."

"In the summers, yes. I've never have a chance to do anything with it during the school year, thanks to *die Quellen.*"

"Well, you could now. I would really like to see that finished before you retire and move out of your office. Also, I've heard that there's a girls' youth basketball league in the Cities that could use a volunteer coach. If you did that, practices wouldn't start until late October. Once they started, you could come up here Tuesday morning, teach classes Tuesday and Thursday, and go back to the Cities Thursday afternoon. You'd have to miss practices on Tuesdays and Wednesdays, but it wouldn't be long until the semester was over. And in the spring, you could come up here Tuesday morning, and go back after the seminar in the afternoon. That would only be for a few weeks. During that time, students could contact you by e-mail if they have any questions. I checked with some of your colleagues. They're willing to help your students if they have any research problems when you're not around. They don't think it would be a problem since it would just be until the basketball season's over in late February. Then you'd be here and available to your students for the rest of the semester. And throughout the year, with that load, you might be able to finish that history of NNC."

"That all sounds great, but I'd hate to impose on my kids to stay with them that much."

"Not a problem! The College has a condo in the Cities, and the Trustees have told me that it's mine to use at my discretion. If I want to let someone from the faculty use it, they don't care. But I don't have any plans to stay there—Owen and I still have our house in the Cities. Whenever he has to go there for work, that's where he stays. We do the same thing if we go down for a concert or to go shopping."

"I thought the condo was Hank's."

"So did Hank! And initially, so did Hannah. She just assumed that it was hers to do with as she saw fit. But I asked the College's legal counsel to look into it. They told me that despite anything Hank may have said, it belongs to the College. He never paid a cent on it. Hannah tried to argue that the condo was part of his 'non-financial compensation.' Our lawyer informed her that THE USE OF IT was part of his non-financial compensation, but it belonged to the College. She made some rumblings about threatening to sue, and he pointed out that if she did, she'd have legal expenses. And she'd take possession of a condo that doesn't have much equity in it—real estate prices still haven't fully recovered after the financial crisis in '08. She'd have to make payments on it, and if she sold it, she wouldn't be getting much. If she just walked away from it, she would have no expenses. She could easily stay in a very nice hotel whenever she came to the Cities for far less money than she'd be paying to keep the condo. And she can easily afford that. So, she agreed—it belongs to the College. The College will probably sell it eventually, but only after real estate values come back up. As I said, for now, it's mine to use at my discretion. So as long as you don't use it for something that's illegal, immoral, or unethical, I'll be happy to let you stay there."

"You make a pretty convincing argument. Let me think about it overnight, and talk to my kids. I want to make sure Erica still wants me to be one of her basketball coaches."

"I did some field work before I came up with all of this, Marty," she laughed. "I talked to Mike, and he said Erica would be delighted. He didn't want to tell her about it until I'd gone over it with you first. It's your life, after all. But he had no doubts about what her reaction would be."

"Well, in that case, how can I say no? You mentioned Hannah—what's she going to do? I saw that she moved out of the President's Residence a week or so ago."

"It's kind of like a chain reaction. Gene Graandsma resigned from the Board of Trustees. He's getting a divorce from Demi. He and Hannah are buying a place in Palm Springs, and they're planning to get married as soon as his divorce is final. Hannah collected a $5 million life insurance policy, so they can live pretty comfortably on that. On top of that, Demi is apparently being surprisingly generous to him in their divorce settlement. Demi sold the majority interest in her exercise studios, though she'll remain a minority partner, which will still provide her with a healthy monthly income. And she's already sitting on a pile of money. Finances aren't going to be an issue for her. She moved to Key West with her pilates instructor, Brandee."

Marty shook his head in disbelief. "I see what you mean about a chain reaction. It sounds like your life's gotten pretty complicated."

"In case you haven't heard, I've been putting out little wildfires all over the place since Hank died. The stop light is a good example."

"What are you doing about that?"

"Me? Nothing. It's my understanding that the College has no control over it. That's not the impression that Hank gave the Mayor, so he called me up, asking me to let the city regulate the light. I told him that the College would be happy to provide a place to meet, but that's the only involvement we could have. It's controlled by the Faculty Association, so he has to talk to them. They have a meeting scheduled next week. In the meantime, the College is going to build a pedestrian bridge across

College Avenue, to connect the dorms to the main campus. The College got $5 million from Hank's life insurance policy. The Trustees put most of in the endowment fund, but I talked them into letting me use part of it for some essential projects. The first one will be the bridge, followed by a small bump in faculty salaries."

Marty nodded. "With a bridge to help get the students across Campus Avenue, I don't think any of the Faculty will object to adjusting the light. All the city will need to do is let the Faculty Association know how they'd like the timing to be set."

"I made a point of telling the Mayor that. The light will still be the responsibility of the Faculty Association. But I assured him that he should be able to expect complete cooperation, at least after we get the pedestrian bridge in place. We're about to let out bids for that now, so hopefully we can finally get this issue resolved."

"You have been busy!" Marty said. "And you've managed to fly under the radar. I hadn't heard anything about most of it. Hank was always out blowing his own horn about every little thing he did. This is definitely a refreshing change."

"At least that was a fairly easy matter to resolve. But it seems like every time someone turns around, they stumble across another scheme that Hank was working on. We still haven't run into anything illegal, but everything he did was definitely designed to benefit him. The biggest crisis was with the van der Kellens."

"What happened with them?"

"I'm sure you remember: after they gave all the money to establish the Dutch Studies Center, they wanted to name the center after Hank and Hannah. I suspect it would probably be more accurate to say that Hank talked them into that."

"Oh, yeah, the 'Henrik and Hannah van Daam Endowed Chair of Dutch Language and Culture.' That doesn't look like such a good idea anymore."

"Not at all. They heard rumors about some of the schemes Hank had been involved in, and somehow they even got wind of Hank's computer application. They threatened to withdraw their money entirely. Mike Nagel and the key members of his Institutional Advancement staff were running around in a panic. Mike met with the van der Kellens several times, and finally managed to 'walk them back' a bit. He assured them that the Chair would not be named after Hank and Hannah, and offered them an alternative, which they agreed to.

"What's that? I hope it's somebody who actually supports Dutch Studies."

"I think you can rest assured about that. The van der Kellens want to rename the chair the 'Annette and Martin Dykstra Endowed Chair of Dutch Language and Culture.' I think that's a pretty good choice."

For one of the few times in his life, Marty was speechless. When he finally caught his breath, he said, "You can't be serious!"

"Oh, yes we are! I told them I wasn't sure if you'd agree, but once Mike told them how hard you've been working to keep Dutch Studies alive on this campus, they insisted. Congratulations!"

"I honestly don't know what to say. I never expected to receive an honor like this."

"Well, I think it's well deserved." She stood up, and gave him a hug. "Again, congratulations! Thank you for everything that you've contributed to NNC!"

She noticed that Marty looked a little embarrassed by the hug, so she stepped back and said, "Okay, that's all I had on my agenda. Is there anything you need to bring up?"

"Not here. I'm like you—I like to keep work and personal issues separate. I was hoping we could get together sometime at Snuffy's for dinner. We haven't had a chance to do that since before Hank died."

"I know—and I'm sorry that I've been too busy to make that happen. But Owen just left for the Cities today, and I'm going to be on my own for dinner. Would tonight work for you? Say, 6:00?"

"Definitely! I'll call Snuffy's and reserve the back table. See you at 6:00!"

*   *   *   *   *

WHEN HE LEFT SARAH'S OFFICE, Marty headed to the CUB. He poured himself a cup of coffee, and picked out a cinnamon roll. Then he joined the other members of the *Kaffee Klatsch*. A few minutes later, Chris arrived. Marty thought he looked very nervous. Before anyone else could say anything, Dirk spoke up. "Say, Chris. I have a question for you. On the way out of the kitchen this morning, I saw that Karen had an appointment scheduled tomorrow with someone named Chris? That wouldn't be you, would it? I tried asking Karen about it, but she gave me some gobbledy-gook about 'caterer-client confidentiality.' What gives?"

Chris held up his hand. "Hold that thought, Dirk. Marty, could I see you outside for a minute."

"Sure," he said, and got up from the table. He looked around the table and cautioned everyone, "That cinnamon roll had better still be on my plate when I get back!"

When they got outside, Marty asked, "What's going on, Chris? You're jumping around like a fart in a frying pan!"

"I was hoping to talk to you before I got over here. But I had to talk to Annika first thing this morning, and then you were at a meeting."

"I was in the President's Office. We must have just missed crossing paths. What do you need? Please don't tell me that you've gotten a job offer someplace else!"

"No, no, nothing like that. Something a lot better than that—at least I think so. Mariah and I are planning to get married this summer! I hope you can make it—we're planning to have the wedding on Saturday, August 9. I know you're usually at the lake then, but I hope you can be there."

415

"That's fantastic news, Chris! Of course I'll be there! I wouldn't miss it for the world! Where's it going to be? Where's Mariah's home town."

"She grew up in central Minnesota, but her parents moved to Michigan when she was in college. She doesn't really have any ties there, and she doesn't have any relatives where she grew up. So we're planning to have it in Edison."

"Where are you going to live? Here, or in Edison? I assume one of you will commute."

"She has a small house in Edison. We'll live there until we can get a house built at Summerfield Meadows. That's what I had to talk to Annika about this morning. We each signed up for a lot, so we're going to try to switch hers with the person who got the one next to mine. That way, we'll have a double lot, and when we have kids, we'll set up a small skating rink in the winter. Mariah played hockey all through college."

"What about basketball?"

Chris laughed. "Annika asked me the same question! We plan to have a nice, big, flat driveway, where we can set up a hoop. But that's getting a long way ahead of ourselves. For now, we're just looking forward to the wedding. We're going out to the Pacific Northwest on our honeymoon."

"I hope you get a chance to do some steelheading."

"Probably just one day. Mariah wants me to teach her how to fly fish, but fishing for steelhead on the Stillaguamish would be quite a challenge for a beginner. We thought we might stop someplace along the way, like in Montana or Idaho, and see if we can find a good stream for her to learn the basics."

"Let me talk to my friend in Montana. Although we were on some pretty big rivers, his son was telling us about some smaller streams that are a lot easier to manage. That's where he takes clients who don't have much experience."

"That would definitely describe Mariah."

"He even has some people on his staff who give lessons."

"Could you get me his contact information? I'd love to arrange something like that for Mariah."

"I have an even better idea. I think I just came up with the perfect wedding present—a day of lessons and guided fishing in Montana for the two of you. You can definitely get her started on the right foot that way, and you can have a great fishing experience, too."

"That would be wonderful, Marty! I know she'll love it! Come on—we'd better get back inside before someone eats your cinnamon roll. But I didn't want to tell anyone else until I talked to you about it first."

"Thanks, Chris. I really appreciate that! After my meeting with Sarah, I have several things I need to talk to you about, too, but for now, let's get back to the *Kaffee Klatsch.*"

When they got back to the table, several more people had joined the group. But Marty's cinnamon roll was still untouched. And his coffee was still warm. Dirk looked at Chris and said, "Okay, why are you having a rendezvous with my wife? I'm not worried that she's having an affair with you—if she were, she definitely wouldn't put it on our kitchen calendar. At least I hope she'd have the decency not to!" he laughed. "What's going on?"

Chris took a deep breath, and looked at Marty, who nodded at him with a smile that spread from ear to ear. "Okay, here goes. I hope all of you can save August 9 on your calendars. I'm sure you can, Dirk, because Karen told me that she'll be around that weekend. She's about to be contracted to cater a wedding."

"And whose wedding might that be?" Johanna laughed.

"An art historian from Chartwell."

"And . . . ?" she asked.

"Yours truly," he blushed. "The formal invitations will be printed in a week or two, and we'll get them in the mail as soon as we can. I just wanted all of you to know so that you can get it on your calendars. I hope you can all join us."

Everyone in the group got up to shake his hand or hug him, and then they all settled back into their seats. "Well, that's certainly exciting news," Terry said. "I'm glad I came over here this morning."

"I've got some more news," Marty said. "I wouldn't put it in the same category as what Chris just told us, but it's pretty good, nonetheless."

He proceeded to tell them about Sarah being named President, and the endowed chair. He didn't bother to mention his reduced course load in the fall. That would come up eventually, but he saw no need to mix that in with the other news.

Johanna said, "This isn't of the same caliber as everything else I've heard here this morning, but I've got something to share with all of you, too. Has anyone heard about the new football coach?"

"Only that Hank hired someone before Christmas. Why?"

"Well, remember how Hank said we had to clean house—fire all of the assistants and start fresh?

"Sure," Marty said. "And as I understand it, most of the assistants are still looking for jobs. Some of their wives have good jobs locally, and they don't want to leave this area. Several of them are getting pretty desperate."

"Apparently they aren't any more," Johanna said.

"What do you mean?"

"Well, the new coach got to campus shortly before Hank died. Hank called him in and gave him a big pep talk, and then proceeded to tell him how he thought he should be coaching the team. He also told him how lucky he was that Hank had cleared out all the 'deadwood' in the athletic department, so he could start with a fresh staff."

"That's what Hank wanted."

"Yes, but the new coach didn't like the idea of Hank trying to micromanage the football team. He also discovered that it wasn't going to be easy to hire a bunch of new assistants to come to New Leiden. Our coaches aren't paid all that well. After Hank died, the new coach called all of the old assistants in. He told them he thought it was ridiculous to lose that 'wealth of experience.' If any of them wanted their jobs back, he wanted to hire them. He even offered Harry Westbrook an associate head coaching position, but he decided he was going to 'pursue other interests,' though he was grateful for the offer. A couple of the assistants also decided they'd had enough of the coaching racket, but the majority of them will be back with the team. Apparently there's a new spirit and high level of morale among the entire coaching staff, and that's apparently spread to the players. Nobody's ever going to get too optimistic about the Flying Dutch football team, but it sounds like this will be a big improvement."

"Wow!" Terry said. "I'm REALLY glad I came over here today. I can't remember ever hearing so much great news in one day on this campus!"

The group gradually dispersed, and Marty and Chris went back to their offices.

"That other stuff was good news, alright," Marty said. "But yours was the best!"

*   *   *   *   *

SARAH GOT TO SNUFFY'S just before 6. As usual, she saw that Marty's car was already in the parking lot. And as she'd anticipated, he was already in the back booth. The waitress had brought a carafe, and he was just starting to pour each of them a glass of wine.

When she sat down, he handed her one glass, and then clinked it with his own. "Congratulations, Madame President! NNC has made a great choice! I almost wish I weren't going to retire after next year. It would be a pleasure to be here under your leadership!"

"Now, that's piling it on a little thick, isn't it Marty? I haven't even been here a year yet, and you're making me sound like I'm ready for sainthood."

419

"No, I just have great confidence in your leadership abilities. Just promise me you won't give up the practice of listening to what others have to say. And don't hesitate to ask people what they think. You don't have to take it, but people appreciate being asked for their advice. Don't isolate yourself from people who might be able to offer you some different perspectives. In other words, don't let your term in office turn into an 'imperial presidency.'"

"Right now, I have Annika to help in that regard, but that's only temporary."

"What do you mean? What's she going to do?"

"Well, you might say that I'm gently pushing her out of the nest. I'm giving her a paid leave of absence. It's kind of a sabbatical, if you will. But after her experience with Hank, I don't think she wants to hear that term used with anyone other than regular faculty."

"For how long?"

"Six months: from July 1 to December 31."

"Will she come back to your office then?"

"No. From July to December, she's going to work on her dissertation. She's sure that she can get it finished in that amount of time. I've been talking to Charles Thompson at Chartwell. He was very impressed with the way she organized the sale of lots at Summerfield Meadows, as well as the aftermath of Hank's death. I told him that she was going to be finishing her degree, but she needed to get some teaching experience. He's arranged with their philosophy department to have her teach a J-term course, and then a philosophy class in spring semester. She'll also teach one section of *die Quellen* for us in the spring. Charles and I think that we should be able to put together a full-time load between the two schools the following year. And then there's going to be an opening in their Philosophy Department. He obviously can't guarantee anything (since he's no Hank), but after teaching for them for a while, if she does as well as we both expect, she should have a good shot at a full-time, tenure track position there."

"That's great news. Although she's the one who kept Hank's office running, I always thought that her talents were underutilized. I'm glad to see she'll have a chance to get back into her field. I have some good news about Chris, too."

Sarah smiled. "I've heard rumors that he's going to get married this summer. That's wonderful!"

"Word travels fast! He just told me this morning. But he also got some good academic news this afternoon."

"Oh? What's that?"

"He got an e-mail from the editor of the journal that he sent his manuscript to. They want him to make a few minor revisions, but nothing serious. If he gets the revision to them by the end of the summer, it'll be published next year."

"That was a pretty quick turn-around. My experience with journals has never gone that quickly."

Marty laughed. "I know one of the editors. Don't get me wrong—I didn't ask her to do anything inappropriate, or to accept something that wasn't up to their standards. But I asked her if she could just make sure it didn't fall into a black hole. As you know, some reviewers take forever to get comments back. They're usually the ones who complain the most about students not getting papers in on time, and then they take weeks to grade them. She made sure she sent it to a couple of reviewers who could be counted on to get their comments back to her quickly. I'd gone over the manuscript with him before he submitted it, so I was confident it would be well received. But I was still surprised that he heard back from them this quickly. That takes a load off his shoulders—especially now that wedding bells are in the offing. Students love him, and he's gotten a good committee assignment for the next three years. With this article, he shouldn't have to worry too much about tenure. That funding you found for him to get to the Netherlands in January really paid off—personally as well as academically."

"I'm glad I could be of help."

"It's amazing how smoothly everything seems to be running now. Problems that used to seem insurmountable are being eliminated, people aren't at each other's throats, and there's a general feeling of optimism around campus that I haven't felt in years. I hate to say this, but I can't help but think that Hank's untimely demise didn't have some positive effects."

"I've noticed that, too," Sarah replied. "It's kind of like when you have a load of wash, and a couple pairs of jeans end up on the same side of the drum. Everything gets off-kilter. Once you straighten that out, things run smoothly again."

"Are you a 'Star Wars' fan?"

"I wouldn't describe myself as a great fan, though I'm very familiar with the whole series. I have to be—Owen's probably seen every one of the movies at least twenty times. I used to tease him that he only started dating me because Princess Leia wasn't available. Why do you ask?"

"One way you could describe NCC over the past few years is that there was 'a disturbance in the Force.' Hank was no Darth Vader, but he was definitely a disruptive influence. That was part of his 'managerial style,' which I think would probably fit well in 'the Empire.'"

When she stopped laughing, Sarah said, "That's a good analogy. I'm trying to avoid anything that might sound like public criticism of Hank, but that's definitely an image that will be in the back of my mind. I intend to have a very different managerial style, as you'll see in a few weeks."

"That's already pretty obvious. But what other surprises do you have in store for us?'

"Well, for starters, I asked the Trustees not to do an outside search for a new Dean."

"If we'd done that with the last search, you wouldn't be here."

"I'm well aware of that. But I've tried to avoid functioning like the rest of my peers around the country.

I've never been too fond of the idea of the professional 'administrative elite.'"

"I don't think anyone here would accuse you of that."

"NNC is like most colleges and universities around the country. Throughout most of its history, things functioned admirably with deans who came up through the ranks of the faculty here. But as you're well aware, starting in the late 70's or early 80's, the cadre of professional administrators emerged around the country, moving from college to college as they climbed higher up the administrative ladder."

"What Disraeli referred to as 'climbing the greasy pole.'"

"You understand what I'm talking about. They convinced faculty that if they turned everything over to professional administrators, that would free them up to spend more time on teaching and research. But then the administrators turned the screws, and started expecting more publications. The 'service' component of faculty responsibilities was reduced to sitting in boring meetings of committees that didn't really do anything."

"Faculty essentially sat in silence while administrators pulled their teeth," Marty said. "That's why that stop light took on such significance to our faculty. It was the last vestige of 'power' that the faculty had. I think most of us would love to see faculty have more responsibility here, like it was when I was a student."

"That's what I think, too. It took some talking, but I've convinced the Trustees that we need to go back to that model. Faculty committees, and especially the Faculty Assembly, need to do something more significant than discussing course proposals. The time-honored concept of 'shared governance' needs to be reinstated here. But that obviously means that faculty will have to take their committee work seriously. If they don't, I'll fall flat on my face. I'm sure the Trustees wouldn't hesitate to bring in a new dean—and a new president—from outside. Then they'll have reincarnations of Hank and Rothman, and the school will be back in the hole I want to dig us out of."

"I think there are plenty of faculty here who will be willing and able to take on that responsibility. It's a pretty radical change from the way things have been run here for the past few decades. I'm surprised the Trustees are willing to go along with that."

"It wasn't an easy sell," she acknowledged. "But I argued that I wasn't suggesting anything new or radical. I was just trying to restore things to the way they used to be."

"Spoken like a true revolutionary!" Marty laughed.

"What do you mean?"

"Just two obvious examples: Martin Luther wasn't trying to destroy the unity of Christendom. He claimed that he was just trying to get the Church back on the right track. The nobles who sparked the French Revolution in 1789 didn't want to destroy the monarchy, or give political power to the masses. They were trying to restore what they thought was the political order of an idealized past."

"That's not very reassuring," she sighed.

"Sure it is—you're not going to bring any significant change by simply trimming around the edges. We've talked about that before. That 'old order' is worth restoring. I'm sure you'll succeed—I know you won't have any trouble finding faculty willing to work with you. I can think of several good candidates off the top of my head—as well as a few who would love the job just to keep you from bringing changes they don't want to see around here. But I'm surprised the Trustees didn't insist on using a 'headhunter' and bringing in an outsider."

"That was a tough sell. Schools are so used to using headhunters these days, they've almost forgotten how to do it on their own. I've never understood how that became the norm so quickly."

Marty chuckled, "Someone went to some prestigious leadership seminar, where they heard some 'professional' say that it was the best way to come up with good candidates. So everybody does it that way now. Then the headhunters groom an otherwise ill-qualified candidate to say the right things in response to the questions they tell the colleges to ask. Rather circular logic, if you ask me. But since the schools are paying the headhunters a lot of money, it must be a good thing, right?"

He winked at her, and continued: "I hate to be the one to remind you of this, but you were chosen in a search that involved headhunters."

"Even a blind pig can find the occasional truffle," she laughed. "But in my own defense, I have to say that I wasn't one of the headhunters' candidates. I responded to the job notice on my own. And I obviously didn't reply to the search committee's questions with the headhunters' canned answers."

"That's the rumor that went around campus. Apparently one of the other candidates couldn't answer a question without throwing in 'enlightened and inspired' at least once—sometimes more. One of the committee members told me it sounded like's she'd memorized NNC's mission statement, and quoted from it whenever she could. This will be a nice change from the 'corporate model.' I hope you'll be inviting nominations for a new dean soon."

"Next week!—I'll be sending out a message asking for nominations. I look forward to hearing your suggestions. But I don't think you wanted to talk to me about deans, or Hank . . . or Annika or Chris, for that matter. What's on your mind?"

"I'd like your opinion about something, from a woman's perspective."

"Sure—that's the only one I have," she chuckled. "What's the question?"

"What would you think about a man dating someone who's fifteen or twenty years younger than he is?"

"Well, that depends," she laughed. "If you're talking about someone Chris's age, then you've got serious problems. But he's obviously occupied elsewhere, so I know that's not an issue. If you're talking about someone who's over sixty, so the woman would be in her 40's or 50's, then I don't see any problem. Unless she's at the lower end of that age span, wanting to have kids isn't going to be an issue for her. If she's someone he enjoys spending time with, and she feels the same way, I say, 'more power to them.' Now, would this person be anyone I know?"

"How'd you guess?" he blushed. "I've been serving on a state historical committee for the past several years. One of the other committee members is in her late 40's. She was widowed about five or six years ago. The last few times we've been to a meeting, we've ended up sitting next to each other at dinner. Then I got brave, and asked her to dinner—just the two of us, rather than with the committee. And we've been 'dating' since then—movies, a concert or two, as well as dinners. I love her company, and she seems to enjoy mine, too."

"So, what's the problem? Are you worried what your kids will think? Or hers, if she has any?"

"Not really. Mine haven't been too subtle lately about encouraging me to start dating. In fact, the last few times I've visited them, I've been worried that they were going to set me up with one of their neighbors. And her kids have been encouraging her to date, too."

"Okay, then, what are you concerned about?"

"She's already lost one husband. I'm almost twenty years older than she is. I don't want to be the cause of more grief for her when I die."

"Are you planning on doing that any time soon?"

Marty laughed, "Not that I'm aware of."

"Then I think that decision is hers. Age is no guarantee of surviving a spouse. She already knows that. So do you. So why don't you continue enjoying her company, and let things develop? If the relationship really starts to go places, I say, 'go for it.' But there's something else, isn't there? Are you worried about what Annette would've thought?"

"You're sharp. How'd you guess?"

426

"Dad went through the same thing after Mom passed away. After five or six years, he met someone, but he was afraid to let it get serious. I told him that no one ever had any doubt about how much he loved Mom, especially not us kids. But she wouldn't have wanted him to deny himself happiness when she was no longer there to share it with him. Any feelings he developed for someone else would never diminish the love he and Mom shared. From what I've heard about Annette, I'm sure she'd have felt the same way."

"So, what happened with your Dad?"

"He's in his 80's now. He and my step-mother are closing in on their twenty-fifth anniversary."

"I'm glad I invited you to dinner," Marty said. "I knew you'd have some wisdom to share with me."

"I hate to correct you, Marty, but I invited you. You made a general suggestion, but I'm the one who suggested we come tonight."

"Only after I planted the seed!" he laughed. "But even though you made the invitation, I'm picking up the tab tonight! After all the good news you gave me today, I don't think you have to worry about me coming around asking for favors because I bought you dinner."

"As long as you take my advice, you can buy me dinner any time!"

17
Epilogue

Monday, August 4

BEFORE THE TREES STARTED TO BUD that spring, Max Cuypers had made an appointment to talk to Sarah. At that point, she was still Interim President, but she was already earning a reputation as a decisive leader. He hoped she would agree with the recommendation he was about to give her.

Max had prepared an extensive review of the condition of some of the campus buildings. He focused particularly on the damage that the ivy was causing on a number of them. When she asked him for his recommendation, his answer was simple: he thought almost all of it should be removed as soon as possible. She told him to get started right away. They agreed that several plants growing on rock outcroppings could stay. In the fall, they'd offer a splash of color, and throughout most of the year, they'd cover up what would otherwise be drab rocks. But the rest of the ivy on campus had to go. Max immediately set his staff to work cutting the plants off just above the ground. In the summer, he'd put several work crews to work clearing the dead ivy from all of the buildings.

Denny Bakken graduated in May, but Max didn't want to lose a worker with his experience until he had to. So he kept him on throughout the summer. Since he was no longer a student, Max was able to hire him as a regular employee, which gave Denny a little more money than he'd earned before.

Denny was on a ladder, scraping dead ivy off the façade of the Carroll Center. When Max saw him working near the President's Office, he thought it might be a good idea to check on him.

"How's it goin' up there, Denny?"

"Not too bad. Some of this stuff is really stuck to the concrete. In a couple of places, where there were cracks, it even pulled small pieces out."

"You've got somethin' to fill holes, don't ya?"

"Sure—I've got a can of plaster. Unless I run into too much more of it, it should get me through this side of the building."

Sarah saw them talking outside her office, so she opened the door, and stepped out onto the terrace.

"How's everything going, Max? It looks like you've assigned your best worker to my part of the building! How are you doing, Denny?'

"Just fine, thank you. It's beautiful weather, and the work's not too strenuous. I get a nice workout, without getting exhausted. I definitely can't complain about the work."

"You're not having any problems working here again, I hope—outside the President's Office, I mean?"

"No, not really. I thought I might, but it hasn't been a problem. One of the things Wanda stressed was looking ahead, rather than thinking about what happened in the past."

"That's great advice! Speaking of looking ahead, what are you going to do now that you've graduated?"

"I'm headed for graduate school," he beamed.

"You majored in biology, right?"

"Yeah, but that's not what I'm going to study."

"What, then?"

"When Torstein and Solveig were here last winter, after the accident, I thought what they were doing was really cool. I kept in touch with both of them after they went back to Bemidji, and they gave me some information about graduate programs in forensic science. Torstein wrote a letter of recommendation for me, and then he even contacted a couple of his professors and put in a good word for me. And I got accepted! Classes start at the end of the month. He's getting married in a couple weeks, by the way. He even sent me an invitation! It'll be just before I start classes, so I'll be able to go to it."

"That's great news, Denny! It's always a pleasure to see students go off to do great things after they graduate. And I have no doubt that you will! If there's anything I can do to help you along the way, please don't hesitate to ask me."

She reached into her jacket pocket, and pulled out a voucher for the coffee shop. She handed it to Max, and said, "When you two are ready for a coffee break, use this and get yourselves a roll and coffee. Some of the Board members were here yesterday, and this was left over. I'd like to see it go to a good cause. Now, I'm sorry, but I have to get back inside. Mary's still learning the ropes as my new Administrative Assistant. It was great that we were able to promote her, but without Annika around to oversee everything, we're still working the kinks out of our new office structure. Fortunately, she seems to be learning faster than I am!"

After Sarah had gone back into her office, Max turned to Denny. "If you're at a good stopping point, why don't we go have that coffee break right now."

"That sounds great, Max. But first, there's something I want to show you. I was about to point it out to you when President Christiansen came out."

"What's that, Denny?"

"Well, you know how I said that the ivy had pulled some pieces of cement out of the wall?"

"And you're fillin' in the holes. What's the problem?"

"Well, I've found a couple of these along the way, too." He pointed at chip in the concrete.

"Whatcha got there?"

"I'm not sure. It looks like somebody chipped it, with a hammer, or pick, or something. They're almost like bullet marks."

Max thought a minute. "What're you suggestin'?"

"Well, Torstein and Solveig were trying to explain what caused the icicle to fall when it hit Hank. What if it fell because somebody shot it? They could've been sitting in the Field House. Hank would've been a clear target."

"That seems even more unlikely than their explanation that he was hit by an icicle. And don't forget that he hit his head on the railing, too. Torstein had the DNA checked on those hairs he found, and they were Hank's."

"Well, it could have happened like that! Somebody could have been trying to kill him, and shot at the icicles."

"But nobody found anything resemblin' bullets—no slugs, shattered pieces of lead—nothin' like that at all."

"Some of them might have been in the snow I blew off the terrace with the snow blower. More likely, they'd have ricocheted off where they'd never be found. Someone could have shot at the icicles to make his death look like an accident."

"Think about it: everybody agreed it was a freak accident. The odds of Hank walking under that icicle just as it was about to fall were pretty high—astronomical."

"But what if somebody shot just as he walked under it."

"And what would the odds be of someone hitting an icicle exactly above him, hitting it just right so it broke off and fell, and that he was precisely under it when it did? Even if somebody'd been sitting on the edge of the roof, and simply tried to drop an icicle on him, they'd have had trouble hitting him. And even more trouble hitting him where he would lose blood quickly—not to mention slipping and hitting his head."

"What if they really wanted to shoot him, and just aimed too high by accident?"

"There's no indication of that—no bullet marks below the overhang, for example. Torstein and Solveig would have found anything like that. If someone were a good enough shot to try to hit him from that distance, they wouldn't aim that high. And you saw that picture—the one where they thought it might have been Hank out on the terrace. As dark as it was, he wouldn't have been a very good target up here that night. I can't buy that argument. But thanks to Sarah, I CAN buy you coffee and a roll! Let's go."

"So, what do you think I should do about this?" He pointed to the chip on the façade.

Max looked inside the President's Office, where Sarah and Mary were both laughing about something one of them had just said. Sarah was putting a photo on the bookshelf next to her desk. Mary looked out the window, smiled, and waved at them. Sarah waved, too.

Max thought for a moment, and said to himself, *"The same thing she's had to do ever since Hank died."*

He turned to Denny and said, "Just plaster over it, and move on."

Who's Who?

("You Can't Tell the Players Without a Program")

Characters, major and minor, in the approximate order in which they're mentioned (family members listed together):

Henrik (Hank) van Daam: President of Nieuw Nederland College (NNC)
  Hannah van Daam: Hank's wife

Annika van Rijn: van Daam's Executive Assistant
  Pieter van Rijn: Annika's husband, Professor of Philosophy

Sarah Christiansen: Dean of the College
  Owen Christiansen: Sarah's husband

Elke Spoelstra: Hank's Secretary

Gene Graandsma: Chair of the Nieuw Nederland College Board of Trustees
  Demi Graandsma: Gene's wife

Carl van den Hoek: Chief of the New Leiden Police Department

Tom Olsson: Director of Campus Security

Charles Thompson: President of Chartwell College

Max Cuypers: Head of Campus Buildings and Grounds
Services

Denny Bakken: Student worker in Buildings and Grounds
Services

Laura van Klees: New Leiden Police Officer
Bob van Klees: Laura's Husband—manager of
Dick's Market

Frank O'Leary: Agent from Minnesota State Bureau of
Criminal Apprehension

Christiaan (Chris) van Zant: Assistant Professor of History

Martin (Marty) Dykstra: Professor of History, Chair of the
Department
Late wife: Annette
Daughter: Elizabeth ("Liese")
Husband: Jerry Cunningham
Children: Tom , Kristy, Eddie
Son: Michael (Mike)
Wife: Karen
Children: Erica, Karl

Terry O'Brien: Professor of Mathematics

Dirk de Vries: Professor of Political Science
Karen de Vries: Dirk's wife, owner of local
catering service

Marianna de Han: Associate Professor of Chemistry

Hannelore van Leuven: Professor of German

Ed Coonradt: Professor of Finance

Johanna Jacobsen: Assistant Professor of Education
Al Jacobsen: Johanna's husband, Librarian

Tim Johansson: Former Professor & Chair of History, now
with an endowed chair at a larger school "out East"
Erika Johansson: Tim's wife

Alf Thompson: Professor of Biology (Ornithology)

Maria Hendrix: Head of Information Services

Francine Reim: One of the senior members of English
Department

Paul Rothman: "el Deano," the former Dean, President of
Zwingli College
Paula Rothman: Paul's Wife

Mary de Smet: Sarah's secretary

Paul and Cornelia van der Kellen: Wealthy donors who
fund center for Dutch Studies

Matt van Baak: Director of Global Studies Office

Harry Westbrook: Head Football Coach

Bill Logan: Athletic Director

Terry Daalmans: Director of Public Information Office

Mike Nagel: Director of Institutional Advancement

Casey van Pelt: Professor of Physics

Sharon Dickenson: Associate Professor of Psychology

Dale Haak: Director of Student Recruitment and Retention

Mary de Groet: Vice President for Finance

Beatrice (Betty) and Arnold Langbroek: Former Chair of
the Board of Trustees, and her husband

Rich Summerfield: Potential donor – head of a successful.
".com" business, asked by his parents to handle a
gift intended for both NNC and Chartwell

Bill Kaufman: Professor of English, Endowed Chair of
Creative Writing,

Walter Braaten: Professor of Business (Marketing)

History Department:

Marcia Holt: Early American Historian, Women &
Gender Studies
Husband: Jerry Fremont – owner of local
bookstore, the "Northern Prairie
Book Haven"

Terry Brant: Modern American History, also Latin
America
Wife: Margaret, works at local bank

Anna di Marco: Ancient History (Greece & Rome),
& Medieval
Husband: Tony, local CPA

Klaas de Graaf: Emeritus Professor of History –
Dutch specialist

Charles Johnson: Emeritus Professor of History

Talmadge Sumner: Professor of Black Studies, teaches African and African-American History courses

Frank Kramer: Works in Jerry's store, formerly in Student Affairs, fired by previous Dean of Student Affairs
Brenda Kramer: Frank's wife

Cynthia Reynen: Former Dean of Students

Craig Watson: Former Controller

Harry Wilson: Former Professor of Psychology

Zoe van den Berg: Professor of Classics

Monica Schutte: Professor of Art – Chair of Search Committee for Classics Professor

Dale McCutcheon: Hank's friend and former colleague, who is starting "Academic Executive Seminars"

Thomas "Tommy" McCutcheon: Dale's son, Hank's favored candidate for Classics position

Mariah Cunningham: Professor of Art History from Chartwell

Mary Anne Fischer: Candidate for Classics position, currently at temporary position in Pennsylvania.

Marie de Beer: Custodial staff, President of Staff Association

Henry Steenwyk: Head Electrician

Wanda Petri: Head of Campus Counselling Service

Solveig Nygaard: Forensic Scientist from Minnesota State
Bureau of Criminal Apprehension

Torstein Haugen: Forensic Scientist from Minnesota State
Bureau of Criminal Apprehension

Nancy van Wageningen: One of the students who had been
out on the football field in the snow storm

Helen Kerkman: Director of Human Resources

Acknowledgements:

I SUSPECT THAT MANY PEOPLE may read this novel and think, "I remember that professor," "I know the guy who did that," or "I remember her!" They will be wrong. As noted elsewhere, this is a work of fiction. My imagination may have been sparked by events on college campuses around the country, particularly those where I have worked or studied. But those have been conflated with others—real and imagined—to create this novel. I've been associated with higher education since I started college in 1965, so I've heard countless anecdotes about college professors and administrators. I've also witnessed many "curious" events personally. Those planted seeds that grew in my imagination. They have, in turn, been amplified by stories I've read in the *Chronicle of Higher Education*, or *Inside Higher Education*. My wife, Mickey, frequently points those out to me, often noting as she does, "You can't make this stuff up!" But I could alter them and weave them together with other events, as well as with "stuff" that I've made up, to create this work of fiction.

Ivy is the product of my imagination. But as with most other endeavors, I could not have created it by myself in isolation. I would like to express my sincere appreciation to several people who have helped me make this manuscript possible.

I am indebted to Kevin Sand, M.D., for his medical insights, and for his comments about the various factors that could have contributed to Hank van Daam's death. In particular, he spared me the embarrassment of attributing it to something which, as Kevin politely pointed out, could not have been a factor until after Hank was already dead.

Jill Oliveira and her colleagues at the Minnesota Bureau of Criminal Apprehension provided invaluable advice regarding the procedures that the BCA and local authorities would follow in a situation like Hank's untimely death. Since my knowledge of criminal investigation is essentially limited to what I've read in mystery novels, or watched in movies or on television, I am indebted to their professional insights and generous advice.

Fred Bohm III and Ed Scofield have been sources of countless entertaining stories over the last four decades. They also demonstrated a true measure of friendship by reading the entire manuscript in its earliest form. I am indebted to them for their comments and insights.

Jack and Mary Garland, Kurtzi Anderson, and Paul Primak also took the time to read my manuscript and offer their reactions, as well as their encouragement. I am grateful for their support.

Jerry Johnson generously offered his insights and experience to help me understand the world of publishing in the twenty-first century. His advice spared me numerous mistakes that I'm sure I would have made along the way. I appreciate the time that he took to meet with me on several occasions—and he wouldn't even let me pay for his coffee.

Manny Palomo graciously shared his talent and background in graphic design to help me with the cover layout, which I appreciate very much.

Hanna Rosholt was my student for two semesters, and took the photo of me in class one cold, wintery morning. She now has her own photo studio in Austin, MN, and she kindly converted her color photo to the black and white version used here.

I am particularly grateful for Mickey's never-ending encouragement and support. In addition to being an excellent proof-reader, she has helped me refine many of my ideas. Also, by recalling conversations with countless unnamed colleagues across the country, and pointing out articles in the *Chronicle of Higher Education* and *Inside Higher Education*, she planted ideas in my imagination which developed into many elements of this novel.

Photo by Hannah Rosholt; courtesy of Luther College

M. G. Slind grew up north of Seattle in the State of Washington's picturesque Skagit Valley. He received his bachelor's degree from Pacific Lutheran University and his doctorate in history from Washington State University.

Dr. Slind has studied and done research at both the University of Oslo and the University of Heidelberg, where he was a Fulbright Scholar. He has served on the faculty of several colleges and universities in the United States and in Europe. His reading interests include European history, contemporary politics, modern fiction, and various modern crime genres, in particular "Nordic Noir."

An avid golfer, he also enjoys fly fishing in the mountain streams of the western US and Canada. Occasionally he serves as a destination lecturer on cruise ships.

M. G. Slind and his wife live in Decorah, Iowa.

54465869R00278

Made in the USA
San Bernardino, CA
17 October 2017